fat girls
fairy
Sue Watson

fat girls & fairy cakes

Sue Watson

RICKSHAW
PUBLISHING

A Rickshaw paperback
www.rickshawpublishing.co.uk

First published in Great Britain in 2011 by Rickshaw Publishing
Ltd, 102 Fulham Palace Road, London W6 9PL

Copyright © Sue Watson 2011

A CIP catalogue record for this book is available from the
British Library.

ISBN 978-0-9565368-2-2

Cover designed by Richard Smith

Printed and bound in Great Britain for Rickshaw Publishing

Acknowledgements

I have lots of lovely family and friends who have supported me on this novel-writing journey and I'm grateful to them all – but I would like to say thank you to those who played a special part in the writing of this book.

To my teacher, friend and fellow writer Sue Johnson, thanks for spotting a tiny spark and encouraging me to light it. Thank you to everyone at Rickshaw for taking a chance on me, in particular my wonderful and talented editor, Jo Doyle, who guided me wisely and killed my 'darlings' with kindness – and strong editorial anaesthetic.

I am deeply indebted to Alastair Bell for his absolute fabulousness, overflowing font of TV and celebrity trivia and his profound knowledge of Gay Swimming.

Thanks to my great writing buddy and inspiration Jackie Dietrich and to Vanessa Jackson for her wise counsel and true friendship. Liz Cox also deserves a mention for her divine turn of phrase as does my dearest friend Lesley Mcloughlin who stayed up until 3am to help me with the ending over several bottles of red.

Thanks to Sir Terry Wogan for those Thursday afternoons at Clivedon making work seem like fun and for telling me I could write comedy. Love and thanks to my friends Nadia Sawalha and Sue Robinson for encouraging me to take the plunge on a hot afternoon in Hoxton and to Linda Robson, for sharing hilarious TV tales and wonderful advice.

A special thank you to James Martin for all the 'cake porn,' and the best chocolate mousse I ever tasted. And to Colin Mcallister and Justin Ryan – thanks for all the fun and fabulousness – and yes, you two still blow my frock up!

The ladies of The Bodacious Book Club, The Worcestershire Wags and my friends at the BBC have all in their own special way contributed to this book. I enjoy and appreciate their friendship, encouragement and funny stories (some of which I have stolen shamelessly and included in this book).

Thanks to Nick Watson for his love and support and for making it possible for me to abandon the real world and write every day – I'm so lucky to have him in my life.

Finally, a special kiss for Eve Watson who always makes me feel like a star whatever I do, with those three little words, "well done mum!"

This is for my Mum, who told me to look
for the lace in the trees

PROLOGUE

Sex in the Dark

"I need sex every day, luv," said Denise, the vicar's wife. I tried to stay calm and focus on the view of Rochdale by night. Las Vegas it wasn't, but the little clusters of starry lights peeping through the driving rain were a comfort and made me think of people safe in their homes; I wished I was. "I have a very high sex drive you see," Denise continued. The 'high' and 'sex' were mouthed exaggeratedly, almost soundlessly, as if to accentuate the *enormity* of it.

It was July, it was late evening and I was standing under a large umbrella in a vicarage garden in Lancashire with a wife of the cloth who, it seemed, had abandoned scones and sermons for sex. Her breath mingled with steam from the greenish tea she clutched to her bosom as she chatted. Sporting a disturbingly transparent crocheted dress, Denise did nothing to conceal a carnal desire for her fifteen minutes of fame. The phallic jewellery and sparkly heels were bizarre, but the TV-producer part of me knew they'd be great on camera. Not your stereotypical vicar's wife, Denise wore a shock of pink hair and a vivid storyboard of tattoos telling of a life well-lived – and loved. "My Bernie's a once-a-month missionary man," she hissed at me in the darkness, referring to her husband, *the vicar*. "It's not enough for me. I have a big appetite – and it's led me to seek pastures new, you see."

I kept a permanently fixed smile on my face as she continued. "It took me a while to settle down at the vicarage, but I'm happy now I've found a group of 'like-minded' folk." She paused and winked elaborately at me. I suddenly felt a bit panicky. Was she looking for some kind of sign? Did she think I was 'like-minded-folk'? I shivered and looked away as she pulled hard on the herbal tea from her chipped mug, on which was printed, rather reassuringly, 'God Will Forgive'. *I do hope so Denise*, I thought.

Claiming to be 52 (but I'd add five), Denise filled me in on her colourful past of banning the bomb, piercing her nipples and catching crabs on an apparently 'long, hot Summer of Love'.

"Mmm, sounds idyllic," I said, desperately trying to walk away, hoping she wouldn't feel the need to elaborate (and also hoping that the catching crabs comment referred to the innocent summer pursuit of fishing in rock pools for crustaceans).

"Don't be fooled Stella, in remote villages...people get lonely," she added ominously.

"Oh, surely not *this* lovely village with its friendly community?" I asked, in what I hoped was my grown-up TV producer's voice. "This place is picturesque." *It's on shortbread tins at Christmas, for God's sake!* I was horrified (if perhaps also a teensy bit intrigued) at the idea that orgiastic activity was nestling in the grey Victorian stonework, tea shops and cobbled streets.

"Oh, this village is very, very friendly Stel. In fact, only last week I was walking through the village and felt a firm hand on my..." she began with a knowing smile.

"Gosh Denise, what a lovely shade of nail varnish!" I tried, desperate to change the subject, grabbing her hand and admiring the witchy, black talons.

"Sex in the dark, Stella..." she was off again.

"Denise, I was talking about the nail varnish."

"So was I," she answered, bemused. "It's the name on the

bottle, look, 'Sex in the Dark', they do a matching lipstick too. I've got it here somewhere..."

As she fumbled around in her tiny sequined bag for 'Sex in the Dark', I gathered myself together and took a good sidelong look at her through the steam and hot breath. I found myself mesmerised by the twists and turns of the now-damp crocheted dress. Then suddenly, like one of those Magic Eye pictures we all once loved, the truth emerged. In 3D, I began to see Denise in all her glory and looked away in horror. I was about to put this lady on TV in front of millions of people, and this vicar's wife wasn't wearing any knickers.

1

Chunky Kit Kats and Leafy Lunches

2 weeks earlier...

It was five past nine when I finally flung myself through the door of the glass-fronted office building in downtown Birmingham on that fated Monday morning in June. As I sprinted to my desk I could see my boss Mary-Jane Robinson, or MJ as she liked to be called, loitering by the coffee machine watching me all the way with a twisted smile. Clad in a tight, black pencil skirt and a pristine white blouse, MJ's taut, wiry frame hinted strongly at self denial and leaf-only lunches. Unhappy and unfulfilled she may be, but I had to hand it to her, her legs looked good in those killer heels.

"Morning, MJ!" I called with fake cheerfulness as I landed at my desk, deliberately taking a huge bite of buttery croissant and slurping my cappuccino.

"Oh, hello Stella," she said slowly as she passed my desk and ascended the stairs that led to the upper level, where her office was situated. At Media World, the space was open plan and the TV executives were positioned on balconies above, from which lofty positions they could see everyone and make note of any battery hen that strayed from its pen.

MJ paused on the balcony outside her office for a moment, sweeping her eyes across the floor below. "Diet Coke!" she barked at her assistant and catching my eye, she gave me a nasty sneer, marched into her office and slammed the door.

The sneer slightly unnerved me but I quickly logged on to my computer, absently removing a collection of crisp packets and chocolate wrappings from the keyboard and thinking that the diet would definitely start now.

"Morning Stel," said Valerie, the producer of *I ♥ the Countryside*, "I see the bitch queen was watching your entrance with her usual venom."

"Hi Val," I said. "Yeah, she was probably wishing she had my fabulous curvy body. I'm only a few minutes late, for God's sake." Val smiled.

"Why is it the execs only seem to notice when you arrive late, never when you leave late?" Val said. "I mean, what time were you here till on Friday, in the end?"

"Midnight," I said with a scowl.

"Wow – that's dedication to duty!"

"Not really. MJ decided that for some reason best known to her, she needed the pilot for *Forgotten Families* biked to her flat before today. "Sometimes I think she only does it to make my life harder." I sighed.

"Well I know that everyone involved thinks it's great – just don't let her take all the credit."

"Thanks Val. I just wish the filming could have been a bit nearer home, I think the title says it all!" I said.

Forgotten Families was a new series I was producing for the daytime TV audience. It involved people being reunited with family members they'd never met before due to adoption, emigration or divorce – think *Surprise, Surprise* on a daytime budget with a genetic twist.

I pulled out my file for the programme, full of dates, case studies and format ideas and began to get to work. I knew MJ had probably seen the programme by now and that feedback was on the way. Even though I knew it was good, the thought of what she might say almost put me off my mid-morning snack of a chunky Kit Kat and a small iced bun...but not quite – a girl needs to keep her energy levels high; it's all about metabolism. Unwrapping the Kit Kat and biting into the solid chocolate coating that yielded to thick, crispy wafer crunch I wondered for the hundredth time how one person could have this effect on me. Over the years, childless, husbandless MJ had cultivated special venom for her own personal antichrist: mothers trying to hold down a career. This venom was directed at all mothers working at Media World but I was special and invited extra-poisonous doses.

Once upon a time (in a land far away) I was deemed to be a high-flyer at Media World with the owner of the company, Frank Moores, saying he loved my creativity and even offering me an executive producer position. Of course I was very flattered and considered it carefully, but I eventually turned it down because it would have meant even longer hours and being away from my daughter Grace and husband Tom. Meanwhile, MJ was snapping at my heels, spending a lot of time around Frank, arriving early, working late and appearing to be very efficient. It was therefore no surprise that soon after I turned the job down, it was given to MJ. I guess it must have seemed like a bit of a hollow victory for her and ever since then she'd seen me as a threat and never missed an opportunity to lash out and knock my ideas or the work I was doing. If she could do this in a public arena, I reckon she gave herself extra points. At first this was just annoying but over the years as she rose through the ranks this became more and more of a problem for me. I wiped my sticky fingers – time was ticking on and I had work to do, so I pushed in a last mouthful of iced bun and with it pushed thoughts of MJ to the back of my mind and got down to business.

I was so consumed by budgets, press plans, facts and figures that time – and several more tasty titbits – slipped past without me noticing. Suddenly I looked up and the clock on my computer said 5pm. I was just thinking about packing up and wondering why MJ hadn't commented on the programme yet when an email pinged through to my computer.

Stella,
I have some feedback for you. Meet at my desk at 6pm.
MJ

Bitch! 6pm was exactly when After School Club closed, as she well knew. My eight-year old daughter already spent more time at the club than I would have liked and now it looked like she'd be the last kid at the gates – again. My stomach lurched and I felt sick. If I could capture that feeling and bottle it I could make a fortune from slimmers all over the world. I swear if someone had offered me a Flake (even a dipped one) I couldn't have eaten it.

I pulled out my mobile and frantically called Tom but his phone was switched off. I felt a flicker of annoyance as his voicemail clicked in.

"Tom, it's me. I need you to collect Grace, something's come up at work. Call me," I said, crossly. I shut the phone and checked my watch. The meeting with MJ was in 55 minutes which would give Tom enough time to get back from the studio and pick Grace up, presuming he got my message in time. Why was the damn phone off?

I tried not to waste time worrying and began pulling everything together for my meeting with MJ. As I looked through the documents I felt my confidence surge; this was a good programme, and even MJ would have to see that. I smiled and allowed myself to daydream about actually getting a compliment from her. I was feeling quite good until I realised that 40 minutes had slipped by without me noticing and Tom still hadn't called me back about Grace. Then to my horror, a hurried early-morning conversation floated out of my subconscious and danced before my eyes. Tom was on location; he was a cameraman and was filming on a late shoot. Christ! What was I going to do about Grace?

I glanced up from behind my computer to see MJ's skeletal form seated above. Her hard, dry meanness seemed to emanate from the balcony, stretching toward me like long, bony witch fingers. I made some hurried calls to some of Grace's friends' mums.

"Hello Lara, it's Stella Weston here. We met once at the school's Bring-and-Buy Sale, I'm Grace's mum. I'm so sorry to have to ask, but..." and I explained my predicament.

"Oh I'm sorry, Stella," said Lara. "Katie's going to Brownies and we're about to leave. Hope you can find someone to help! Bye!" I felt another wave of guilt; Brownies was just one of the things Grace couldn't do because she was always at After School Club.

I made another couple of frantic calls, all the time watching MJ casually slurping Diet Coke, laughing with executive colleagues, watching a bit of TV and picking at a miniscule sandwich. If I wasn't so upset, I'd have been furious. She obviously had nothing to do all afternoon and had put my meeting right at the end of the day just to cause the utmost disruption to my life. Yet I couldn't bring myself to call her to say I couldn't make 6pm because that's exactly what she wanted me to do. That would prove that I couldn't cope and give her more ammunition with which to take pot-shots at my career.

At 5.55pm, five minutes before Grace would be the only child left at the school gates and just as I was contemplating jumping in my car and driving like Jenson Button through the outskirts of Worcester, I got through to Emma Wilson. Grace was friends with her daughter Alice and I had her mobile number in my phone from some long-forgotten party or outing.

"Emma? Hi, it's Stella Weston here. I am so, so sorry to ask but I'm desperate. Grace is at After School Club and I'm stuck at work. Is there any possibility you could save my life and pick her up?" I held my breath. I couldn't believe what I was doing. I hardly knew these people because I never had time to stand and chat at the school gate and here I was asking them to collect the most precious thing in my life.

"Oh, hi Stella. Erm yes, that's fine – we're not too far from the school so I'll take her back to my house, shall I?"

I could have cried. "Emma, you're an angel. I will pick her up as soon as I am done here. Thank you so much." I hung up the phone and had to take a few seconds to compose myself.

Val was back at her desk and had overheard the frantic phone calls. She was shaking her head and putting on her jacket. I looked at her enviously – Val would be home in time for her kids tonight. In the same boat as me, Val knew exactly how hard it is to reschedule when a late meeting is 'popped' into the diary. It would be easier to organise a full-scale war or a royal wedding, complete with catering and security.

"They make you feel nothing but guilt in this job," she said, "guilt if you can't go to the meeting because you have to pick up your kids, guilt if you go to the meeting and don't pick up your kids – you just can't win." She shook her head sadly and grabbed her handbag. "Speaking of which – I've got to go, the childminder leaves in ten minutes. See you tomorrow!" And Val hurried out of the door. I watched her leave, and wondered what I was doing. Why was I still here, when I should have been at home with my child?

There was no use putting it off any longer. Having had all day to stew and with the stress of finding someone to pick up Grace I was feeling very tearful walking up the stairs to MJ's lair. *Fee-Fi-Fo-Fum*. My mouth was dry and I could barely swallow, and when I tried to, it felt like my throat was folding in half.

When I finally reached her office MJ saw me but didn't acknowledge me. This was a woman who would have excelled in Nazi Germany. I stood awkwardly at her desk while she continued to deliberately ignore me, gazing avidly at a piece of paper. Another Diet Coke was delivered by an almost-invisible lackey and suddenly a flicker appeared under the fiercely straightened brown hair that framed her face. I moved to stand directly in front of her, eager to get it over with – but she was enjoying this too much so she twisted away from me a little more and carried on studying the paper. She eventually glanced up, feigning surprise and looking me up and down with deep, thin-girl disapproval at my love of chocolate and lack of control.

Unsmiling, she said; "Take a seat Stella," gesturing towards a very low chair on the other side of her desk. As soon as I'd sat down (my knees almost touching my chin) she picked up the DVD of my programme and slammed it down on to her desk, glaring at me.

"Unbroadcastable!" she said.

I felt my chest tighten. What the hell was this?

"Why didn't you get her to cry on camera? I *told* you I wanted tears!" MJ glared, grabbing the disc and waving it aggressively, her forehead creasing in anger. She was referring to the contributor who had been dramatically reunited with the child she'd given up for adoption 40 years before. My fear was suddenly replaced with fury and injustice, and my brain filled up with all the things I knew I should say.

I could have made her cry, MJ. I could have told her she was a bad mother. I could have added that she was a stupid bitch and had ruined her child's life – she'd probably have cried for the camera then. What you said you wanted were 'real people, feeling real things'. They are not performing monkeys and, as programme-makers, we have a responsibility to the people we film. Not that you'd know that, as you're just an inexperienced, talentless bully!

But as usual, I didn't say what I really felt – I pushed it back down. As MJ glowered at me over her desk I felt my confidence slipping away and made a vain attempt to defend my work.

"MJ, the woman is beside herself. Anyone watching this can see on her face the torment that she's lived with for 40 years. She had to give her baby away; her life has been torn apart."

MJ didn't respond, it was as though I hadn't spoken. She just carried on in her usual, tight tone. "This programme isn't good enough. I won't allow it to be broadcast."

I felt a huge weight suddenly pressing down on me. All those hours, all the work the team had put in – not to mention me being away from Tom and Grace – and it was all for nothing. I knew she was wrong; it was a damn good show.

"Stella. I will have to get someone to rescue this – someone who knows what they're doing."

My eyes were stinging and my chin was seriously starting to wobble. I couldn't speak.

"Anyway, there was another reason I called this meeting," she suddenly announced in a more composed, almost triumphant voice. "I'm making some staffing changes in my department. As you are clearly not suited to working in Documentaries, I have arranged for you to work in another area."

I watched her thin-lipped mouth in close-up; she was salivating.

"The producer on our forthcoming live show, *Gardens of Prayer*, seems to have had some sort of breakdown. You will replace her. Report to Peter Willis first thing tomorrow morning," she said, licking her lips, unable to contain the dribble. She looked straight at me, a sneer dancing across her face; "Gardening and Religion – you'll be *perfect* for it, Stella."

I was speechless. At Media World, TV gardening was

considered to be the care home for ageing TV producers. This was where infirm, incontinent, invisible, forty-something female producers went to die. For years I had tried to fight it by wearing dangly earrings and calling everyone 'honey.' I even gave up cake for a while and squeezed into size twelve suits, carried a Blackberry and contributed vigorously to brainstorms for 'the next' *Big Brother*. Even though it was all a sham and beneath the veneer there was a rather desperate, middle-aged woman clinging hopelessly to the career ladder, I still wasn't ready to go yet. I knew I had years of creativity left, and the prospect of being sucked into the black career abyss of *Gardeners' Universe*, *Bulbs in my Barrow*, and *The Rough-Handed Horticulturalist* made me shiver with horror.

"I'm not happy about this," I began, weakly, trying to move into a more dignified position than the low seating would allow.

"Then take your 'problem,' to the big boss," she smirked. "Though you'll find that, with my recommendation, Frank approved this move wholeheartedly – over dinner last night."

What could I do? There was no one to complain to or plead with. She was 'in' with Fast Frank and my career was officially over. I opened my mouth but nothing came out, tears filled my eyes and if I stayed any longer they'd burst. I wasn't going to let her see me cry. I rose awkwardly from the seat and shakily gathered my notes, dropping some on the floor, almost falling as I bent down to pick them up.

"Oh yes, and just to let you know, *Gardens of Prayer* is starting with a live show in two weeks' time, so you'll be expected to head straight to Rochdale and stay there for that time to prevent the show turning into a disaster live on air," she smirked.

I froze. "MJ, no, you know how hard I worked on the last project. I was away such a lot and I promised my family I'd spend some time with them, I can't go away now."

"I'm *so* sorry Stella. The matter is decided. Rochdale awaits," she raised her brows and smirked again. "Enjoy!" she called after me as I fled towards the stairs clutching my notes to my chest. I glanced back and for a couple of seconds the world stood still as she caught me in her glare before reaching for the can of Diet Coke and pushing it hard into her face.

Returning to the relative safety of my desk, a floaty feeling enveloped me like thick cotton. My finger hovered over an imaginary trigger as from behind my computer I watched her tight, tangerine-lipsticked mouth sucking hard on the defenceless Coke can. I looked around, moving my imaginary gun along the balcony. I would shoot her like a target at a fairground, hook a duck, hit a can and win a teddy. And as her veins bulged and her malevolent, orange lips slurped the calorie-free liquid I slowly pulled that imaginary trigger and blew off Mary-Jane Robinson's head.

2

Jam Doughnuts and Jewelled Tiaras

Still fighting back tears of rage, I headed straight to a nearby café. As I walked into the brightly-lit, plastic coffee bar smelling of warm pastries and sweet coffee, the floodgates opened and I started to cry. I sent out an emergency text to my two best friends.

TXT: Am in cafe – need caffeine and a friend x.

Within minutes of my text, Lizzie was walking towards me with two big, sugary doughnuts and large cappuccinos as I sat numbly at the sticky, Formica-topped table. Lizzie worked at Media World too, producing a makeover show called *Home Dreams*. With Lizzie's son all grown up, MJ didn't have the hold over her that she had over me, but she still knew how evil she could be. Looking at me with concern, Lizzie placed the foaming coffee and sugar-encrusted dough in front of me and jumped right in.

"I just heard about what happened and Gardening isn't *that* bad. It doesn't *always* mean the end..." she offered, trying to sound jolly and handing me a tissue (I'd started again).

"Not that bad?" I said, raising my voice and blowing hard into the proffered tissue. "Lizzie, it *is* the end. MJ is a bitch. She knows what she's doing, it's like saying: 'you're too old, you're past it, get out'."

"Come on, Stel. It's what you make it. Don't be so negative

hon, it's not like you," she started, taking off her wrap and fanning herself with a menu.

"I hate gardening," I ranted, "it's so predictable and boring. Autumn is bulbs and planting and waiting. And digging and waiting. And summer is roses and flower shows. And digging and waiting. Spring follows winter and we wait for more bloody summer and that's how it is – year in year out. Bulbs in, bulbs out." I stopped for breath and a sip of hot cappuccino. She'd let me get it off my chest, munching on her doughnut quietly, now she saw a chink and leapt in.

"Well, yes, gardening is by its very nature cyclic Stel, but...it's actually pure *sex*...its birds and bees and..." she tried, but I was off again.

"Avoid early frosts. Avoid late frosts, pocket frosts, big frosts, little frosts, Jack-fucking-Frosts. Bulbs in, bulbs out, on and on, dictated to by the seasons and the RHS."

Lizzie raised both hands in the air and in a raised voice said; "Stella, get a grip. Be calm!"

"How can I be calm? My final years will pass by in a relentless loop of generic bee-hovering-on-bloom shots and close-ups of gardener's calloused hands patting down filthy soil. And that's if I even make it past the first show."

"Look Stel, I'm not belittling your situation but in this climate – well, at least you have a job," she tried.

I wasn't convinced. "God knows how many tortuous years of pruning, preening and pricking out lie ahead," I whinged, between mouthfuls of sweet, bready doughnut, which was starting to have a calming effect.

"I think we need to approach this from a different angle," she started, adjusting her ample bosom and running her fingers through her shiny, auburn bob. "It might not be a complete disaster. If anyone can fix it, you can. Think *Thorn Birds*, think Richard Chamberlain, honey. Come on Stel, I mean, bodice-ripping men of the cloth, well some of them are pure eye candy."

There are times this would have made me smile, but I just gave her a look. Richard Chamberlain wasn't going to do it for me today, or any other day for that matter.

"Lizzie. I don't care if the minister is bloody Brad Pitt, I can't do it."

I could see out of the corner of my eye that she knew she was running out of positives and started concentrating on stirring her coffee. "I have to face it, MJ has bought me a ticket for the fast train to career death!" I wailed dramatically, getting a second wind. "It's not just the gardening, there's the religion, for Christ's sake! I'm hardly what you'd call spiritual and I can't travel the country giving up evenings and weekends in search of the Garden of Eden. Clearly, if there is a God: he hates me!!"

"Wash your heathen mouth out with soap," squealed a high-pitched voice from the doorway. It was Al, who'd also heard the news of my dark, alfresco future and arrived to comfort me over yet more cake.

Waving his arms in the air, he rushed over, hugged me and placed a large, double-chocolate muffin on the table – which made me want to cry again.

"I'm sorry babe, that bitch MJ is out to destroy you! And at *your* age, you'll never get another job."

"Thanks, Al." Ever the drama-queen, he went straight to the point.

"I've just seen François from Fashion who has his finger on *every* pulse and word is, it's a *disaster* zone. The last producer was found at 4am running around the set with her underpants on her head. I mean, gardening and Jesus? In the same programme? Hello?!"

He was scaring me now. As he clutched at my arm and stared intensely into my eyes with genuine (though admittedly somewhat theatrical) concern, I saw a half-smile form on his lips. Had he finally thought of something positive? I licked the sugar from my lips in anticipation and swapped plates for the muffin.

"On the plus side Stella, some of those clergy are complete *babes*," he breathed, searching my face for response and not getting one. Lizzie waved her hand.

"I've already tried that one Al," she said, slurping the last of her froth.

Al looked down at his beautifully manicured hands and pretended to pick at them.

"Well, they wouldn't be interested in *you* anyway, my darling."

"Cheers Al, that's just what I need right now," I mumbled through chocolate cake crumbs. "Would it be the fact that I'm overweight, over 40 or just repulsive?"

"Darling, darling, you're completely ravishing but, well, I have to tell you, they're all *gay*," he announced, flicking his fringe, feigning nonchalance and launching into yet another vibrant story from his gay folklore collection.

"We had a vicar once, in Swimming Out." (Al's gay swimming team.) "He was tall, dark and *gorgeous!* Anyway, one afternoon after a rather *vigorous* team breaststroke he invited us all round to the vicarage for tea. Well, we didn't need asking twice so piled into cars and headed to his. Thing is, he didn't expect so many of us to take him up on it and he hadn't come out to any of his parishioners. You can only imagine the scenes: a convoy of screaming queens turning up in pink trunks at the vicarage. The parishioners nearly collapsed. You should have seen their faces – you should have seen *his!* Hilarious, what an outing!" he squealed, shaking his head and giggling to himself at the memory. "That's vicars for you. Yep...they're *all* gay, doll."

He continued to regale us with more anecdotes condemning the whole ecclesiastical arm to a life of choirboys and cottaging, then sipped elegantly on his espresso, my plight completely forgotten. Al was one of those gay men who believed that gayness was inherent in all males and that men's lives were spent concealing this from everyone else, particularly their wives and girlfriends. 'WAGS? More like FAGS!', was his current favourite phrase. In Al's world it was merely a matter of time before the England football team came screaming out of pink closets to team bond over Joan Crawford movies and Vogue to Madonna.

I didn't want Al taking over and turning this into some sort of gayfest of jewelled tiaras and Judy Garland, so I carried on whining.

"Not only will it destroy my soul, it will wreck my marriage. I desperately need some time at home and now I'm off again!" I said, waving my coffee spoon for extra emphasis. Just then Al's phone rang.

"Look Stella," continued Lizzie, "at least one positive is that MJ's not your boss anymore. She may have been able to request your transfer, but she has no authority over you in Gardening."

"Hmmm. I suppose that's something," I grudgingly conceded.

I suddenly sensed a new silence at the table and looked across at Al. He was staring at his mobile in horror.

"What is it, Al?" I asked, concerned.

"Oh doll. It's horrible. I've been reassigned too! Apparently I'm going to be your co-star in gardening hell." He wailed.

"Looks like we'll both be spending some time chasing God in a garden!" I said.

Lizzie sat up. "That's not a bad idea for the title," she said, "*God in a Garden*." People in TV are always doing that.

After I left the café I picked up a tired and unhappy Grace from

Emma Wilson's and tried to communicate with her about her day. It was raining and the traffic was heavy, so it took about 45 minutes to get home and in that time she didn't say a word. She wasn't speaking to me because I'd let her down again.

"So, who did you play with, darling?" I asked, in my Julie-Andrews voice as I swept into our kitchen and started pulling out baking ingredients from the cupboards. I'd learnt over the years that fantasising about the murder of colleagues was probably an overreaction and just a teensy bit dangerous for both parties. It may have provided temporary relief, but on the whole it was not healthy. MJ wasn't the first person to put me in this state. There was a time when a fellow producer stole my brilliant programme idea and blatantly passed it off as her own. This hurt because I had trusted her but I found comfort imagining an anonymous, gloved hand (just like in an old Columbo movie) shaking a sachet of something highly toxic into her coffee.

Gloved-hand-poison-therapy worked – for a while – but I learned to manage my murderous thoughts and bury them in my all-time favourite hobby – baking. Yes, in my darkest hour I'd always dragged myself back to sanity with the deep joy of a light sponge, moist banana bread or cute cupcakes. There was something so comforting about cake. Eggs and flour and sugar didn't let you down in the same way that people did. So, with my coat still on, I started measuring and weighing. Grace still hadn't answered.

Then my mobile rang. It was Tom. "Stella, what's going on? I've just got your message. Did you get Grace?" he said, sounding worried.

"Yes, someone picked her up for me. When are you coming home?"

"I'm not, sorry. The shoot's run late and I'm going to have to stay in a hotel."

"Oh," I said, disappointed that I wouldn't be seeing him and knowing he'd be less than happy with my news. I took a deep breath.

"Tom, there's something I have to tell you. I'm not happy about it, but I've got no choice. I have to go to Rochdale for a couple of weeks, to rescue a gardening show."

"What?! We've barely seen you for six months. You promised you'd be spending more time at home."

"I know, but what can I do? If I don't go I'll lose my job. Tom, I've had a terrible day, I just need your support and understanding," I almost pleaded.

"Well we all need a bit of that," he said bitterly. "Look, I have to get back to the shoot, let's talk when I get back."

"There's nothing to talk about Tom, I have to go, I..." Then I realised he'd gone. I slammed my phone onto the table in frustration.

I grabbed my largest mixing bowl from the cupboard and without a word I threw in the ingredients I had measured. Flour fell in, unsifted, and was quickly covered in crunchy brown sugar, followed by cold, yellow butter straight from the fridge. I viciously stabbed the butter with a wooden spoon to break it up and began to cream everything together. I could have used a mixer but as my wrists and arms started to ache with the effort my frustration flowed through the spoon and was stirred and stabbed along with the ingredients. I hurled spicy cinnamon into the bowl, threw in a large glug of vanilla essence and a few fistfuls of dried fruit and put down the spoon. Rolling up my coat sleeves, I plunged my hands into the sticky, gritty mix. Glancing round, I could see that Grace had taken off her coat and was standing by the kitchen table watching me.

"Mummy's making a fruit loaf for tea, darling," I said, as I squeezed and pressed and pummelled with feeling. After a good rummaging around the bowl I scraped out the mix and smacked raw dough down onto my wooden bread board. MJ's face swam into focus as I was shaping and I slapped it, hard. It felt like cold flesh under my palm, so I pulled it then slapped it again and again, thinking, *take that, you bitch!* Suddenly the mixture warped and became Tom, his raisin features scowling at me disapprovingly. I pushed my knuckles into the dough with such force I broke out in a sweat. Then MJ's smirk rose from the cinnamon-scented mound once again, her tangerine mouth mocking me. I leaned all my weight on her, squishing and mashing her face into the board until I couldn't see it anymore.

"Mummy, what are you doing?" asked Grace. Her tight little pout had softened. "Are you fighting the cake?"

I smiled. "Ooh I am and it feels sooo good. Would you like to try?"

She broke into a smile. "Yes please Mummy."

"Go on then, you give it some welly too, Grace." She licked her lips and rolled up her sleeves, taking a few steps back to get a good run-up. With a roar, she threw herself at the embryonic fruit loaf with such force that I started laughing. She started to giggle and hit the dough even harder. I joined in, and we took turns in kneading and slapping. We both suddenly felt much better.

"So sorry I didn't collect you sweetie, but my boss is really mean and she made me stay behind," I said, putting my arms round her and burying my face in her soft hair.

"Were you naughty Mum? Is that why your boss kept you back?"

"No. She's just nasty. And I'm so sorry but it looks like I may have to go away again." I said, pressing the battered dough into a loaf tin and opening the oven door. Grace smiled sadly.

"It's ok Mummy, it's just that...I miss you. Daddy does too."

And all the emotions I had mixed into the fruit loaf suddenly rose, boiled, and bubbled over.

3

Sex-fuelled Romps and Revolting Vicars

So there I was, in darkest Rochdale, up to my neck in compost and Christ, reluctantly producing the department's latest offering, now titled *Is God in the Garden?*, billed as 'a seasonal exploration of the influence of God on and around nature against the backcloth of a church garden' but which was rapidly becoming 'a sex-fuelled romp through the boggy English countryside' (with a few bulbs and a bit of Jesus). The basic format was a sort of Sunday morning *Songs of Praise* meets *Gardener's World*. It was a live show, which was always a risk – especially as this one relied heavily on the vicar, Bernard, and his wife, Denise, as pivotal characters. Bernard would be interviewed at the beginning of each show and then go off to do his Sunday service and the show would end with his live sermon, direct from the pulpit. The idea was that this would reflect on the events of the week and tie up gardening, God and any significant goings-on in the parish. All of this would be interspersed with footage filmed during the week, of the vicarage garden and village life in general.

This all looked fine on paper but Bernard the vicar had only agreed to do the show if a) we donated to the Church Roof Fund and b) if we didn't make any significant changes to the vicarage garden. Al had sworn on his own life that the garden wouldn't be altered in any way and Bernard had agreed on those terms.

However, this was a blatant lie because the gardening team were under strict instructions to create a weekly 'theme.' This meant that Bernard would wake up each Sunday morning, pull open the parish curtains and likely discover the Hanging Gardens of Babylon on his lawn. Current ideas being tossed around were 'Mediterranean', 'Japanese' and 'New York loft style roof gardens' – all to be jigsawed together in a surreal garden maze by the final show. Suffice to say, Bernard would be bailing out by show two and, as his wife was insisting on going commando, we'd probably be taken off air anyway. First thing was first and I needed to share the Denise-lack-of-undergarment horror with someone so I tracked down Al across the muddy ground, who as ever had got over the shock of being assigned assistant producer and thrown himself into the project with gusto.

"Ooh darling, that should get the phone lines buzzing," was his response when I finally found him flirting with the sound man by the catering tent.

"It's not funny Al," I said, grabbing his meat pie and taking a very big bite. "I know it's late and I'm tired but don't tell me I'm overreacting to the fact that the vicar's wife can only talk about sex, doesn't wear pants and is likely to share all this with the viewing public as soon as we go on air."

"Why Denise, how lovely you look..." he suddenly gushed loudly for my benefit. Denise was behind me and within seconds she had embraced Al and had embarked on some sordid tale of three-in-a-bed bell-ringers involving the doubles, the triples and the *Bristol Surprise*.

I had to walk away.

It was very late and the rain was still falling lightly. We'd all had a long day and as usual we were behind schedule and working into the night. I was desperate to phone home but it was after ten and Tom and Grace would probably be asleep. I tried to fight the urge to reconnect with my family, but couldn't resist. I convinced myself that Tom wouldn't mind being woken up. I needed sanity and the sound of his voice telling me all was well and our little girl was safely asleep having lovely eight-year old's dreams.

I popped behind a tree, opened my phone and dialled. Just as it started to ring, a voice called out from the darkness. "Stella? Where's Stella?" I closed my phone and reluctantly emerged from behind the tree.

Belinda, a young researcher with straight blonde hair, long legs and clear skin was running like an Olympic athlete across the grass towards me. "Stella we've got a real problem..." I put my phone back in my pocket, with a sinking heart.

"Tell me," I said, really not wanting to know.

"Well you know we've been waitin' for this ten-ton compost? It was finally delivered this afternoon – to the wrong address! The woman's goin' bonkers. She's on the phone now. Says she's left loads of messages but no-one's got back to her. She's losin' it big time."

"Compost? Hell. Er, give me a second Belinda..."

"Stella," a new voice demanded in the darkness. This time it was Dan, one of the gardeners. "Do you want us to have the bulbs item over here? If you do we'll need to dig it out and put sleepers down. Who's going to do that?"

"Erm...I haven't had chance to think about that yet Dan."

"Have the sleepers been ordered yet, Stella?" he continued shouting.

"Sleepers?" I answered. "Ask Al."

"He said to ask you."

"*I* don't know. *He's* in charge of ordering."

"Stella if we don't get those sleepers..."

"Hang on a minute Dan. I just need to get my head round 'compost-gate'."

"But the sleepers'll need time to settle, *this* is the

emergency."

"I know Dan, I know, I'll find Al..."

"Stella, the woman's still goin' bonkers down the phone about the compost..."

"OK. Tell Mrs Bonkers we'll get the compost moved tonight. Send her a bouquet and two audience tickets to *I know My Mrs*. If that doesn't do it I'll go and see her and let her scream abuse at my face for seven minutes when I have a window," I added with a deep sigh.

"And where's Al? Has he ordered those bloody sleepers?" I screamed into the darkness, spotting Al's silhouette in the dim middle distance. Backlit by a halogen light, which gave him a rather unlikely halo effect, he was chatting animatedly, waving his arms in the air no doubt telling an outrageous story to the crew and some kind, innocent parishioners who'd stayed late to help out. *God help them*, I thought. As I approached, I could see that Al was now thrusting his hips backwards and forwards in an obscene gesture, to a mixed roar of amusement and bewilderment from his gathered audience.

"Ooh you are a terrible boy," squealed an old lady in a knitted hat.

"And you're a naughty girl, Edna," he retorted, waving a finger at her. She squealed again, slapping his bottom in mock chastisement. I couldn't help but smile at this until I noticed some of the older parishioners who clearly weren't taking too kindly to Al's floor show.

"We've planted all the bulbs. Now we're just waiting for you to stop messing about and give us our instructions," said a stern, Sergeant-Major type. His team of pensioner parishioners nodded and my heart sank for a second time. The Major didn't look like he'd be fobbed off with any TV show tickets, least of all to *I Know My Mrs*.

I couldn't face it, I needed somewhere quiet to think in

peace, but while desperately looking round for an escape route, I caught Denise in the corner of my eye heading straight for me again. I wasn't in the mood for more tales of Babylonian goings-on in the local pie shop, so I did an about turn and trudged in the opposite direction. I could feel a billowing mist of rising panic. We had only a short time before our first live show. Nothing was ready. It was a technical, logistical nightmare. The assistant producer was a Butlins Redcoat, the vicar was revolting and his wife was a crazed nympho. My list of 'Ten Things That Could Possibly Go Wrong' had just reached twelve. At least it had stopped raining.

I trudged through the walled garden and towards the church, walking away from the vicarage and all the queries, questions and demands. I needed to sit quietly and plan the running order.

It was more peaceful near the church and finding a low wall to sit on I started jotting down timings in my notebook, illuminated by the halogen lamps. I'd only been there a few minutes when I heard a conversation nearby. I could hear the voice of one of the researchers talking to Bernard the vicar. The girl, Sacha, was barely out of her teens and in combats and a heavy fleece with an iPod strapped to her hip. She was holding the compulsory bottled water in one hand and a mobile phone that was so clever it could land spaceships, with the other. It seemed Bernard was getting cold feet about becoming a 'TV vicar' and I could hear her desperately trying to convince him that God was 'cool' with the filming.

"I'm just not sure I'm comfortable with the intrusion, dear. My wife urged me to take part because she feels it would be good for the Parish and well, she likes this sort of thing but I'm beginning to regret it. The church should be a peaceful place and I'm really not sure I can continue..."

I felt sick; without Bernard we didn't have a show. Forget

settling sleepers and wayward compost – we were in danger of losing our star and as the producer I needed to deal with it. I put down my notebook and staggered across the grass behind the church. It was horribly muddy – as it wasn't going to be in shot, it had been used as an access point by the TV trucks and the once manicured turf was churned up and slippery.

"Hello there Bernard, the rain's finally stopped then?" I called, planning to use my smooth-as-silk producer's people skills to allay Bernard's fears.

However, within a few seconds of striding across the boggy ground, I could see this was going to be harder than I imagined. The church grounds sat at the foot of the hill so all the recent rainwater had drained into it and turned parts of the soil into virtual sinking sands.

In the darkness I hadn't noticed how bad this particular section had become and despite making several attempts to set off determinedly, my feet kept sinking into the squelchy earth. Each step took me further down and threatened to suck my new Boden polka-dot wellies into muddy infinity. I panicked and tried to turn round to go back before anyone noticed, but I'd come too far. *Be calm, you can do it,* I told myself firmly, and forced my feet to make strong, quick movements which, to my horror, made the most obscene noise. Each excruciating attempt to lift my wellied foot out of the gloop became louder and more profane. This sudden noise in the darkness had the effect I'd been dreading and began to attract the attention of my fellow workers, who, I noted, giggled and stopped what they were doing to stare rather than help. Bernard (a true man of the cloth) was the only one to step forward and help me in my moment of need. He held out his big paw of a hand and, relieved to have something firm to cling to, I lunged enthusiastically at it. Unfortunately, Bernard wasn't quite ready for my gusto and this vigorous rugby tackle brought us both down into the mud.

"Oh Bernard, I'm so sorry," I cried, grabbing at him in the darkness to try and help him up.

"Stella, are you alright dear?" he said, shocked and breathless.

"I'm fine!" I cried, lurching at him for more support and slipping further in the mud.

Despite the situation, our politeness meant we both tried to help each other up but in doing so, we each simply pulled the other back to the ground. As we grappled and slid, a mass of twisted limbs and polite yelps, I was suddenly aware that camera lights had been switched on and a small crowd of researchers, runners and crew had gathered to watch the indecent, mud wrestling spectacle involving their esteemed producer and the starring vicar. "Oh my God it IS! It's Stella!" "What's she doing with the vicar?"

I tried to ignore them all and concentrate on getting out of this mess but the more we tried to heave ourselves from the mud, the more unwittingly intimate it became as I clung to Bernard for ballast. Trying hard not to swear and scream, I could hear Bernard shouting, "Oh...Oh I say... Oh..." and going under again. Throughout this whole mortifying episode I was praying that Denise wasn't watching and coming up with new ideas in sexual entertainment for the parish.

Suddenly, Al appeared at the sidelines, shouting, "Go Stella. Go Stella," and wiggling his hips in a cheerleading mantra.

"What the hell do you think I'm doing here, Al?" I yelled angrily.

"You tell *me* babycakes?" he screamed. "Whatever gets you through the night." This contribution delighted the onlookers, who roared with laughter. Even in the middle of this muddy doom, my legs wrapped round Bernard in a most inappropriate way, I managed a 'look' under my brows. Al's expression changed; he knew I meant business and throwing off his designer jacket and rolling up his jeans, he screamed "human chain!"

Within seconds, several burly crew members were clutching his waist (he told me later he couldn't believe his luck). I grabbed at Al and was dragged to safe ground, closely followed by a muddy, bewildered vicar.

"Bernard, are you OK?" Al asked, grabbing his arm and escorting him to safety.

"I'm fine. Just a bit of a surprise. I didn't expect that...in the dark...bit of a shock."

"Stella, you should be ashamed of yourself, the vicar's in shock." Al glanced over at me; even in the semi-darkness I could see his eyes dancing with laughter.

"I'm so sorry Bernard, the ground just sucked me in. Gosh I can't believe I pulled off your dog collar," I said, brushing at his chest in a vain attempt to wipe away the mud and reposition the collar, which was now hanging limply across his chest.

"You two need coffee," said Al. I could see his shoulders going up and down in mirth as he walked away. I looked round to see everyone staring in disbelief at what had just happened. I wanted to shout 'just fuck off' at everyone, I was so embarrassed, but instead I rolled my eyes, feigned a giggle and curtseyed. Then I shouted in a mock-announcer's voice; "Go back to your work, there's nothing to see here."

Once everyone had dispersed, I gathered what was left of my dignity and Al returned with refreshments.

"Al, the next time you see me up to my waist in mud and clinging to a vicar, would you help first before you make hilarious comments from the sidelines please," I hissed.

"My darling, I do hope that's the first *and* the last time I find you *in flagrante* with the vicar of the parish," he giggled, with fluttering lashes and a flash of cosmetically-whitened teeth.

I was soon furnished with a towel, a Mr Kipling and a hot

coffee. The cake revived me and despite being very muddy I was able to move on and attend to Bernard's concerns about filming.

A pleasant chap in his late fifties, our Bernard was no George Clooney or Brad Pitt, or even Jack Nicholson. He was more of a Jack Duckworth, really. After what we'd just been through together, I felt an intimacy I hoped he shared. I could see I had to convince him that God and his parishioners wouldn't desert him and that the garden makeover would be in keeping. Mind you, I had my work cut out with the new 'Punk Paint' range that was currently being slapped up and down his fencing and which promised on the tin to, 'bring out the Johnny Rotten in you!'

"This will be an amazing experience for everyone involved," I said. "And the garden will be a triumph." Who was I kidding? Even I could see that 'violent violet' paint wasn't the obvious choice for the vicar's garden showcase of Victorian art, featuring sculpted stonework, encaustic tiling and wrought iron. But I'm not one to give up.

"God would *want* this on television; he *created* this garden... why not show off his handiwork?" I heard myself saying, scrabbling at random concepts in an attempt to prevent him backing out at this late stage in production.

"Stella. There's paint everywhere, there's noise from the catering truck and shouting until all hours. There are cables and cameras all over the place and lights still full-on at midnight. Poor Denise hasn't been able to sleep because the crew keep her awake all night, banging away."

I looked away and managed to refrain from commenting.

"My biggest anxiety, Stella, is the parishioners' access to the church. I'm afraid none of us feel very close to God with a big microphone and a cherry picker bearing down on us at Evensong."

"But Bernard, I can assure you it'll be worth all the pain.

Instead of 30 or 40 parishioners at your services, you'll be on TV with more than a million!"

"That may well be true Stella, but my concerns are with my congregation and their relationship with Jesus."

I saw his point and couldn't help wishing that I had more in my armoury, that I'd paid attention in Confirmation classes or was more familiar with the writings of Patience Strong. I needed the holy approach because I realised Bernard's main concern around being on telly was God. He didn't want to piss God off (my words not his) and who could blame him for keeping in with the boss? The Lord was his bread and butter, after all.

"I was told the makeover would be minimal. Just some 'tidying up,' your colleague told me. That turned out to be rather misleading to say the least... Then there's colour scheme Stella. It's rather 'punk-rock-ish'. Do we really think scarlet and purple are the most churchlike of choices?"

I spluttered to give myself time, then went for it. "I'd say that violet is very ecclesiastical, Bernard," I tried, wiping at my mud-covered wellies with wet leaves in an attempt to hide the horror on my face and think of something else to say.

"As for the punk look," I continued, not meeting his eyes, "well, I'm sure I read in *Hello!* that Johnny Rotten has just become a born again Christian, hasn't he?"

I lied to a vicar and I may burn in hell but it was for a good cause and anyway, my fingers were crossed behind my back. I had no choice because in TV terms this was life or death and Bernard had to buy it, because we didn't have time to find another church.

"I'm worried what the Bishop's going to say about all this," he went on.

"Bernard, I promise you this will be good for you and for the church as a whole. As for the makeover, the vibrant garden will put you on the map and bring people flocking to see the garden and to Jesus."

I was just thinking that I couldn't get any lower in my desperation to make this work when I heard the dulcet tones of Gerard, the garden designer, who Al had brought in at the last minute to bring some more 'pizzazz' to the proceedings. He was hammering scarlet trellis onto the lurid lavender to the tune of Tom Jones' *Sex Bomb*.

"A charming man," Bernard said, nodding in Gerard's direction. "Though, it would be nice if he sang something a bit more appropriate while in the vicarage garden. I was under the impression he was a religious man, but I have to say his choice of music doesn't indicate this."

"Really? I hadn't noticed," I said weakly, feigning surprise. But I have to confess I was also slightly troubled by Gerard. Selected by Al for his gardening prowess and religious piety, Gerard would be making over a different aspect of the garden each week. He'd been singing pretty much since he arrived, but despite a huge and varied musical portfolio, he hadn't sung one hymn. I should have known better. Phrases like 'suitable' and 'appropriate', have always eluded Al when selecting contributors to take part in TV programmes.

There was the alcoholic tenor who drank three bottles of Tia Maria in the green room and gave an operatic performance live on *Great Morning* that was likened to the late Ollie Reed's live-and-inebriated rendition of *Wild Thing*. Then there was the narcoleptic Al booked to talk about his condition on live telly. Not surprisingly, our studio guest slept through most of the interview while the hapless presenter 'filled' for six whole minutes – which may as well be a year in television. And my own personal favourite, the psychic with Tourette's that Al booked for *Have a Dead Good Morning*. There had also been naked decorators, gay gardeners and bulimic dieticians, all with their own unique way of stealing the show and blocking phone lines with viewers' complaints.

I reassured Bernard once more that all was OK and went to find Al in the makeshift and optimistically-titled catering tent.

"Al, can you assure me that Gerard wasn't the result of a trawl through one of your favourite gay dating websites?" I said as I joined him at a table where he was eating a rather delicious-looking chip butty.

"My sweet, it's a bona-fide garden company and Gerard comes highly recommended," he answered, taking a huge bite of hot, chip-filled bread. I knew what he was up to – he was trying to dismiss the whole subject with chip distraction.

"That looks nice. But I've started a diet," I muttered, refusing to be drawn into the hot chips and melting butter on thick, white, doorstep bread. I pictured the 'delicious, nutritious' Lighter Lift shake that was waiting for me back at the B&B and felt even more depressed. I grabbed a black coffee and returned to poke again at 'the Gerard problem.'

"I know you think I'm completely paranoid," I said, sitting down at the table and letting the steam from my coffee provide warmth and a mini-facial, "but Gerard's not your typical gardener, is he?"

Al shrugged, "What is a typical gardener Stel? I mean he's got all the qualifications..."

"Mmm, it's fine on paper but it's something else when Gerard, in his twenty-two-stone glory is brandishing a pitchfork and working it to the tune of *Smack My Bitch Up* on the vicar's grassy knoll," I spat, now deeply resenting the way the butter was melting around Al's chips.

"You said you didn't want the same old gardeners with their boring old trugs and terracotta, so that's what you've got. His designs are just a bit different and the garden will be fabulous, you old drama queen!" With that he stood up and blew me a kiss before rushing off for an overdue and much-needed conversation about sleepers with Dan.

I decided that for my own sanity I needed some space and time alone. I wandered out of the catering tent and stood for a moment in the vicarage garden, just wishing I could blank it all out like I wasn't really there. I longed to escape the pressure, move up and away to see it all from the safety of the cherry picker high above the trees.

But I couldn't. I had to stay on earth and watch close up as Denise resurrected Sodom and Gomorrah, Al screamed and flirted, and Gerard and his pack of 'heavenly heavies' turned God's garden into something resembling a steamy night in Bangkok.

4

A Rainy Night in Rochdale

I changed out of my mud-covered clothes and had a quick shower as soon as I got back to my cheap B&B and even though by now it was well after eleven, I called home. I missed Grace so much; sometimes just speaking to her on the phone helped, but there was no answer. Before, when I'd worked away, Tom had called me at night and passed the phone to Grace. When she was tiny these calls involved a lisping voice lost in a confusing jumble of baby words involving 'teddy' and 'Daddy'. The novelty would wear off for her quite quickly and within about 45 seconds I'd find myself talking to no-one as she dropped the phone to investigate something far more urgent and interesting.

"I'll have to go, she wants to play," Tom would say apologetically. Putting down the phone, my heart would break and I'd return to writing the scripts I seem to have spent my life doing. I loved and hated those calls; they were a tantalising glimpse at the home-life that was going on without me. I always felt a deep compulsion to jump in the car and drive home and I had to steel myself to turn my heart off and my laptop on.

Grace was now eight and if she did deign to speak to me it was about the score she'd achieved on the latest Nintendo game or a confused retelling of something that happened at school. A slight in the playground or a recrimination at fruit time can cause ripples of hurt until afternoon break when you're that age.

I tried the phone again, wondering why it was that Tom didn't call me these days. No answer, just an incessant, empty ring followed by my embarrassingly fake posh voice: "Hi, this is the Weston house. Please leave your message and we'll get back to you."

I sighed and opened the can of Lighter Lift, swirling the 'Passionate Pineapple' around and taking a big swig. It certainly didn't seem to me to have the 'aroma of the tropics' – more like paint stripper. The cheap Custard Creams thoughtfully left for me by what was laughingly referred to as Room Service suddenly looked very appealing. They stared up at me from the nasty, chipped saucer with diamond-shaped edging, willing me to eat them. I turned back to the phone hastily.

After the tenth ring there was still no answer. Suddenly it all started to get a bit 'Violent Violet' in my head. Had Grace had an accident? Had Tom fallen off a ladder onto Grace, pinning her down, neither of them able to get to the phone? Had they disturbed a deranged burglar and were they now both tied up? As my call rung, – cruelly, mockingly – were they trying to reach for the phone with their fingers inches away, so near and yet so far?

I promised myself this would be the last time I dialled (knowing deep down that it wouldn't be). 'Ring, ring,' for an eternity, 'ring'. Then, just as I was about to hang up, 'click.' I heard Tom's abrupt voice: "Hello?"

I was filled with overwhelming relief, warmth and love which naturally manifested itself in an angry, clipped voice: "Tom! Where the hell have you been? I've been so worried."

"Stella, we're fine. I've only just got Grace to go to sleep and now the phone has woken her. Thanks, it's late enough as it is."

My relief was replaced with a nice cold splash of anger. How dare he speak to me like that? How dare he tell me what time *my* daughter goes to bed?

"Oh, I'm sorry if I've been worried sick all night about my family. If *you* had phoned *me* Grace wouldn't have been woken up. Where the bloody hell have you been?"

"Don't start, Stella," he said, with simmering anger. "We went to the cinema. She wanted to see that film about the penguin. It went on quite late. I finally got her off to sleep and now you've woken her up. I can't believe you're ringing this late," he muttered.

I was furious. How could he be so unfeeling? I knew it wasn't just about waking Grace either – he just wanted to finish the conversation and get back to watching sport on the TV – bloody balls on pitches.

"How is she?" I asked firmly, trying to cut through the bubbling rage on both ends of the line. This was my daughter and I needed to be kept informed of her well-being. It was my right as a mother.

"She's fine and I'm fine," Tom said in an irritated voice. "I've just got her to bed and I'm about to have my dinner – it's getting cold. I'm knackered, Stella. It's not easy working and looking after a child at the same time you know. It's all right for you..."

That put me on the ceiling, red mist pumping into my brain like dry ice, at the point of no return.

"Oh, yes it's great for me. Do tell me about being a working father, Tom. After all, I love being here working my tits off and feeling like a crap mother. Then when I'm home and working all day at the office, I also work my tits off and feel like a crap mother. Tough isn't it? Welcome to my world."

I slammed the phone down, tears of hurt and rage stinging my eyes. Most of all, I was disappointed. All I wanted was to have a normal conversation with my husband and to know my little girl was safe and happy. I wanted anecdotes and quotes. What did she do? What did she say? How did she say it? I wanted some of Al's colour and fun. It wouldn't have taken too much effort for him to give me a few highlights – but it's all Venus and Mars and I'm convinced straight men just don't do colour...or fun.

Not having a fully-equipped kitchen in which to bake away my stress, I reached over to the nasty saucer and grabbed the packet of Custard Creams. I ripped off the cellophane and crammed both of them into my mouth at once, which made me feel a bit better – for about a nanosecond. My Lighter Lift counsellor –'Jemma with a J' – would go into a spasm if I confessed I'd actually let real food pass my lips, and filthy biscuits at that. When I'd dared to suggest during my Lighter Lift Induction Day that I might be hungry drinking only three 'highly nutritious yet delicious,' shakes she had almost hyperventilated.

"Stella, you couldn't possibly be hungry. These shakes are medically formulated. My goodness!" she had exclaimed, breathlessly patting her tiny, washboard tummy.

I sighed and slowly threw the wrappers in the bin. Sat in my lonely little room, I was beginning to think that I'd turned up in someone else's life. Part of me couldn't believe I wasn't eighteen anymore and I was slightly worried that time was running out for me to do everything I wanted to. I'd always believed my destiny was to be a successful film producer with a walk-in wardrobe, Persian pussy and second home in the Bahamas. My only problem would be what to wear for my spot on *David Letterman* in a life of gilt-edged glamour and gleaming flesh. In between the parties and Pilates I'd adopt left-wing politics and rainbow babies from Third World countries. And after the book signings and Botox lunches I'd squeeze in a bottle of Dom Perignon and a couple of torrid toy boys.

The reality, of course, was that at the age of forty-ish, I was digging a vicar's vegetable patch and forcing crazy people to smile for the camera all day. At night I killed time by trying not to eat cake and stalking my wrinkles far from home in a very cold, very single hotel room on the outskirts of Rochdale. I could hear Tom's voice ringing in my ears: '*You want too much. You are setting yourself up for disappointment. Life will never live up to your expectations*'.

He's right, I *was* disappointed because it didn't matter how hard I searched the dingy hotel bathroom, or how tightly I shut my eyes, I just couldn't find the Dom Perignon or the toy boys.

5

Trouble in Paradise

I didn't call Tom again that night. I decided to give him some space and leave it until the next morning. But I needed to sort it early so I could be free to concentrate on the last rehearsals before the first live show in the afternoon. Again I waited and waited for Tom to answer and when he finally did, it was clear that he was going to continue to be vile. Again the one-word comments, the gruff voice and the sulky demeanour, so I tried to approach things from a different angle.

"Tom, what is it? Why do you always seem so abrupt? It's like you don't want to talk to me."

"You always ring at the wrong time, Stella," he answered. "We're in the middle of breakfast. And I'm tired – with you away, I never even get a weekend lie-in."

"Oh, I'm sorry. I thought this would be a good time." I said, crushed. "I don't seem to be able to do anything right at the moment." Silence. "Mind you, I find your lively telephone banter irresistible, it has me hanging up laughing every time," I added.

He laughed. If in doubt, make them laugh. I always used to make him laugh. Tom and I had been married for ten years. I could still remember the time we would be excited just being together – when we made each other laugh, stayed in bed all day, stayed up all night. I often wondered where all that intensity and spontaneity went to. On second thoughts, they were probably hanging out with my firm skin and pointless dreams – too far out of reach.

You'd think there would have been more understanding between us with us both being in the same business. I remembered the day we met, when we were both working in London at the BBC. We'd done a few shoots together so would say hello and perhaps chat if our paths crossed, but I was obsessed with someone else at the time and didn't really notice Tom, he was just another cameraman.

It was at Steve the soundman's leaving party that things changed.

The party was in a rough old pub in the backstreets of Shepherd's Bush and I went along with some of the girls for a first drink. We'd planned to go on to a wine bar and end up at The Groucho for last drinks and a bit of star spotting. I was coming out of the toilets and as I passed the bar I saw Tom, who smiled, so I peeped under eyelashes, Princess-Di-style, while sashaying past. He was tall, with short, thick, black hair and a smile that filled his face. I went back to the girls but I kept catching him looking at me. Eventually he wandered over to our table. We started chatting and he made me laugh.

"We could go and see a film one evening after work?" he suggested after we'd been chatting for about an hour. "There's a new film club opened in Camden and they're showing old black and white films. I think there's a Hitchcock season coming up."

So as the girls waltzed off to The Groucho that night I was happy to stay in the smoky bar with Tom and the whiskery locals. In the next hour we discovered a shared a passion for old films, dark chocolate and black humour. Kismet.

We saw *Dial M for Murder* on our first outing, on the second date we went to the zoo (a cliché I know) and on the third date I moved into his flat. It was a bit of a whirlwind, but it just felt right. And at the wrong side of thirty, I wasn't letting this one go.

We laughed a lot then in Tom's cramped, rented flat. We

watched TV on an old portable and lived on takeaways and cheap plonk. When we weren't in bed, we'd spend weekends at the cinema watching films back to back, our only sustenance being popcorn, chocolate and each other. After we'd lived this completely carefree, self-indulgent life for about a year Tom suggested we get married. I loved him, loved big parties and *really* loved big cake, so I said yes.

"Stella, we miss you," he said suddenly. "I'm bored spending every evening and weekend on my own. Grace needs you and I'm tired of living like a single parent."

I dreamt of spending time alone with Grace and I often wished I were in his shoes, especially after I had been demoted to gardening hell. But this was the most he'd said in weeks, so I resisted whinging about *my* feelings for once.

"Well, I bet you love being a single parent outside the school gate with all those Yummy Mummies!" I half-joked (Tom meeting another mum outside the school gate and falling madly in love was number three on my 'Things That Could Possibly Go Wrong,' list).

"Stella. You don't take anything seriously," he started. This was sounding like a gear change so I leapt in for damage limitation, scared of losing the warm wave of telephone intimacy.

"I know it's tough for you," I soothed, "but Tom, I've just had a wonderful idea. Why don't you and Grace come and visit me in Rochdale next Saturday? We could have a proper family day, just the three of us."

"Oh Stella. You're working and it's a long way for Grace to travel and..."

"Yes, I know all that but as it's the first show today the pressure will be off. It's going to be a small series, tucked away on a Sunday afternoon, so by next Saturday I'll have everything in place and I can work on final script changes when you go back on Saturday night. I know it's a couple of hours' drive but you're both off and Grace will sleep in the car, she always does."

"Mmm, I don't know. It's not like she's a two-year old anymore who will nap all day you know."

That hurt, of course I knew that. I realised she was eight, it's not like I hadn't seen her for six years. Recently I'd only been able to see her every couple of weeks and I knew I'd missed a lot, but it wasn't by choice – he didn't need to rub it in. I bit my tongue.

After a little more persuasion and me promising faithfully to take the whole day off and not do *any* work – or even answer my mobile – Tom agreed. He put Grace on the phone and when I told her she'd be coming to see me she screeched with delight: "Yay, we're going to see Mummy!" I thought my heart would burst. Then Tom came back on the line.

"I hope it goes well today. We'll be watching the programme, so good luck." I hung up the phone, feeling positive and happy – and then I noticed that I had an answer phone message. It was from Peter Willis, the head of Gardening and executive producer of the show.

His message was all tight vowels and deep voice.

"Stella, I'm on my way to the location. I have some concerns we need to discuss urgently– I shall be with you at noon."

Whatever the problem was, it was clearly bad enough for him to travel up for an urgent meeting on the day of the first live show, which indicated that it must be quite serious. Peter may have been absent for most of the programme preparation, but as the executive in charge I'd hoped I could rely on him for support on today of all days.

When MJ first sent me to Gardening I'd reported to Peter Willis and, still feeling very bruised, did little to hide my incredulity at the latest programme idea; "Religion and gardening? This is a joke, isn't it Peter? No-one is really expecting this programme to work. Are they?" He was uncomfortable, but could always come up with a soundbite or stock phrase to cover himself and the fact he hadn't a clue.

"It's all about funding and a need to please the God-Squadders, Stel my love," he said, with no eye contact but a louche smile at a passing young shoot.

"And you come highly recommended from Ms Mary-Jane Robinson, no less."

"Mmm, so I gather..."

"Stella my love, the programme's fine editorial content will be to question and embrace the meaning of God, life, death, humanity. Not forgetting to remind our viewers about late frost in spring and early frost in autumn."

I was about to launch into a tirade about MJ and my concerns about this project, but he knew what was coming and didn't want to hear it. I took a wild guess and thought to myself *when this all falls flat on its face, over-budget with garden manure hitting fans in every religious establishment in the country, there'll be a scapegoat and there'll be a Judas. No prizes for guessing which one I'll be.* MJ had left no stone unturned. I had to hand it to her – she'd surpassed herself.

Back in Bernard's (and God's) Garden, I was in deep panic. Peter turning up at short notice with something serious to declare had me worried. This led to the copious consumption of hot, thickly-buttered toast, two Star Bars and several mugs of hot chocolate before 8am. So much for the Lighter Lift diet – this morning's oh-so-delicious 'Amazing Apple' was a distant (and rather revolting) memory.

Al appeared and was, as always, very excited. He didn't take any of it seriously and every now and then said unhelpful things like, "Stel, it must be *really* serious if he's coming all this way," and in an annoying, mock-American accent "Oh girlfriend. I hate to say this – but you *is* in trouble!"

I ignored him and as I waited for Peter's arrival I tried to cast my mind back to the last time I'd spoken with him. It was long before Rochdale and he'd given me some advice, in fact the only advice he'd ever given me; "Be careful with Islam." He'd whispered this, placing a conspiratorial arm around my shoulder.

I think there was a message here, albeit in code. I think he was saying that it would be nice if the gardening programme didn't cause an international incident resulting in street riots and my effigy on fire. I would second that.

"Its bibles and bulbs then," I'd shouted after him, smiling bravely and trying not to sound ever-so-slightly murderous or suicidal. The head gardener had smiled back as he walked through the door and stopped for a second.

"Hey, that's not a bad idea for the programme title," he'd said, and left.

I was in the vicarage with Denise when he arrived. It was about 12.30 and we were in the kitchen enjoying a herbal. Well, she was enjoying it, along with her usual topic of conversation while I tried to work. When she heard the car pull up outside, Denise leapt up and lifted the chintz curtains (apparently the vicarage had come ready-furnished so there wasn't much of Denise's unique style).

"Ooh, *he* means business," said Denise, peering over her bifocals and giving Peter the once-over through chintz and old netting.

"Is he your boss Stel? Wouldn't mind a bit of that – the power's quite a turn on, isn't it?" she looked over her glasses and winked at me. I smiled nervously. I had to keep her away from him. Her nocturnal goings on atop the Church organ could be the reason for his visit and I may need to play her proclivities down. "You should see his face, Stella," said Denise, twitching the curtains. "He's not happy. I think yer in fer a bollockin' love. Good luck!"

As the door bell chimed I laughed weakly, reassuring her there were no problems at all, then almost knocked her over dashing to answer the door before she could.

"Hi there, welcome!" I shouted in the Head Gardener's face, trying to sound enthusiastic but actually having the demeanour of someone on drugs. I noticed him stepping back stiffly, unsmiling. I knew then it was bad. I saw Belinda walk past out of the corner of my eye and I'm ashamed to say that for an instant I considered throwing a young researcher under this carnal bus to save myself. Peter had always had a weakness for the ladies and missed the 'big promotion' long ago after being caught in an edit suite with a bottle of Gordon's and a redhead from Graphics. At the time, he claimed he was showing her 'the flexibility of digital editing', but she told *The News of the World* a different story. It wasn't long before 'TV Boss in Gin-Soaked Sex Tape' was on everyone's lips and he found himself on top of the dung heap in TV-gardening.

"My dear," he began ominously. "This is a matter of extreme urgency. Is there somewhere private we can talk?"

Denise had rushed off to polish the altar (a euphemism I guessed, but didn't pursue) so I offered Peter tea in the vicarage kitchen.

"Come in. Hope you had a good journey. Isn't it cloudy today?"

"Stella. A matter has been brought to my attention and as executive of this programme I am- well, frankly, I'm horrified," said Peter theatrically as I filled the kettle with pounding water from a leaky tap and placed it neatly on the hob. I found some chipped mugs in the cupboard and arranged them too carefully near the tea caddy, aware that Peter was glowering at me from the other side of the kitchen. Everything was in slow motion on the outside, yet inside I was screaming and tearing around. I had a programme to prepare, including a running order, script, phone calls, safety checks and rehearsals. Everyone was relying on me and waiting for my signature/go-ahead/decisions on everything. Even without his visit I was on borrowed time but having wasted the morning waiting for him I was now seriously behind. Pouring boiling water onto fragrant tea bags I felt as though I was trying to run at two hundred miles an hour but barely managing to keep up.

Is this what a breakdown feels like? I thought, grimacing and proffering tea and biscuits to Peter.

"HobNobs!" he announced with unbridled joy, forgetting solemnity for a second and cramming his mouth with golden crumbs.

"Everything's going really well here," I started while his mouth was full. "Great team...we're so busy getting ready for the first show..."

His raised his hand to stop me talking and he sucked hard on hot Earl Grey. Eventually, he took a seat at the table and after an eternity of crumb-wiping and mug-moving like he was playing chess, he spoke.

"It would seem," he started, "that Media World's most stringent Health and Safety policies have not been adhered to and the public and crew have been exposed to a dangerous criminal." He banged his mug onto the table dramatically and tea slopped over the rim.

My heart skipped a beat. What the hell was he talking about?

"A – a criminal?" I spluttered, my voice breaking slightly. This was going to be tough to get out of.

He nodded, slowly and deliberately.

"I had no idea, Peter. Who? I mean..."

The hand went up again and he raised his voice, "Your garden designer, Gerard Wilkins, is an ex-con. You realise that this contravenes all our health, safety and social regulations. It is NOT our policy to employ serious offenders," he said, in full Shakespearean mode now.

"For God's sake, Stella, there are some very young, vulnerable women on this production team. They could be taken in by this...this potential serial killer."

The thought of all those young, vulnerable girls had stopped him mid-sentence and he was clearly conjuring an image for his own use later. It gave me a few seconds to collect myself. I was genuinely shocked about Gerard – despite his musical interludes he'd seemed such a kind, gentle man. I wondered what he could possibly have done to be deemed a serious offender.

"I'm so sorry Peter, I knew nothing about this. What do you want me to do?"

Peter gazed into his tea; "Stella, unfortunately this matter has gone further than I would have liked. I was advised by a trusted colleague to take the matter higher – I mean, I need to be crystal-clear and think of my career. I can't be held responsible for this. Now the big boss is threatening all kinds of..."

"Oh, you went *that* much higher?" I said. Obviously the fact that I had compromised the whole production was now not only public knowledge back at Media World, but Frank Moores had also been told.

"Peter, please. We'll pull the shoot immediately." I said, my chin trembling slightly.

"Pull the shoot? I don't think so! I've bought a whole new wardrobe for this show," screamed Denise as she burst into the kitchen, followed by a very sheepish Al. Sporting her 'workout' gear, which consisted of a very tiny top and fluorescent cycling shorts, Denise had obviously dressed up (or rather, down) for Peter. As he turned to speak to her I swore I saw a light flicker in his eyes.

"Well hello," he said, Latin Love God taking over, kissing her hand rather vigorously. "I'm Peter. I'm the Executive Producer."

"And I'm Denise. We haven't met but I've heard all about you!"

He went from angry manager to lustful lothario in a millisecond. "And I'm sure you will be on everyone's lips too before long," he oiled. It was actually quite impressive.

"Ooh, thank you kindly Peter," Denise said, coquettishly pulling a seat up right next to him.

"Now what's all this about?" she asked, all wide-eyed innocence and tight top.

"Denise, Denise, Denise," he smiled, playing with her name on his tongue in a rather inappropriate way. "We have a teeny-tiny staffing problem. Nothing for you to worry about."

"Well Peter," she paused, making full eye contact, her tongue pushing hard through chewing gum in a very provocative manner. "Al was filming me doing me push-ups in the hall and we couldn't help overhearing your conversation. Now who's been saying that lovely Gerard's a criminal? That's slander isn't it? I happen to know he *did* spend time in Strangeways a few years back but he's hardly Jack-the-bloody-Ripper."

"Really Denise, do tell," Peter leaned forward, his eyes at cleavage level.

"Well, years ago, Gerard had a panties stall on Sheffield Market. Fabulous stuff Peter, lacy thongs and teeny-tiny little brassieres," Denise said, waggling her breasts for emphasis. "The problem was, he was buying it cheap and selling it cheap. He says he didn't know they were hot – stolen – but fifty pence for a pair of frillies? He sold 'em for a pound a pair and made a bloody fortune!"

Peter was staring at Denise, mesmerised.

"He got twelve months," she went on, "the judge was making an example of him. Did him a favour really, 'cos that's when he got the gardening bug. He learned all about garden-design in prison."

My head was spinning. If this was true, then I might be off the hook but would it be enough to save the shoot? I looked over at Peter and to my relief he was looking more relaxed.

"Are you sure about this, Denise?" he said, without taking his eyes off her fluorescent top.

"Ooh yes Peter," she replied. "He's really quite proud of how he's turned his life around after prison. It's quite inspiring," she added, with an exaggerated arm stretch.

"Well. It's still less than ideal but perhaps not quite the disaster I feared. You still should have checked this Stella, it's very unprofessional – but maybe, in light of this, we can carry on for the time being. I'll see if I can sort this with the office, "he said, still staring at Denise. They were gazing at each other intensely, as though Al and I weren't there. I felt like a gooseberry and could see Al was about to open his mouth, so before he told them to get a room I grabbed him and we went to find Gerard. We needed him to confirm he wasn't a mad, spade-wielding sex-murderer, just an ex-market-stall holder who couldn't resist bargain lingerie. Career crisis had been averted – for now.

"This whole Gerard thing could have caused me a massive problem Al," I said angrily, as we walked back to the garden together.

"I know Stel, and I feel terrible about it," he said shaking his head.

"I've told you before, you can't just find people for the

screen off the Internet. It's not safe and they can tell you anything about themselves. As it happens Gerard isn't dangerous, but he might have been."

"Stel, I told you earlier, I didn't find Gerard on the Internet. He was a personal recommendation."

"Where the hell from? Some ex-convict convention?"

"From MJ."

I stopped in my tracks and pulled him round to look at me.

"I'm sorry Al, what did you just say?"

"MJ told me just before we came here that she knew a really brilliant garden-designer who would make our programme special. And, well, I knew she wasn't your greatest fan but I never thought..." started Al, looking as if he wanted the ground to swallow him up.

"That scrawny, manipulative witch!" I yelled. "She put Gerard our way, and then when he was settled and the programme was about to be filmed she told Peter that he'd been to prison."

Al bit his lip. "I feel awful. And stupid."

I put my arm around him, still shaking with anger. "Fortunately for us, Denise knew the truth and is a shameless flirt. It's lucky she's so nosy, or we'd both be packing."

"I know," said Al. "I'm so sorry Stel. I promise never to listen to MJ again."

"Let's get back to work" I said, taking a deep breath to calm myself and turning towards the melée, "we've got a show to run."

And with only hours to go until the first live broadcast, we needed every spare second.

6

Showtime!

By teatime I was in a cold sweat. I drank ten cups of coffee and
went through the final script. Bernard was the main man and yet
he'd barely ever *seen* a TV-camera before. We were asking a lot
of him but I was just hoping he'd recruited some heavenly help –
after all, it was Sunday. Just before the final run-through, my
phone beeped. It was a text from Lizzie.

   TXT: *Good Luck darling. Remember, Jesus loves you.*

   I smiled, and put the phone in my pocket.
   I met up with the presenter, a brunette news anchor called
Debbie who I worked with as a humble researcher on *Good
Morning Britain* many years ago. She'd been an absolute bitch to
me then and had treated me with the utmost contempt.
   Debbie was a competent presenter but she didn't have that
elusive star quality and as we had a rather elusive budget we
were stuck with her. She'd never made it to prime time and that
had always made her bitter and tough to work with. She hated
anyone under 35 and had a charming way of asking researchers
for refreshment, which was: "Coffee. Now!"
   Funnily enough when she'd turned up a few days earlier in
full make-up, Barbour jacket and pink wellies, it was *she* who
brought coffee to *me*. How things change. "Darling its *ages* since
we worked together," she exclaimed, too enthusiastically. She
was over-the-top delightful and hugged me like we were old

mates. I felt sick.

"I think it was *Good Morning Britain*," I ventured politely. "I was a researcher then and as all good presenters know, today's researchers are tomorrow's producers," I added, pointedly. Then I sipped coffee, waggled my pen and talked through the script authoritatively. She nodded and smiled and fawned. I was civil but cool and made a mental note to keep my eye on the nasty piece of work should any unsuspecting young researcher come into her orbit.

"It's lucky you have no work on and are free for this series. We were trying for Nadia Sawahla but she's far too busy." I said, smiling sweetly. *I'm becoming a twisted TV tart*, I thought. *Maybe it is time to get out.*

If Debbie was nervous about the live broadcast, she hid it well. I wished her luck and she staggered off through the mud while I climbed into the satellite truck. This is where a live programme is transmitted from for an outside broadcast and where the producer and director and the more vital people like technicians sat during the programme. It's always small and hot and cramped in those things, but the excitement and nervousness was tangible. It was 'live' and anything could happen.

Our director Sam told the cameras where to be and the vision mixer switched between all the different cameras, showing off the garden and checking everything was working before we set off on our first 'journey'. I could see from the monitors that Denise was ready for her close-up and Al was also in the garden giving Bernard a pep talk. I noticed Bernard looked a little pale and pressed the 'talkback' button in front of me to find out from Al if all was ok.

"Mmm, he'll be fine honey. Just a little bit of vomiting. I'm mopping him up now."

"Christ Al, we're coming to him in about three minutes,

we're about to go on air. Make sure he's clean." My heart was in my mouth. This first show needed to be brilliant so that people watched again. The thought of our leading clergyman vomiting in his own flowerbed seconds before we went on air made me want to be sick too.

As the music started my stomach filled with butterflies and the PA began counting down from ten. It felt like I was in the cockpit of a small plane about to take off. The weather could be calm or stormy and I was filled with exhilaration and dry-mouthed fear at the same time. There was nothing quite like this feeling and for those ten seconds it was actually almost worth all the crap and hard work.

As I watched on the monitors, my heart racing, I could see (with great relief) that Gerard's violet garden looked a little less lurid on camera. It actually added a bit of colour to a potentially boring backdrop and it was certainly different.

Surprisingly, everything started well. Debbie did an opening piece to camera introducing the programme and establishing our location. She then introduced Bernard; "What a beautiful setting you have here, Reverend Butterworth. How long have you been vicar of this parish?"

Bernard looked straight at the camera and opened his mouth then he looked back at Debbie and back to camera. For what seemed like half an hour – but was only a few seconds – Bernard stood in front of the camera opening and closing his mouth like a goldfish. He'd been fine in rehearsals, but like so many people he'd completely clammed up as soon as the camera was whirring.

I looked at Sam and he looked at me; "Shall we do a tight on Debbie?" I was loathe to cut Bernard's part so quickly in favour of waffle in close-up from Debbie but it had to be better than dead air and it was becoming horribly clear that nothing was coming out of Bernard's mouth.

I could feel heat rising through my body and the blood rushing to my head. Debbie may not have had star quality, but she was a safe pair of hands on air and with my guidance on talkback we could get through it with Bernard still in vision. "Hang on Sam," I said, calm taking over. I leapt onto the talkback that Debbie could hear in her ear.

"You've been at this parish for twelve years now," I said in a presenter's voice over the talkback. Debbie looked calm and repeated the sentence.

"Get the wife on, quick!" I shouted, hoping that crazy Denise in the role as 'tainted Angel of Mercy' would be able to step in and talk lucidly and colourfully (but not too colourfully) about a vicar's life in a Northern town. She'd been schooled by me on what would be appropriate and warned not to talk about ecclesiastical orgasms or the verger's weakness for whips.

"Hello Denise. As the First Lady of this parish, what's life like in this lovely village?"

Everyone in the garden and in the OB truck held their breath.

Denise stepped forward, wobbly on high heels. She was sporting a full-length, tangerine frock which strangely complemented the purple hard-landscaping, albeit in a hallucinogenic-hippie-on-acid kind of way.

"We love this village and its people, there's such a sense of community here that you don't always find these days," was her opening line, which sounded surprisingly sane for Denise. "We also love the rugged landscape round these parts. We like our garden to reflect this with no pretentions, using local stone and native planting, as God intended. The television company have certainly added something different with the vibrant colours – but it works."

She went on to talk about the seasons in the garden and some of the produce from the vegetable patch; I held my breath throughout. To my amazement and relief, it went brilliantly. Debbie guided Denise expertly through about ten minutes of planting, preening and plucking interspersed with charming (and non-sexual) anecdotes about village life. Then the show cut to some previously filmed footage and my air exploded out of my mouth in relief.

"We roll VT footage for six minutes thirty seconds," I said to Debbie over the talkback. "So you're OK for five, then stand by." On the monitor I could see her relay this to Bernard and Denise and they visibly relaxed. I watched the footage. It was some nice shots of Bernard visiting sick and elderly parishioners, which would hopefully compensate for his stage fright. As the nation watched Bernard dispensing comfort and kindness, Sam and I exchanged a smile. Against all odds, everything was on cue and the end was suddenly in sight. It was all going brilliantly, in fact – right up until the point it went horribly wrong.

Just as we were about to broadcast live again I suddenly spotted our garden designer making his musical entrance and dancing right up to Debbie, holding out the watering can needed for the next shot and humming Britney to himself. "What the hell is Gerard doing? He's in the wrong place! Get him off the set now!" I hissed over the talkback.

But it appeared that Debbie had become busy with Denise who had just 'adjusted' her dress and managed to drop the clip-on mic down her cleavage. "Can I have some help here please?" Debbie yelled, as she plunged her hand between Denise's voluptuous breasts. "I can't find it!"

Some of the production crew ran over and Gerard stopped humming long enough to offer some advice. "It's all right love," he said to Denise, "just jump up and down and it will fall right out." Denise began jogging up and down and shaking her breasts left and right to free the mic, with no notable success.

"Live in ten seconds, Stella," the PA called urgently.

"Debbie!" I yelled. "*We are on air in ten seconds!*" But Debbie clearly couldn't hear me. She was shouting at Denise to stand still, all the while wrist deep in cleavage and her earpiece must have got dislodged in the scuffle. Gerard's humming turned into full on singing as three of the crew plus Debbie tried desperately to extract the mic. "Oh dear," Denise beamed at one of the very red faced male runners, "It does seem rather stuck, doesn't it?"

"Five seconds, Stella!" The PA screamed.

"Debbie!!! Just clear the set!" I yelled. But it was no good – I could see her earpiece dangling uselessly over her shoulder. "Somebody get on set, now!" I shouted, jumping out of my seat.

"Two seconds!"

I lurched uselessly towards the door. But it was too late.

"And we're live!" said the PA.

Everything went silent in my head. On screen, everyone carried on, unaware that we were broadcasting live to the nation. I could see Debbie thrusting her hand further down Denise's top and from his excitable gestures, Gerard appeared to be cranking the singing up a gear. I watched them for what seemed like hours. Then suddenly the sound flooded back to me and the full horror of what we were beaming to the nation sunk in. Far from preaching or even pruning, the live TV audience was being treated to the glorious spectacle of Gerard waving a watering can and singing *Oops I did it again* at the top of his voice and the presenter and three runners groping the vicar's wife. Not realising we were back on air, Debbie finally managed to grasp Denise's wayward mic and she pulled it out with a flourish. "Got it!" she shouted, "And for God's sake Gerard, SHUT UP! Jesus!"

At which point my heart stopped. I was probably clinically dead for about six seconds.

I mutely watched Debbie as she realised her earpiece was

dislodged. I saw her find it, adjust it, and stand stock still as she listened to someone out of shot. Then Debbie's 'safe hands' flew up to her face in horror as she finally realised we were broadcasting live to the nation. This time, everything really did stop. Denise stopped talking, Gerard stopped singing and our presenter was mute. Everything seemed to go deathly quiet and I could almost see the tumbleweed rolling over the set.

"I knew it," I spat and glanced urgently at Sam, who had his head in his hands.

"Well this wasn't in rehearsal, Stella," he said, looking up.

"Petunias," I yelled into the talkback, "we need to talk about the vicar's PETUNIAS."

As I screamed down the talkback and Sam frantically pressed buttons and moved the cameras around, all hell was breaking loose in the garden. We cut to the petunias, which is where Gerard should have been to give tips and advice. Instead, the petunias sat unattended and the viewers could just make out Bernard in the corner of the shot, once more retching over the flowerbed.

"Debbie!" I yelled. "Leave bloody Denise and get Gerard over to the petunia bed!" Debbie grabbed his arm and sprinted over the lawn, sliding gracelessly into shot and tripping Gerard, who slopped the contents of the watering can all over Debbie and himself. "Argghh! Sam, cut to the next recorded piece whilst we sort this out!" I screamed.

Then, just when I thought it couldn't possibly get any worse, I glanced at the monitor to watch our next VT of Denise drawing the raffle at the WI but to my utter, utter horror all I saw was myself grappling in the mud with Bernard. For a few seconds I tried to process the shots of the vicar/producer mess now being beamed across Britain's airwaves. I could only imagine this little 'out-take' had been meant as a joke for me at the after-show party but some idiot had loaded it into the wrong place.

I wanted to cry. All the planning, all the late nights structuring the programme, all the rehearsals and readings, and then *this*. It was supposed to be petunias here, tease a bit of Jesus to keep them on the edge of their seats there, then launch into huge sunflowers, ornamental cabbages and end with a starry sprinkling of The Holy Ghost and a word from our vicar. When we cut back to the church for said last words from Bernard it seemed that his nerves were actually some form of food poisoning and his sermon – our grand finale – was being punctuated with various ungodly sounds.

As I watched the vicar trying to find words of wisdom whilst battling extreme flatulence on one monitor and an overweight, karaoke Britney-wannabe trying to mop up a terrified presenter on the other, I threw my hands up in the air and gave up. The PA began counting down to the end of the show. "Thank God," I sighed.

Sam looked at me. "Roll the fucking credits," he said, "before I die."

In the little van we just sat there in shock. Outside all was silent. Then suddenly Al's voice came on talkback. "Er Stella, the vicar's been sick again, I think we might have to get a doctor. It's all over the altar." I looked at Sam and after a few seconds of mutual horror I just started to laugh, then he started to laugh. As we climbed out of the van the crew were looking at us, waiting for a reaction and when they saw that the director and producer were holding each other up and howling hysterically they started too. It wasn't long before the whole crew were rolling around in the mud and Denise was pole dancing round the sound mic.

"I will never work in telly again," I announced, to anyone who would listen, "but what a send off."

7

Family Fun Day

The next morning I woke to the sound of a ringing telephone cutting like a knife through my skull. I was so hung over I couldn't even think of breakfast – which is usually my first thought of the day. Our response to the disastrous show the previous evening had been to fall into the nearest pub and get wasted. As I gently picked up the receiver, snippets of the evening came back to haunt me. Al and Gerard singing karaoke, both fighting to be Lily Allen, and me and Denise drinking weird cocktails until way past last orders. I was wondering what a glass of 'Rampant Monkey' actually consisted of as I held the phone gently to my ear.

"Stella, its Peter here. I insist you come down to the set immediately," was all I heard. This had the effect of a bucket of cold water and I just knew this was bad news and I was about to be sacked.

I gathered myself together, dragged on some clothes and staggered to the set. When I arrived the garden was empty, with no sign of Peter, or anyone else for that matter. In the silence I heard the hopeful chink of crockery and my Pavlovian response was to head for the catering tent. At times like this I never saw the point of fight or flight – why do any of that when you could eat? I decided to wait for Peter and console myself with something tasty. Approaching the tent, I swept back the canvas doorway and was greeted with loud crockery rattling and shouts of "Hurrah!" I couldn't believe it: everyone was there and the catering tent was decorated with balloons and streamers. Through the many faces I could see Peter holding a glass of what looked like champagne. Was I still dreaming?

"We're a hit," came Al's excited voice from my side. "The ratings are through the roof! We're already the most watched on BBC iPlayer, and don't get me started on You Tube."

I half smiled, by now convinced this was definitely an alcohol-fuelled dream. Then I was enveloped by Peter; "Stella! My love! Congratulations and thank you. That was pure comedy. Another series will be in the bag by lunchtime!" It slowly dawned on me that I might actually be awake after all and my jaw hit the floor. "Everyone's talking about it," he continued. "It was so *real,* they're saying. Glad you took my advice, I told you to keep it loose, my love." He gave me a sleazy wink. I couldn't remember the Head Gardener ever giving me that bit of 'advice'.

Oh well, I thought, *now isn't the time to resent him taking the credit, I should just enjoy the success.* I sipped the glass of cold champagne thrust into my hand by Al and tried not to move my aching head. I nodded and smiled at everyone and laughed along politely at the amazing – and frankly, unexpected – positive comments. A disaster live on air had turned into an overnight success and instead of being sacked, I was applauded. That was TV for you.

I looked round the tent at all the smiling faces and at Al jumping up and down and hugging Gerard. Of course I was delighted the show was a success but I found I couldn't completely enjoy the moment without worrying about the havoc it would cause at home. I was happy and relieved, but my underlying emotion was panic. If this series was going to be as big as Peter was suggesting then the producer would need to be here 24/7 for the next hundred years!

Mum called me the next day to congratulate me on the success of the first show. I was just sitting down with Al to plan the filmed footage for the week when my mobile rang. I checked the display and smiled.

"It's Mum," I said to Al. "I'll be five minutes."

"Ok doll, I'll grab a coffee. Say hi to her for me." I nodded and picked up her call.

"Love, it's Mum" she announced (she'd never quite got the hang of caller ID). "I saw your show last night and tried to send you a message on eBay but it wouldn't go through...bloody technology. Anyway it was great dear. That vicar's wife is hilarious – has she had Botox? I was saying to Beryl, she looks very good for her age."

"Thanks for calling Mum, was it really OK?" I said.

"Oh yes, it was great, love. I was saying to Beryl, we should get some of that," she started.

I sensed someone behind me and as Mum wittered on about the advantages of Botox I turned to see Al waving at me. Peter Willis was standing next to him, obviously keen to have a production meeting. "Mum, it's a bit crazy here, can I call you back?" I said, signalling to Al that I was winding up the call.

"Well you can, but I won't be here dear – I'm stripping for the old soldiers."

"Oh?"

"Yes, I told you about it last week. The over-fifties are redecorating their sheltered homes, don't you remember? Lovely old boys. I'll ring you tomorrow then. Bye dear."

I hung up and smiled. Ever since Dad died five years ago, Mum had been like a woman possessed. She was desperately trying to claw back some life for herself and, as she put it, 'taking what's owed to me'. I knew we were in trouble when at Dad's funeral she got pissed on Babycham and did a spontaneous rendition of Rod Stewart's *Hot Legs* in the vestry. Five years, a 62-year-old toy boy and two cruises later she declared that 'sisters are now doing it for themselves'. And it seems that now they were doing it for old soldiers, too. I put my phone in my pocket and went over to join Peter and Al. *Perhaps our next series should be about life after bereavement featuring Mum as the star turn*, I thought with a smile. That would certainly be a ratings winner.

A busy week followed our first live show and despite my joy at our success I had a sinking feeling it was going to become even more manic. It's all very well being the producer of a ratings-winning show but as the cliché goes, you need someone to share it with. As I planned and rehearsed and shot footage in the week, all I could think about was Tom and Grace coming up the next Saturday; I was almost beside myself with excitement. But then the Friday before their visit I received a call from our Press Office that changed everything.

"Stella, I know that it's short notice," announced Ella the Press Officer, "but I've arranged a photo shoot and press call for first thing tomorrow. It's a quiet news weekend and it would be amazing if we could get stuff in the Sunday papers."

"That sounds great Ella, but I won't be around tomorrow. My family are coming," I started.

"Oh Stella, no, you have to be there. You're the producer," she said, alarmed. "We need to strike while the iron's hot, everyone's talking about last week's programme and there's a kiss-and-tell from one of Denise's ex-boyfriends rumoured to be doing the rounds. This is all great publicity for the programme and you're a major part of it – in fact quite a lot of the papers have requested an interview with you, especially after the mud-wrestling scene."

After some negotiation with Ella, we agreed that I would be available from 8am for two hours. During that time I would be around to answer questions and help 'supervise' our contributors. After that Ella was on her own in the mud with our cast and the World's press and I would be able to spend the day with Tom and Grace who would arrive at 10am.

Of course as often happens with these things, when Saturday arrived the press junket went on far too long and photographing Denise in her various outfits took an eternity. I was talking to a reporter from the TV pages of *The Mirror* when I saw Tom's car pull up and out of the corner of my eye saw them greeted by Al who I'd asked to take them on a tour of the set, with promises that I would be there asap. At eleven o'clock, an hour after our agreed time, I rushed anxiously from my last interview and found them outside the catering tent. I almost burst with joy. Grace ran across the grass to embrace me shouting at the top of her voice, "Mummee, Mummee!" I swept her into my arms and hugged her for so long and so hard and it felt wonderful. I buried my face in her shampoo-scented hair and kissed her a hundred times.

I looked up from Grace to see Tom standing next to us and I held out my arms for a hug. He moved awkwardly towards me holding out his arms and we embraced stiffly. It didn't feel right and I had a dipping in my stomach. "I've missed you," I whispered in his ear, still locked in our uncomfortable hold.

"Me too," he whispered back. "Let's get out of here. I saw the vicar's wife on telly – she's scary, let's make for the hills," he smiled.

"Oh Tom, I know. I just need to do one more interview, two at the most. The show's really taken off!"

Tom's response was to roll his eyes and turn away from me. I felt sick, but I had no choice so I carried on, turning to Grace and avoiding eye contact with Tom.

"I've arranged for Daddy and Grace to have hot chocolate and muffins in the tent while Mummy just sorts something out quickly."

"Yummy, yummy," she squealed, clapping her hands together and jumping up and down.

"It's vital that I just deal with this now, while we're on the up," I said, looking pleadingly back at Tom. "If I can stay on top of this I'll be offered the next series and I reckon I'll be able to name my price and my working hours and you and Grace must want a drink and something to eat after your journey. We really didn't expect it to be such a success. I had no idea the world's media would descend on us today." Tom smiled reluctantly and took Grace's hand.

"Come on sweetie. Let's go and get some hot chocolate."

"But what about Mummy? Doesn't she want hot chocolate too," I heard her ask. As I walked away in the opposite direction, Grace was clutching my heart in her little hand.

Feeling a little weepy, I trudged back over to the throng of journalists, cast and crew. I could see Denise waving her skirt around and Bernard looking decidedly uncomfortable. I couldn't believe I was walking towards this rather than away; I was horribly torn. I was deeply grateful for finally receiving recognition for all my hard work, yet if this was only the beginning it obviously came with a price. *Be careful what you wish for*, I heard my mum saying.

After three more interviews I saw my little family standing patiently waiting on the other side of the garden. Muffins and hot chocolate now a distant memory, Grace in her red T-shirt was sitting in the warm June sunshine, staring up at the trees and Tom, his hands in his pockets was nodding towards a squirrel, to Grace's delight.

I finally extricated myself from the melée and almost ran across the grass towards the two of them, apologetic and tearful. Even Tom could see how distressed I was and for once, held out a life raft.

"Don't worry about it," he smiled. "You're here now. Come

on Gracie, let's take Mummy out for lunch."

This was a rare glimpse of the old Tom, the one I'd fallen in love with. He was essentially kind and caring and never used to bear a grudge. After the weeks of telephone silences and sulky conversations this glimpse of the old Tom overwhelmed me and as he started the car and we moved down the drive, I burst into uncontrollable tears.

Grace was confused and kept asking; "What's the matter Mum? Why is Mummy crying?" and each time she asked, a fresh wave of sobs enveloped me and I became engulfed in so much emotion I just couldn't control it.

"Mummy's fine. Sometimes grown-ups cry when they're happy," I heard Tom say, looking at me with some concern, patting my knee reassuringly with one hand and holding the steering wheel with the other.

We drove for at least half an hour, trying to find somewhere to eat. Then just when it all looked like it was going pear-shaped a Harvester appeared, like a mirage in the Rochdale desert. I wouldn't normally be so delighted at the sight of a Harvester, but Grace loved them and it was well after lunch time. We were all hungry and at this restaurant I could fill up on salad from the cart and tell them 'no chips, please'. Once at our table, Grace placed her paper napkin neatly on her knee, sipped on cola and created a city on her Nintendo.

"I've missed you both so much," I said, kissing her cheek and grabbing Tom's hand in mine. "Thanks for coming all this way to see me."

"We've missed you too Stel. I know this programme is important for you and it's great it's done so well, but I – well, I wonder, is it worth it?"

"I know, I've asked myself the same question every day. But it's hard to just give it up and say goodbye. It's who I am. Mum always said 'you have to have a career, Stella', and to be honest, I don't know what else to do."

Tom smiled at Grace and concentrated on folding his napkin into a tight little roll.

"You're Grace's mum and my wife. That's who you are too. We've talked about this before, you could go part-time or at least try to work from the office more, rather than working away. Yes we need two salaries but we could manage a pay-cut if it meant you could spend more time at home. You get so involved in everything Stella, you really throw yourself into it, always promising to slow down 'after the next series', but then there's always another and another."

"I love that you want me home and..." I started.

"I suppose what I'm really saying Stella, is – can't you just get an *ordinary* job somewhere that doesn't involve long hours or being away?"

I felt the familiar stirrings of anger that Tom seemed to evoke in me these days. For a moment there I thought he understood. I was wrong.

"Look, I worked bloody hard to get a job in TV and now I'm working bloody, bloody hard to *keep* the job in TV. I am not prepared to throw it all away for what you call, 'an ordinary job', riding the tills down the sodding slave-driving superstore."

Grace looked up, alarmed at Mummy's sudden swearing and raised voice. I smiled at her and hunched my shoulders as though this were all a bit of a game Mummy and Daddy were playing.

"Stella, I just think that you should put your career on hold and consider Grace and I for a..."

That did it. "*Consider you*? Do you know how much I *consider you*? Have you any idea how bad I feel about spending all my time working and not being the perfect wife and mother?" I hissed at him as the waitress placed half a chicken with piri-piri sauce in front of me. And chips.

"I bet you've never considered giving up being a cameraman, the career *you* always wanted to do and trained hard for have you?" I said, ignoring the fragrant chicken. "Why don't *you* get a fucking *ordinary* job!" I hissed.

"Mum just used a swear called f..."

"That's enough Grace!" Tom shouted. Her little face started to pucker and she burst into floods of tears.

"Don't speak to her like that," I yelled, getting up and comforting Grace, who was sobbing into her napkin. "Now look what you've done with your temper!" I threw at him, as I mopped her eyes and started crying myself.

"We were being silly. Take no notice of Mummy and Daddy darling. If you eat all that you can have an ice cream," I said.

Tom was silent. Crushed by my anger and Grace's tears he picked up his knife and fork, defeated. I sat back in my chair, feeling full but stuffed my mouth with big, golden chips and thought *you stupid cow, you've ruined it – again*.

For the rest of the day, I desperately tried to keep a lid on my feelings which made me act like someone else and didn't make for a great atmosphere. There was so much to say and not enough time to say it. Our day was supposed to be about being a family, laughing at stuff and bonding over in-jokes. It was about creating a memory for Grace about the time she and Daddy had an adventure and visited Mummy on location. Now all she had was the memory of Mummy swearing at Daddy and crying all the time.

When you don't see the people you love every day, you can't share the minutiae of each other's lives. Whole episodes of our real-life soap operas are missing, so comments are misunderstood and feelings and motives become suspect. A huge chasm had formed in the middle of our relationship and, despite its unlimited salad cart and unbeatable prices, the Rochdale Harvester wasn't the place to close it.

After lunch we'd walked through a small village and bought some black pudding and Eccles cakes which lifted my mood slightly. So much for Lighter Lift! While in the shop I bought Grace a strawberry milk lolly – her favourite. Tom and Grace were outside the shop when I greeted her with it.

"Thanks Mummy, I'm quite full, not sure I can eat it now," she said, looking rather awkward.

"But it's been ages since lunch and you love these, don't you?" I said, beginning to feel uncertain.

"Actually Stella, she's gone off them. She made herself sick at Megan's party by eating about four and she's not been able to face them since," Tom offered apologetically, like I was a kind auntie they didn't want to offend. I felt like an outsider; being away had excluded me from their lives. I suddenly felt like a stranger as I realised that during my absence, things had moved on and I didn't even know what my daughter's favourite ice lolly was anymore.

I wondered what else would change while I wasn't there to see it. In another year, would I still know her best friends, her teachers, her favourite books? Grace's birthday was in a few weeks and she'd carefully made a list of friends to invite to her party. There were names I didn't even recognise. I didn't even know what she wanted, but I was sure that Tom did.

They left at about 7pm. The summer evening light was soft and I would have given anything to just climb in the car and go with them. Tom wound down the car window and kissed me.

"Sorry Stella, I always seem to say the wrong thing to you these days."

"I know," I said, "I'm sorry for getting upset and angry." I could feel tears forming and I didn't want to cry in front of Grace again. "Don't forget to feed the fish," I said to her, smiling through my tears and blowing kisses. I stood and watched them leave, then turned and trudged back to my lonely little B&B.

8

Lesbian Lust and Lemon Curd

For the next few weeks the show went from strength to strength. Denise and Co were hilarious and the garden bloomed under Gerard's care. Facebook pages were set up by fans and it became the unexpected hit of the season. No-one watching knew what was going to happen next and quite frankly, neither did I. Every week produced a new and outrageous happening. If Gerard wasn't singing Rihanna's back catalogue he was tripping over compost heaps and demolishing a trellis in one hefty fall live on air. And as he tiptoed through the tulips, Denise made it her mission to reveal all the scandal parish life had to offer, not least of which was a colourful tale detailing lesbian lust and lemon curd in the WI.

One week she must have had too much altar wine and made a pass at the choirmaster, egged on by Gerard and the crew. Al had to step in, which of course he loved and was making all kinds of eye-rolling faces on camera and milking it for everything he'd got.

Every Sunday afternoon phone call of congratulations from the Peter Willis and every write up in the press made me feel fantastic. Ok, so I was lonely at times and missing half my life, but this was what I'd always wanted: to be part of a successful show – wasn't it?

Peter seemed to have dealt with the Gerard situation back at base – and despite a few newspaper headlines from kiss-and-tell girlfriends, 'revealing' he'd been to prison, we got away with it. In fact, I had a call from an agent who reckoned he could find him presenting work and was talking memoirs if he could sign him up. He said it was 'very courageous' of us to employ an ex-convict and we had sent out a good message to people who believed their lives are over after a prison sentence.

Bernard the vicar was delighted because the publicity meant his flock had expanded and the church was crammed every Sunday. Lots of mad old ladies in hats turned up to sing loudly and get their faces on camera. Al said it was like a geriatric *X Factor*. Denise was also enjoying her new-found celebrity. She even did an 'at home' with *Hello!* where she got to spread herself across the vicarage kitchen worktops like a Page-Three wannabe.

We had made religion and gardening the new sex, drugs *and* rock and roll so I was very excited when we finally left Rochdale and I got a call to come back to Media World for a meeting to discuss the show's future – and mine. Surely now I will have the respect I've always wanted, I thought, and be able to negotiate child-friendly hours. Maybe even a promotion so I could take a more office based role and see my family much more. I had been furious with MJ when she moved me to Gardening, but it had worked for me and backfired on her. The great thing was that, as head of Documentaries, she had no jurisdiction in Gardening, so had no control over my career anymore.

However, the downside was that things between Tom and I had become even more strained. The success of the first show meant that I had been so busy I hadn't been able to get home at all, but as I travelled home from Rochdale, I was sure I could fix everything if we could just get to spend more time together.

By the time I got back it was getting dark but I could just make out some kids doing all kinds of stunts on bikes in the middle of the road. As I climbed out of the car, I couldn't believe it – one of the kids was Grace. She looked so different, so grown up. My eyes filled up as I remembered her first ever bike – it was bright pink and she was really wobbly, even with pink, Barbie stabilisers. Now she was riding a shiny black one covered in skulls. How things had changed.

I waved and called to her and as soon as she saw me she shrieked with delight (OK, *partly* because I usually bring her a present). She abandoned her bike in the middle of the road, yelping and rushing to me, shouting; "Dad, its Mum...she's back, Mum's home!"

Tom was sitting on the doorstep with a cup of coffee in the fading light, laughing at her mad greeting. Gosh. He looks so handsome, I thought.

Tom helped me from the car with my bags and embraced me like he'd really missed me. Grace put her arms round my hips and all three of us walked and hugged at the same time up the path. As we climbed into the hall and dumped my bags, Grace disappeared into the kitchen, swiftly followed by Tom.

"Thanks everyone," I teased. "I would have liked a bit more attention. Hello – anybody there?"

I walked slowly into the kitchen, to be greeted by Grace proudly holding a big, pink iced cake. "It's for you, Mum," she said walking towards me.

Tom was beaming; "She said it's just what Mum would like when she gets home. She baked and iced it all herself."

Grace smiled at him and added grudgingly, "Well, Dad helped a bit."

"It's lovely," I whispered, feeling a lump in my throat at the sight of the almost illegible, wobbly words saying 'Welcome home Mummy!'

Grace and I sat round our big old wooden kitchen table while Tom put the kettle on. Grace cleared some space for the cake by moving the homework, magazines and camera pieces, and got some plates out. It felt so good to be home, amongst familiar things. I felt a rush of happiness as I looked around at the warm cream walls and lovely oak worktops. I smiled to myself as Grace and I cut three huge slices of sponge and began to devour ours.

"Tell Mum your great news," Tom said, bringing mugs of hot coffee to the table.

"Mum, Mum, I've been picked for the gymnastics team!" Grace squealed, jumping up and down in her chair.

"She did so well," Tom added, "she was up around the bars and jumped right across the horse."

Grace folded her arms and furrowed her brow, looking straight at him, "Dad, it's called a vault, and I didn't *jump across it* – I did a long fly. You're just so uncool!"

Tom laughed and ruffled her hair, "Silly Dad, I don't know what I'm talking about, do I?"

"Tom, you're just so uncool," I said, resting my tired head on his shoulder. It was good to be home. We just needed time together so I could catch up on everything that had been happening and discover exactly what a 'long fly' consisted of, in the name of cool!

That night after Grace's bath I went upstairs to read her a story. As I got to her room I overheard Tom and her talking.

"Do you like having Mummy home?" I heard Tom say.

"Ooh yes, I love it. I don't ever want her to go away again. I just wish she could collect me from school every day."

I felt that familiar pang in my heart. I walked in and gave her a huge hug.

"You're not going far away again, are you Mum?" she said, her brow crinkling into a frown.

"I don't think so, sweetie. I think my last programme's done so well that my boss will let me come home every evening to be with you."

"Mmm, just don't be naughty again, Mum, or that mean

lady might make you stay behind."

"Oh no, I don't have to work with that mean lady anymore," I smiled, thinking, there *is* a God after all.

"I bet if we ask Mum, she'll play cricket with us at the weekend," Tom said. He was rubbing his hands together and giving me a wink. Grace jumped up and down clapping. I smiled in agreement. I wasn't sure about the cricket, but I wished we could be happy and sensitive to each other like this all the time.

"OK, sleep time madam," I said, ruffling her hair. Tom kissed her goodnight.

"See you in the morning darling," he shouted from the landing, off to attend a cricket or football match from the sofa.

"Mum please, please, pleeease will you read me a story?" Grace asked, her hands together in prayer. It was ages since I'd read to her so we rifled through her library of Jacqueline Wilsons and settled down with *Sleepovers*. We'd read it so many times before we both knew exactly what happened next and as I read aloud, Grace's 'I love this next bit' punctuations became fewer and fewer and sleepier and sleepier. She was fast asleep long before the final climactic sleepover but I kept on reading and watching her sleep, just bathing in the sheer pleasure of the moment.

After a while, I tiptoed downstairs and Tom and I shared a bottle of wine and laughed at *Father Ted* and fought over the toffee Revels just like we always had. "Thank you for keeping Grace safe and happy," I said, as the credits rolled and the Revels came to an end.

"That's my job," he smiled.

"Well, it's my job too but I haven't been around to do it."

As we went upstairs and lay together in our own big bed I felt us start to reconnect. I felt Tom's hands on my body, a little awkward and hesitant at first but moving with growing passion. After we made love we lay there, breathless, next to each other.

"If someone had told you fifteen years ago that this is how your life would be, would you be happy Tom?" I asked, sitting up onto one elbow and looking into his eyes. This was really just a formality for me, an affirmation that what we'd just shared was the truth. He put his head down and ran his fingers through his hair. He appeared to be thinking. I wondered if he was joking, but when he lifted his head and looked directly at me I felt a sudden chill go right through me.

"I honestly don't know, Stella."

I moved slightly apart from him and sat up. The 'Stella' bit sounded serious. This wasn't good. I needed him to say 'I love you, it's all fine. Night, night.' But he didn't.

"I've been feeling unsettled for some time. I don't know what it is, but I just keep thinking that something's missing – it's not enough. You *know*?"

I was stung, completely taken aback by his answer. No, I didn't *know*! For Tom to talk like this about how he'd been feeling was new to me. I didn't like it and I wanted him to piss off back to Mars while I stayed safely on Venus.

"You mean you need more...at work?" I asked, hopefully.

"Yes, work. Well...*everything* really. I don't know. I hate how life's become so complicated. Sometimes I'd like to just go and live on a remote Scottish island."

"Do you think things would be any easier in the wilds of Scotland?" I asked, a little too sharply, still smarting and noting painfully that he'd said 'I' and not 'we' on the island. I was now kicking myself for spoiling things by asking for confirmation of his feelings. *We were still married weren't we? Wasn't that enough? Why did I have to open up a new vent of hell?* After all, ignorance is bliss.

"I don't know," he continued, in his own thoughts, "but I always said I'd never live *this* life. I never wanted an overdraft, a mortgage and two cars."

"Nobody *wants* a mortgage," I answered tritely. I was hurt, but trying to keep things friendly and honest and open. After all, I started it.

"I suppose I feel a bit tied down," he went on, the floodgates opening and gushing all over the duvet. "We've stretched ourselves with this house and, despite us both working, we're not exactly rolling in it. And you talk about what you want all the time but you know I always wanted to film wildlife and work in Natural History. My plan was to shoot polar bears in the snow and whales in the sea. As it is, I'm shooting people painting walls, losing weight and planting bulbs."

"Welcome to my world," I answered sulkily and rather unsympathetically. Sometimes I became so obsessed with my own feelings I forgot that Tom had dreams too.

I turned over and tried to sleep, telling myself it would all be OK. On Monday I'd go into work and get a big promotion. It would mean more money and I could work in the office and spend more time at home. Then I would be happy and so would Tom. I was the producer of a ratings winner and should be able to name my price and my hours. I could look after Grace more and perhaps Tom would get his turn to take filming jobs further afield. There wasn't much call for wildlife cameramen in the Midlands, let's face it; there aren't many rainforests or polar ice caps in West Bromwich and Tom needed his dreams too.

9

Perfectly Peachy

On Monday morning I power-dressed, made packed-lunches, ironed school clothes, put a wash on, fed the fish and Grace, kissed Tom and headed to the office for my triumphant return.

Arriving at the office I walked past all the familiar faces to be greeted with high fives, 'well done on the show,' and 'we've missed you,' and as I turned on my computer I felt warm and fluffy inside. Within seconds an email pinged through from MJ. For a moment I felt the same panic I'd had before, but reminded myself I was in charge now and didn't have to be scared anymore.

> *Stella,*
> *Congratulations on the success of 'Is God in the Garden?'*
> *I always knew it would work, which is why I recommended you for the role of producer. You couldn't fail with such a great team. I think it would be useful for you and me to have a talk about the future of the show and other projects. Can you come to see me at midday.*
> *MJ.*

"I wonder what she wants." I said to Val. "The gardening show has nothing to do with her."

"I expect she's trying to climb on the back of your success, Stel. Maybe she wants you back in her department. After the gardening show, having your name around will no doubt help her out."

"Mmm. You're probably right. In her email she even takes the credit for putting me on the programme, like she thought it would be good for me."

"You know what she's like" said Val.

"Yeah..."

"...a bitch!" we both said together and laughed.

I refused to let it get to me and remained unperturbed by the prospect of my meeting with MJ throughout the morning. I was now safe from her clutches in the Gardening Department where my career was finally on the up. I'd heard that the second series had already been commissioned and I was delighted to be in the glow zone. I'd been out of it for so long I'd been feeling quite chilly.

I turned up as requested at 12pm to see MJ. I was feeling unusually confident for this meeting, wearing a suit and heels (so unlike the wellingtons and waterproofs that I'd been used to wearing recently). Even the timing seemed much more geared to suit me, with no end-of-day child-collection worries. Maybe this was MJ's attempt at a peace offering?

I knocked on the door confidently and MJ's assistant Cynthia came over.

"Hi Stella, would you like to wait here for a few minutes? MJ has someone with her. They're running a little late," she said, gesturing to the chair outside the office.

I didn't mind at all. While I was waiting I had the chance to think about how I would turn MJ down. I suspected she was going to offer me a role back in Documentaries, so that she could take credit for my work. As much as I would enjoy saying no, I really didn't want to make an even bigger enemy of her than I already had. I decided I would be polite, say I was flattered and perhaps even offer some ideas and even contacts for their latest doc, but no way could I ever work with her again.

I must have waited and contemplated for about fifteen minutes before MJ's door finally opened. I was rather surprised to see The Head Gardener shuffle out of the office, sheepishly shutting the door and keeping his head down. He looked a little flustered and though he saw me, he didn't speak or make eye contact, just nodded in my direction. I began to get nervous, but assured myself it was nothing. Whatever he was up to, I was responsible for the success of the show and not even MJ could deny that.

I knew there was nothing she could do to me, she wasn't my boss anymore, so I distracted myself by thinking about what I'd make for pudding that night. I was just covering the sweet mixed berries in Delia's summer pudding with thick clotted cream when MJ appeared in the doorway. "Come in, Stella," she held a frozen smile and ushered me to a low, hard seat.

She cleared her throat and sat down, tidying papers and pretending to be transfixed by one every now and then. Still using her old technique she made me feel that I was merely an irritating interruption as she had lots more important stuff to deal with. Yet it was *she* who had invited me to this meeting. My heart started palpitating. As I'm sure she knew it would.

"I have some news for you about a big promotion," she started. My heart leapt. "Everyone on a very senior level is in agreement with this."

Woohoo! I wished it wasn't MJ giving me this news but I had been the one who turned *Is God in a Garden?* around and made it a hit. I had worked so hard after the initial show to ensure we focused on the comedy of the contributors and it had really paid off. Now it seemed that everyone who mattered was finally acknowledging it.

"As a result of this – I have to say, well-deserved – promotion, there will be some staff changes," she added.

"OK. I'm sure that's fine." I said, half-smiling, a little

concerned this might lose me the second series, but perhaps my promotion meant something even bigger?

"Yes. There will be lots of changes round here," she glared straight at me. "Starting with you."

Oh no. She wanted me back in her department. This was going to be harder than I'd thought. I gathered all my strength and launched into my well-rehearsed speech.

"MJ, I don't mean to be rude but I have no intention of returning to work with you in Documentaries. I realise that my new-found success means that I would be a good name to put next to a new series and may give the company a bigger chance of a commission, but I'm now committed to Gardening." I looked straight at her, waiting for a reaction, but she just continued talking like I hadn't said a word.

"It's been decided that we need fresh blood in Gardening and a young producer with new ideas has been appointed for *God's Garden*," she sat back, licking her lips. "As you know, we're always looking for something new and different, Stella," she said, with a twisted smile.

I was confused, but hopeful. "Oh, am I going to be promoted to *executive* producer?" This was beyond my wildest dreams.

She shook her head incredulously and, tilting it to one side in mock-concern, said; "Oh Stella, I'm sorry. Did I give you the impression that *you*'d been promoted?" Fake, theatrical horror filled her face.

A chill ran down my spine. "No, I er...I suppose, I assumed..."

"Well, you know what they say about assumptions, Stella," she licked her lips with unadulterated, unconcealed joy.

"MJ, why are we having this meeting?"

"Well Stella, because I wanted to tell you the wonderful news myself," her mean lips sipped on Diet Coke to prolong my agony further.

I held onto everything I'd got. I needed to keep calm and above all not allow her to get to me. She wasn't going to turn me to jelly and make me cry this time, however hard she tried.

"Exactly what is the news?" I asked, willing myself to stay calm.

"The news is that I've just been confirmed as the new Executive Programming Director of Media World. I'll be reporting directly to Frank Moores – the owner, no less. You know what that means, don't you Stella?"

I didn't answer.

"It means I will be in charge of *all* the programmes in the company's portfolio. Mmm...I can't wait to get my hands dirty in Gardening!"

"It looks like you already have." I said in monotone, not even attempting to hide my despair at this news.

"No congratulations, Stella? I'll be your boss again."

I stared at her, numb, stunned. For about thirty long seconds I didn't say a word. I just let it all sink in.

"And this brings me to the real reason for this meeting. Unfortunately, my first task in my new role is not a happy one. As I'm sure you know, Media World has a strict policy on Health and Safety and all contributors are to be thoroughly checked prior to allowing their involvement in any programme..."

It took me a moment to realise where she was going with this.

"...and as the producer you have to take ultimate responsibility for all decisions regarding the programme."

Bile rose into my throat and my eyes stung. Surely this couldn't be happening? MJ was watching me intently, her eyes glittering, as she steamrollered over my career.

"Failure to account for Gerard's criminal background, however minor it turned out to be, and to complete the relevant safety documentation is a serious mistake, one which can endanger all Media World's current contracts..."

The room started to swim around me. MJ's face blurred and twisted.

"There were children on the show, Stella. What if something had happened? All senior management here are in agreement..."

When the words finally came, I barely heard them.

"Stella", MJ said, her face twisting into an evil smile, "you're suspended, pending a full investigation."

I stood up in a daze. Part of me was screaming: *You put fucking Gerard on the programme. You fed him to Al. This is your doing, you evil, miserable old hag!* But I said nothing. There was no point. She had me; I was the producer and the buck stopped with me. I had to hand it to her – she had finally got what she wanted. I was finished at Media World. With my eyes swimming, I turned away from her and made my way to the door.

I stumbled back to my desk and slumped into my chair, feeling tears pricking at my eyelids. It was only just sinking in – my career, all that I had worked so hard for, could be over.

As I was staring blankly at the computer screen in front of me, my eyes wandered to the postcard stuck in the top right-hand corner. It was from Mum, sent from one of her many holidays. This one was from Malaga and I pulled it off the screen and turned it over to read the back. *Blue seas and wall-to-wall-waiters*, it said, in Mum's usual jokey style. *Just wishing that I'd come here sooner.* I looked at the shiny picture of frothing waves and white sands and thought about how Mum had taken almost 65 years to get to where she wanted to be. In that moment I knew I wasn't prepared to wait that long and spend my life wishing that 'I'd come here sooner'; it was time to take control.

Opening up my desk drawer, I took out the folder

containing all gardening contacts and information and then I opened a bottle of 'Perfectly Peachy' Lighter Lift. The smell of fake peaches filled the air as I poured the orange slime into the cardboard folder. Rubbing it in like a lotion, I massaged and pummelled every bit of paper, every telephone number and every permission document associated with the series. The liquid worked like cleaning fluid (God knows what it had done to my insides) and I swirled it and mashed at the soggy paper, everything washed away on a sea of 'Perfect Peach'. I dumped all the soaking, peach-scented illegible mush into a wastepaper bucket and headed up the stairs to MJ's office – for the final time.

I opened her door without knocking.

"MJ, I believe that as I am suspended, you'll be needing all the paperwork for *God's Garden*?" I said.

She looked up and I don't know what surprised her most – the fact that I was holding a wastepaper bin or that I was smiling warmly at her. "Yes, I will need everything." She clipped, lips extra-tight.

"Well, here it is, all the vital information I've been working on for weeks that will be invaluable for my *excellent* replacement." I said. With that, I walked up to her desk and, leaning over, slowly turned the bin upside down over her perfectly groomed head.

Orange goo and mashed paper landed with a squelchy thud and the air in her stuffy little office was suddenly permeated with the chemical stench of fake peach. It took her a couple of seconds to realise what was happening, but as the peach slime ran down her white designer blouse and seeped onto her knees she leapt up, screaming in horror. The gloop dripped off her, landing in fluorescent globules on her new office carpet and creating an instant neon stain.

"No need to sack me, MJ," I continued, "the pleasure's all

mine. I quit. I quit Gardening, I quit Media World, and best of all, I quit you. Goodbye, you miserable cow."

For the first time in her life, Mary-Jane Robinson was lost for words.

I marched out of the now sickly-smelling office, head high, and suddenly felt delirious, relieved, liberated. I wanted to kiss everyone. MJ's assistant was staring, open-mouthed and several people on the office floor were stifling their giggles. I hadn't shut MJ's door – and I hadn't spoken quietly, either. I ran back down the steps, waltzing on air. I had finally taken control of my own life.

Back at my desk, I gathered papers and souvenirs from all the years I'd given to the company and put them in several carrier bags, then I skipped all the way to the car park. Tomorrow would be the beginning of a new me, I thought as I drove away from Media World for the last time. I couldn't wait.

10

Cake Volcanoes and Marital Eruptions

Tom's reaction to my departure from Media World was not the one I'd hoped for.

"That was a bit hasty, Stella," he said when he got in late, hanging his coat up and pouring a beer, "are you sure it was the right thing to do?"

I was surprised and hurt. He'd banged on at me so much about giving up work and being the perfect wife and mother, I had expected him to be as pleased as me.

"But Tom, now I can be at home with Grace every day." I said, incredulous.

"That's all very well, but what about your salary? I didn't mean you to quit your job without something else to go to," he muttered.

Surprise descended quickly into anger. "Tom, you were the one who went on about me not fulfilling my duties as wife and mother and anyway, that suspension was just a smokescreen whilst MJ worked out how to get rid of me for good. My career was over from the moment she was promoted. I'm now just trying to do the right thing, for me and for us!" I yelled.

"You don't know that your career is over, you've just had enough. All you ever think about Stella, is yourself."

"What? But I thought we'd talked about this?"

"No Stella, YOU talked about it. How can you just throw in your job like that? In this climate?" he ranted.

"How can you say I just threw it in? You aren't listening

Tom – MJ *suspended* me, pending investigation. Even if I was reinstated, I would have had her on my case 24/7 and that would have been unbearable." I said, amazed.

"Stella, 'unbearable' is working down a mine eight hours a day."

"Oh that's right, belittle everything…"

"I just don't want to hear any more of this. I have to sort out my camera batteries for the morning as I'm the only breadwinner now – or had you forgotten?"

With that, he stormed out of the kitchen and I heard slamming upstairs. I sat down in the sudden quiet and laid my head on my arms at the table. What had just happened? I thought he'd be pleased. I thought he'd agree that I could now be a proper mum – and a proper wife. I thought this would be good for our marriage, but right now it felt like another nail in the coffin.

Tom and I didn't really speak over the weekend. I was still annoyed and I think he was sulking, but we had a good time with Grace.

On Monday morning the phone rang as I made breakfast.

"Oh Stella, it's all over Media World!" yelled Lizzie, the second I answered. "I got in early and people are already talking about it. The cleaners are still trying to get peach out of the carpet. And MJ – well, let's just say she hasn't appeared yet. I am so proud of you!"

"Thanks Lizzie!" I beamed. "I'll call you later. Got to go – I'm taking Grace to school."

I took Princess Grace to the school gate and chatted to the other mums. So immersed was I in this new role that before I knew it I was asking if a few of her little friends would like to come to tea that evening and to my delight, three of the mums seemed very eager to have an evening off. I walked home, contemplating my new goal, which was to reach new heights in mummy-ness. I would achieve this by attending school assemblies, peeling two kinds of organic veg and baking a Victoria sponge all in the same day – every day! On a slightly selfish note, I could see that my emotional and celebrity well-being would also be taken care of because, as I discovered to my deep joy when I got back to the house, I now had precious time to analyse *Heat* and *Hello!* from cover to cover each week without merely flicking and rushing through the juicy bits.

Once I had devoured the magazines and come to the conclusion that celebrities didn't have cellulite, 'Demi's Ageing-Knee Nightmare' required a double above-knee amputation and that 'Posh's Bony Body Hell' would be cured by the regular consumption of cake, I thought I would have a little experiment in the kitchen. I was in need of something sweet so I pulled out all my ingredients and created a fabulous, honey-scented chocolate cake with a gooey, frosted topping worthy of Delia. I even had the time and patience to make tiny striped sugar bees to decorate it. The sponge was dense and moist, yet – though I say it myself – had a delicious lightness.

Chocolate cake and soap stars aside, money was clearly going to be another matter. My husband seemed to be under the impression that I wasn't taking our financial position seriously enough. I decided to extend the olive branch but when I called his mobile at lunchtime to let him know how well I was doing in my new career as a Yummy Mummy, I didn't get the reaction I hoped for.

"Now you've left work you need to tighten your belt, Stella," he said, mouth full of sandwich. "I've got to go. We'll discuss this later." I hung up, feeling annoyed again.

All afternoon I kept checking the time, leaving home at exactly 3pm so I could be the perfect mummy waiting outside the school gates at 3.15 to pick up Grace and her friends Emma, Lauren and Katie. OK, I was actually there at 3.20, but that was only because some 80-year old man in front of me in his car decided to drive at five miles an hour the whole way down the high street. Grace still seemed happy (and I have to admit a little surprised) to see me arrive only slightly late. She was so used to my life of chaos it would take time for us both to adjust.

I had spent much of the day planning this evening as I wanted everything to be perfect. I planned to make little pink fairy cakes with the girls so had all the ingredients and everything laid out ready to go. When we arrived home, everything was pink and gorgeous and the girls threw themselves into the project with gusto.

"Mmm, your Mummy makes such nice cakes, Grace," I heard Katie say later as I popped to the kitchen to refill the plates, and my heart swelled with pride. Once they had finished eating (I tried to ignore the food fight that ensued) we started on the 'craft' element of the party: I had planned for us all to make lots of pretty things with sequins.

I really should have known I was onto a loser with the pink arts and craft, when at breakfast, Princess Grace announced that she was now a 'Goth.' It seemed that whilst I'd been busy working, my little princess had moved on from her baby-pink fixation and turned into a dark, shadowy figure of the night. In denial, I continued to wax lyrical about pink napkins and matching crockery for tea, but my only daughter cruelly rejected my pastel advances.

"Mum, can we have stick-on tattoos instead of those boring old sequins? Pleeeease – they're so uncool?"

So my dream of a pink and perfect teatime ended with me painstakingly sticking glitter onto polystyrene 'Fabergé eggs' while tattooed children rode the neighbour's cat round the garden and fed the fish 'magic-sequin' food.

Whilst Grace and her friends were screaming obscenities at each other outside, I abandoned the eggs and gave Mum a ring.

"Grace has taken to wearing burgundy lipstick and studded wrist-bands at the weekend, which I tell myself is all about healthy self-expression – isn't it?" I wailed.

"Hmmm. Stella, I think she may be having a 'mid-childhood crisis'." Mum replied dramatically. "I read an article about it in this week's *Womans Own*."

Within minutes we were both in a frenzy and at the end of the conversation I was convinced Grace was going through an emotional life-stage trauma. I needed a large slice of my bee-covered sponge after that call.

Al, who I called straight after, my mouth full of gooey chocolate, was more optimistic: "My darling, inside every Emo, there's a cheerleader just itching to get out. Give it time honey, you'll see."

I hoped he was right. Just before the first mother arrived to pick up her sequin-covered child I went onto the Internet and bought a set of pink pompoms which I would stash in the back of my wardrobe to wait in the wings for that glorious day.

Anyway, whatever she currently was, I refused to take on any ex-working-mother guilt about Grace's 'individuality.' Yes, of course I'd rather she was more Hannah Montana than Amy Winehouse but a mother couldn't have everything. And I was now doing my bit, as from that day I resolved that she'd be delivered to school on time (most days) that we wouldn't ever forget her games kit again (well, rarely) and I would always be a well-groomed, calm and unruffled Yummy Mummy (sort of).

After Grace's friends left, the two of us collapsed exhausted on the sofa. Grace cuddled up to me.

"Thanks for today, Mummy, it was great having you pick me up. I like it much more than going to After School Club."

I smiled at her. "I love being at home with you too, sweetie."

I thought I would burst with pleasure. After Tom's negative reaction about my departure from work I was beginning to wonder if I'd done the right thing; this confirmed it. "I'm so glad you're happy. You must tell Daddy," I said, rather sneakily.

Despite my warm mother-daughter glow it wasn't long before Tom's financial paranoia crept to the forefront of my mind. This made me worry about Grace's forthcoming birthday so, as we picked sequins up off the kitchen floor, I broached the matter with her.

"Sweetie, now I'm not working, I don't think we're going to be able to buy everything on your pressie list," I said, waiting for the bomb to go off. Grace looked at me thoughtfully.

"I'm ok with not having EVERYTHING on my list," she conceded, to my huge relief. "As long as I can still have my big, birthday disco-party."

She fluttered a handful of sequins into the air and they landed on the floor at about the same time as my heart, which landed with a bump.

"But sweetie," I started, "I think we might need to have a smaller party now, at home."

"Mummy, you promised we could have a big room. Don't you remember? It was last year when you couldn't do a party 'cos you were at work. You said, you did," and her bottom lip began to tremble.

"But Grace, now I'm not working we won't be able to afford..." I started.

"You said, you said we could wear grass skirts and flowers round our necks and...and that I could have a reeeeally big cake...like a volcano. Don't you remember? I've told all my friends now, Mummy!"

I did recall invites and something vaguely Hawaiian being discussed when Tom and Grace visited Rochdale a few weeks before and Grace clearly remembered it all in detail. I felt so bad.

"I know we talked about it but we don't have enough money now. I'm so sorry sweetie." But I could see she had started crying and I wasn't far from tears either, plus I couldn't bear to have my 'Best Mummy' badge ripped from me so soon. "I'll talk to Daddy when he gets home and I'm sure he'll say it's OK." This seemed to stem the tears – temporarily at least – and Grace wiped her eyes and stomped upstairs to get ready for bed.

As I carried on picking up sequins one by one, my mind was now filled with strategies and schemes. How could I not grant my daughter her only wish? But this was going to be a tough one; since Monday's big departure, Tom's financial sanctions were now in full throttle and there was no way I could get a full-blown 'big birthday disco' under his all-seeing radar. Perhaps the only way to approach this was with complete honesty. I knew room hire, a cake and buffet would set us back £400 minimum.

Aware I needed to start this ball rolling immediately, I waited until Tom was home and Grace was safely in bed. I decided to bring up the 'big birthday disco with price tag' as Tom wrestled with the remote control and gasped with something akin to sexual excitement at a ball and twenty-two men on the screen.

"Tom, we need to talk," I said, sounding like some psycho-babbling glamourpuss from an American mini-series. He didn't look up; apparently they were doing something with penalties and he lunged forward to save one and at the same time blocked me out, waving his hand at me like he was swatting a fly.

"Tom," I said, louder and more angry now. "It's Grace's birthday next weekend and she wants a party."

He glanced vaguely in my direction and muttered the two words that it would appear were closest to his heart: "How much?"

"About two hundred-ish," I answered, knowing that the real price would cause heart failure, extreme distress and quite possibly an emergency call to the Air Ambulance to have him choppered out.

"Two *hundred* pounds? You *are* kidding?" he said without taking his eyes off the ball.

"No. I'm not kidding. This is important. I promised her she could have one and..."

"Aaagh," he shouted, bouncing off the sofa and thumping the floor with his open hand. Apparently the other team had scored.

"She wants a Hawaiian theme and cake volcano and we *owe* it to her," I said, through gritted teeth. "And Tom, we need to hire a venue, I mean, it just wouldn't be possible to create a Hawaiian haven in the back garden."

"Stella, we are *not* hiring a room. For God's sake, it's only a ninth birthday party! We can't afford it and that's final!" he yelled between goals. Then he must have felt bad shouting at me because he looked over and said, more calmly, "Why can't she have her party in the garden like other kids?"

"Tom, you can't hold a disco in a garden. What about all the lights and things? And besides, it would probably rain!"

"I'd love Grace to have a big birthday party, but I think it's more important that we keep the house," he said sarcastically.

"Tom, you're so bloody practical – and selfish – and boring!" I screamed, storming back into the kitchen to arrange decorative limes on the granite worktop. He couldn't see that this wasn't just about Grace's birthday party; it was about me wanting to do right by her after all the time I'd missed and about us doing something fun as a family. I was still racked by unworthy-mother guilt. I didn't agree with Tom, Grace *did* need her Birthday luau, and I was going to make sure she got it – with or without her father's help.

I woke up the next day and decided to take matters into my own hands.

Grace was going to a friend's house after school (and would no doubt be painting her lips and nails black whilst planning her first tattoo) so I took the bull by the horns and approached a small local hotel regarding her party. They came up with what I considered to be a very reasonable Mount Etna-style buffet for thirty children in a Honolulu-style setting for £250. I booked the venue there and then but nearly fainted at the price of creating a spectacular volcano cake. They wanted a further £175 so I promised to 'talk it over with my husband' and left.

As I arrived home, clutching my receipt for the venue, I felt slightly nauseous. I knew I was still working on the Oprah-esque 'take charge of your own destiny' thing but I couldn't stop myself worrying about what Tom would say and dreading another eruption over grass skirts and cake volcanoes.

Walking into the sitting room, I saw that Tom was home from work and hard at it, about to bat against Pakistan. I watched him twitching in the chair, knowing I needed to get him off the pitch and convince him that Grace's party was absolutely vital for all our emotional well-being. He also needed to get it into his thick skull that Hawaii was not a theme to be taken lightly; we were talking tropical fruit-filled paradise in the bowels of Bromsgrove, and believe me that didn't come cheap.

"Hi," I ventured, sitting on the sofa nearby and trying vainly to attract his attention.

"Christ, they're giving us a run for their money!" he announced, to no one in particular.

"Talking of money," I saw the opening and raised my voice, "I've just booked a hotel, for Grace's birthday. It was only £250 which I think was quite reasonable," I gabbled and biting the bullet added, "plus another £175 for the cake."

His initial response, in between runs, overs and wickets, was silence.

"I said, I have just paid for..." I started again.

"I heard what you said," he snapped. "I just don't believe it, Stella."

I felt the tremor underfoot – this was going to blow, so I stomped out of the sitting room and into the kitchen. On safer ground, no leather on willow here, I switched on my nice, comforting kettle but to my surprise, Tom appeared in the doorway. For him to abandon England to carry on without him during a vital cricket match was unprecedented, and for just a moment – a teeny tiny one – I realised the enormity of what I'd done.

"Have you any idea how much money we have?" he said. Then without waiting for an answer, he continued, "We have almost nothing Stella! We've had a couple of expensive years and now, without your salary, there will be nothing left in the bank at the end of the month. Do you understand? NOTHING!"

Even in this awful moment I was amazed at how animated this made him and couldn't help but think it would be nice to see this kind of passion in other areas of our life.

"You have no income Stella – what if you were on your own?" he continued, more calmly, like he was about to die or something. *God*, I thought, *he's been coughing a bit recently, I hope he's OK.*

"You and Grace are a huge responsibility and it worries me."

This was the perfect opening to make him see my point. "Tom, I told you it's what Grace wants, and I feel..."

He slowly walked towards me, his hands held out in despair.

"You feel? Always about you, isn't it, Stella? What about how I feel? About how I lie awake at night worrying about the mortgage, bills, car tax, all those boring things that don't interest you? Go on Stella, tell me, what do we do now? You're the one who tossed her job down the drain and instead of trying to find something else, you've immediately spent several hundred pounds we don't have." This was becoming ever so slightly scary because Tom always knew what to do. For him to ask my advice on monthly finance issues was bizarre and unsettling. "You must have a plan," he continued, "because I sure as hell don't!"

"If you have a problem with a birthday cake shaped like a volcano and costing £175 then perhaps you shouldn't have had a child!" I shrieked, slamming plates into the dishwasher like something from a Greek wedding. Tom just stared at me and walked back into the living room.

After a few minutes I popped my head discreetly round the door to see if he was still alive. I watched him slowly turn off the TV (this was serious, he *never* turned the TV off), pick up his jacket and walk out of the door. I was shocked and hurt – how dare he just walk out like that! So I ran to the front door and hurled a couple of decorative limes at his car as it screeched off. I got the last word of course, it was something eloquent and highbrow, along the lines of, "Yes, you can just piss off, you tight bastard!" But by then, he'd gone.

As I walked slowly back into the kitchen, I wondered what was happening to us. I'd made huge sacrifices already and stopped buying ready-meals from M&S. I had cancelled my order for *wild* salmon from the Orkneys and *organic* pork by post from Nigella's preferred butcher. Yes, I was slumming it now; I'd put my money where my mouth was and was making ends meet but did Tom give me any credit? Did he hell.

At midnight Tom still wasn't back and I was starting to get worried. Perhaps if I lost a stone he'd fall in love with me all over again and things would be like they used to. Dieting would definitely start the next day. Lizzie had also lent me the new Paul McKenna book and CD: "Babes, you can just lie there and it will happen," she assured me and I have to admit, Paul looked very serious and somewhat tantalising with promises of 'I Can Make You Thin,' so it must work. Yes, I'd get rid of this blubber by simply lying back and letting Paul McKenna have his hypnotic way with me again and again until I was an eight-stone supermodel.

Tom finally came in at about 2am. I felt it was perhaps time for me to compromise, so in the light of all the recent Hawaiian themed dramas, I conceded.

"Tom," I announced. "I am sorry I haven't been a bit more understanding about money. I will make the Princess's volcano-shaped birthday cake myself and save us £175. It won't be as good as a professional cake and I'm not completely happy about it, but I do want to help."

"Yeah...whatever," Tom sighed in monotone, accepting my sacrifice with a nod but without the gushing gratefulness I'd hoped for. As he climbed into our kingsize bed (with dove-grey over-quilt that matched the John Lewis curtains perfectly), I gave him a warm smile and took his hand. But Tom just switched off the light and turned away from me.

It made me feel so sad, the way everything was turning out. Grace was a Goth, Tom was miserable and I couldn't talk to Mum about it all because she had gone away with friends she met on eBay (she posted herself on there, thinking it was a social-networking site – and for Mum it became one).

"Are you OK?" I asked Tom in a wobbly voice.

"Yeah, I'll be OK. We just have stuff to sort out," came the reply from the darkness.

"I was worried when you left," I said. "I shouldn't complain about having no money, I'm here at home as I wanted, a Fifties housewife and organic meatball-making mother." I joked half-heartedly, realising that instead of being a fulfilled wife baking flapjacks in a flowery apron as I'd dreamed, I felt completely worthless.

Closing my eyes, I comforted myself with the thought that I was the same age as the Desperate Housewives – and they were having a ball. Teri Hatcher reinvented herself and came back for a second bite at that big, juicy old cherry; in fact she was rubbing cherry juice all over that forty-something body of hers – and the boys *and* her bank balance were loving it. I told myself I wouldn't give up my dreams, but as Tom's snoring pierced my bubble, I realised that without a Hollywood makeup artist, dentist, plastic surgeon and a lifetime's supply of Botox I would have to try a slightly different road to Teri and her neighbours on Wisteria Lane.

11

Hawaiian Heaven in Suburban Hell

The next morning I decided it was time to stop feeling sorry for myself: I had a volcano cake to plan and only three days to make it. I rang Al; he always loved a drama and I needed to share a little panic-time before I embarked on the volcano.

"Al, I am about to create an artwork in confectionery and I need cocoa beans from Argentina, vanilla from Madagascar, butter from Normandy and raw cane sugar from the Caribbean," I announced.

He didn't let me down. "Oh My God doll! What you need is Candace Nelson on speed dial!"

"Who?"

"*The* Candace – of Sprinkles Bakery? Beverly Hills? Do keep up my love."

"Well, I'll have to make do with Tesco," I sighed. "I'm just not sure about quantities and stuff."

"Well, just think big. If the recipe says one kilo of sugar, buy two."

"Recipe? Gosh I don't always follow a recipe for cake – I just throw it all in from memory then add flavours I fancy." I said, concerned.

"Sweetie, you need to be focused. Do you think Candace created Sprinkles' dark chocolate cake with marshmallow frosting and bittersweet chocolate ganache by 'throwing it all in'?"

"Probably – I mean that's how you discover new flavours

and..."

"Doll, I'm off work tomorrow. You obviously need help, so I'll come over and advise," he said.

I was beginning to regret calling Al. There was such a lot to think about and Al flouncing round the kitchen in an 'advisory' capacity playing, 'Candace of Beverly Hills' didn't sound like help to me. Anyway, I drained the last of my coffee, got in the car and headed out for the supermarket. On arrival I grabbed a very large trolley and zig-zagged it to the Home Baking aisle.

Loading the trolley with flour and sugar I couldn't resist hurling in lots of vibrant crunchy hundreds and thousands and tubs of silver tooth-breaking balls. I fell in love with some little sugar pigs and also couldn't resist a long tube of delicate lemon and white icing flowers. However, despite my deep joy at discovering these little cake decorating treasures it was clear there wasn't anything that said 'cake volcano.'

I was just loading twenty packs of unsalted butter into the trolley when I heard "Stella, is that you, with 200 kilos of fat?" Al had warned me about the 'food police' that supermarkets were now employing; I knew I should have shopped online. I turned round expecting to see some sort of police/Tesco uniform but was equally horrified to see athletic 'Jemma with a J', my Lighter Lift counsellor, swinging her way down the aisle. She'd lost seven pounds once by taking off her cardi and cutting out biscuits for a week so felt it gave her the right to be superior and talk down to anyone over nine stone. "You should be enjoying a good brisk walk and a chilled glass of Perfect Peach," she said, wagging her finger.

I smiled sheepishly; "Jemma, hi. I'm, er, making a birthday cake for my daughter's party," I offered, feeling like a school kid caught skiving by the headmistress.

"I hope you're not going to eat it," she said, smug in her size-ten jeans and tight little top.

"Lovely to see you, got to go," I said, grimacing and hauling the trolley in the opposite direction. It was resisting strongly under the weight of ingredients and its insistence on veering to the left was almost dislocating my hip. In my desperation to escape I yanked it forward, staggering past 'Continental Cheeses' in agony but with a determined gait, refusing to let her witness my pain.

Driving home with five million calories-worth of cargo I thought *a woman is never free from guilt. If it wasn't my work or family I am letting down it is my own body. How could skinny Jemma think it was OK to jog up to me in Tesco like a bloody Olympic runner and tell me what I should be putting in my mouth?*

Heaving the gargantuan butter, flour and sugar mountain from the car to the house, I reckoned I must have worked off at least three slices of carrot cake. So I duly refilled as soon as I got in. Telling myself it was filled with carrots and therefore healthy, I opened up my favourite cookery books and devoured cake-porn over hot coffee and moist, spicy sponge.

I found a recipe for a large square cake but my biggest problem was that I didn't have a cake tin large enough. I did have two smaller ones and after much thought (and more carrot cake) I decided I would simply have to make four squares and join them together under a huge blanket of sugarpaste. This would form the base for the mountain but I still had to make the volcano itself. I hunted out a pen and paper and made a few quick sketches then decided that the easiest way to do this would be to make three light, round sponges and stack them on top of each other. I would join them with delicious buttercream, then shave and shape the edges with a sharp knife and cut a crater in the top layer. Once this was placed in the centre of the base, I could use textured icing to create a mountain effect on the outside of the cake and use marbled yellow and orange icing inside the crater itself.

First I weighed the flour, sieving it high to add air for the lightest sponge possible. I then sieved cinnamon onto the top of the huge flour mound in the bowl, creating snow-capped mountains in negative, the snow beneath and the earth dusting the top. Pineapple juice and brown sugar sweetened the mix as whole eggs landed hard into flour and softened butter thudded onto mountainous, sugary terrain. I used to watch Mum bake like this, anticipating the reward of a loaded wooden-spoon to be licked clean of creamy, sweet batter. I wished Mum was with me, I wished we had more time together and like a child I rewarded myself with a curative lick at the spoon. The cool, sweet, creamy mouthful filled me with warmth, obliterating the guilt and grown-up doubts with a poultice of brown sugar and butter.

Laying greaseproof paper into the square tins and pressing it into the corners I thought of Tom and me – were we the snug, perfect fit I'd always thought we were? I'd blamed working life for the obstacles in our relationship, but perhaps we weren't as happy as I'd thought after all. I dropped the gloopy mixture into the tins and opened the oven which blasted me with a waft of boiling air, almost taking my breath away. As I closed the door on the mixture and watched it slowly level I realised that I couldn't blame work anymore for our failings as a couple. Unlike the cake batter, my marriage wouldn't just settle on its own. It needed help. Tom and I had nothing left to hide behind anymore and I knew I had to do more than just spectate.

45 minutes later, the first two squares of fruit-scented, golden sponge emerged and suddenly things didn't look too bad. I tipped them onto wire cooling racks and started the second batch; the warm, sweet air went to my head and I found myself giggling insanely at nothing. Eventually I took out the second batch of steaming cake and tearing myself away I set off

to collect Grace from school. Waiting with the other mums I smiled and opened my arms as she and the rest of her class burst out into the playground.

"Mum!" she squealed, with barely-concealed horror; "What are you wearing?" I looked down to see I was still wearing my cinnamon-dusted floury apron and furry slippers. We both giggled, her embarrassment tempered by the fact that I was so 'uncool' it was hilarious. I hugged her and threatened more outrageous outfits for future school collections as she covered her face in mock horror. Holding hands, we rushed home together. I couldn't wait to get back and start working on the plans for the decoration and the icing flavours.

Once home, I made the three sponges for the volcano and we slapped them with buttercream and joined them together. I then began carefully shaving sections off, to create the volcano shape.

"I think the top is too big," said Grace after some consideration. "And I think we need to slice more bits off to make it smaller...and then eat those bits," she smiled, raising her eyebrows hopefully." I agreed that we should neaten the top up and scoop out some cake to make the crater. Grace was enthusiastically testing the shavings when Tom arrived home. .

"Dad, Dad...I know what I want to be when I grow up," she announced, running to him and spraying a mouthful of sponge crumbs into the air, "I'm going to be a cake taster."

Tom picked her up and whizzed her round. "That cake smells good Stella," he said, smiling and winking at me. *Click*, I thought; this was the snapshot I'd longed for – my family home together, an effortless and happy scene.

As threatened, Al came in an 'advisory capacity,' the following day. He had lots to contribute and was still in the kitchen washing up two days later.

"I feel permanently sticky," I announced over the volcano.

"Yes doll, I can see that and I hate to say it but the sweating is more Gordon Ramsay than Nigella Lawson."

I giggled.

"But at least you seem to being enjoying yourself," he observed, with a smile.

He was right; it was fun. My absolute favourite bit had been deciding on the marriage of flavours and textures for decorating the cake.

"I'm thinking coconut and pineapple with a little lacing of vanilla?" I suggested to Al.

"Mmm, I think the vanilla may be one ingredient too much, doll," he said. "Let's keep the vomiting children down to a minimum and stick with the basic piña colada flavours with a hint of cinnamon spice."

Once we'd applied the sugar-blanket coating, our four joined-up cakes were like a huge blank canvas on which we could paint anything we wanted. We then carefully placed the three, now almost conical, joined sponges in the middle. I held my breath as I was worried they might be too heavy and that the base would sink but to my relief they were fine. Then I got to work slapping thick chocolate buttercream around the sides of the volcano. Grace joined in excitedly and watched Al, who was finally utilising his degree in Graphic Design and working on the intricate, arty stuff.

"At the base of this magnificent, pineapple beast we will carefully place twenty-five grass-skirted sugar figurines dancing on white chocolate sand frosting," Al said in a regal voice, much to Grace's delight.

These sugar-crafted beauties dipped tiny toes into azure seas (blue food colouring with white frosty tips). The rolling waves were framed by sugar palm trees so real you could almost hear them swishing in the breeze. Behind them, the mountain rose majestically and near the top we positioned a Hawaiian flag, stuck to a cocktail stick. The crater of the volcano smouldered in marbled yellow and orange and little flowers were dotted around the mountainside.

Al had even added a perfect, tiny pair of sparkly flip-flops made from marzipan. "They are yours, Grace," he said, positioning them on the beach. "I think you've just gone for a swim."

It was the middle of the night when we finally completed it and Al and I just sat drinking tea and staring at the amazing spectacle we'd created. "Not bad for two old telly tarts," he smiled, wiping a tear from his eye. We hadn't slept for two days and he was tired and emotional.

When we finally unveiled the completed Mount Etna-by-the-sea (not geographically correct I'll admit), Grace shrieked with delight. Even Lizzie, who had come to the house pre-party to help screamed in amazement and Tom had to pop his head round the door to see what all the noise was about.

"Wow, that is really good," he said, genuinely surprised. At that moment I could have cried (Al did). After all the stuff I'd ever done in life, this cake felt like the high point of my achievements. As she danced round the kitchen I could see it made my daughter very happy too.

If I had ever had any doubts about fighting Tom for this party they were completely washed away by the look on Grace's face as she entered the room we'd decorated in Hawaiian beach party-style. 'Happy Birthday Grace' was plastered all over the walls, with huge vibrantly-coloured paper flowers dotted everywhere and huge blow-up palm trees in every corner.

"I am soooo excited!" she squealed, unable to contain the bubbling hysteria in her voice.

The party started at three and as her friends arrived, Grace greeted them at the door accepting beribboned gifts and cards and placing them on a trestle table to be opened in a frenzy of happiness later. "Mummy this is just amazing," she said with shiny eyes as she grappled with an armful of gifts.

As soon as all the guests had arrived the disco started and several of the more confident dancers started wiggling their tiny hips with little regard to the musical rhythm. I watched from the sidelines with amusement as Tom secured the piñata and everyone queued up politely, just like at school. Given a pole and faced with an inanimate object packed with sugary treats, however, even the shyest children transformed instantly into savages. I exchanged smiles with Tom who ducked the pole as a tiny, red-haired girl whacked the poor piñata with such force that her feet lifted off the ground. It didn't stand a chance and spewed out tubes and packets of sweets to the delight of the little girls who roared like beasts and wrestled each other to the ground. "They're fighting to the death for a packet of Parma Violets," Tom laughed.

After the piñata abuse, the food was served and the children ate ice cream and fruit cocktails like they'd been on a fast. Grace's grass skirt soon became sticky with icing and spilt fruit juice but she was oblivious, happily dancing and laughing.

"She's having a wonderful time isn't she," I said to Tom, who was smiling at his daughter playing the clown.

He looked at me and smiled, not ready to admit I was right, at which point Al came over. He had embraced the occasion with a tinsel Lei over a Hawaiian shirt. He was followed by Lizzie, who'd gone for a slightly more 'out there,' grass skirt with a T-shirt stating, 'I need a good Lei,' emblazoned across her ample bosom.

"I am loving Hawaii," she whispered. "Even Tom's smiling – haven't seen that for a while."

Tom was great, organising games for the kids and really

getting involved. He was like the old Tom who could be great fun when he wasn't dragged down by work and money worries. Meanwhile I socialised with the other mums as they nibbled on Hawaiian-chicken skewers and bite-sized pineapple pavlovas.

I was pleased to see Emma Wilson's mum, Alice. She was going through a particularly painful divorce and I hated to say it, but it was showing on her hips. She was enjoying the pavlovas a little *too* much and as she crammed in the crumbling meringue and licked the oozing, sticky pineapple syrup from her fingers, she raved about the volcano.

"It's just the most gorgeous cake I've ever seen," she yelled, competing with Lady Gaga who was now full throttle as grass-skirted disco divas took to the floor. I confessed I'd made the cake with a friend and she looked quite surprised. "Are you taking orders?" She asked, mid-meringue mouthful.

"Emma's having a birthday party soon. Since Jack left it's not been much fun for her so I've promised her that when the divorce money comes through we'll celebrate her birthday properly. I don't suppose you'd consider making a special cake?" She said, clutching at my wrists in a rather desperate way.

"I'm flattered," I said, "but these days I barely seem to have time to do anything except look after Grace and Tom!" I felt a bit mean because she was having a rough time with the divorce and everything but it was such a big commitment.

At the end of the party it was obvious that all the kids had had a great time and as their parents cleared the last of the grown-up finger buffet we gathered our stuff together. I helped Al into his VW Beetle (he was having a tussle with prickly tinsel and pink hibiscus) and the manager of the hotel came out, holding the cake board with what now looked like an erupted Mount Etna. "Amazing cake," he commented, as he handed it to me.

As I drove back home with a happy little girl and an

unusually smiley husband, I thought maybe things weren't so bad. I'd never forget her jumping up and down on the dancefloor, shouting along to the music. I was still smiling when we returned home and as we got through the door, the phone rang. Grace rushed to answer it. "Hi Nan," she squealed. It was Mum, calling to wish her a happy birthday.

"Where's she calling from?" I asked.

"New York!" squeaked Grace. I smiled. I'd almost forgotten about Mum's latest jaunt – she'd joined an amateur dramatic theatre group in Bolton and they were doing a two-month experimental life swap with another ageing Am-Dram off Broadway. I couldn't remember the play but I was sure it was something inappropriate for her age.

Grace spoke to her for a few minutes then hung up. "Mum, can I play with the rounders set that Emily bought me?" she asked, still jumping up and down with energy. It was almost dark but it was her birthday; I was about to say yes when Tom cut in.

"Grace, honey, it's late and we're all very tired. Let's play tomorrow." I could see she was disappointed. But she'd had a good day, so she accepted it and went to bed.

As soon as she'd gone up, Tom went into the lounge and turned on *Match of the Day*. I sat down next to him and put my head on his shoulder. It really had been a lovely day and I was feeling closer to him than I had in a while. I turned my head and started kissing his neck.

"Stella, I'm very tired," he said. "I really just want to catch up on the scores and go to bed."

He gave me a quick, dismissive kiss on the forehead and turned back to the TV. Clearly the day hadn't had quite the same effect on him as it had on me and I couldn't understand why. I thought we'd had such a perfect time together, as a family. Was Tom really that tired? Or was it something else?

I moved away from him and watched mutely from the doorway as he groaned and cheered the teams on, hoping that he might change his mind, or at least talk to me for a while. But even though he must have known I was standing there, Tom didn't look up from the screen once. So after a while I closed the living room door behind me and with a sigh went to bed.

12

Mum, Mountains and
Midnight Blue Lace

Over the following weeks, the distance between us increased. "I'm sorry, Stella," Tom said one Friday morning before leaving for Leeds (he was freelancing for *Emmerdale*). "You know how tight money is at the moment and I just can't turn work down." He pecked me on the cheek without even looking at me and as he walked out of the door, I knew I needed to do something, so I called Mum in New York.

"Hello love!" she shouted (she always shouted long-distance). "I'll have to be quick, it's nearly curtain-up!"

I told her about Tom.

"You need to get away for a bit," Mum yelled. "A family holiday for the three of you. Spend some time together dear."

"You must be kidding." I said. "Tom still hasn't forgiven me for spending a few hundred pounds on Grace's birthday party. I don't think a family holiday is on the cards!"

"Yes but it doesn't have to cost much love. Look, I meant to say a while ago, but I forgot. I have lots of those flying miles thingies..."

"Air Miles?"

"No, I think they're for BA. Anyway you can use them if you like. Then you won't have to pay for the flights."

"That's very kind of you Mum, but even the accommodation would be too much."

"Well it's up to you dear. But if you want my opinion, you should seize the day and a stitch in time saves nine you know. I was talking to Beryl the other day and..."

"Thanks, Mum, I'd better go, the potatoes are boiling over," I interrupted, before she could trot out any more clichés.

However, the more I thought about it, the more I realised that Mum could be surprisingly lucid sometimes. I suddenly had a vision of Tom and I, hand in hand, Grace running alongside us, on a sun-kissed beach, like something out of a Thomas Cook ad. Could a holiday be the answer? Essentially, apart from our honeymoon over ten years before we hadn't actually spent much time alone together – perhaps that was the problem? When I was working away he'd be at home with Grace and if he had to work away, I'd cover the home front. I knew Tom would initially balk at this, given his concerns about cash but surely he couldn't say no to a free holiday. And once that chilled white wine and warm sunshine trickled in, he'd take me in his arms and realise that some things were special and worth working on.

A few days later I was preparing dinner when Tom came back downstairs and sat at the kitchen table to read the news. I thought again about our honeymoon in Greece – all blue water, sunny white beaches and burning cocktails suffused with love and longing, but our money troubles seemed to be getting in the way lately and we just weren't communicating like we used to. I glanced at him squinting over his paper and belching and I was suddenly desperate to recreate some of the romance Tom and I had once shared. If Mum could sort the flights then all we needed was accommodation and I had a card up my sleeve for that. Kath, an old friend from the Drama Department, had inherited a little place on Kefalonia, the same island on which Tom and I had spent our honeymoon, and she'd said in the past that I was welcome to use it. I snuck upstairs and called her.

"Money's a bit tight so I was wondering how much it would

be to rent it from you and head off in Grace's October half term," I asked her, hopefully. Tom had rather reluctantly agreed to take some time off so we could do things as a family and this would be the perfect time to go away.

She sounded doubtful. "Well, there's no air-conditioning and October can still be very warm. The hot water's a bit iffy too. It's also very isolated Stella – it's halfway up a mountain. You're welcome to stay there for free – it's very basic," she added.

This was great – surely even Tom couldn't say no to a totally free holiday? I went back into the kitchen and mashed the organic sweet potatoes. As I stirred the rich onion gravy for the home-reared pork sausages, I considered the best way to approach this whole thing. As the three of us were round the table, eating my perfectly-prepared dinner I dived in. "Tom, I have some great news. Mum has offered her Air Miles so we can all go on holiday in Grace's half term."

Grace looked up, delighted. I explained Mum's offer and she said, "Yay Nan! Are we going then?"

Tom's shoulders sank. "No we're not, we can't afford it and I just wish you would accept that." Grace crumpled and I wanted to scream at him but this would cause a huge row and that would be the end of any family holiday.

"Oh Tom, don't be so grumpy. It would be really good fun. Grace would love it and if you just thought about it, so would you. I mean, we can do it for almost nothing. Free holiday – free flights?"

"Daddy pleeeease," started Grace. *That's my girl*, I thought proudly, with both of us onto it we'd soon wear him down.

"We can't afford it because we will still spend more than we would here," he was shaking his head, adamantly.

"Tom it can be done on the cheap and I promise I won't complain if we don't eat out. We can cook and have picnics. We can really keep the cost down."

"Oh God! I don't know." He looked up at Grace, who was smiling hopefully and had her fingers visibly crossed. How could he refuse? "Oh, well I suppose if it doesn't cost anything. And you have to sort everything, Stella," he muttered, going back to his food and shaking his head like a family holiday was something to be endured.

His reaction was a bit of a downer, but Grace was ecstatic and I refused to let it spoil things. Grace and I danced around the kitchen. I knew this holiday would bring us back together – it was something we all needed and given time, Tom would come round to the idea and realise it wasn't going to break the bank.

"It's all about sex darling," said Lizzie, who I called as soon as Grace was in bed and Tom was safely stationed in front of the TV.

"What's about sex?"

"Well, if there's a problem, that's always the first thing to go," she said, and I heard the click of her Zippo as she lit a cigarette.

"We haven't had sex for ages – weeks and weeks." I said uncomfortably, taking a large gulp of the red wine I'd poured to console myself for Tom's lack of enthusiasm.

"I don't care what they say, if things ain't going on in the bedroom – well, they ain't goin on," she announced.

"It's really not about sex, Lizzie."

"Sweetie – EVERYTHING is about sex," she said, exhaling loudly and no doubt blowing out a mouthful of smoke. "If you can sort the sex side of things out – everything else just falls into place."

I wasn't convinced, "Yeah, but when someone's distant it's

the last thing you want to do. I just feel so vulnerable and unattractive and..."

"Stella, whatever it takes, you need to get him back into bed. And back into your life."

I had a week before we were due to leave and as I hung up I realised she was right. We'd only had sex once in the last few months. At first it was a relief – all that jerking around when all you want to do is curl up in bed with a good book and a bar of chocolate but I was starting to feel paranoid. I'd never been the: 'come and get me, my name's Temptation', kinda gal in the bedroom. I was more Janet Reger than Ann Summers and not into Rampant Rabbits, baby-doll nighties or fluffy handcuffs. I'd rather be pursued courteously, like an early Mills and Boon heroine with a gentle teasing off of the bodice rather than any lewd ripping scenarios. And I think it went without saying that for me this tasteful encounter would always be followed by a post-coital cup of tea and a slice of homemade date and walnut.

But maybe Lizzie was right. It would have been good for my self esteem (but not my bank balance) to buy something utterly fabulous with ribbons from Agent Provocateur. However, I decided that the cost – when revealed on our credit-card bill – would probably give Tom permanent droop and therefore defeat the object of the exercise. I nipped to our local M&S instead. Arriving at the store and trawling through Ladies Lingerie to reignite the passion in my marriage, I lighted upon a midnight-blue polyester affair with matching dressing-gown. Nothing too raunchy or expensive, more Joan Collins than Jordan, with a little bit of what my mother would call 'important' lace here and there.

As I secretly inserted it into my suitcase I got a little thrill. Passion was on the menu...

13

Lost in Translation

We arrived on Kefalonia very late in the afternoon and it was just as magical as I'd remembered with the sun beating down and the skies a shattering blue. We picked up our hire car (the cheapest, oldest car Tom could find) in the port of Argostoli, a beautiful, quietly bustling place, colour-washed, with a warm, pine-scented breeze. Afternoon siesta was over and the square was slowly coming to life as shutters opened and tablecloths unfurled for evening trade in the warm open air. I looked at Tom, he smiled and I just felt so good; we were back where we belonged, a little older and wiser, but still in one piece, still together...just.

This time however, we'd brought a little person with us and our little angel wasn't as enamoured with the place as I was, letting it be known that she was tired, cross and hungry. At times like this, Grace could cut up rough and she held my holiday hopes in her nine-year-old palm. I watched my dream of sipping cold white wine and nibbling mezze alfresco as the world went by slip suddenly from my grasp. Something that had seemed so simple years ago when we were alone and first married was now insurmountable.

"I want a crêpe and a Coke," Princess Grace demanded, rather ungraciously. I wanted lemon-drenched calamari, tzaziki and a feta-and-olive filled Greek salad.

"Sweetie, don't be a pain. There's nowhere here that does crêpes," I said, really hoping our first night wasn't going to involve some huge family row over pancakes.

However, Grace was clearly old enough to read and knew when Mummy was telling a barefaced lie. "There *is* somewhere that does pancakes, Mummy," she declared, pointing and defiantly jangling her skeleton charm bracelet (a gift from my mother). "I can see that sign – it says, 'World of Crêpes' over there, over THERE," she urged, "and *that's* what I'm having." With that, she stomped across the square, a girl on a mission who quite clearly wasn't going to take 'no' for an answer.

"I won't have this," I said to Tom, "it's our holiday too."

Tom, as always, was far more reasonable and understanding of our daughter (and possibly more scared of her) than I was. "She's tired and it's easier to just let her have a crêpe," he said to me in that cajoling way which made me seem very unreasonable and even younger than Grace. Irritatingly, he had a point, so we trawled after her and I reluctantly sat down on a green plastic chair in the neon-lit 'World of Crêpes.' When the crêpes arrived they were less than impressive and chewing on flabby, tasteless batter I thought *this isn't going to be like our honeymoon at all*. I felt hot, itchy and absolutely fed up.

'Crêpe-gate' had started us all off on a bad footing and it was about to get worse. After filling ourselves with cold, duvet-like pancakes and warm fizzy cola we wearily climbed into the hire car and set off with a loud bang in a plume of black smoke to find our villa. I was navigating and it was dark, two things that just don't mix. Once he'd worked out the gears, the mirrors and the lights by banging on the dashboard and swearing a lot, Tom began driving cautiously through Argostoli. He didn't actually ask me any navigating-type questions so I naturally assumed he knew where he was going. I settled in my seat to point out all the stars and the full moon shimmering over the water to Gracie who didn't really give a toss because she was playing *Mario Bros* on her Nintendo and I was just being irritating.

An hour and a half later, we were still driving. By now I'd stepped into the breach and was in full 'navigating' mode – keen for Tom not to notice that we'd been going round in circles and just passed 'World of Crêpes' again for the fourth time. Praying he hadn't spotted the big neon crêpe sign, I glanced over discreetly to discover that God had let me down again and my prayers had been ignored.

"No, no, no, we're back where we started. That's the crêpe house!" He banged his head on the steering wheel. *Here, let me do that for you*, I thought, irrational hatred suddenly pulsing through every vein.

"How hard can it be to read a bloody map?" he snarled.

"It's pitch-black," I raged through gritted teeth. "How hard would it have been for *you* to read the bloody map in daylight before we set out and – call me old-fashioned – plan a pissing route?"

"I do everything," he spat, "so when something goes wrong it's always *my* fault."

This just wasn't true, and as much as I'd have loved to expand on my critique of his holiday planning there was really no point in arguing with him in this mood. And right on cue, Grace was now screaming from the back seat, "I want a wee!"

We eventually arrived at the so-called villa and as we pulled up and got out of the car we were engulfed by the heavy stillness. My heart sank; I truly, deeply hoped we'd got the wrong place. It was completely deserted, on a steep hillside and probably as old as said hillside. The 'villa' was little more than a grey shack with shutters, the only light a bare bulb hanging outside in the mothy blackness. As we tentatively approached, hoping we'd got the wrong place frantic shouting came from inside and it seemed that Yannis the caretaker had arranged a welcome committee. A bearded bear of a man, he appeared on the worn, wonky steps of the building waving a set of keys and laughing maniacally. Apparently delighted to see his 'guests', he rushed towards us with wife, chickens and various children in tow.

"Great," I said. "Tom, where's the nearest hotel? If this is the reception desk I don't want to see any more."

Despite their enthusiasm and friendliness, we just weren't in the mood. Tom and I were tired, disillusioned and filled with a dark, mutual hatred. Grace, who had just woken from her slumber on the back seat, had her hair on end and a truly horrified look on her face. She was prone to a bit of nocturnal wandering and saying incomprehensible things if woken abruptly and now wasn't the time for her to do the sleeping-walking-talking thing. It occurred to me that it might put the wind up Yannis's kids if Grace suddenly started speaking in tongues like the child in *The Amityville Horror* so I glided quickly over to her side. In an attempt to keep her under control, I clutched her arm. I was relieved – if a little embarrassed – when she shook my arm away and snapped, "Mum, get off me you freak!" She was obviously wide awake and behaving as normal.

Yannis ignored the mother-daughter scuffle and did his best to introduce us to his wife Anna. He opened the door to the villa, ushering us in with both hands like we were livestock. "Krevatokamares, krevatokamares," he insisted, still ushering us forward and nodding enthusiastically.

We smiled wretchedly through our tiredness; "What's he saying?" Tom hissed.

"How should I know? I'm not fucking Greek," I spat under my breath while continuing to nod and smile at Yannis.

"I'm aware you're not Greek," Tom spat back, over the noise of all the chickens and children, "but you've got the bloody phrasebook!"

I grappled with my shoulder bag and gestured for Yannis to speak slowly, which I think he got. "Krevatokamares," he repeated, pointing to an open door, off which I presumed was the chicken-shed living room (Cath Kidston would have had a heart-attack). I lifted my hand in a 'wait' gesture and balanced the guidebook on my knee, rifling through Greek words beginning with K. "K...K...K..." I said uncertainly, feeling just like I had earlier when 'navigating'.

"What's he saying?" Tom was such a stresser and it was infectious.

"I'm, er...here it is," I said, relief sweeping over me.

"Come on, the holiday'll be over by the time you..."

"Thanks as always for your patience and support Tom," I said, sarcastic and slightly cocky now because I had found the word.

"Krevatokamares," I announced, "means bedroom!"

"Oh, of course!" Tom gestured for Yannis to show us the 'master' bedroom, which – when we all poked our heads round the door – looked like a Greek vent of hell.

Completely deflated, we all trooped back and as Tom and I prepared for a confused 'goodnight' conversation with Yannis and his brood he pulled out a bottle of urine-coloured local wine, some glasses and plonked himself at the table. My heart sank. Tom and I were obliged to sit down with him, quickly followed by a smiling and nodding Anna.

"Stella, look in the book. How do you say, 'We're tired and need to go to bed now?" Tom said quietly.

I opened the book desperately, scouring the English words and trying to find something. "Ooh, I remember – bedroom is 'krevatokamares'," I said in a low voice as Yannis poured me a huge glass. I took another peek inside the guidebook. "Yannis," I said, waving my hand in what I felt was a Greek way to get his attention; "Thelo....na....koymitho   mazi   sou   er....stin krevatokamara tora," I said slowly and carefully, smiling and nodding throughout as is apparently customary when abroad. Yannis gazed at me with what I can only describe as a whimsical look and Tom gulped the last of his wine in an effort to bring proceedings to a close.

"Well done," said Tom under his breath. "You see, you can do it when you put your mind to it. I think he's got the message." There were a few moments of silence, when no-one knew quite what to do and to our deep joy, Yannis rose from his chair. Within seconds however, our elation at the thought of sleep turned to horror as Yannis reached into a cupboard behind him and brought out another bottle.

"*Christ* nooo," breathed Tom. "But I thought you just told him we wanted to go to bed?"

"I did," I hissed, "Perhaps it's my pronunciation."

I was now dreaming of a bed, any bed. We were all so tired from the flight then the hellish car journey, the last thing we needed was more animated signing with foreign strangers in a hut up a hill. Looking around the dingy room and smiling inanely at our new friends I could see that they were here for the evening so I let Yannis refill my glass. "You like?" he asked, with a wink.

"Lovely," I winked back. This went on for some time with Yannis and I winking and raising our glasses as Tom sank deeper onto the table, his head now resting on his arms. Grace (being a child vampire) was wide awake and playing happily with Yannis's kids despite a complete lack of common language. The kids didn't need words but I was struggling with the winking and the benign gestures as Tom snored on the table.

After a couple of hours of mimed-conversations, forced laughter and smiles that made my ears ache, we finally bid goodnight to our new Greek best friends and fell, exhausted, into a rickety double-bed.

"I'm not sure we did the right thing... coming here," Tom said, sleepily.

"You mean this villa?"

"I mean coming away on holiday when neither of us really want to."

My heart lurched; neither of us? But I wanted to! "Give it a chance Tom, it's only the first night," I said, painting over the cracks with my usual whitewash of hope.

"I can't believe Yannis kept pouring drinks. He knew we were tired," his voice was fading as he dropped off.

"I thought they'd never go. And we went to the trouble of speaking in his language to tell him we were tired and wanted our beds," I said, indignantly picking up the guidebook and turning to 'translation' for a quick swot.

Leafing idly through 'English to Greek in a jif' I came across the section I'd used to tell Yannis we were 'tired and wanted to go to bed now' and felt the heat rise from my toes to my face. According to the, 'Jiffy Quick' section where you could apparently attain 'fluency in a jif', what I had actually said to Yannis in Greek was; "I want to sleep with you in the bedroom, now!"

I didn't wake Tom to tell him.

14

Noisy Cocks and Strappy Nighties

Barely four hours later, the dawn broke over our Greek retreat and we were rudely awakened by the sound of a cockerel crowing in the back garden. Even Tom, who sleeps through most things, was disturbed by the constant noise. I decided there was no point in lying there trying to sleep so I staggered into the kitchen. Grace was sitting at the table, Nintendo in hand.

"Mum, I can't find the pool," she said, without taking her eyes from *Nintendogs*.

"Erm, there isn't actually a pool. What would you like for breakfast, Grace?"

"No pool? But you can't go on holiday and not have a bloody pool!"

"You can, and that will do young lady. You do not say that word."

"*You* do."

"What would you like for breakfast?"

"A pool!" With that she opened a window and leaned out, looking hard in disbelief. At this point, Tom staggered in scratching his head and his groin (yes, at the same time – quite a talent).

"What's for breakfast?" he asked, like he was a six-year old and I was his mummy.

"Well, did you buy any food? I didn't, and my magical powers are limited abroad. I can't conjure it from nowhere and

the bloody 'breakfast fairy' hasn't appeared, so I would guess –
erm, give me a minute – there isn't anything!"

"No need to be like that."

"Like what?" I asked, wanting to be all mature but pushing
him for a reaction.

"Mum, Mum, the bloody breakfast fairy *has* appeared."

"Grace, I will not tell you again."

"No Mum. Look, look!"

Grace was pointing frantically at something beneath the
window and with some trepidation (Grace's idea of a fairy was
likely to be a creeping lizard) I opened the door and stepped
out. There, in the shade of the house, lying on the ground was a
basket covered in a cloth. I handed it to Grace who was still
hanging out of the window, who lifted the cover and began
whooping with delight.

"Ooh Mum, it's yoghurt and honey, yay!"

Yannis or Anna had kindly left us this little 'Red Cross'
parcel, placed in the coolest part of the garden.

"That's kind of them," Tom said, almost smiling as he poked
his finger into the thick, white sheep's yoghurt. I spooned it into
some cracked bowls plucked quickly from the cupboards and
Tom poured the golden, syrupy honey into each snowy puddle.
Grace found a handful of almonds in the basket and made it her
job to sprinkle them on top of the bittersweet breakfasts. We
took our bowls outside like the three bears and sat in the warm
breeze at a rickety table looking out upon hills and olive trees.

The yoghurt was cool and rich, the tangy sharpness relieved
by the sweetness of honey and crunchy with nuts. "It's not *that*
bad here," I said, lifting my face to the sun.

"Yeah," Tom nodded, looking out onto the golden
landscape. But I could tell that he wasn't convinced. We both
looked and felt like hell, but at least I was trying. This was the
island where we'd spent our honeymoon and I couldn't help but

keep making stark comparisons between then and now. Could this couple who barely make eye contact be the same two people who once slept all night in each other's arms, afraid to be apart?

Later, as we washed the breakfast things there was a knock on the door. It was our friend Yannis. "You OK? You sleep?" he asked, putting his palm to his face, his head on one side in a sleeping gesture.

I was concerned we'd be woken by the cockerel every morning so I thought it would be a good opportunity to ask if Yannis could perhaps put him in another field. However, after my faux pas the night before, I wasn't prepared to risk a hurried translation of 'noisy cock' in Greek (it could have gone *so* wrong) so I smiled and made a 'cock-a-doodle-doo' sound several times, rubbing my eyes in a charades fashion to try and let him know we'd been woken and were now very tired.

"Ah," he said, nodding his head. "No problem." I looked helplessly at Tom who just shrugged.

"You can remove the noisy cockerel from our garden?" I asked, nodding madly – and unnecessarily.

"Yes, yes," he said, turning to leave. "No problem, noisy. I do now," he said, making strange shapes with his hands as he started to leave. As I turned away and picked up the tea-towel, my eyes and brain decided to communicate and I suddenly understood his sign language. He was twisting his hands and nodding, clearly on his way to end the cockerel's life by strangling it with his bare hands at my request. "Noisy. I do it now," he repeated over his shoulder, already starting up the dirt track that led to the cockerel's lair.

"Wait, wait, don't *kill* the cock!" I screamed running after him uphill, starting to sweat and pant in the early morning heat. Yannis turned round, looking confused.

"Kokoraki? Kokoraki?"

I guessed this meant cockerel but there was no time to

check. An innocent bird was about to be strangled just so I could have a lie-in and something needed to be done. I grabbed Yannis by both arms, shouting, "No! No! Don't kill cock. I like noisy cock." He was surprised but clearly not averse to this and for a moment, I suspect he thought I was continuing my previous night's pursuit of his no-doubt hairy body. I saw Tom's shoulders shaking out of the corner of my eye.

"You could actually help me out here, Tom," I yelled.

"You're doing fine on your own," he shouted back, clearly enjoying the show.

Still clutching Yannis I saw that strange, whimsical look on his face again and followed his eyes to note with horror that I was still sporting my strappy summer nightie. I almost died. Not only was it way too short for a woman with my knees but it barely contained my wayward breasts that since the age of 40 had lived a life of their own. One false move and Yannis would be forced to call the police about the crazy English lady who demands to sleep with him and accosts him on dirt tracks screaming about how much she likes cock. Appalled at myself I decided to leave, thinking, *I am half naked and these people are decent. They have religion and 'the evil eye'.*

So while I still had a modicum of dignity left, I walked slowly back down the hill, still insisting in a less animated way (i.e. keeping my arms firmly by my sides and therefore my wild forty-something breasts in check) that the cock be saved. Yannis smiled, shrugged and walked away.

I lumbered back down the hill towards Tom, who was clapping my performance. As I smiled and took a bow, he walked back inside the villa. I watched him disappear and stood alone in the heat and dust feeling stupid.

Well, we may not have had a pool, but we did manage to find

the sea and actually ended up having a pretty good day. Tom and Grace played together in the water whilst I topped up my tan and texted Lizzie to find out what the weather was like in the UK. After all, there's nothing more satisfying than being somewhere hot when the weather at home is bad, is there? I soon got a text back.

TXT: Bloody freezing here darling. Grey skies and rain. Are things hotting up in the bedroom?

I read her text thoughtfully and glanced over to the water where Tom was swirling our daughter round, dipping her in and out of the sea and laughing as she shrieked. I quickly texted Lizzie back.

TXT: Not yet. Maybe tonight.

Very soon my mobile pinged through a response.

TXT: You go girl. Don't put it off or it'll be too late.

I put my phone away and picked up my book – but I couldn't help thinking about what she said for the rest of the day. So that night, with Lizzie's warning ringing in my ears and as Tom lay in bed reading *The Private Life of the Chinese Panda*, I slipped into midnight lace and slinked around the bedroom.

Feeling sort of hot in midnight blue, I tried to swish a bit, thinking *tummy in, bust out* and refused to be put off when I caught a fleeting glimpse of an overweight, middle-aged blonde in the cracked bathroom mirror. I immediately banished her from my head and whispered, 'J Lo' over and over in my head like a mantra. I was in full view, pretending to be unaware but aiming to catch Tom's eye and create spontaneous fireworks. I didn't look directly at him because I wanted it all to be very natural and not seem like a planned seduction. If Tom thought I was trying to inflame him with my M&S polyester it would be a turn-off and the Chinese Panda would have the upper hand. I wanted a love scene in the vein of *From Here to Eternity*. I wanted lashing, thrashing waves and tidal passion.

However, what you want isn't always what you get and while I wanted Deborah Kerr and Burt Lancaster, it was beginning to look more like George and Mildred. I pondered this and nearly put myself off the whole idea but with an alarming stab of false confidence I slipped between the sheets and seductively slid my fingers under the coverlet. I felt surprisingly shy after all this time, but reached out with the tips of my fingers for Tom's lower abdomen. On reaching my destination, I allowed my fingers to run gently yet seductively along the border of pubic hair between day and night. At first he didn't respond and I started to feel a bit silly.

I was just considering a return to the my decadent airport purchase of the *Good Food Magazine* and Jamie's 'pukka prosciutto pasta' when I heard a slight moan coming from Tom's direction. Oh yes, apparently I'd still got the touch. I sizzled silently and turned my gaze to him. He was biting his upper lip, eyes closed in ecstasy. *Yes! He still wants me*, I thought as I moved slowly down the bed, making small rodent-like nibbles at his neck causing another moan, deeper this time. He began to move his arms upwards, hands reaching for his face as the sexual joy began to build, and he cried: "Oh! Yess!" It did occur to me that this was a bit much at this stage in the proceedings but I was prepared to go with it. Yet as I looked up to meet his eyes I discovered to my horror the real reason for his unbridled emotion.

A glint of silver in each of Tom's ears told me that he was oblivious to my advances and was in joyful receipt of audio sporting action. Yes, Tom's orgasmic groaning had been evoked by a game of cricket on the other side of the world. Someone had just done a googly. And it wasn't me.

For the rest of the holiday we spent our days arguing and sweating and our nights drinking to forget the days. Meanwhile, nothing stirred in the bedroom which was silent save the piercing shriek of Yannis's cock, which continued to wake me every morning without fail. Despite my best efforts and planning, it looked like the marriage repair-job was not going to be as quick a fix as I'd hoped and as the holiday drew to a close my veneer of hope cracked. I didn't understand why this was so difficult, or why I felt more distant from Tom on our family holiday than I had at home.

On Friday, our last day, Grace and I sat in the airport with our hand luggage on uncomfortable plastic chairs whilst Tom was in the bookshop, flicking through a sports biography.

Grace suddenly turned to me and said "Mum, do you know Dad's friend Rachel?"

"What sweetie? Do you mean the Rachel that works with Daddy?" I said, smiling vaguely.

"Yes. Daddy was talking to her on his mobile phone yesterday. He was laughing a lot." I tried to force myself not to jump to any conclusions and quickly swallowed the lump that had suddenly formed in my throat. So Tom had a female colleague at work who shared the same sense of humour. And who rang him on holiday. What was wrong with that? It was nice to know *someone* could make him laugh these days.

15

Bowling a Maiden Over

The morning after our return home I got up early and made a huge breakfast in an attempt to console myself for our disastrous holiday. I made light, fluffy pancakes and dug out some of my homemade blueberry jam – not as sweet, and fruitier than the nasty, bought stuff. While Tom, Grace and the batter rested I made a batch of vanilla cupcakes. They came out of the oven before everyone was up and the warm, sweet smell filled the kitchen – and my heart – with 'home'. I had to taste a couple and the hot, buttery sponge scorched my tongue but it was worth it for the explosion of soft, melting vanilla – which for a very brief moment made me indescribably happy.

Tom and Grace eventually got up and wolfed the pancakes in silence, Grace on her Nintendo (which seemed to be surgically attached to her these days) and Tom flicking through the paper and grunting every now and then. I could tell he wasn't really concentrating though and I had the feeling something was wrong. "Are you OK, Tom?" I ventured. He looked up at me, almost guiltily.

"Mmm. Did I tell you I have to go to work today?" I shook my head.

"But it's Saturday, Tom. We've only just got back from holiday, and..."

"Sorry Stel." He cut me off. Tom had planned to take Grace to the cinema and I could see from her face she was really disappointed.

"Aagh, Dad!" she said, looking from him to me.

"Tom, you know how much Grace wanted to see this film. You can't let her down at such short notice!" I huffed. "I suppose now I'll have to take her and cancel my hair appointment."

He looked at me in disbelief. "I have to work – don't be so unreasonable. I need to go, or I'll be late. Sorry Grace, we'll sort another time, yeah?" and without even waiting for her response or mine, he threw down the rest of his juice, grabbed his coat and headed for the door. I was disappointed about my cancelled hair appointment but I didn't mind taking Grace to the cinema and in truth, after recent events, I was glad to see the back of Tom. He stormed off in a big huff and slammed the door behind him.

He'd been gone about half an hour when I heard his phone upstairs; he'd obviously forgotten it again. It kept making a reminder-noise so you knew there'd been a call or text and this was annoying me so I followed the sound upstairs into our bedroom. He'd left it on his bedside table and the screen was intermittently lighting up. As I picked up the phone I could see '1 new message'. I hesitated to press the select button because I didn't want him to think I was checking his calls, but what if it was something important to do with work?

Hi darling
Where R U? Am waiting!
Luv u, Rachel x

Ten words that would change my life forever.

My heart was pounding in my head and my stomach. I held onto the phone, rooted to the spot, just reading the words over and over like they might be different by the hundredth time. I tried desperately to reinterpret what was pretty obvious. *I call people 'darling'* I thought, trying desperately to drag myself from the pit of despair and sheer panic. *Perhaps she's supposed to be*

working with him today and wants to know where he is?
However, the three little words I was having real problems
reinterpreting were 'Luv u, Rachel x'.

Tom came home at about seven o'clock. I didn't know
exactly what was going on with him but I had a pretty good idea.
I felt very devious but I deleted the text from his phone so he
wouldn't know I'd read it; he'd think it just hadn't arrived. I
couldn't bear to be in the same room, let alone have any kind of
eye contact or conversation with him. I took a bath and washed
my hair (wondering what Rachel's hair was like) I washed
Grace's hair (wondering if she had any kids) and stayed in her
bedroom all evening to avoid Tom. We read stories about
witches (they were all called Rachel) and by ten o'clock even
Grace despite her baby Goth tendencies said; "Mummy, can I
please go to sleep now?"

"Love you," I said as I kissed her goodnight, and thought,
Luv u, Rachel x. I left Grace and crept into bed. Tom was already
asleep with a huge tome outlining David Attenborough's 'Zoo
Quest Expeditions' open across his chest. *How dare he sleep so
peacefully?* I thought to myself. *How dare he concern himself
with bloody zoos at a time like this?* I had to staunch the anger
rising from the pit of my stomach, resisting the urge to beat my
fists on his chest, kick him awake and shout, 'Fuck David
Attenborough! Who's bloody Rachel?'

In all this I needed to be rational though. If he was having
an affair – he didn't know I knew – and I therefore, in a round-
about way, had the upper hand. I lay all night with my fists
clenched and my heart pounding, my mind covering every
possible scene from the past, present and future. With 'Bitch
Rachel' as leading lady.

On Sunday morning I woke early and rose from my bed,
having not slept a wink. During the long night I created a
million scenarios in my head, all of which were fighting for pole

position. The majority, it has to be said, were concerned with the death or imminent demise of Bitch Rachel. I didn't know her and had never even seen her but at that moment she was ruining my sleep and pipping MJ at the post for winner of the 'Most Painful Death Award'. As I sipped my coffee and checked the post, I settled on Bitch Rachel being a single, thirty-something size ten with long fair hair, an airbrushed complexion, a worktop full of limes and a celebrity, cellulite-free arse. I really wanted to talk to Mum, but she was still living the life of an Am-Dram thespian in New York. Instead I phoned Al.

"She obviously has a warped, damaged, twisted personality and can't get her own man so steals another woman's", was his immediate reaction on the other end of the phone, but he didn't stop there. "I can't believe the stupid tart would text him! I mean you could check his texts any time. Bloody stalker! She's no better than Glenn Close in *Fatal Attraction*," he continued, "a raging bunny-boiler who'll turn up on your doorstep tomorrow trying to buy your real estate then wham! Before you know it, Gilbert and George are bubbling away in your Le Creuset."

I pointed out that firstly, Gilbert and George were goldfish, which kind of negated the bunny-boiling thing and we didn't have real estate as such in Worcestershire. I wanted him to tell me I was overreacting and just being silly. I wanted him to tell me it wasn't happening, that I was just imagining everything, but as usual, his imagination had got the better of him.

When he called back two minutes later, I'd rather hoped it was someone else, or at least that he'd calmed down. "Stella!" he shouted as I picked up the receiver. "I've just remembered what happens next. Glenn Close in your bathroom, slashing herself and staining your fluffy, white towels with her adulterous blood. Don't go in there, I'm coming over!"

He arrived with Lizzie a whole hour later, which would have left plenty of time for Glenn Close to rise up from the bath bubbles and slash me with the kitchen knife. After he'd checked the bathroom for 'adulterous tarts', we all settled down to discuss the 'Bitch Rachel Situation'. Tom had left early to 'go to work' again (on a Sunday? Ha!) and Grace was playing upstairs.

I prepared several butter-slapped, freshly-baked scones and sat at the kitchen table, eating them quickly to soak up the pain, while pouring my heart out while Al and Lizzie listened.

"Half of me wants to call him now to make him confess and demand to know everything about her, down to the type of tampons she uses. The other half of me is so scared and irrationally hopes that if I ignore it, she'll go away," I said, stuffing a scone in my mouth to stem the tears.

Lizzie was every bit the supportive friend; "Look, it will all be fine with Tom. Trust me, he'll come to his senses," she said, wiping warm butter from her chin.

"It's not about him coming to his senses, I won't have it – I was trodden on by MJ for years and I'm damned if I'll let my own husband take over where she left off," I wailed into a big, floury scone. "But I can't bear thinking about life without him and I keep thinking maybe it will be OK. He's my husband. He's Grace's dad!" I sobbed.

"I remember having a relationship with a guy called Frank, or was it Frankie," said Al "he was gorgeous anyway..." and he went on to describe in detail several of his own 'tragic' experiences of infidelity, before announcing he had to meet another friend for coffee.

"Come on Lizzie my love, I'll drop you home on my way to David's," he said, throwing on his new leather jacket. "Now my darling Stel I don't want you to worry about anything. And you know where I am if you need me," he said sincerely, giving me a big hug.

Lizzie smiled at him. "I'll call you later, Stel," she said gently, winking and blowing me a kiss.

Tom took Grace to school the following morning before he headed off to work. It all seemed so normal, so mundane as I kissed Grace goodbye and wrapped her scarf around her neck to ward off the late-autumn chill. I'd tossed and turned all night and I still didn't know what to do. I wasn't sure how long I could keep up the pretence. Tom may have been sensing my anger. I didn't explain why but I refused to make anything for him to eat. It was irrational, but I just felt that whatever I cooked for him would taste bitter. If Tom wanted a hate sandwich with vitriol chutney then that was fine, but I couldn't trust myself not to put rat poison in his food or antifreeze in his coffee, so not making meals for him was a selfless act, essentially for his own good.

Wiping the kitchen worktops I wasn't concentrating on what I was doing, rather allowing images of him with her to swirl through my brain. *Was Tom the love of her life? Did they already have a shared history? In-jokes and secret smiles? Or was he simply a shag? Was he a diversion from work, an ego-boost and someone to fill a void until another one came along?* What a shame if that were the case, because a family would have been ripped apart for nothing. I sat at the kitchen table with my head in my hands. I hoped she loved him, I really did, because the price we'd pay as a family would be too high for anything less. Whoever she was and whatever she wanted, her actions were going to cause collateral damage.

I sat at the table for some time, wondering what to do. I was filled with hurt and anger yet afraid to lift the lid on my feelings in case I couldn't force it back down. *If he was having an affair, what was he intending to do? If I told him I knew, would he finish it with her? Could I ever truly love him again, even if he dumped her and declared undying love for me? Could it ever be the same?* One thing I was sure of – I had to confront him and get this

whole thing out in the open, but I felt like I had nothing left –
no energy, no self-confidence and no courage. And through it all
I kept wracking my brain for an innocent explanation to 'luv u,
Rachel x'.

16

Low Flying Turkey and Twisted Tarts

The following weeks flashed by in a blur and before I knew it, the festive season was upon us. Everything was about Christmas and razzle-dazzle. Lizzie and I went shopping for Grace's presents and for a little while, among the glitter and the Christmas music, I almost forgot about Tom and *her*. We chose some Christmas cards together and as Lizzie pondered over different Christmas scenes I spotted a glittery, red card with the picture of a cosy log fire on the front and 'To My Loving Husband at Christmas' written in red glitter. I looked at Lizzie, "Tom's loving," I said, waving the card in the air, "he's loving someone else!" Then my eyes filled with tears and the card became a blur.

She smiled and gave me a hug; "He's a stupid idiot. You really need to decide what you want to do babe," she said handing me a tissue.

I was living on a knife-edge as he still didn't know I knew. I felt helpless but in a strange way, I was ultimately the one with the power to light the touch-paper that would urge us all forward into an unknown future. Things had happened that I hadn't wanted or planned but knowing still gave me that modicum of control. It was pretty scary to know that it was down to me and that, at any time, I could press the nuclear button.

So many times I'd almost done it. One evening, we were having a Christmas dinner party with friends and as we 'worried' about A Qaeda and enthused about the chocolate mousse, I thought, *I could say it now. I could suddenly announce over the coffee and homemade star-topped mince pies that my husband is shagging another woman.* I thought about it as we drove home and looking over at Tom it was on the tip of my tongue to say 'who's Rachel?' but I shuddered with fear and looked away, seeking sanctuary through the curtain of rain at the car window. I just couldn't bring myself to set in motion a whole cataclysmic process of events that would change our lives forever.

And then it was Christmas Eve. Mum came to visit early in the morning. She was dropping off our presents on her way to the airport; she'd decided to spend Christmas in Norway with Beryl.

"We're going to watch the Northern Lights from a roof-top Jacuzzi," she announced, over a large slice of Christmas cake.

"Well I don't blame you Mum – it sounds more fun than sleeping in our spare room and spending Christmas Day watching satellite reruns of *Only Fools and Horses*." We both smiled. It wouldn't be the same without Mum and I wondered what the hell Tom and I would find to talk about, locked in the house with Del Boy and a giant tin of Quality Street for two whole days. I was aching to tell her about Tom's text and ask what she thought I should do – but Grace had joined us for cake so I kept it light. We talked about the past and giggled about family Christmases and how every Boxing Day Gran would get tipsy on Snowballs, insisting they weren't alcoholic whilst sliding slowly off her chair. Mum and I told Grace about the handmade *Blue Peter* decorations we'd made one Christmas when I was little; "They looked like alien spaceships but your mother insisted on putting them all over the house," Mum told her; "she was about your age Grace. It seems like yesterday."

When Mum left, Grace and I waved goodbye on the step and I thought about how hard Mum and Dad had worked for all those years to make Christmas special for me. Mum shopped and cooked and baked and Dad worked overtime, yet it all appeared like magic in the morning and I ripped sparkly paper and squealed with delight at a new doll or selection box crammed with chocolate bars. I thought about Grace's first Christmas and her bemusement at all the presents and food and attention. We'd bought her a big plastic car to ride in – she was far too young but Tom and I couldn't wait. We'd laid her in it and while I held on to her he had pushed her carefully round the living room, beaming all the while.

Closing the door, I suddenly felt all the Christmases I'd ever known, rushing in and drowning me with tinsel and love and laughter. *What was going to happen next? Would Tom and I still be together next Christmas? Did I want to be with him a year from now, knowing what I knew?* Telling Grace I needed the bathroom, I ran into the downstairs toilet and locking myself in I quietly sobbed and sobbed for the past, until there were no tears left.

After a short while, I decided to pull myself together and finish wrapping the last of the presents. I climbed into the messy spare room and began pulling out boxes and wrapping paper. Just touching the smooth pattern on my matching metallic paper and glittery silver bows cheered me up a little. For Grace's presents, I'd bought pink and blue paper with angels and scattered snowflakes and I gathered the rolls together with the gifts and sticky tape and started to wrap. Folding the corners and ripping at tape with my teeth I thought that although my marriage may have been in deep trouble, Christmas was coming and I needed to rally for Grace. I spotted my dusty old stereo in the corner and joy of joys, an old Johnny Mathis CD was nestling inside. I continued wrapping to the sound of *The Little Drummer Boy*.

The music was soothing and reminded me that this really

could be a wonderful time of year. I started to wonder if things were really as bad as I thought they were. Perhaps there was an innocent explanation after all and I had got things horribly wrong in my own head? I was running out of paper and as I stumbled over near to the window to get more I heard Tom's voice coming from the garden. I was surprised to hear him; he must have come back from work early. At first I thought he was chatting to the next-door neighbour but then I stopped dead in my tracks with a handful of gold ribbon and reindeer wrapping when I heard the softness in his voice.

It was the voice he used for Grace, the one he used to use for me. Grace wasn't there, so I clambered over tinsel and presents and very, very carefully opened the window. I gasped as the icy air blasted into the room and almost whipped the window from my grasp. I grappled with it then slowly, and as quietly as possible, placed it on the latch. I was sure he must have heard and I held my breath. For a while he seemed to go quiet. I crouched down by the window so if he looked up he wouldn't see me. A piece of holly was digging into my thigh but the sharp, prickling pain was weirdly reassuring.

After what seemed like ages, but was probably only a few seconds, he started talking again. My face was hot and itchy despite the chilly blast coming through the open window. "I miss you too," I heard, "I know, I know but we have to wait... after Christmas... Can't do it to Gracie..."

My heart was in my mouth and my stomach had turned upside down. I was about to explode with hurt and tears and anger, but in a flash the fog of the last few weeks cleared and the truth stared me in the face in the fading December light: it was true – everything I had imagined and probably more. I couldn't move, rooted to the spot under the window, with the cold air blasting through my hair. It wasn't just what he was saying, it was the way he was saying it. The tone of his voice took me back through the years to when we first met, filled with kindness, softness and sex. Suddenly I knew that there was no way back from this. And there, under the window, crouching like a wounded animal in the reindeer wrapping and tinsel, my heart split in two.

There was nothing to hide behind now. What I had heard had removed all doubt, all other possibilities and had left me with only one option: I would have to face Tom. But I couldn't say anything on Christmas Eve, surely? I couldn't do that to Grace. So instead that afternoon, I found myself making festive mince tarts. I grabbed the flour from the cupboard and desperately creamed it into lard and butter, my knuckles white and my head spinning. Suddenly, white-hot anger seared through my brain. *That Bastard. How can he do this to me?* Throwing the doughy wedge onto the flour-topped table I reached for my rolling pin; surely, this would help? Rolling it out with gusto I imagined it was her, Rachel, flattened to the table with my huge wooden rolling pin, again and again – smoothing it over and rubbing her out. But somehow it didn't help in the way it used to with MJ.

Twisting open the jar of brandy-scented mincemeat sent a whiff of pure Christmas to my nostrils and reminded me of home and Mum. I began to cry as I carefully spooned the sweet, jammy lumps into pastry circles before plunging them into the hot oven. But even the slow drift of warm, cinnamon air that rose from the cooking pastries didn't make me feel better, so I made another batch. And then another. By 3pm, the tart count was 60 and rising. I knew if I didn't deal with this Tom problem soon, there was likely to be a European mince-tart mountain emanating from a small town in the Midlands. Added to this, the more anxious and heated I became the more the pastry was suffering at my hot hands. The tarts took on the kind of floppy, warped appearance that would have had Salvador Dali reaching for his easel. I knew I would have to speak with Tom, and soon.

Tom went to collect the turkey from the butcher's down the road. He did this every Christmas and Grace always made a big fuss like he'd fed, bred and killed the bloody bird himself. It was the perfect Christmas scene, me rolling out pastry for yet more surreal tarts and Grace carefully placing pentangles on the Christmas tree (I told you, there was something of the night about her). We had on our usual Christmas CD and with a huge carrier bag of bird, Tom sauntered in to the tune of *God Rest Ye Merry Gentlemen*, shouting "Ho, ho, ho!"

What a fucking tosser you are, I thought coldly, vigorously rolling out pastry as he appeared in the kitchen doorway wearing a white beard and a red hat. I ignored him and carried on rolling, with some fierceness now as he stood in the middle of the kitchen.

"Gracie! Santa's here with the turkey!" he shouted cheerfully. I glanced over at him in the daft hat and the ridiculous white beard waiting for accolades and high-fives from Grace and I thought *How could you? Our lives are hanging in the balance and you're standing in the kitchen dressed as fucking Father Christmas.*

Apparently very pleased with himself, he proudly offered me the plastic turkey-filled bag. "There you go, Stella. Ho ho ho!"

And to be honest, I'm not sure quite what happened next. All I remember, through a mist of searing mincemeat, brandy and rage is that I couldn't keep it down any longer. I don't know where it came from, but I suddenly grabbed at the bird bag, putting all my weight and resentment behind it and swung six kilos of juicy Christmas bird high in the air. I needed to take the fucking smile off Tom's smug, white-bearded face. Even through the mist I could see a half smile of incredulousness under the cotton-wool beard; he was probably under the impression this was some new festive tribal greeting I'd perhaps picked up from Mum. Even mid-swing I could see a sort of bemused grimace forming just before he ducked but as six kilos of prime turkey meat whipped past his face and came crashing down on his head, I think he realised: I knew.

"Christ Stella!" he said, a trickle of blood running down the side of his face. "I'm...I'm sorry."

"You should probably go to A&E," I said flatly.

"Can we talk first?"

"Just get out!" I spat.

He staggered out to the car, holding a Christmas napkin to his head.

Fortunately, Grace had gone upstairs, so had missed the spectacle of 'Mummy wrapping the Christmas bird round Daddy's head'.

"Where's Dad?" She asked as she came back into the kitchen.

"Daddy has fallen over, darling, and he's gone to see the doctor," I sniffed, still reeling from the shock of it all. She nodded, satisfied with the explanation – not that she needed one. With her promised gift of 'Tokyo a Go-Go Bratz Sushi Lounge with Karaoke and Moving Parts' on the horizon, Grace clearly had more important stuff on her mind.

Whilst Tom was in casualty, I cried and cried and baked more and more mince tarts. "Is mincemeat like onions Mum?" Grace asked as she wandered into the kitchen and saw my tear-stained face. I grabbed some kitchen towel and dabbed at my swollen, red eyes.

"Yes, a bit sweetie. Mincemeat always makes my eyes sting." Grace nodded and picked up a tart from the still-warm pastry mountain then went into the lounge to watch TV.

Now Tom knew that I knew, something had to happen. We

couldn't go on pretending everything was fine and Grace and I had to face an uncertain future during panto season at the hands of Prince Cheating-Tosser and Bitch Rachel the Wicked soon-to-be-Stepmother.

As the mountain of crumbly sweet pastries continued to rise, my rage slowly turned to despair. If he left us then Christmases, holidays, school fêtes and Sports Days would all be fatherless for Grace. Nocturnal visits from moths and daddy-long-legs, heavy lifting and tuning in the TV would all be husbandless for me. Who was going to unblock drains, put the bins out, push the car and bury dead goldfish?

I wept as I thought about him with her, kissing her like he used to kiss me, telling her his jokes, his hopes and his darkest fears. Worse still, telling her about me, about us. His version. Mind you, on the bright side, this would also be peppered with his hour-long theories on why Test-Cricket is better than One Day and how football's all about money and not about the game anymore. I thought about all these Tom-things and cried into luxury, brandy-soaked mincemeat. When I finally stopped baking, I started eating. Well, I had a mountain to move.

At about eight o'clock on Christmas Eve, after a seven-hour stint in A&E, Tom came home. This time a rather subdued figure walked through the kitchen door. Wisely, he was without white beard and Santa hat but with bandaged head and mild concussion. He didn't say 'Ho, ho, ho!' this time. Inexplicably, I felt a sudden rush of sympathy for him, standing in the kitchen bandaged amid the Christmas clutter and mince tarts. I walked on wobbly legs towards him and put my arms round his waist. He felt strange, like a new person I hadn't touched before, suddenly not mine anymore. His outdoor clothes felt chilled in the warm kitchen and I pressed my face against the cool prickly cloth of his coat. I eventually let go and stepped back to look up at him.

"How long have you been seeing her?" I asked, and even in that moment I surprised myself at the clichéd script. How else can you say it? Stupidly, a part of me was hoping he'd come up with a look of surprise, followed by some complicated-yet-plausible, innocent explanation for the phone calls and the texts. I was willing him to say, 'Don't be stupid. You've got it all wrong, she's just someone I work with,' but he didn't. Like a stinging smack in the face I saw it all in his eyes. It was true.

"I've known her for some time, Stella," he started. "We were friends, just work mates," he said without emotion. "Then things...developed about six months ago. It was something that happened. Stella I'm so sorry. The last thing I wanted was to hurt you. We just couldn't help it."

I couldn't cry. I was numb. Their feelings for each other were so strong they *just couldn't help it*.

"Is it too late?" he asked, his voice breaking.

I wasn't sure what to say. Too late for what? Tom and I? Tom and her? Was he telling me there was a possibility that he would still choose us over her? If so, could we be together now, for Christmas? It could almost be wonderful – couldn't it? Then I thought beyond the next few days; once the fairy lights were down and the Christmas tree back in the loft I'd wonder if he was seeing her, imagining her, texting her. I'd be filled with insecurities, worrying he was comparing her to me every time I put on lipstick, read a book, drank coffee or made love. Would he always be looking at me and wishing it was her?

I couldn't live with him – and this. It was too big for me. I'm just not a grown-up enough, strong enough person to forgive him, so despite the safety of his arms and sixteen years, I pulled away.

"Yes, it's too late. *Things have developed*. You need to go."

He was visibly shocked. Maybe he'd hoped he could hedge his bets and keep us both on a string until he'd decided, eenymeeny-style. It was very hard for me to do that, to say goodbye to my husband, to Grace's dad, to the man I still loved – but it would be much harder in the long run for him to stay.

"Can I stick around at least until Boxing Day? Let me spend Christmas with you and Grace, please?" he asked, his voice cracking.

I knew how much Grace meant to him and how upset she'd be without her dad at Christmas but – selfishly – I couldn't go through that. I shook my head, unable to answer through my wet, runny nose and cheeks stinging with tears. The CD was now playing *I'm Walking Backwards for Christmas* which – even in the middle of all this – I noted added a surreal quality to the proceedings. My marriage was ending and Spike Milligan and The Goons were providing the musical backcloth. I think that said it all.

"No way are you staying for Christmas," I said shakily. "If you go, you go now. I'm not spending the next two days counting down to when you walk out of the door. I'm not going through Christmas thinking this is the last time he'll sleep in this bed, sit in that chair, eat from these plates."

"You can't deny me Christmas with Grace," he said, his voice raised in panic. He could see I wasn't budging on this and his tone was pleading, "She'll be heartbroken if I'm not here for Christmas. She'd want me here."

"What she would want is for you to be here forever," I said, "but you're not doing 'forever' are you? You're just doing *for Christmas*."

Tom looked down at his feet, "You can't do this, Stella."

In a way I was glad he'd said that because it felt like a cold shower and turned any sadness I felt into brittle anger. I was blinded by rage and couldn't believe the sheer hypocrisy, the injustice of all this. He was bloody lucky there were no more dead turkeys around.

"How dare you say that I can't do this?" I hissed, hating him all over again. "You're the one who did this, the moment you fell into bed with her. You're the one who's leaving us, but then, you left months ago. Every time you phoned her, every time you went near her, every time you got into her bed, you took another step further away from us. So don't ever say this is down to me Tom. Don't ever forget it was you," I spat, "because I won't."

I turned away and looked through the kitchen window. I couldn't bear to look at him. I never wanted to see him again.

He walked away and didn't say another word, though I think deep down I kind of hoped he would. I thought he might plead a bit more after all these years, I thought I might be worth a bit of begging, but then Tom knew me well enough to realise he'd hurt me so much there was no turnaround for me. I heard him moving about upstairs, probably packing. *I can change this,* I thought to myself. *I can go up there now, ask him to stay and make this a good Christmas for Grace. I can stop her heart from breaking. It's within my power to make things right again, at least for the next two days.* In my heart I knew that things hadn't been right for a long time. If I was completely honest my rational-self knew, even in the middle of all this, that Bitch Rachel wasn't the cause; she was merely a symptom.

Tom's voice came from the hall, "I'm so sorry Stella. I'll speak to Grace. Shall I call her tomorrow?" I didn't answer. "I'll call her then. Perhaps we can talk next week when things are...well, bye."

Brimming with agony, you would think I couldn't have squeezed in any more pain but I felt a fresh stab when he didn't come into the kitchen to say goodbye face to face and a new wave of tears enveloped me as I heard the door slam. And after sixteen years of black and white films, dark chocolate and a beautiful baby, he left.

17

Pinot and Pole Dancing

Christmas was a muted affair for me and Grace. I was still reeling from the shock of it all, though I did go through the motions. I cooked the turkey (I believe it's called 'eating the evidence'), we pulled crackers and opened presents. Al came round for a few hours in the afternoon and tried to engage Grace in Monopoly whilst offering me silent sympathy. But it wasn't the same without Tom, and Grace hardly said a word all day. I was relieved when bedtime approached and I turned on the television so I didn't have to think anymore. I opened several boxes of chocolates and mindlessly pushed them into my mouth allowing the *Eastenders* Christmas special to wash over me. Here was a whole community in crisis and it was a comfort to know that there were people more miserable than us on Christmas Day, even if they were just acting.

Tom called on both Christmas Day and Boxing Day and tried to speak to Grace, with little success. She refused to take the phone from me when I said 'it's Dad' and although I knew she was angry that Tom had ruined Christmas, we were both worried that she was in denial. As painful as it was, we needed to help Grace come to terms with it eventually, so Tom and I agreed that he should speak with her face to face and attempt to explain things.

"I'm happy for you to see Grace, as long as you don't bring that bitch anywhere near her," I said, sounding immature and I think, justifiably bitter.

"I won't bring anyone," he agreed. "Grace and I need to spend some time alone together as father and daughter. I'm not a fool Stella, I can see how important that is."

He came over the day after Boxing Day. As Grace put on her coat to go for a walk with him he turned to me and said sheepishly; "If I can just talk with her, I'm sure she'll understand."

"Mmm. I'm sure she will," I muttered, with a theatrical snigger.

Snow had started to fall in soft, white flakes, the blanket of silence muffling Grace's squeals of delight at the promise of enough for snowballs later. Grace seemed happy enough to see her dad and as Tom walked and Grace danced in the falling snow, I sat in silence watching them, wondering what secrets they would now have without me. This was a fractured part of my family I didn't belong to anymore and all I could do was wait, until my daughter was returned to me.

After their walk, Tom left and Grace was quiet but I think she was OK. "Did you have a nice time with Daddy?" I asked.

"Yes, it was fine Mum."

"Well what did you talk about?"

"Just stuff," and she turned on the TV and zoned out.

Grace went back to school after the Christmas holidays and the house suddenly seemed really quiet and empty. After a couple of weeks of crying into a mixing bowl, I decided that some retail therapy was just what I needed. But when I checked my bank balance outside Tesco I nearly had a heart attack. There was minus nothing in there. Tom and I had yet to sit down and sort out all our finances so he'd agreed to cover the basic bills until we could work everything out. But I knew I *needed* to go back to work and my life plan to spend time with Grace, get to know her and grow with her for a little while was out of the window again. Ironically, this was a time when I needed to help our daughter feel more secure, but in order to survive, I had to disappear into that big work cloud again. We'd once more be swallowed up by child-carers, After School Club, before-school clubs and kind neighbours.

I realised that all the lecturing from Tom about our finances had been his way of preparing me for this. *He knew, he bloody knew he wouldn't be around for much longer.* I climbed back into the car and as I pulled out of the car park noticed that, to my consternation, the needle on the petrol gauge was hovering dangerously close to empty.

When I got home, I put the kettle on and logged on to the computer. I thought I would scan the *Heat* website to cheer myself up, and just as I was zooming in on Jen's latest squeeze, an email pinged through from Lizzie:

Now then Darling,
Put down your whip, tear the mantilla from your tresses and get that rippling male model off your ruby-red lips. Al the diva and moi have decided that tomorrow evening is perfect for one of our chaste little soirées at yours. I shall be bringing a new liqueur I have discovered on my travels and I am sure we can count on you to provide something suitably virginal – even if it's six foot and aged nineteen! Hope to Gahd that you can make it. Much to catch up on and Al will be bringing a little surprise..!
Will be at yours by 7.
L x

That cheered me up. I hadn't spoken to Lizzie for ages, save a few brief telephone chats and emails. She'd been busy travelling the country transforming homes and lives and would no doubt have lots of stories to tell. I desperately needed to share the unplugged version of my own Christmas pantomime with her – I knew she'd love the bit where I slapped Tom over the head with the turkey.

Al arrived first, loaded with pressies, flowers and his surprise: a new boyfriend. I was amazed to see them both, standing on the step with arms full of gifts and flowers; I had no idea.

"Stel, this is Sebastian," said Al, beaming. I was actually a little taken aback as I'd hoped to talk freely about Tom with my two best friends. But after one look at Al's face and how happy he was holding on to Sebastian's arm, I put those thoughts aside. Al gave Grace a massive hug and a teddy dressed in a tutu. She grabbed Al's hand and led them both into the living room while I opened the wine.

"Sebastian, would you like red or white?" I shouted from the kitchen.

"Could I just have a glass of mineral water please? I'm driving," he replied.

Then Lizzie arrived and I rushed to open the door." Al's here and he's brought Sebastian." I said, with a raised eyebrow.

"Ooh he said he had a surprise!" Lizzie squealed and rushed in. "Hello Sebastian! SO lovely to meet you," she embraced him with a big kiss on both cheeks, which made him blush.

"Well, tell all?" she said, looking from Al to Sebastian, who was now seated primly in the corner.

"Seb and I met at the swimming club," said Al with a huge smile. "He's a brilliant swimmer, he's won awards."

"You're a good swimmer too," Sebastian countered. This gave me the excuse to look at him properly and I could see what Al had fallen for. Tall with black hair and a boyish, *Brideshead Revisited* look about him, Sebastian was quite a heartbreaker.

"Oh Seb, I'm not a great swimmer, I only use the cocktail lane," Al giggled, flirting and batting his eyes at his new beau.

Lizzie saw a gap in the conversation and produced a bottle of Champagne. She popped it open, screaming "Glasses, Stella!"

Champagne dripping, she followed me into the kitchen. I passed her some glasses, watching as she lifted the bottle aloft allowing foaming champagne to douse the prawn pasta with delicate lemon and dill sauce that I'd slaved over for supper. "Lizzie. You're making the sauce runny, take that bottle away," I said, holding out the flutes for her to fill.

"What do you think about Sebastian?" I whispered.

"He seems nice – but we'll see," she said, raising both eyebrows.

Lizzie went back into the living room and from the raucous laughter I guessed she was regaling everyone (including my nine-year old daughter) with a tawdry tale from her travels. I took a big gulp of Champagne and made a mental note that when she asked later I'd tell Grace that an orgasm was a drink made from coconuts.

Lizzie took Grace up to bed as I spooned out the pasta and opened more Pinot. Then everyone came into the kitchen to sit around the table. As Sebastian smiled and ate and politely drank his mineral water the three of us consumed all of the Champagne then started on the red wine. It wasn't long before Lizzie was demanding to know all about the current situation with Tom.

"Tell us all about that Bitch Rachel," she said with venom. Al and Lizzie listened intently and said all the right things in all the right places. Al, as usual, had been asking around Media World and had some interesting gossip to share.

"One of the researchers on *Dream Homes* knows Bitch Rachel," he revealed. "It seems she's a complete tart and apparently chases men all the time. Tom's not the first married man she's had either."

"Who? When?" I begged, wanting but not wanting to know the details.

"I don't know exactly, but apparently she's had her eye on

Tom for a while, and was always playing 'helpless' around him. I'm sorry to tell you, Stel, but she decided she was going to have him and she did."

He went on to say that Rachel was chameleon-like in her adulterous adventures. It would seem she was prepared (for a short time) to become whatever the bored husband wanted. "Apparently, she developed a passion for cricket and a deep desire to live on a remote Scottish island the week she met Tom," he spat. "She did her homework and turned up everywhere he went, appearing on shoots and arriving in the office all breathless, saying her car had broken down or her cat had died."

"Yes, and he's a sucker for a damsel in distress," I added bitterly, finding it hard to believe this was *my* Tom we were discussing.

"What a complete knob he is," slurred Lizzie, who was warming to the theme and becoming quite aggressive, "to believe her when she told him she shared his dreams of England winning the bloody Ashes and life in the fucking Highlands, the bastard!"

"Exactly!" hissed Al. "He fell hook, line and sinker. Especially as she was wearing figure-hugging tops and swishing past his lens every five minutes with her tits out. Tom didn't stand a chance. Darling, you are Jennifer to their Brangelina!"

Despite having a macabre fascination for all this – I had to make them stop. It was all too painful and I didn't want to hear any more of Al's colourful analogies or Lizzie's announcements about Tom's likeness to the male organ. Al and Lizzie were still hissing and spitting about the whole thing and, being more sober than they were, I felt we should move on so offered to make coffee. As I got up from the table I realised that Sebastian had gone to the toilet ages ago and hadn't returned. "Al, is Sebastian OK?" I said; I was the hostess after all.

"I'm sure he's fine," smiled Al, "he's very low maintenance. He's lovely, isn't he girls?"

"Yes he is," we both chimed.

"But it must have been really boring for him to sit and listen to my marital woes all night," I added, feeling very guilty. "I'll go and find him and apologise for being such a drunken, boring old cow."

"It's OK, doll. I've told him what you're like. He knows," giggled Al.

I put the kettle on then discreetly popped upstairs to knock on the bathroom door and ask Seb if he'd like coffee. However, as I walked towards the bathroom I could see the door was wide open and the light was out. I hoped he hadn't gone home, bored and horrified by his hostess. Standing outside the bathroom I became aware of soft voices coming from Grace's room. "Grace, are you OK?" I called softly. I tiptoed into her room and there was Sebastian, sitting beside her and reading from her latest Jacqueline Wilson book.

"Stella, I hope you don't mind but Grace called out and well, we got chatting and..."

"And Sebastian wanted to be a chef just like the boy in my book and now he is – how cool is that?" Grace chimed excitedly.

"That is *way* cool," I said smiling at Sebastian, "and now I want Sebastian to come and talk to his *other* friends downstairs because you're hogging him."

He stood up and patted her hand. "Goodnight Grace, we'll carry on with the book another time."

"Ooh yes please," she said then she turned over and was almost immediately asleep. Sebastian left the room with such a tender look on his face I felt quite touched. Linking his arm as we walked downstairs together I said; "Thanks for reading to her, Grace loves that story." He smiled and I wondered if he'd deliberately left us alone so I could talk privately with Lizzie and

Al; if I was right, Al was definitely onto a winner.

Over coffee I felt I needed to bring Sebastian into the fold. "So Sebastian, you're a chef?"

"Yes I am," he answered, clearly a bit uncomfortable to have the spotlight on him.

"He's being modest, he *owns* a restaurant," said Al proudly. "It's in Worcester, it's called 'Sebastian's', it's French, and the food is delicious."

Sebastian smiled shyly. "I'm lucky. My father was French so he taught me how to cook. You must be my guests one evening."

"You bet," said Lizzie slurping on her wine. "Ooh, all that butter and garlic, French food is so creamy and rich, not like those bloody vegan joints, where cheese is a dirty word."

"So, what about your work situation, Stella?" Al asked, changing the subject and cutting to the chase as usual.

"Well, I don't have any work as yet but I have applied for a few things," I lied.

Lizzie then stepped in. "Have you thought of working that fabulous body of yours up a pole sweetie?" she said, giggling into her wine.

"Oh doll, I can see it now, you with your Vaselined thighs, sliding up and down like a woman possessed and gyrating in laps," screamed Al, slapping Seb's back.

They were all laughing hard. "Thanks guys, for your vital input," I said. I thought Al was going to choke on his Merlot.

"OMG! At one pound fifty a dance she'll be dancing on laps 'til dawn." This descended into the two of them conjuring up 'hilarious' images of me as Page Three girl, Playboy Bunny and kissogram.

Once the laughter had died down regarding my pole-dancing career, Lizzie staggered into the garden for a cigarette accompanied by Sebastian, who was attempting against all the odds to keep her upright. Al and I were smiling at him through the window as Lizzie leaned on his shoulder and told him her life story while blowing smoke in his face.

"Seriously, Stella, you know I could lend you some money to keep you going for a bit," Al said, leaning across the table and touching my hand.

"Thanks Al. I really appreciate the offer, but I need a more long-term solution." I replied. The problem was, I just didn't know what it was yet.

18

Fat Brides and Fairy Cakes

As spring blossomed and the days got warmer the money situation got more and more desperate. Grace and I spent weeks eating out of the freezer and raiding the cupboards for old packets of Cup-a-Soup and Alphabetti Spaghetti. It wasn't easy, but we discovered some new and interesting food combos that were surprisingly tasty when you were hungry and had no alternative. For example, I didn't realise one could create such culinary delights from a tin of tomatoes, a jar of herbs and four frozen pitta-breads. Grace had also created her own concoctions involving fish fingers, frozen peas and ice-pops, a sure favourite with child nutritionists everywhere. However, there was definitely a silver lining; I couldn't bring myself to eat some of the more adventurous combos so lost six whole pounds.

Tom and I also finally had the awkward discussion about money and access to Grace, which made everything seem horribly real. We met on neutral ground at a coffee shop in town one Saturday, while Lizzie babysat. Apart from when he picked her up some weekends, it was the first time I'd really spoken to him and my stomach churned as I waited, breaking up my skinny muffin nervously. He walked through the door looking almost as tense as me.

"Hi Stella," he said, and smiled hopefully.

"Hello Tom," I replied, stonily. "Let's talk."

We agreed that Grace and I would stay in the house as it was her home. Tom had worked out a monthly maintenance payment figure and when he showed it to me, I snorted in disbelief.

"That's hardly realistic, Tom," I spat.

"It's all I can afford, Stella. I have to pay for two places now. It's not easy." I had to hold on to everything I had not to throw my double skinny latte in his face.

"I'm sorry", he said, looking like he genuinely meant it. "But I think you are going to have to get a job, Stella."

After our meeting, I did apply for a few jobs, but without much success. I didn't want to go back into telly again and besides, I suspected that after the 'Perfect Peach incident', MJ would do everything she could to prevent me working in that industry again. What I really wanted was something that was interesting but with child-friendly hours. To my dismay it seemed that there were very few 10am-to-3pm jobs out there and if I had to pay for After School Club I wouldn't have much to show for my efforts. I did click on a couple of jobs that said 'flexi-time' only to discover they were shifts in the supermarket – and I didn't feel ready to go down that road just yet.

However, logging on one day I noticed that there were one or two office-based jobs with suitable hours so I excitedly sent off my CV to the recruitment agency handling the position. I didn't hear anything back for days, so in desperation I rang them and got put through to Mandy.

"I'm sorry to tell you that you'll be hard to place, Stella," Mandy said, cheerfully.

"Why?" I replied, incredulous. "I've worked all my life!"

"Yes I know. But you've worked in a specific industry, which you say you don't want to go back in to. You aren't really qualified to do anything else, you know."

"But I type well, and I'm a wiz on the computer," I lied.

"Even so – most of our jobs are nine to five and require specific experience. So sorry about that!" she said, and added thoughtfully, before she hung up; "have you ever considered check-out work?" Ironic really – I'd spent all that time wishing I could be at home, and now I needed a job it seemed I wasn't suitable for anything. Each time Tom's money came through into my bank account I was desperate to go to the supermarket and splurge on goodies. But I was almost too scared to spend it. I had to eke the money out and make it last, as there was nothing edible left in the house. I knew we couldn't go on like this much longer or it would all end in tears and a Gilbert and George sandwich.

When Easter came around and I couldn't afford to buy any eggs – or worse – make any biscuits, I finally decided enough was enough. It seemed I'd given up everything for Lent without even intending to. It's one thing not being able to feed yourself and your child, but quite another when you have to use your credit card to bake. I'd arrived at the last resort and with Mandy's reference to my 'job situation' still very much on my mind I sat at the kitchen table and made a call to the local supermarket about check-out work. The woman on the other end of the phone was very nice but seemed a bit surprised and decidedly unimpressed with my TV career. "Put it all down in writing and send in your CV," she said, fobbing me off. Presumably in an attempt not to raise my hopes in these recession-ridden times, she added: "We're actually laying people off, dear."

I put the phone down feeling very deflated because it had taken all my courage to call.

On a more positive note, Mum had finally returned from her latest trip to Africa and was coming to stay. Before she arrived later in the afternoon I nipped out for some essentials and did some therapeutic baking as a special treat for her visit. The cake was mocha-flavoured and I swirled rich, coffee buttercream into the middle of the two fat-but-light-as-afeather sponges. I piped it with the coffee buttercream and wrote in dark chocolate, 'I must get a job' on the top.

Mum arrived at about 4pm in a flurry of excitement. She trundled down the hall with her wheelie bag and tribal feathers shouting "Hola! I've returned from the wars because those bastards at the Embassy want to mess with my vista again."

"You mean your *visa*, Mum," I said, hugging her.

"Well, both, I suppose," she laughed, then yelled, "Where's Gracie?"

Grace heard Mum's voice and crashed down the stairs into her embrace. "I like your feathers, Nan," she said and Mum put them on her head.

"They suit you, Gracie," she said, "I'll ask the Chief to send some more."

"Chief?" I asked.

"Of the Hi Hi tribe. We got quite friendly."

Once we'd unpacked her bags and settled her in, Mum, Grace and I sat together in the warm kitchen.

"Lizzie texted me while I was away," Mum announced over a cup of tea and the welcome-home cake. This took me by surprise, because Mum can't text and Lizzie hadn't mentioned it to me.

"What did she want?" I asked.

"There was a bit of confusion with the texting," Mum muttered, sipping her tea. "Anyway, in the end, Lizzie phones me up and says 'Is that you Ellie? Stop sending me full stops!' She's a card!" Mum giggled, shaking her head, like Lizzie was the crazy one.

"Now, what did she say?" Mum said, gazing round the kitchen like the answer was written on the buttermilk walls. "I remember there were *two* things." This wasn't about Mum's age; she'd always been like this.

"Oh yes, the first thing is, she wants to take you to Spain for a holiday and asked if I could come and look after Grace." My heart sank. I love her to bits but a holiday with Lizzie was the last thing I needed.

"Er that'll be a big, fat no. Moving on, you said there was something else, Mum?" I asked, hoping for better news.

"Oh bugger! I've just remembered – the other thing Lizzie said was not to tell you because it was going to be a surprise."

Perhaps telepathically sensing Mum's slip Lizzie called a short while after and sang down the phone, "I've got a big surprise for you." I couldn't go through the charade and told her Mum had spilled the beans.

"It's a lovely idea, Lizzie, but I really can't go. I haven't got any money and besides, I am far too busy at home," I lied.

Mum was ear-wigging; it was funny how she suddenly became quick as a fox when it suited her.

"I don't know about being busy around the home love. You're the original 'lady who lunches' – constantly. You haven't put your fork down long enough to pick up your sweeping brush, looking at the state of this place."

I ignored her and returned to Lizzie who was never going to take no for an answer.

"Lizzie. It's really kind of you and it would be nice to enjoy some sunshine but I really am too fragile for anything else."

"Absolutely my darling – you need rest and relaxation. We fly to Ibiza next Thursday and it's my treat so get your teeny bikini packed."

I smiled. So I was fated to visit a hot country that sold alcohol with Lizzie – who, live and unleashed, would make Pete Doherty look like an altar boy. I hung up the phone and went back to my tea and cake.

"I don't know what you're doing with your life, Stella," Mum said as she bit into the thick, coffee-cream frosting, "but I'll tell you something I do know – you bake a mean sponge cake, love."

The following Tuesday morning, in the middle of trying to get Grace ready for school, finding her games kit under the kitchen table and making a cup of tea for Mum, the phone rang. It was a woman's voice.

"Hello, is that Stella? It's Anne here. I'm Katie's mother – Grace's friend, Katie Richards?"

"Of course, hello Anne," I said, desperately trying to put a name to the face and a face to the name.

"I wonder if you can help, we've got a bit of a problem," she said. "My eldest daughter Jessica's thirteenth-birthday party is three days away and we have had a disaster."

"OK," I said, unsure of where this was going.

"We had ordered a special birthday cake and unfortunately the company we approached to bake the cake have taken our deposit and gone out of business," she wailed. "Not only have we lost money – but we have no cake. Then Katie remembered Grace's beautiful birthday cake and we wondered if you would be prepared to make a cake for Jess. She wants a big pink and green-iced cake with pink ribbons and roses?"

"Well, I don't know. Grace's cake was a one-off, I don't..."

"Look, I know it's really short notice and a massive ask but Jess is so upset, please say yes?"

She sounded distraught and I felt really sorry for her but the thought of trying to bake, compile *and* ice a proper cake was daunting to say the least – not to mention in two days. "I'm so sorry Anne, I can't – I'm going on holiday on Thursday," I said, truthfully, and very relieved to have this perfect excuse.

"Oh no. You were our last hope. I'm at my wits' end – it's such a special birthday. Well, thanks anyway."

She was about to put down the phone when I heard myself say; "Hang on, let's check the dates. It's now Tuesday – I *might* be able to do something before I go away."

"Oh Stella, if you could that would be wonderful! You've no idea what this will mean to her."

It was at this point, reality set in and I panicked. "I have to point out, Anne, that I've never made a professional cake before – I can't promise miracles, but I will make *something.*" She tearfully thanked me and we discussed cake flavours and colours and I agreed to make and ice the cake by Thursday and drop it off on my way to the airport.

"So, let me get this right, honey. You're going to shop for, bake and ice a big fuck-off birthday cake in *two* days, then deliver it without incident on route to the airport where you will get on a plane – without using the sick bag – all the way to Ibiza? Good luck with *that!*" Al commented sarcastically when he called in for coffee later that day.

"I couldn't say no could I? I felt sorry for her. And they'll probably cover the cost of the ingredients."

"Oh, they'll *'probably'* cover the cost will they? That's sooo nice of them. And you didn't talk about dirty money did you lady? Ew, no – filthy stuff. Who do you think you are, the bloody *Queen?*"

"No, there's only room for one queen round here," I said blowing a kiss with my left hand and reaching for another chocolate digestive with my right. "Al, I know it's stupid but I couldn't bring myself to start demanding money over the phone could I? Poor woman, I didn't want to upset her all over again."

"But my sweet, you've hardly enough money to feed yourself. How can you possibly lay out money for ingredients?"

"I'll try my credit card – it's almost maxed but there should be enough to get some basics."

"Look, 'try' isn't good enough. You need to shop *now*. You

need to bake *now*. I'll loan you something so you can buy ingredients and make a start and stop yourself and Grace from starving. I could also drop the cake off for you, to save you rushing from there to the airport. Seb has a small van and so he'll help me. But only if you promise to get the money for the ingredients back off her!"

"But Al, I couldn't let you..."

"Oh sweetie, there's no point in me having money sitting in the bank earning virtually no interest when you need it. I'll arrange a transfer today."

I hugged him and tried desperately to quell the lump in my throat. When things aren't great, it's friends like Al and Lizzie who get you through the tough days. As soon as Al left I trawled through some of my many cookery books to get an idea of quantities. I worked it out by taking a basic sponge-cake recipe and tripling it to make three tiers. That would give a little extra because the tiers would stack on top of each other and get smaller as the cake grew higher.

I collected Grace from school and we headed straight for the nearest supermarket. She pushed the trolley and announced the contents of each aisle like a town crier until we reached our destination. "Flour and Home Baking over here, Mum!" she screamed at the top of her voice and whizzed the cart around display stands on two wheels like it was an Olympic event. We filled the groaning trolley with kilos of butter, dozens of eggs, one and a half kilos of flour and tons of icing and caster sugar (courtesy of Grace, who started filling the trolley in the sugar aisle while I stopped to say hello to one of the mums from school. When I turned the corner to see a trolley heaving with various sugars and Grace struggling to get the thing moving, I gave up on quantities and just threw stuff in.)

Next, we caught the local Icing Emporium just before it closed. Here I took advice from Marjory, the owner, about quantities and types of icing like I knew what I was talking about. During this, I felt a surge of adrenalin – I was in control again, planning something, being creative. Kind of like being back at work, but in a good way. Grace and I saved the best bit until last and chose the ribbons and roses from all the myriad shades and textures the Icing Emporium had to offer. "Ooh Mum, Jessica will love these," Grace said, waving a chunky little bride and groom decoration. "They are just sooo cool Mum – we *have* to get them."

Marjory and I laughed; "I think I can throw those in free of charge, love," she said. "I can't sell them. No-one wants a fat bride!" Grace was delighted, but as we bid our farewells to Marjory I did wonder how I was going to break it to her that Mr and Mrs Chunky wouldn't be adorning Jessica's thirteenth birthday cake.

On our return home, we filled the kitchen and hall with crammed carrier bags and I dragged out the largest mixing bowl I had. I couldn't wait to get started and immediately began adding all the ingredients slowly and carefully, incorporating as much air as I could to keep the mixture light and fluffy. I held the sieve high and white flour landed gradually like chiffon into the bowl. Grace smashed the rich, gooey, yellow eggs into the flour and as I began my folding, the symphony of sugar and flour and eggs just sang to me. I'm a Delia 'all-in-one-sponge' girl, so it all went into the bowl together and I mixed for England. God it was so good; pure therapy. This time, MJ's head was back in the bowl being smashed with the eggs and Rachel's face was being slowly folded into flour and butter with strong, definite movements coming from the elbow.

Grace and the bride and groom cake decorations were in attendance throughout and she proved to be invaluable when it came to licking the spoon and asking relentlessly, "Is it ready yet, Mum?"

Grace was just asking the question for the twentieth time as I finished mixing and to my horror realised I'd forgotten something vital. "Christ!" I exclaimed, my hand over my mouth.

"Mum, you're not supposed to say..." started Grace, but I didn't hear.

"Grace, I didn't hire any cake tins," I said shakily, "and none of mine are nearly big enough!"

I sat down, collapsing into the chair. It was 8.30pm and there was nowhere I could hire any from now – and even if I could it was Grace's bedtime and I couldn't leave her alone. I racked my brains. If I left the mixture in the fridge overnight the sponge would be flat and hard but I couldn't cook it now as I didn't have any tins the right size. I put my head in my hands, completely lost. I thought about buying ingredients and starting again the next day – but the cost aside, I knew I wouldn't be able to bake and ice them in time.

"What are you going to do, Mum?" asked Grace, worried.

"I don't know Grace. I just don't know" I said tearfully. We sat in silence at the table for what seemed like ages, as I put off what I knew had to be done. Eventually, I couldn't delay it any more; I picked up the phone.

"Mum, what are you doing?" said Grace.

"Calling Anne. I'll have to tell her I can't make the cakes after all," I said shakily. Grace bit her lip as I dialled the number.

"Mum, wait!" Grace shouted suddenly, hopping up to sit on the kitchen table and waving her hands in my face: "I have an idea!"

"Grace, get off there. You'll get flour all over your bum," I warned, not really listening.

"But Mum, listen to my idea. Why don't you just make millions and billions of little cakes and make a fairy-cake mountain like the ones in your magazines?" she said. My mouth dropped open. Just then, someone answered and said "Hello?"

on the end of the line.

"Sorry, wrong number," I said in a fake posh voice and hung up quickly. I scooped Grace up off the table and hugged her.

"Grace! You are a genius! That's exactly what we should do. Well done!" I said and covered her with kisses.

And so, at midnight as my brilliant daughter slept (with the bride and groom cake decorations on her pillow) I put the last batch of what seemed like a million fairy cakes into the oven. Thanks to my addiction to baking, MJ et al were safe from murder *and* I had a lifetime's supply of fairy-cake cases. My plan was to bake all the cakes that night, then decorate them the next day in pink or green icing, tie ribbons round them and stack them high and tight on a tiered cake stand, like one big cake.

By 9pm the next night the cake mountain was just about complete. There had been a few hairy moments, like when I'd set the timer wrongly and nearly burned an oven-full. I also realised when I started icing that I'd need to make extra cakes because it wasn't as easy to apply as I'd thought. The icing also drank up so much icing sugar – thank goodness Grace put what I'd imagined would be far too many bags in the trolley at the supermarket. I also had to hire a huge, tiered cake stand which involved another mad dash to Icing Emporium once I had dropped Grace off in the morning. But after lots of lip biting, sweating and holding my breath, it had all worked out and the cakes looked beautiful. Before I finally got round to packing for my holiday, I positioned the last tiny pink rose and tied palest green gingham ribbon round the final fairy cake. I arranged them on the stand and marvelled at the 4ft-high tower of pistachio-green and rose-pink fairy cakes, dressed in matching gingham ribbons. Against the odds, it was now all ready for Al to collect in the morning and deliver in time for the party. Lightly positioning a pretty little pastel pink and green cake on the top tier of the stand, I felt exhausted and elated.

Grace wandered in looking for food and was completely mesmerised by the sight of them.

"Well done Mummy," she said, which made me feel suddenly weepy and actually proud of myself.

"Well done *you*," I said. "What a brilliant idea to turn a disaster into a mountain."

I thought about how much Grace and I had pulled together since Tom left. She seemed to have developed a strength and empathy that was impressive for her tender age. As painful as it had all been, Grace had certainly grown up and – fingers crossed – I thought I might be starting to do the same.

19

Social Paralysis in an Incomprehensible Universe – or 'Holiday'

We arrived in Ibiza the following evening. As the coach roared to a shuddering stop in our resort I thought *what fresh hell is this?* How can a place that looks and sounds so beautiful, calm and restful in the brochure be so different in the flesh? When I'd mentioned to Tanya, one of the younger and trendier school mums (she Twitters and has her own page on Facebook), that I was off to Ibiza she raised her eyebrows.

"I love the Med and I can't wait to relax and eat tapas at little cafes and watch the world go by," I announced outside the school gate.

Tanya's response had been a little disconcerting; "Oh you'll have a great time. But you won't be sitting in cafés. It's a party island and trust me, you'll want to *partay!*"

I wasn't quite sure what she meant and, trying to sound young and laid-back, said I was happy to go to a few 'partays' while I was there. She continued to enthuse about the place, reassuring me that I'd have a 'really cool' time. I should have cancelled then and I really *should* have gone home when hundreds of eighteen-year olds in hipster jeans, cowboy hats and boob-tubes with 'The Best F*ck You'll Ever Have' emblazoned across their chests, appeared at our check-in desk (and that was just the reps). And I sooo *should* have got off that plane when Lizzie and I asked for a G&T, a bag of dry-roasted peanuts and a Kit-Kat and everyone else ordered Tequila slammers, flavoured condoms and staggered to and from the toilet in twos. However, it was only when the girl in front on the coach ride to our resort offered me some 'bubble' and told me to 'chill' that it finally hit me: I was in trouble.

So at 2am we pulled into the beachside village that was to be my parallel universe for the next seven days. What the brochure had described as a 'lively' resort was in fact 'Planet Party' and it wasn't like any 'partay' I'd ever been to. As soon as the coach stopped everyone – including Lizzie – leapt off, stripped, threw their pants into the sea and chased after them, splashing and screaming. I declined. I was too old and my pants were too big but I didn't want to be an old frump so over Lizzie's shrieks of delight from the spray, I shouted, "I'll chill in our den and crash the travel kettle for something hot," but she didn't hear me. In the dark I could see her clamber onto a young man's back and as she rode him hard through the black, moonlit water, I knew in my heart it was only a matter of time before she was pissed and naked on a dancefloor covered in foam.

Trying to convince myself that everything would be OK I struggled with my old-lady suitcase, now abandoned by Pedro the coach driver on the side of the road.

Once on terra firma and dragging my pink wheelie behind me, handfuls of tickets were suddenly thrust in my face. I looked up to see that the perpetrator was a bronzed girl with long, sun-streaked hair, incredibly tight denim cut-offs, a butterfly tattoo and too many bangles, with a whistle round her neck. She smiled and enquired in a husky, educated, very Home-Counties voice; "Amnesia?"

"I wish," I answered, thinking perhaps she'd been sent by Pissair, or whoever bloody Lizzie booked this nightmare with, to look after older travellers suffering from confusion brought on by early dementia.

"Amnesia is fabulous," she continued.

"Well, I suppose it depends from which perspective you..."

"It has an ice-cannon," she added, like this would clarify *everything*.

"That's nice dear," I answered, in my mother's voice. This must be how Mum felt most of the time: socially paralysed in an incomprehensible universe.

"There are three or four parties every night," the girl assured me, introducing herself as Cressida.

She then opened the zip of my handbag and pushed yet more flyers in, while hurling names and places at me like bullets.

"There are loads of parties happening, Pure Pacha is Fridays with Sander Kleinenberg and Trentemøller, Tong also has Timo Maas, Luciano and Dubfire."

"What?"

When I was her age, a party was a Malibu and pineapple, crescent moon-shaped nibbles and George Michael crooning in the background. To Cressida a party was probably crystal-meth, poppers and Babyshambles throwing up in the toilet.

I walked on, now very worried about what lay ahead. Gone were the days of a glass of Cinzano and a quick dance round your handbag. Party nights in Ibiza apparently involved ice cannons, amnesia, whistles and foam. I wanted flight times and the next plane home.

Having mounted a million steps and teetered around the edge of the pool, my suitcase wheels veering dangerously close to the water, I landed at our apartment. After a little tussle with the key in the lock I was in and relieved to see that the room was basic but clean. Two neat beds stood side by side, covered in matching rust-coloured blankets. A plain dressing-table and mirror were opposite (where I spotted an overlarge, overage blonde plugging in the travel kettle). I looked at myself; I felt so

old and wanted to call Tom. Despite her initial nocturnal frolics
in the sea, I was even starting to wonder if Lizzie would survive
seven days and nights in this hedonistic heaven of suntanned
bodies and impenetrable Veejays.

At 43, she'd clearly decided to have some 'me-time' and who
could blame her? At the tender age of twenty-two she fell in love
with a married man. Of course, he'd promised to leave his wife
and of course she'd believed him. Then, when she became
pregnant, of course she had expected him to marry her. He
didn't. Instead, he dumped her and she had to struggle on alone.
Her son Marcus had recently gained his degree and found a job
in the City. He was making a fortune and probably sleeping with
hundreds of girls so with her 'baby' now making his own way,
Lizzie was determined to make up for her twenties and thirties; I
just hoped she wasn't planning to cover both decades that week.
In her own words, Lizzie was 'young, free and single' and, unlike
me, she had the time and the money to apply body cream, and
have regular hair and beauty sessions. As she was constantly
reminding me: 'I'm out there, girlfriend'.

I stared at my reflection in the small mirror. I realised that
if I wanted to begin life after Tom, I needed to think more like
Lizzie. I was just warming to this idea when I opened up my
suitcase and took out a pair of enormous M&S linen trousers.
Gigantic floral tops followed and it was clear that I was in
serious danger of looking like Veejay Dubfire's grandma. As I
placed a million pairs of dangly earrings on the dressing table,
glancing at a ham-like upper arm and blaming myself for not
losing twenty pounds, Lizzie appeared. Like a tsunami she burst
through the door, wet through, laughing loudly and screaming
obscenities at her new found buddies.

"Sorry babe," she laughed as she fell over my hand-luggage
and staggered like Dick Emery across the tiled floor. "I just had
to feel that seawater on my skin. Get that kettle on babe, am

gaggin' for a cuppa." She slipped off her shoes and as she towelled herself dry in the bathroom shouted enthusiastically; "Ooh, I spotted a couple of what you might call *'older gents'* in the bar as I came up, and when I say *older* I'm thinking twenty-something as opposed to nineteen!" and she roared with laughter.

"What happened to 'relaxing in cafés and watching the world go by'?" I half-joked, but she was singing away and slipping into her baby-doll in the bathroom, oblivious to my pain.

"The brochure described our resort as 'famous for its old town, cobbled streets, tasty local sausage and fine linen'." I called through, adding dried milk in big blobs to the swirling tea.

She laughed; "Sweetie, it is a bit younger than I thought but on the plus side, it's just full of *young* men. Babes, it's *Cougar Town* out there!" I drank my tea in silence. So, Lizzie had already discovered what the brochure referred to as *'tasty local sausage'* and it was only the first night.

When we woke that first morning to the distant-yet-insistent beat of 'Veejay Bobbi' I stood on the steaming, concrete balcony and surveyed the scene. It was incredibly warm already and not yet ten. By the pool, a few late-night revellers had abandoned themselves to the sun-loungers and were sleeping off last night's orgasms on the beach and long hard screws against the wall (and no, I *don't* mean the cocktails).

As I sipped yet more comforting hot tea I heard Lizzie singing and rummaging around in the room. She was so used to travelling with work, she never bothered to unpack and by the end of the week her suitcase would look like an explosion in a dress shop, but as she pointed out, "a *designer* dress shop, darling." Anyway, from the already-detonated suitcase Lizzie had extracted a really stylish lime-green tankini which she was now sporting on the balcony with a matching silk sarong and a golden layer of 'Fake Bake'. "Lizzie, you look gorgeous," I said, almost as green as her outfit with best-friend envy.

"I have a turquoise set too," she said. "You can borrow it if you like. It would go great with your blonde hair." I looked at Lizzie's full, curvy shape, chin-length auburn bob and (despite years of Merlot and Marlboros) perfect skin, and smiled; she was so kind.

"I couldn't possibly look as lovely as you Lizzie. I'd never get those lycra shorts over my bum. I'll stick to my big black upholstered costume, thanks."

Lizzie put down her cup and saucer and grabbed my wrist, gently but firmly dragging me inside the room. "Madam," she said, in a mock-stern voice. "You and I are the same size and I have to say you're looking a little skinnier since that cheating bastard husband of yours did the dirty. There's nothing better than a bit of marital trouble to make those pounds melt away." She plucked the turquoise beach set from her exploded case and handed it to me. "Just try it on."

I was sorely tempted. I'd only ever worn a big black bathing costume and black sarong on holiday. I'd once bought a pink sarong to try and liven up the black when we went to Majorca but Tom said it was 'too young' and that I didn't want to look like 'mutton dressed as lamb', so I'd pushed it to the back of the wardrobe forever.

Lizzie pushed the turquoise set at me and pushed me into the bathroom. "Put that on. I think you'll be surprised what it does for your tits, darling," she said, clutching at her own bosom with both hands and talking in her 'Trinny' voice.

I had a wobbly moment and wished I could climb into big black lycra and sit by the pool with Tom and Grace. I'd been comfy with Tom; our marriage wasn't about how we looked but about the people we were (at least, that's what I'd thought anyway, until he ran off with a younger, slimmer model who looked much better than I do). I tried to stop torturing myself – what happened had happened I had to move on or I'd drown in the past and the pain.

Anyway, the first step to moving on and grabbing life by the balls was to fit into the little beach-belle number. Forgetting Tom, I slid into the soft, sea-coloured fabric which wasn't as tight as I'd thought it would be. The tankini covered the tummy area and the bikini shorts hid multiple lumpy bits around the thighs. I stepped back and was rather pleased with my reflection. "That big old blonde must be by the pool," I said quietly to the mirror. "Cos she ain't in here."

Lizzie raved about my 'look' and insisted we go down to the pool immediately and try it out. She was right, I had lost a bit of weight with all the drama and was slightly exhilarated, tripping down the steps in Lizzie's silver flip-flops with matching beach bag. "You look fabulous," she kept saying, as we climbed down the steps to the pool. It was like a mantra, but I loved hearing it and it was drowning out the echoes of Tom's voice saying, 'are you really going to wear that...?'

Lizzie skipped round the pool to find two sun-loungers while I went to the bar and ordered breakfast: coffee and croissants. Then we sat by the turquoise water with our sun cream and books, listening to the musical beats and primal screams of the other holidaymakers. "I'm feeling happy," I said, sinking into a warm, buttery croissant.

Lizzie smiled and coughed over another fag. "That's great, babe – me too. And you look hot in that outfit!" I wasn't so sure, but as I lay back on my lounger and soaked up the sun, I thought maybe this holiday would be good for me after all.

20

Cocktails and Cannons

For the next couple of days, Lizzie and I swam and read and chatted and applied sun cream. I'd have a light salad for lunch and Lizzie would have several Marlboros, half a bottle of Merlot and a couple of vodkas. "Hair of the dog," she'd announce huskily, like it was somehow medicinal and therefore OK to drink a bucket of spirits at noon. We found a couple of nice bars in the evenings that weren't *too* young and trendy where we sampled the local vino under the stars and watched the perfect party people go by.

"It's hard to think we were once like that," mused Lizzie one evening as we watched the slim-hipped girls trip by in next to nothing. We were on our third glass of wine and both waxing lyrical.

"It seems like yesterday," I said, "and I still feel as young as they are. I don't feel older than eighteen really."

We both laughed and Lizzie (who by now was very tipsy) suddenly looked straight at me and said, "Amnesia?"

This sobered me up like a slap in the face. "You mean the nightclub?" I whispered, hoping against hope she was talking about an inability to recall past events.

Before I knew it, I was being led in the direction of Amnesia and its ice-cannon. When we reached its hallowed portals I couldn't believe it – we had to wait in a queue! This added insult to injury for me; not only was it the last place on Earth I wanted to enter, I had to queue up to get in. I kept telling myself it would all be fine because Lizzie and I were together and we were both old. We would have one drink and then go – that's what she'd said, hadn't she? I comforted myself with the thought that it would be interesting to see what it looked like inside and experience some of this, even if only for about 45 seconds and a quick glass of Pinot while ducking the ice-cannon.

Slowly the queue of tight young things moved forward. Screaming girls in tiny shorts and young, shaven-headed tattooed men jostled in the crowd, all dying to get inside. I prayed the club would be full by the time we reached the door. However the friendly bouncer reassured everyone (and upset me) by saying we'd all get in and 'no need to push'. Who was pushing?

Eventually we were pressed up against the door and after a few very uncomfortable minutes it was suddenly opened and twenty of us were counted in, like schoolchildren. With everyone's impatience to get into this hellhole, people were surging from the back and thrusting us forward at a breakneck speed. I lost Lizzie in the scrum and, barely able to stay on my feet, I staggered forward into thick, techno-trance-blackness. I heard someone shout 'Stella' and as I looked down I saw Lizzie sprawled on the floor. I leaned towards her trying to grab her arm but couldn't see properly and flailing around on the beery-wetness I slipped and ended up on top of her. We started laughing and were soon in a hysterical heap, unable to move as people fell over us in the darkness. Terrified that this was some form of lesbian floor show/middle-aged mud-wrestling scenario a bouncer stepped in and helped us back to our feet.

"Woohoo!" yelped Lizzie as she straightened her unforgiving lycra vest and ran her hands over her shiny bob. "What an entrance!"

Our eyes now used to the darkness, we wobbled over to the bar, where Lizzie ordered four bottles of Smirnoff Ice. I didn't argue – it's what everyone else was drinking. *When in Rome...* I thought, knocking back the sharp, chilled sweetness, longing for a cold Pinot and desperately trying to work out where the ice-cannon was hiding.

I gazed across the collective madness, the whole dancefloor crowd was moving together in a trance-like state. My plan was to stay safe by the bar hugging my drink, observe, placate Lizzie and then leave. However, it wasn't meant to be. To my horror, Lizzie picked up her two bottles and one in each hand, began wiggling her hips and semi-dancing into the throbbing cloud of zombie people. Why was I surprised? Lizzie was drinking and her alter-ego was now out there in a skimpy vest with a trick pelvis. I suddenly felt very alone and very uneasy in the middle of the sweating, snogging and thumping music.

Lizzie had been swallowed up into the dancefloor, so I decided to wait and take refuge against the wall. It was bare brick and felt cool on my hot, wet back. Two girls were arguing by the cigarette machine and I could see from where I stood it was getting quite heated. Couples everywhere were kissing, someone was being sick and a group of guys were hurling themselves into the dancing area, just landing on people and roaring like wild animals. I felt completely out of place. I knew Lizzie was more used to this kind of thing because she'd been single most of her grown-up life, but I wanted Tom again and I felt that urgent need to be at home with Grace watching TV.

As the music became more frenzied, the whistles started up and the club became hotter. *I'll find Lizzie and we'll go back now,* I thought. I looked for her everywhere and after too long in the heat and the mist I finally spotted her through bobbing heads and dry ice. Lizzie was talking to someone. I screwed up my eyes and got closer. It was a man and they were very, very close. I had that old feeling I used to get at school discos. My friend had met someone and I was the wallflower, dumped on the side. I was seventeen again – and not in a good way.

I had to get out. I couldn't stand it any longer. I fought my way into the dancing mass and reached Lizzie's bare arm. I patted it to get her attention but she was oblivious so I tugged gently at her vest top and shouted over the pulsing thud that I needed some air and would see her back at the apartment. She was sober enough to feel that 'friend responsibility' that girls did with each other. "I'll come with you," she offered half-heartedly, but I insisted she stay. We were both grown women and I didn't want to spoil Lizzie's fun. I also had a desperate need to be on my own, to have some space to think. As I left, I could see that she and the guy were now dancing very close, albeit to a strange, spacey sounding beat which meant they were bobbing up and down a bit. Through the mist, I could tell they were about to kiss – and the ice cannon was about to blow.

I walked back to the apartment slowly, the cobbles hard under my flip-flops, the hot night air giving little relief from the sweating, pulsating insides of Amnesia. As I heard the cannon roar and ten thousand muffled screams of delight coming from the club I thought that maybe it had all been too much too soon and that I wasn't ready to move on after all.

To reach our apartment I had to pass the poolside bar. It was only about 11pm and there were one or two people sitting around drinking. Time was different on this planet; some people were having a drink at this hour *before* going out.

Walking along the pool, I glanced across and caught sight of a dark-haired guy, dangling his legs in the pool. Our eyes met so I feigned nonchalance and tried to walk like I was in heels (flip-flops are so unflattering for short legs like mine). I kept walking, holding my stomach in and raising my head so I might lose a couple of chins or pounds should he care to glance in my direction again. I had to walk right past him and was taking a discreet peek when he looked up and smiled. *Wow! Twinkly brown eyes.* I felt a very slight flutter in my chest, a feeling I'd almost forgotten about.

"Hi," he said, as I stumbled past. "Having an early night?"

I looked round first to check he was talking to me. "Amnesia," I said casually, like I went there every night. He nodded and looked back into the navy-blue water, lit by the fairy lights from the pool bar.

"D'ya fancy a last drink before bedtime then?" he asked, in an irresistible Irish accent. My gut response was to say no, to make some excuse and head back to the travel kettle, but in a moment of daring I changed my mind.

I couldn't believe this was me walking to the pool bar with this gorgeous stranger. He ordered a bottle of wine and we went back to the side of the pool with it and two glasses. He told me his name was Alex and he was from Dublin.

An hour later, another bottle arrived and I heard this new Stella say, "OK, just one more glass." Alex was a few years younger than me but he didn't seem to mind and I certainly didn't. Apparently his friend had also met someone and Alex was now alone that night too. I didn't care who he was or why he was there, I just melted into those chocolate brown eyes and basked in the soft, Irish brogue. He told me he'd been divorced after only three years of marriage and had no children. I could tell that it still hurt, but again like me he was looking for something new and a way to move forward. We talked and talked – and at about 2.30am he gently took my glass from my hand, placed it on the table – and kissed me.

It was amazing and hard to describe the fireworks that were going off inside my chest when his lips pushed against mine and his tongue forced its way into my mouth. My stomach exploded with forgotten feelings of lust and joy and the combination of kissing and wine began to make me feel slightly out of control: this wasn't Stella kissing a man she'd just met. It was as though there were two of me and one was behaving in a completely outrageous way, while the other looked on in shock.

"Would you like to take a walk on the beach?" he asked.

"Yes" she answered, in a voice croaky with lust.

Stella knew what was happening, but the wine and the warmth and the fact she hadn't been with a man for a long time conspired to render her helpless. Her legs were shaky as they stood to leave and she leaned on him in a way the old Stella wouldn't have dared as they walked slowly across the cobbles to the beach.

Lit by the moon, the sea looked on as couples murmured in the sand. Walking along the water's edge, they were part of a different world where there were no rules in the moonlit darkness. She could make out the silhouettes of lovers lying on the sand, a head appearing from behind a dune then being gently pulled back down by an urgent partner wanting more.

They paddled as they walked along, holding hands. Drinking him into her alcoholic, lust-fuelled stupor Stella pushed away the feeling that Alex had been this way before. He had a destination in mind, and when they slowed down and walked towards a closed ice-cream shack she knew exactly what was on the agenda...and it wasn't a Cornetto.

"I don't normally do things like this" she slurred. Wordlessly, he pulled her behind the small brick building plastered with posters offering all flavours of ice cream and hundreds of different lollies in Spanish that she could barely see in the dark. She knew she shouldn't be doing this on a strange beach with a man whose surname she didn't know. Yet she wanted him so badly.

He lowered her onto the cool sand and they rolled around on the floor kissing for a long time. Tearing off each other's clothes, they had wild uncomplicated sex. And for the first time in her life,

Stella had an orgasm on the beach.

So that's how it was, *almost* like in the movies. Had there been any white-capped waves we'd have rolled around in those for a bit, like Burt Lancaster and Deborah Kerr, but you have to work with what you've got and an ice cream shack sufficed.

"You're special Stella," he said, kissing me as we walked back to the hotel, hand in hand.

"Go for it girl," Lizzie encouraged when I told her about Alex as she crawled back into the room at dawn.

"Lizzie, I met someone," I heard myself say into the darkness.

"Christ Stel, you made me jump," she squealed, still buzzing from Amnesia's Smirnoffs and ice-cannon.

"I met someone too. His name's Joe and I reckon he's at least ten years younger than me. I should be ashamed," she giggled.

"He looked nice. I saw you with him when I left Amnesia," I said, feeling like I was back at college, comparing boy-notes.

"Oh no, that wasn't Joe," she laughed. "Joe arrived about three men later."

I told her about Alex, but missed out the bit about the ice cream shack. I couldn't even admit that to myself yet.

Next morning Lizzie and I went down to the pool and I was incredibly nervous. Alex had said he'd see me down there, but I had a feeling he might not turn up, after all, I hadn't exactly played hard to get. So while Lizzie slapped on sun cream and sucked on ciggies, I lay on the sun-lounger in a way that made my stomach look slightly flat. Unfortunately the sacrifice for this was that I would need to remain horizontal all day, on the off-chance that he appeared.

"What are you doin' Stel?" Lizzie asked, knowing full well

what I was doing. "Don't you think he'll be a bit surprised when he rushes over and you just lie there like you're dead?" she asked with a smile.

"No, because I'm pretending he's caught me by surprise and I'll reach for sarong if I have to sit up, that should cover it."

I spent three hours on my back that morning – and not in a sexual way. As Lizzie puffed away and devoured the latest Marian Keyes I lay in turquoise waiting for Alex, but was filled with that familiar, sinking feeling.

By noon I was fed up and hungry. "Let's get chips, Lizzie," I said, gathering myself together, slipping into flip-flops and trudging across to the pool snack bar. Once there, we clambered onto stools and ordered two Diet Cokes and two cones of chips covered in ketchup.

"Well, this is new and different," I said filling my mouth with soft-yet-crispy hot chip, laced with salt and tangy tomato sauce. "Stella's disappointed with life – so she eats."

"Yeah, well chips don't stand you up like men do," Lizzie lamented. She'd been expecting a text from Joe to make plans for that evening, but so far none had arrived.

Filled with hot chips and Coke I had just taken ownership of a double-scoop, choc-chip cone and was consuming it with some gusto when I spotted him out of the corner of my eye.

"Lizzie, it's him quick!" I squealed, thrusting the huge, dripping cone at her – which was tricky because she had one of her own and was now holding two. I pretended I hadn't seen him and chatted animatedly to Lizzie, who was trying to suck on her fag and staunch the flow of two double-scoops in hot sunshine. *That's* what best friends are for. Within seconds I felt a shiver of excitement as I felt him approach the bar. What would happen? Would he ignore me? Was he so drunk last night he wouldn't even know me? The horror of my teens came flooding back in those few seconds and part of me just wanted to grab back my cone and bury my head in it. But I needn't have worried. As soon as he reached my side his hand was on my arm.

"Hi Stella," he said in that gorgeous accent and kissed me on the mouth. Lizzie stood by in delight and surprise, smiling like a proud mother whose daughter had just got ten A's in her GCSE's.

"This is my friend Lizzie," I gestured, "she likes ice cream." Lizzie giggled. "Actually I couldn't decide on which flavour, so I had them all," she said loyally.

"Well, I'm sure I can help you with one of those," Alex offered gallantly. She carefully handed the now dripping cone to him and they both began eating the ice cream (greedily – or perhaps I was just jealous – I really wanted the chocolate chip).

"Do you girls fancy a drink or lunch?" he offered, when he'd polished off my cone.

"No thanks Alex, I'm going into the resort to meet a friend," Lizzie lied. I so owed her *big* time.

"I go home the day after tomorrow," he said, "and you promised to take me to that wine bar."

"OK, let's go," I heard myself say, kissing him first and feeling all that warm, sweet stuff come flooding back like the feeling you get from the very best chocolate fudge cake (warm with thick, cold fresh cream).

For the next 48 hours, Alex and I were inseparable. During the day we walked along the cobbles, shopped for souvenirs, sipped cocktails by the pool and looked into each other's eyes for hours on end. We drank wine on pavements in beautiful sunsets and everyone else seemed boring and stupid and a waste of our precious time together. With Alex, the sea was bluer and the sun hotter. I didn't need Amnesia to feel like I'd been shot between the eyes by an ice-cannon. Every sensation was heightened and intensified because we were filled with new lust and knew that the clock was ticking; it would soon be time for him to leave and I didn't want the magic to be over.

We were sitting in a dark cocktail bar surrounded by women younger, slimmer and prettier than me, but I was the lucky one because I was the one sitting next to Alex.

"I know it sounds like a line," he said, looking into my eyes, "but I've got really strong feelings for you."

"It's not 'a line' to say you have feelings for someone," I said, feeling an electric jolt pass through me. It was late and warm and I'd drunk three Tequila Sunrises. I felt like a teenager again.

"Alex, I feel the same," I blurted. And we kissed and talked and talked and kissed, then went back to his room.

Our relationship was just like *Brief Encounter* (but he was better looking and less posh than Leslie Howard) and because we knew we were on borrowed time, everything took on an intensity I'd never felt before. On his final day we didn't part, I even waited outside the Gents for him, which Lizzie said was a bit sick, even for me. When he left at 2am to catch his flight home we hugged outside the coach and he promised to call as soon as I got back to Britain.

After he'd gone, the place just wasn't the same. I know it had only been three days and nights but I felt such deep loss. The days dragged, it was lifeless by the pool and the sunsets were washed out and pointless without him. Every song playing in every bar reminded me of Alex. I felt empty and at the same time elated, revisiting the places we'd been to feel his ghost, going over the things he said, the way he said them, the way he kissed, the way his eyes were constantly laughing. For the first time since Tom and I started going downhill I wasn't lonely and just thinking about him was enough.

Then, the day before we left, the bubble burst. I was thinking about Alex as I sat by the pool and I watched idly as a young dad and his daughter were playing with a beach ball in the water. The dad reached up to catch a throw from his daughter and from that angle he looked so like Tom when we were younger that my heart nearly stopped. The memories of our family holidays came flooding back and Lizzie sat up in alarm as tears began to stream down my face. My fling with Alex had been fun and possibly what I needed to try and move on – but it wasn't love. It wasn't the love I had shared with the father of my child.

"What's the matter, hon?" asked Lizzie, passing me a tissue.

"Oh, Lizzie. I had fun with Alex, and he made me feel so attractive, but..."

"He wasn't Tom," she finished, putting her arm around me.

"No," I sobbed.

"I've been waiting for this since Alex left," said Lizzie.

I wiped my eyes and looked at her in surprise. "Really?"

"Oh, sweetie. You had fun with Alex and he gave you confidence which is a really good thing. But you don't just get over a marriage in the space of a holiday – even if you are in Ibiza."

I covered my face as the tears began again.

"I'll get us some drinks," said Lizzie, fishing out her purse. "Come on, a vodka and some chips will make everything seem better."

I nodded gratefully, feeling very lucky to have a friend that knew me so well (even though I wasn't too convinced about the vodka). Lizzie went to the poolside bar and ordered and I did my best to compose myself. My time with Alex had been great – it was good to feel that kind of desire for someone again – but in my heart I knew that whatever Alex had said, he probably wasn't going to call me and I wasn't sure I even wanted him to. I needed to leave my thoughts of him here and move on.

21

Brazilian Boys and Baking Blues

I arrived home at lunchtime, put Mum on her train back home and was in plenty of time to pick Grace up from school.

"Did you have a nice time, Mummy?" asked Grace, over a healthy tea of cheeseburger and chips at McDonald's.

"Hmmm it was lovely," I said, trying not to think about the more inappropriate moments whilst imbibing caffeine and burying my face in a McFlurry.

"Ew, gross! Mummy, that boy's putting chips up his nose!" Grace shouted, pointing at him in deep disgust.

"So what have you and Nanny been up to while I was away?" I asked, grateful to change the subject.

By 9.30pm that night, Grace was sleeping soundly when the phone rang. "Hi love, it's me. I got back safely. Thought you might be interested." It was Mum. "How's Gracie? Have you heard from that Tom?" I was tired and this was all I needed – a bloody interrogation.

"She's fine and no I haven't."

"Good. Now, I met a very nice doctor today at the hospital. I took Beryl this afternoon, with her leg."

Go away Mum, I thought. *I need to go to bed.*

"I've always thought you should have married a doctor or a lawyer. So reliable and intelligent – I wish you had," she said with a sigh. "Anyway, Beryl's doctor is from South America. He's come to Britain because his daughter's here, which is nice isn't it? I told him you make lovely cakes. I said you were going through a divorce."

"That's great Mum. Now I must..."

"I gave him your mobile number."

This wasn't the first time she'd done this. Grace told me over tea that while I was away, Mum took it upon herself to log on to dating websites on my behalf in a desperate (and no doubt very confused) search for my soulmate.

"Mum, I need to get off the phone. And will you stop giving my phone number to complete strangers?" I grated, losing it ever so slightly.

"Beryl's doctor's called Diego," she continued, ignoring me. "Lovely man, he's going through a divorce and he's got a daughter who will be twelve soon, I think."

"I'm sure he's very nice Mum, but you always told me not to speak to strange men. And I really don't need any psychos in my life right now."

"He's not a psycho – he's a surgeon."

"Get off the phone!" I heard myself yell. "Grace is climbing out of the window and about to throw herself off the roof. I need to call an ambulance."

"OK dear. Tell her to have a nice time and give her a kiss from me."

I put the receiver down and rubbed my tired eyes. It was only just after nine thirty so I made a cup of coffee and thought about how coffee granules made delicious icing when you poured hot water over them and mixed with icing sugar. The sweetness of the sugar and rounded bitterness of the coffee beans always blended together so well. I watched the coffee swirl in my cup and felt a touch of the post-holiday blues. Even though I knew Alex would never call – and to be honest I wasn't sure I really wanted him to – he had made me feel special, even if only for a short time.

The following morning, I was back to looking at the jobs

section in the paper when the doorbell rang. It was Jessica's mum.

"Stella, I'm so glad to catch you. I didn't know when you'd be back from Ibiza" she said, stepping in and hugging me like a long-lost friend.

"I only got back yesterday. Come through to the kitchen. How was the cake?" I ventured, holding my breath.

"Well, that's why I wanted to see you in person. We really didn't expect anything quite like..."

"Oh no! I'm so sorry! I wasn't sure. I knew I should have stuck with a whole cake, but, but...You hated the cupcakes?"

"They were the most beautiful birthday cupcakes I've ever seen," she smiled, "and Jess was beside herself, she said it was just like the cakes you see celebrities eating in *Hello!*"

"Praise indeed," I smiled, deeply relieved. I'd been worried they didn't like them and had hoped Al would have left a message about her reaction when he'd dropped them off, but he hadn't.

"Coffee?"

"Coffee would be lovely," she sat down and began rummaging in her handbag while I made the drinks.

"When your friend Al dropped it off, I wasn't home and he left it with my son who, typically, didn't even peep in the box," she smiled. "When I got home and saw it – I have to tell you Stella, I cried." I handed her a mug of coffee and she cried again telling me all about how she'd cried at the cake. I cried too.

"I have to rush, Stella – I'm on my way to work," she said eventually, wiping her eyes, finishing her coffee and placing a white envelope on the table. "There's the money for the cake," she said, gesturing to the white envelope as she got up from the chair, "please let me know if it isn't enough."

"Oh, I just wanted to cover the ingredients. I'm sure it will be plenty, thank you," I said, slightly embarrassed. When she'd gone, I went back in the kitchen and opened the envelope – it contained £200 – and I cried again.

Later that night, I put Grace to bed then sat at the kitchen table looking at the thank-you card from Anne and Jessica. I was so pleased that they had liked the cake. Since making Grace's volcano it had been my biggest creative achievement. And as I sat in my warm, homely kitchen thinking about how lovely it had been to profit from my handiwork an exciting idea slowly started to form in my head. Shaking slightly, I rummaged through one of the drawers and found some of Grace's felt tips and a piece of paper and sketched an oblong. Inside it I wrote 'Stella Weston – Professional Cake Maker' and drew a little picture of a cake. OK, so I would clearly need help with the business card design, but – why not? I loved baking, I needed child-friendly hours and I desperately wanted to enjoy my job. But as I looked at the badly-drawn picture my old friend self-doubt put in an appearance. I couldn't even get a job at a check-out – how could I start my own company? I was hardly going to win 'Businesswoman of the Year'. I folded the piece of paper up into a tiny square and stuffed it back in the drawer. I was just making myself a hot chocolate when the phone rang.

"Hi babes, just giving you a quick call, I'm packing my bags again hon." It was Lizzie and apparently she'd been given the role of director on a new cookery programme filmed in Australia, called *Barry's Barbie*.

"That sounds fab, Lizzie. Did MJ agree to it? I thought a plum job like that would have gone to one of her cronies." I said.

"Mmm. I wondered about that too but I've heard Barry likes to work with female directors and let's face it – how many of us are free to just drop everything and travel round the world in search of 'barbie heaven'? I'm single with no ties, so MJ probably had no choice."

"Well, you be careful out there," I said seriously. "I'll miss you."

"I'll miss you too sweetie. Ooh and Al's got the assistant-producer job so he's coming as well. Great news for us, but not much fun for you stuck here while we're filming juicy meat on beaches around the globe."

After she hung up, I called Al and congratulated him on *Barry's Barbie*. He was happy about the job, but sad to leave Sebastian.

"Look after him for me, will you Stel?" he asked.

"Of course I will. Oh Al, by the way, I can't thank you enough for lending me the money and delivering that cake. They paid me £200 for it."

"That's fabulous Stel. It did look gorgeous. I'm so proud of you."

"Anyway, how are you?" I said changing the subject to one I knew he'd be happy to move on to. Having listened to Al's current life story for some time I finally ended the call and went back to the job section when the phone rang again.

"Hi is that Stella Weston?" a woman's voice said.

"Yes," I mumbled, through crumbs.

"My name's Emma, I hope you don't mind me calling this late but Anne Jackson gave me your number – you make cakes?" My heart skipped a beat.

"My daughter Alice is having a tenth birthday party next week and I wondered if you would make the cake?" She continued. I had a moment of indecision. It was as if my fate was teetering on an edge and I finally needed to push it in the right direction. I reached for the kitchen drawer and pulled out my sketch.

"Yes, I think I can fit that in." I said firmly, unfolding the paper and smoothing it out.

"Alice wants a cake like the one Ashley Cole gave to Cheryl on her 25th," Emma started. "Now I don't expect you to know what it looked like, but..."

"Mmm. It was a handbag with lipsticks and make-up, wasn't it?" I *knew* there was a reason for reading celebrity magazines other than a puerile need for lascivious, cellulite gossip.

"Wow, I'm impressed," she laughed. "Actually, we sort of know each other – well, our daughters do. My daughter came to Grace's Hawaiian birthday party last year and I picked her up from After School Club for you a while back." I remembered now, Emma was the woman who was having a hard time with her divorce at Grace's party. "I heard about your problems," she stuttered, "your husband leaving. Grace told Alice."

"Yes. I suppose we're both in the same boat now," I said, feeling a little guilty about the way I'd brushed her off at Grace's birthday party. Such a lot had changed; I didn't have time for anyone then, especially sad losers who couldn't keep their husbands. I was now Chairwoman of *that* club.

"Why don't you come over and have a coffee one morning this week? Tomorrow would be good. We can look through some cake pictures and talk about Cheryl Cole's man trouble," I said.

"I love talking about other people's man trouble," she laughed. "I'll be there about ten."

Emma arrived the next morning and we Googled images of Cheryl's cake and decided that if *she* couldn't keep a man there was no hope for any of us. Emma told me about how her husband had walked out on her for his secretary three years ago. "Such a cliché," she said. "I went to the office to surprise him on his birthday and take him for lunch and when I walked in, he wasn't alone and his secretary was – well, you know the story."

"Mmm," I nodded, "giving him a birthday surprise."

Emma is so attractive; slim with spiky black hair cut in a trendy short style complimented by a gash of bright red lipstick that only a truly perfect face could get away with. Even after all this time, it was clear to see she couldn't talk about her ex without becoming tearful. *I like her*, I thought after she left, *but I don't want to be like her. I don't want the rest of my life to be like a bed imprinted with the shape of the man who used to lie there.* I needed to move on now.

A week later, Emma brought Alice over and the girls played in Grace's bedroom while we shared a bottle of wine. I only drank one glass because I was icing and needed a steady hand but it was lovely to share a drink with a friend and have some company while I worked.

Emma, Alice, Grace and I all had input in the design and planning of the 'sponge bag' as Grace called it. The girls wanted fake lashes and hair-straighteners in sugarpaste but I wasn't sure I could do it, so I convinced Alice that edible jewels and scarlet lipstick would be classier.

Anyway, we amalgamated our thoughts and came up with a huge sponge cake filled with jam and buttercream, covered in black and white sugarpaste and studded with edible jewels. I'd almost finished the handbag, which appeared to be open and contained a bottle of perfume, a lipstick, a pair of sunglasses – all edible save the jewellery (Emma's surprise gift to Alice, a silver charm bracelet).

"It reminds me of a handbag Grace Kelly would carry," Emma commented, as I pushed the tiny diamonds and pearls into glossy, patent-look black icing.

"Tom and I loved *Dial M for Murder*," I said, suddenly feeling a pang.

"You seem so together Stella, considering what happened with Tom," said Emma carefully. "Are you OK? Or is it just that you're in denial?"

I sighed. "I'm not over it yet, after all it's not been very long. I still have sleepless nights thinking about Tom and *her*. It's the anger that keeps me awake, then the hurt, then the tears. It's ridiculous really."

Emma listened as I talked, and for the first time I felt someone really understood. It was good to spend time with someone who had been through a similar experience, even if it was over a giant, sponge handbag.

"Sometimes I want to hug him and say 'come home Tom', then other times I just want to kill him."

"Ah, so many men, so few patios," Emma said and we both laughed loudly, two scorned women united in their pain. Judging by the way she laughed, perhaps there was hope for Emma yet.

I arrived at Alice's party, Grace in tow, with some trepidation. I was so nervous about the cake, more than I thought I would be. By the time we got to Emma's house, a lovely old Victorian terrace with a sprawling back garden, I had convinced myself that no-one would like my creation. There were quite a few people there, and whilst the kids played in the garden supervised by Alice's older brother the mums had a cheeky glass of wine in the kitchen and I started to relax. As I looked around, I saw the cake covered in a cloth in the centre of the dining table. I was outwardly cool but secretly delighted to hear the gasps when, after we'd been there about an hour, the kids were called in from the garden and the cake was unveiled. Alice discovered the charm bracelet and blew out the candles, while everyone sang *Happy Birthday*. It's hard to be objective about your own stuff, but I have to say, it looked amazing.

After the unveiling, I was stood by the window when one of Emma's friends rushed over to me and said "Emma says you're responsible for the cake. I am *loving* the diamonds and the *darling* lipstick. Can we talk?" This was an odd comment, seeing we were already mid conversation, but I nodded politely.

"Sangita Singh," she said, offering me a delicate and bejewelled hand. "I run Events Inc. We cover film premières, product launches, corporate events packages and themed parties."

"So, you're very busy?" I said, lamely, trying to keep the conversation going but panicking about what to say to this scary woman who talked like a corporate video.

"Absolutely, I've worked with Madonna, George Michael, Katie..."

"Price?" I said, gulping my wine, impressed but feigning nonchalance at this woman's career and client list.

"What?!"

"Katie...you said Katie *Price* was on your client list?" I tried, hopefully.

"Oh my God no – Katie *Cruise!*" she said, looking horrified.

"Oh, I'm sorry, I..."

Mentioning the artist formerly known as Jordan had clearly upset her and as she turned her back I could see I needed to move, but had no escape. I didn't know anyone there and Emma was busy being Mother-of-the-Birthday-Girl.

Just as I thought she was walking away, Sangita turned round to face me. "I may have work for you re cakes," she announced. "My company is expanding and we have a developing project. I need to see figures first, do some number-crunching but I might be in touch." With that, she swept across the kitchen, hugged Emma and with a rustle of silk and a clatter of chunky bracelets, she donned her pistachio-green pashmina and left.

In the end I charged Emma £60 for the cake. I know it didn't exhibit great business credentials but I couldn't ask for any more. It covered costs and as she was now a friend I couldn't profit from her but when I arrived home after the party I noticed an envelope in one of my cake boxes. Inside was a thank-you card from Emma and Alice and enclosed was a cheque for £150. I smiled; maybe I could do this after all.

22

Life Changing Phone Calls

A few days later things started to move – beginning with
potentially-life-changing-phone-call number one. At about
eleven o'clock in the morning I was busy making fresh
gingerbread people for Grace's school summer fête later in the
day. I'd always enjoyed making these chubby, spicy little boy
and girl biscuits but I found myself getting carried away
imagining they were Tom and Bitch Rachel. Consequently, I
ended up wasting a lot of dough because gingerbread men with
mangled genitals and maimed faces didn't go down too well
with the strawberry cream-teas on the school lawn. The phone
rang during a particularly vigorous ginger-bread-face-maiming
scenario and as Grace had obviously joined a religious sect and
taken a vow of 'not moving from my chair when the telly's on' I
ran to answer it.

I was a little breathless and when a male voice with a faint
Spanish accent said "Hello, is that Stella speaking?" I felt a rush
of warmth to my chest which went straight into my voice.

"Hello, this is she," I said coming over all Scarlett O'Hara.

"I have your phone number. From your mother."

"Oh yes," I quivered, suddenly remembering who this might
be. "Mother mentioned you, is it Diego?" I asked, trying to
sound firm yet sensual.

"Yes, I'm Diego. Hello".

"Mum says you're living locally and have a young
daughter?" I offered. "I also have a daughter around the same

age," I continued, at least attempting *some* background small-talk.

"Yes, she told me. And you used to work in TV? Your mother says you make very nice cake."

"Mmm." *Thanks for the PR Mum*, I thought. Most mothers would describe their daughters to would-be suitors as 'pretty,' or 'clever' but I just 'make very nice cake.'

"Do you think we should meet?" Well, he wasn't wasting any time. But who was I to reject an eager Latin Love God? Let's face it, I wasn't exactly turning them away at the door and this would be the nearest thing I'd had to a date since Tom left (Alex didn't really count). Diego had a sexy Spanish accent and he was a doctor. What was not to like?

"Yes. It would be lovely to meet up," I heard myself say.

So, amid the full-on flirting (him) and fake breathlessness (me), we arranged to meet in an Australian bar on the following Wednesday at 8pm.

I suggested 'Bruce's' because it was the only trendy-ish bar I'd been to in the last decade. It was on Broad Street in the centre of Birmingham and surrounded by other bars and cafés so we could always move on if we wanted to. Lizzie and I once had quite a night in there, referring to each other as Sheila, singing *Waltzing Matilda* and getting plastered on 'Aussie Wallbangers.' Lizzie had always had a thing for Antipodean men and hoped she'd find her *Crocodile Dundee* amid the stale Foster's lager and smelly kangaroo pelts. She was into *ER* at the time, had a huge crush on Doctor Doug and insisted (as she often did) that all Aussie men had a look of George Clooney. Unfortunately there wasn't an Aussie or a Clooney in sight and we were chatted up by two salesmen from Bradford with bad breath and loose morals. When Lizzie asked why one of these 'single' guys was wearing a wedding ring, he said 'it's my dead mother's', which was a conversation stopper.

Before I could contemplate the full implications of a blind date set up by my mother with an unknown Brazilian in an Aussie bar, I received potentially-life-changing-phone-call number two. This time it was a woman's voice and she sounded very business-like.

"Hello, Stella Weston?" she barked down the phone.

"Yes. Who is this?" I asked politely.

"Sangita from Events Inc. Emma's friend, we met at a birthday party." I recalled the beautiful but haughty Asian woman who had admired the cakes and said she might have work for me. Before I could say anything else, she was back at me.

"Costings," she ordered, getting straight to the point and talking at a hundred miles an hour. "I have a huge event coming up. Three hundred fashion delegates for one big Fashionista Afternoon Tea Party. Cucumber sandwiches and Earl Grey are Harrods and The Ritz but Bertrand at Parisian Pastries has returned with a *profane* pricing for fairy cakes. I'm looking for something new and fresh so I've called you instead. I'll need hundreds of individuals, tasteful not twee. Think Cath Kidston, pink polka-dot *with* edge. I want kitsch with a lingering scent of Parisian chic. I also need a big cake in the shape of a Vivienne Westwood-style basque. I want big, busty, lacy, but tasteful. Vivienne's receiving an award on the night so think full-on kitsch married to chichi chic. Don't even *try* to palm me off with Pucci – that was a hundred years ago and I won't buy it. I'm thinking Carrie in The Magnolia Bakery à la *Sex and the City*, with gingham trim."

She spoke like a medium channelling a spirit, a relentless stream of consciousness. "Hang on," she suddenly shouted; "think Naomi Campbell in *those* heels. I need you to understand the importance of this, it's stellar, Stella. The fairy cakes must be the bridesmaids...but the cake is the bride. It can't be just a cake

– it needs to be an *installation*."

"Er, ok," I tried to join in, but I couldn't. She was like an express train.

"Think 70s with a contemporary fringe. Beautiful, funky, kooky," she continued, like I wasn't even there. This was making me very nervous; I wished I'd recorded the conversation because I would never remember everything. If I could pull this off, though, I could be on the verge of making cakes all day for a living. But *could* I pull it off? Suddenly, MJ's mean face flashed into my head telling me that my work wasn't good enough. Could I make cakes for an event this large, for a company this connected? And who, or what, was Pucci, anyway?

Sangita was what Lizzie would call a 'conceptualiser'. She had magical ideas but needed someone else to execute them. I was salivating from excitement and fear at the same time but felt I should explain that I wasn't Sprinkles in LA or Harrods Cake Hall, merely a woman in her kitchen who made interesting birthday sponge, but she didn't want to hear it.

"Sangita, this is great but I really should tell you I..."

"Have two o'clock conference call with with Gaga. Need to shoot. Will text email address and list of what I need and you send costings asap." Sangita didn't do small-talk. In fact she didn't even do whole sentences, just instructions and celebrity names.

This was a daunting request, but it wasn't going to do any harm to start pricing up the cost of a few hundred fairy cakes, some glittery sugar strands and a sheet of gold leaf. There was also the big cake in the shape of a Vivienne Westwood-style basque. *Making a cake for a big function is scary, but how hard can it be?* I thought. I was sure it would also be fun. I started to think about rich cream ruffles, juicy scarlet cherries folded into dark chocolate lace, and of course, riding crops.

Within minutes of the manic call, Sangita texted

requirements, dates and an email address to send my pitch to so I started to work things out. By the end of the afternoon, I had the costs for two hundred pistachio and rose macaroons, two hundred pink and blue handbag-shaped fairy cakes and two hundred coffee-ganache and gold-leaf high-heel fondants.

From my time working in TV I was used to doing written pitches for work. This included writing treatments for programmes regarding the tone, the format, the look, the branding and how much each episode would cost to make. How different was a cake sell? A pitch is a pitch.

Al phoned just as I was typing up my concept. "Al, you won't believe it," I started to take on a Sangita-like persona, screaming, 'new business', 'Vivienne Westwood,' and 'chichi handbag cakes'. I was met by silence.

"Stel, that's great, but are you sure you know what you are doing? It's not so easy setting up a business, doll. There are lots of things to think about and this one sounds like a big deal."

After my previous elation, this brought me down to Earth with a bump. Al was right – this was a big deal.

"I think I've got it all covered. But I do need to sort brandings and costings. And source ingredients...oh God, there's actually masses to do!"

"Look babes. There's been a delay on *Barry's Barbie* so I'm in limbo until they sort my flights. I'll come over and help you. Maybe I can check your maths and money – I am the queen of the Excel sheet, after all."

"That would be wonderful Al. Could you come over tomorrow night?" Then I processed what he'd said. "Why is there a delay in you going out to *Barry's Barbie*? Lizzie's already there, isn't she?"

"Oh it's something about that twisted bitch MJ demanding to be on the shoots. She's flying out first and checking out all the bloody beaches so they don't need me for about a fortnight.

She's just taking a bloody holiday on the Media World dollar if you ask me."

"Yeah, when it comes to budgets, none is too small for MJ to enjoy a free ride," I said, feeling that familiar anger welling up inside.

"Oh and talking of twisted bitches – it looks like Tom and the tart are on the rocks my love."

"Really?" I suddenly felt giddy.

"Mmm, apparently they had a huge row at work. François from TV Fashion – you know, raging queen, fake tan, Botox – overheard the tart saying that she was fed up competing with Tom's ex-wife. *You!* How fabulous is that?"

I put the phone down feeling far more pleased than I should and wandered upstairs to see how Grace was getting on in the bath.

"You OK, Mum?" she said, looking up from Malibu Barbie, who was showing her versatility by playing Gabriella, the lead female in *High School Musical*. Grace was using the bath as the set for the summer camp swimming pool and in my opinion, California Ken was being a bit over-familiar in the deep end with one of the cheerleaders, but I was textbook and didn't react.

"I'm fine sweetie," I smiled. "It's just that Uncle Al's pointed out there are lots of things to think about if I do this event and now I'm not sure."

"Mummy, if it's what you want to do, why don't you just do it?" She sat there all wet and soapy with both hands out in a 'so what?' gesture looking just like her father. I kissed her soapy head. Sometimes kids were the sensible ones – they saw a bigger, clearer picture.

"You're right, Grace, thank you. I *am* going to just do it," I said, giving her a high-five.

"Shall we watch *Masterchef* on my bed with hot chocolate and marshmallows?" I said, trying to put Tom, tarts and MJ firmly from my mind.

As we snuggled up after her bath, Grace had obviously guessed I still had my mind on the event and said perceptively: "Mum, don't worry about it. Don't feel sad if that lady doesn't choose you – it doesn't matter," she sucked up the cream and mallows in one go, deliberately creating a cream moustache and feigning surprise when I laughed and pointed to it; "Mmm, I love hot chocolate. No-one else makes it as good as you do, Mum."

"That's because all my love goes into your mug," I said as I tickled her with a warm feeling in my tummy, a lump in my throat and a sugar-coated Vivienne Westwood basque whirling around in my head.

23

Fatal Attraction

After the initial excitement about corporate cup cakes and chichi chocolate creations, I submitted my pitch and heard precisely nothing from Sangita. Al had helped me with the practical stuff and as a result the pitch was creative *and* businesslike and I couldn't believe she'd just turn me down flat without even a rejection call or email.

I phoned Emma; "Perhaps she didn't like my ideas? Perhaps I'm just too small time for her?" I wailed. But Emma had worked in this field and known Sangita for years. She reassured me that Sangita would be doing ten million things at once and would get back to me one way or the other.

Feeling fat, fed-up and broke, I decided to cheer myself up and email Mum regarding Diego the Doctor, my hot date for Wednesday:

> *Hi Mum,*
> *I just wanted to let you know, Diego called and I'm meeting him in Birmingham on Wednesday.*
> *Could you describe him to me?*
> *Love Stella x*

She emailed me back a couple of hours later (no doubt with the help of someone more technically able):

> *Glad Diego called, you must bake him a nice cake.*
> *Love Mum x*

Typical Mum, I thought, *she always says that 'a way to a man's heart is through his stomach'*. That may have been the case in her day, but he'll have to prove himself before he gets his mouth round my 'Frangipane Surprise'.

I emailed her back:

I was wondering what Diego looks like? Could you describe him?

I waited for another hour and when I heard my email bleep I leapt onto the computer, eager to read details about my luscious Latin date.

Glad Diego called, you must bake him a nice cake.
Love Mum x

Mum and technology were not friends. I'd never had an email or text from her that made sense. Why did I think today would be any different? I wasn't in the mood for email volleyball and anyway, I wasn't shallow enough to make a decision about a man purely on his looks (*who was I kidding?*).

The day before my hot date I was rooting through my wardrobe whilst doubting my future as a businesswoman and having second thoughts about meeting up with Diego. I was still not really over Tom and there was also Grace to consider. She spent every other weekend with her dad whom she adored and she might not take kindly to another man at the breakfast table, let alone in her mother's bed.

Lighting on a dress I hadn't worn for at least five years I dragged it from the wardrobe and took it off the hanger. It had been a favourite of mine. It was navy blue and crossed over at the bust, giving, I'd always hoped, a perky-breasts-slim-waist effect. I held it against me and decided to try it on. I hadn't been able to squeeze into it the previous summer but I'd lost a husband and a few pounds since then. And hurrah! It fit! I whooped, which brought Grace running from her bedroom still in her school uniform. "Look at me, Grace, I'm in a dress I thought was too small." I gave her a twirl.

"Yay Mum, you're like one of the ugly sisters, squeezing into Cinderella's old shoe."

"Yeah, thanks Grace," I answered, a little deflated. Just as I was giving a second twirl in front of the mirror and checking for unsightly bulges, the doorbell went.

I was about to rush and get it when whoever it was decided to let themselves in anyway. Grace had run on ahead and shouted up "It's only Daddy!" I heard some chatting and laughter from Grace followed by Tom's voice calling to me up the stairs.

"Stella, I've come to get some of my stuff, as requested." Oh, he knew how to wind me up. Not only had he just walked in like he still lived here, the 'as requested' comment was a reference to the fact that last time he dropped Grace off I had asked him to make arrangements to take away his 'nasty mugs and other sad collections' that were 'cluttering my house'. *Let Bitch Rachel live with his loser rubbish; after all, he was shacked up with her now.*

I wanted to stay upstairs until he'd gone but I had to supervise his packing, lest he mistake any of my Emma Bridgewaters for one of his cheap crocks. I wasn't letting that tart get her mouth round my cream mugs with pink hearts on. I stomped downstairs, still sporting the navy 'date dress' that I intended to wow Diego with and walked into the kitchen to find Tom on his knees at the open cupboard door holding a 'I ♥ Menorca' mug. My anger turned to a sticky lump in my chest and I thought I would cry.

"Hi," I said, trying to smile, looking at his hands and imagining them holding someone else.

"Oh hi. You look nice. Er, I'm just getting my stuff. I don't know where I'm going to put it."

"Don't tempt me," I answered sharply. I walked towards the kettle, then seeing Grace out of the corner of my eye, almost holding her breath waiting for the inevitable argument I said; "Would you like a coffee, Tom?" Grace looked relieved and nodded encouragingly; I wanted to cry again watching her little face filled with hope and anticipation. Things had been so hostile recently; for Grace a cup of coffee was akin to us getting back together.

"Thanks, er yes, I will. Two sugars, please."

"I haven't forgotten, Tom, after sixteen years there are some things you don't forget, even if you want to," I said, without smiling, torn between wanting to make Grace happy and wanting to substitute his sugar for cyanide.

Tom winced, then lifted the Menorca mug he was holding and said, "That was a good holiday, wasn't it?"

I softened at the thought of the holiday in Menorca. Grace was three years old and happy, and so were we. "Yeah, I remember Grace falling in the pool, fully-clothed," I said, bringing the coffee cups to where he was and joining him on the floor to view the famous mug collection for one last time.

"There was a good slide that went into the water," I said.

"Yes and you were so light you came down it at about a hundred miles an hour, Grace," Tom laughed, shaking his head. The telephone rang and Grace went to answer it – when she didn't return immediately I heard her chatting and knew it was one of her friends. Still smiling from the memories, our eyes locked for a couple of seconds.

"We had some good times, didn't we?" I said looking down, away from his eyes.

"Yeah," Tom answered, obviously unsure where this was going and making a big thing about sipping his coffee. I watched his eyes close as they always did when he took a drink. I used to love that when we were first together. I hadn't noticed it for years.

"How's Rachel?" I blurted. I don't know what made me say this but I think I wanted him to say he was desperately unhappy and he missed me. I also longed for the caveat that Bitch Rachel had gained three stone, grown thick, dark, facial hair (and would 'grown a penis' have been really sick?).

"Erm, OK," was all he offered.

"What's she like?" I heard myself say, sitting in the middle of the kitchen floor and feeling a strong urge to put my head on his shoulder, to lean on him like I always had.

Silence.

"Is she slim?" I heard my fifteen-year old self ask.

"Stella, this is silly. It doesn't matter what she's like." He moved to get up and I caught his arm. I didn't want a row, I wanted to know why.

"Don't you understand? I need to know what it was that took you away. I need to know what she had that made you want to leave us. Is she really pretty? Is she fun?"

"She's attractive and she can be fun, but...I do have days when I think 'you idiot, what have you done."

"Do you?" I said, my voice croaking with suppressed emotion.

"Yeah, I miss you and of course I miss Grace, but then perhaps it was for the best. I'm finally getting there. Rachel's OK. She's difficult sometimes, insecure, you know – but we have some laughs." I could feel the heat of rage and hurt rising from the soles of my feet and had the lump in my throat I hadn't felt since Christmas when he'd left.

"Look, despite what you might think, Rachel's a good sort," he said, looking at me like he was trying to convince me to vote for the bitch.

A good fucking sort is she? Gosh, that's funny, I thought she was a husband-stealing slut, was what I wanted to say. So I went one better. "I'm glad you're finally getting there," I said, clamping down the anger and relishing the next bit, "I'm moving on too. In fact I have a date tomorrow night – with a doctor."

The look on his face assuaged a good deal of the stinging and was better therapy than any swearing and bitching on my part. He looked like he'd been hit by a truck, but soon composed himself enough to slap me back.

"Doctor? Ha – is that someone your mum fixed you up with, on the Internet?" he said, rather cruelly (obviously Grace had been blabbing).

"No, this is someone I met at a party," I lied, staying calm, getting up off the floor and resisting the urge to kick him hard in the head from my now-higher vantage point. A little stiff from sitting on the floor but damned if I'd show it, I veered towards the sink and begin rinsing the cups.

"And who's looking after Grace?" he started, with a whisper of indignance, which kind of roused my old friend, Mr Angry.

"Since when have you been concerned about who's looking after Grace?" I said raising my voice and only just stopping myself from hurling pink polka-dot coffee mugs across the kitchen. "I don't recall you saying 'Stella I'm going out to have sex in every possible position with my girlfriend tonight, but don't worry, I've sorted a babysitter'." I hissed, as I frantically rinsed.

"I just meant that if you're going gallivanting off with..."

"Don't you even go there Tom. How dare you suggest that I'm 'gallivanting'! How fucking dare you? Or that I'm putting my daughter second on the list when you've been nailing the office slut for the past year without a thought for your only child!"

"That's right, it's all my fault..."

"Damn right it is!"

"Stella, I just think it's a bit much – introducing another man into her life. Isn't it a bit soon?" Not for the first time in our relationship I was deeply awed by his gift for sheer hypocrisy, which always achieved an incendiary effect when used alongside his complete lack of empathy.

"Get out." I spat.

"Stella..."

"Get out Tom. NOW." He huffed, and gathering his carrier bag of mugs he went off to say goodbye to Grace while I crumpled into a navy-blue heap on the kitchen floor.

Eventually I heard him leave and within a couple of minutes Grace wandered into the room. "What are you doing, Mum?"

"I'm just wiping this mark off the floor sweetie," I said, desperately trying to hide my tears.

"Dad's gone now."

"Yes...er, he'll be back on Friday to pick you up," I looked up and forced a smile, but she wasn't fooled. She nodded, patted me on the head and went back to the relative safety of Miley Cyrus and her double-life as a schoolgirl/pop-star.

Meanwhile I brushed myself off, wiped my eyes and foraged for a pen. According to the latest issue of *Celebrity Psychology*, a ballpoint was better than anger management therapy. You used it to avoid a conflict by inscribing your angry thoughts somewhere on your body. The way it worked was you write the name of the person or issue that's causing you anger and pain and if you began to feel that anger rising you glanced at the written word and apparently it had a deep, calming effect.

I couldn't bring myself to write Bitch Rachel so sitting at the table in my date dress with swollen cheeks and red eyes I wrote, 'bunny boiler' ten times on the inside of my left wrist. I couldn't say it was instant but I felt slightly better and at least it would help prevent me committing a double-murder – I hoped.

24

The Doctor, the Damsel and the Date

Against my better judgement, I decided to go on the date. I'd
been veering between feeling wobbly and furious since my
confrontation with Tom and it took Lizzie to finally persuade
me to go. She was back from Australia for a few weeks and gave
me a pep talk about moving on. Grace also approved, so with
some reluctance I decided to go for it.

I wore the 'date dress', which as far as I could see showed no
signs of the kitchen floor. I also wore some very high, very
expensive black strappy Gina shoes, courtesy of Lizzie who was
going to babysit Grace. Added to my date doubts I couldn't help
but feel that Grace's approval was influenced by the fact that she
got to spend the night with her favourite auntie, eating millions
of E numbers and watching unsuitable DVDs way past her
bedtime.

Jostling for space with inappropriate DVDs, Lizzie's
overflowing overnight bag contained at least one hundredweight
of chocolate and a bag of knitting. The chocolate and DVDs
were nothing new but the knitting needles poking out of the top
surprised me; I couldn't imagine that the woman who'd braced
herself for the ice-cannon in Ibiza would be the same one sitting
in her arm chair knitting and purling.

"It's the latest thing," she said when I asked her. "I've joined
'The Stitchin' and Bitchin' Club' with Al. We are the new
'Knitterati' – it's the woolly way forward honey." Lizzie was the
original fashion victim and if someone told her that Stella

McCartney had taken up dog-handling, Lizzie would be on the back field with an Alsatian and a big whistle before you could say 'down girl.'

"Al's making a lovely long purple cardi for winter and I'm creating a little cashmere number," she continued, opening up her knitting bag and draping a rather luscious mink-coloured half-knitted pashmina round her shoulders. "I'm loving the stitchin' and the bitchin' is a *revelation*. You wouldn't believe the swingers, the affairs, and, yes – the *transvestites* living in our community," she announced loudly, warming to the theme. "Respectable neighbours indulging in afternoon delight and Al says he's scared to go out at night now after hearing the lurid tales of car keys thrown on laminate floors and every man for himself in fishnets."

"I'm impressed with your handiwork," I said, caressing the costly thread and trying to change the subject before Grace enquired about the nature of transvestism or love in the afternoon. Too late: "Mummy," she piped up, "what's Afternoon Delight?"

"It's a sort of dessert," I answered vaguely, crossing my eyes at Lizzie and going back to the softness and safety of cashmere. "Such delicate work Lizzie. I didn't think you could do stuff like that."

She smiled proudly, "It's funny how everyone has a talent. Al's a great swimmer, you're a great cake-maker and I seem to knit like a dream. Talking of your fabulous cakes," added Lizzie, delving into her overnight-bag for extra ciggies, "I hope you've left a little something in Pandora's Box?" She winked hopefully and nodded towards the cake tin.

As it happened I'd just been practicing my pastel macaroons in case scary Sangita ever called. I opened the plastic container and laid two pretty, pistachio discs on a plate. Held together with the softest, most delicate rose-scented buttercream, made with unsalted Normandy butter and sugary pink crystallised rose petals, the macaroons were crispy on the outside with a surprisingly soft centre. The pale green discs complimented the almost pink of the cream which looked and tasted gorgeous.

"Darling, you wouldn't get finer in the salons of Paris," Lizzie enthused, munching away. "They sell macaroons in the French coffee house in Harrods and I'm telling you, these are just as good, if not better. You should be on the phone to Al-Fayed sweetie, or whoever the hell owns the place now." I was glad she approved, I'd been experimenting with the colours, texture and flavours for days and felt I now had something else to add to my growing cake repertoire.

After a quick cup of coffee and more macaroon-sampling with Lizzie and a hug from Grace, I applied lipstick, a cloud of Chanel and left for my first date for many years, feeling very nervous.

I took my time arriving at Bruce's. I didn't want to be too desperate and arrive before Diego so I sauntered down Broad Street which was buzzing, with bare arms on the street and music and aftershave on the air. My chest was fizzy with excitement (and fear) as I tripped past the busy bars, their doors wide open to allow the last of the summer evening to waft in. Anything could happen tonight and that felt scary – but good.

The bar was dimly lit with Australian beer signs in coloured neon lights and as I opened the door to walk in I was met with blackness. It took a few seconds for my eyes to adjust and assuming he was already there waiting, I needed to compose myself quickly. This would be the first time that Diego saw me and if it was love, he would recall this moment for many years so I walked slowly, trying hard not to stagger, with my arms out to steady myself – not a good look on a first date.

Once my eyes had refocused I spotted a man at the bar who I hoped was Diego. He was standing under a lit Foster's kangaroo and I thought *wow* and as he smiled expectantly in my direction I thought *thank you Mother*. Standing against the bar, he looked about six foot (nice), in his early forties (another tick) with shiny brown hair and the sweetest smile (fasten your seatbelts, ladies).

Along with relief that he wasn't one of mother's axe-wielding madmen, I was overcome with nerves that turned my legs and stomach to jelly. As I wobbled towards him on Lizzie's unfamiliar Gina heels I felt the same as I did on my very first date as a chunky fifteen-year old with acne and terminal shyness. It was imperative to walk quickly and keep up the momentum in the heels but as he turned to greet me he was clearly surprised at the speed I was approaching and let out a little yelp as I sailed into him. I think he was slightly winded, but it broke the ice; I blamed the shoes and he laughed.

There was really no need for my nervousness because from that first moment he was just so lovely and warm and smiley. He couldn't do enough for me, helping me with my jacket and ordering drinks while directing me (with a guiding hand on my arm to prevent any more sudden moves) to a seat. Once I was safely deposited with a large glass of red, I asked him about the hospital he was currently working in. "Crazy, crazy, crazy," he said, waving his arms about in a very cute way, obviously bemused by the NHS way of doing things. We laughed about my mother (what's not to find funny?) and after another large glass of wine I was ready to share with him the information that my husband left me for another woman at Christmas.

"She's older than me and some say, much bigger," I lied. I didn't want him to think I was rejected on the grounds that I was too old or too fat. He smiled and nodded enthusiastically. I found him so easy to talk to – and what with the wine and those big, brown understanding eyes, I went into some detail about the break-up (editing turkey violence, I didn't want him to think was unhinged).

"He walked away from us on Christmas Eve – the presents half-wrapped, the carol singers unpaid," I waxed, trying to give this some context and feeling.

He was fascinated. "My heart goes out to you," he said, touching his heart with both hands and then extending them out to me. How cute was *that*?

Regaling him with my life story and reaching for another slurp of red, my sleeve rose slightly to reveal 'bunny boiler' etched in biro on my inner wrist. Spotting it, I nearly choked on my Merlot. I'd freshly applied it earlier during an 'I'm going to kill all Bitch Rachel's bunnies' moment and had meant to scrub it off before the date. I cringed and covered it up but I think it was too late – he looked away, but he'd spotted it. I decided to keep going and tried not to think about it and as Diego smiled and listened I told how Tom and I first got together, our wedding, honeymoon, Grace, even MJ. All the time I was talking and enjoying the wine and the atmosphere I was looking into his lovely big brown eyes. I lost myself in their warmth and twinkle and began to imagine kissing him.

"I'm now planning my own business, making cakes; professionally and personally I need to move on," I stressed, keen to let him now there was a vacancy in my heart.

"Yes, your mother she says your cakes are *mwah*," and with this he made a kissing noise involving his mouth and fingers that I'd defy any woman to resist.

Trying not to be completely distracted by his gorgeous mannerisms and delicious accent, I talked him through Sangita and the cake order. He listened intently throughout showing real interest.

By the time the bar closed I was feeling like I'd got a lot off *my* chest, but still didn't know his second name. I hadn't asked him about his daughter, his life in South America – or even the million-dollar question, 'could you see yourself marrying a blonde Englishwoman with a lot of issues and a weakness for buttercream?' Never mind, I'd save that for our next date. I hoped there would *be* a second date. He must have bought me about six (or was it seven? *eight*?) glasses of wine and I never once offered to go to the bar. What must he have thought of me?

I think I was a bit tipsy when we left because as he walked me towards a taxi I fell off the pavement and the only thing I can clearly remember is sitting in the gutter laughing. Diego offered to help me up but I shouted, "No Tom, I'll be fine," and managed to get up without any help by using the taxi door as a hoist. I couldn't remember what we had arranged for our next date. I wish I hadn't drunk quite so much, I wish I hadn't fallen over – and I *wish* I hadn't called him Tom.

The next day started out as a hangover day and turned into something completely different. I was feeling pretty rough after my hard-drinking date with Diego and had almost given up on Sangita and her diva cakes when I got the call. As soon as I picked up and heard her barking orders, I guessed the news was good.

"Stella. Sangita here. We're looking at a 'yes' on the cakes for Fashionista Tea. I will send all requirements in writing. Will call later. LA is on the other line."

With that, she was gone and I danced round the kitchen. They wanted my fairy cakes and, despite my inexperience, were risking the curvaceous, basque-shaped confection too. For the privilege of creating, nurturing, cajoling and baking these cakes to perfection in record time, the company would pay me a small fortune. I was so happy I just couldn't believe it, after all the bad stuff that had happened. It was about time my luck changed.

I picked up the phone and called Al. He was due to finally fly to Oz the next week and I was dying to tell him the good news about Sangita's call – after all, he was a big part of the pitch. I'd tried his home number about six times, on the seventh, he answered.

"Al I have the most brilliant news," I exploded. "I've got the 'big bun' contract, the one with the 'busty basque'. The big one," I laughed.

"That's fabulous, doll," he said, sounding subdued.

As always, it looked like Al had some bigger event unfolding and he launched straight into "Oh babes, I hate to rain on your parade. I'm so excited for you really, but yesterday – well I had some bad news."

"What is it, Al?" I asked, worried.

"I lost my job, Stel. They fired me."

I was shocked. Al was a great researcher. Yes, he went out on a limb sometimes but as in the case of vicars and tarts he put his finger on the nation's zeitgeist discovering Bernard and Denise in a garden in Rochdale.

"Al, I'm so sorry. Why? What happened?"

"Mary-Jane Robinson is what *happened*," he said, through gritted teeth. "I made the mistake of suggesting some ideas to her about *Barry's Barbie*. As you know, it's always good with a successful series to come up with the next idea pronto and I thought for the next series it would be good to get real people involved. A sort of barbecue *X-Factor*, if you will. We'd call it *Barry's Real Barbie*, do a big cook-out with lots of interesting punters to bounce off Barry then Barry and a couple of celebrity judges would choose the winner."

"That sounds brilliant."

"But yesterday MJ said my ideas for the current programme

weren't strong enough so my contract was not being renewed. Then this morning I hear that all my 'weak' ideas are to be included in the new series – and get this – MJ is credited with every single one of them."

I couldn't believe it – well I could actually. She'd got rid of Al so she could take all the credit for his ideas. Once more the woman had committed an incredible act of injustice in the workplace and was living to tell the tale.

"Al, I don't know what to say. My mum believes in karma and is always saying that if someone does you down an opportunity will present itself to get them back."

"Mmm, it's a nice thought – but sometimes you just have to call it a day," he said dejectedly. "I need to move on anyway. MJ saw me, you and Lizzie as a little group, and she's picking us off one by one. She's threatened by us all and I worry for Lizzie because I reckon she's next. François in Fashion – you know, raging queen, Botox and..."

"Yes, fake tan."

"He says she's an unforgiving bitch and she holds a grudge for years," he added with his usual drama.

"But what about Lizzie? She's due to fly back in a few weeks," I said.

"I know doll. And I think the only reason she's hanging in there at the moment is this rumour that she's having a relationship with Barbecue Barry." Al announced theatrically.

This came as a complete surprise. Lizzie hadn't said anything to me last time I saw her, and we usually shared everything.

"Are you sure, Al? I saw her yesterday and she didn't say anything."

"Well she wouldn't, would she doll? He's married. But rumour has it that MJ daren't get rid of her, or she may lose Barry, her star."

I hung up, feeling a little sad that Lizzie hadn't shared with me but more than anything worried for her. It looked like Lizzie was going to have to watch her back – or she might find herself on the receiving end of one of MJ's poisoned daggers.

25

You're Never Alone with a Box of Coffee Creams

By the following weekend, I was exhausted. Diego hadn't called, but I didn't have time to think about it as I was worried about Lizzie which lead me to think about MJ, then Tom, then Bitch Rachel and I spent the rest of the week in an emotional daze. Grace was with Tom that weekend and I was really looking forward to a leisurely Saturday having my hair done and in the evening having a curry with Lizzie and Al. The plan was that everyone would head back to mine for lots of drinking and talking. However, on Friday night Lizzie called to say she had to work on some new recipes with Barry all weekend. I was a bit disappointed and I could tell that there was definitely more to it than 'recipes'. I just hoped she wasn't being stupid, believing everything he told her like I had with Tom. Lizzie wasn't saying anything because Barry was married and given my feelings at that time for 'the other woman syndrome' I think she was being sensitive.

In truth I was happy if she was happy, however hypocritical that made me. It was unfortunate that the man she loved happened to be married but I wasn't prepared to make judgements on all 'other women', everyone had their reasons – except of course, Bitch Rachel.

On Saturday morning, Tom came to pick up Grace and I barely made eye contact with him. I certainly didn't invite him in for coffee. Since our argument about my date, I had been going out of my way to avoid him.

"I'll have her back in time for her tea on Sunday," he said, standing rather awkwardly on the doorstep.

"Fine," I said, kissing Grace on the top of the head and practically slamming the door in his face.

Once I had watched his car trundle down the drive and turn into the road, I went out almost immediately to the hairdressers. It was a nice day, and once I was in there, I started to relax a little. As I was lapping up Jordan's latest lover in *Hello!* whilst waiting for Jo to finish with her current client, I had a text from Al.

TXT: Sorry Stel, have terrible cold. Staying in bed all day.

I immediately texted him back.

TXT: Shall I come over and feed you hot soup?

Just as Jo was showing her latest client the back of his hair in the mirror, a text pinged back.

TXT: It's OK doll. Seb's being nursemaid. Have a nice night x

I sighed. Since being sacked by MJ, Al had been helping out in Seb's restaurant and things had definitely moved onto the next stage for those two which was great, but I was disappointed not to be seeing him.

Thinking about Al and his partner and Lizzie and hers, I suddenly felt panicked at the idea of spending the night alone, so as Jo started to snip away at my hair and scream intimate details about her colleagues (embarrassingly within earshot) I did some desperate texting. Emma was working for scary Sangita tonight, helping out at an event, so I knew she wasn't free. I trawled through my phone numbers and found Marie, a new friend I'd met at the school gate. We sometimes went for coffee after the morning drop-off. I sent her a 'we haven't caught up 4 ages. R u free tonite?' text. Within seconds, she'd texted me back, reminding me she was away with her husband on a special anniversary weekend (*damn, she'd mentioned that last week and I'd forgotten. Some friend I was*).

I randomly texted a few other people I used to know on my phone list and waited.

"...so then he was practically eating her face!" yelled Jo, just as the hairdryer to the right stopped. I looked up and humoured her with a horrified face and a "gross." I hadn't a clue what she was talking about, I'd almost forgotten she was there. I wished she'd shut up and concentrate on my new look. A black look from a colleague silenced her (momentarily) and she went back to pulling my tresses, as the responses came through. Sophie was in a cottage in Wales spending Saturday night with friends, husbands and children. Gemma was 'going 2 Petit Blanc 4 dinner with nu man' and Kate and Laura had obviously changed their mobiles and not bothered to let me know because I wasn't getting any delivery receipts. I think that said it all, I was now deleted from most of my working friends' lives.

Missing Grace and wishing she wasn't away, I even started to think fondly of how Grace, Tom and I would enjoy a Terry's chocolate orange with *The X Factor* on a Saturday night. *I hope they aren't sharing a chocolate orange with Bitch Rachel tonight*, I thought.

In absolute desperation I texted Fiona, a friend I used to go to college with. I hadn't spoken to her for years but surely she was still unbearable and therefore available? She moved to the Midlands a couple of years ago and threatened to visit so I'd never contacted her in case she turned up. Her text came back within minutes to tell me she was having friends over for dinner and Danny her husband was celebrating his promotion. They'd also got a brand new car, their kids' IQs were through the roof and they'd just bought a property in Spain – all in one text.

I remembered then why I'd avoided her and with one push deleted her from my phone; time was too precious to waste with people like that. Life wasn't a competition about who had the biggest salary, fastest car and brainiest kids. Then I realised, that's what Tom used to say. Finally I was starting to understand him – how ironic was that? And for a nanosecond, I really missed him.

As the dryer whirred in my ears and Jo's chatter merged with the swishing water and the beating music, my eyes started to fill up. In the middle of this busy place full of chattering people and chopping hair, I suddenly felt very, very lonely.

I bought two bars of chocolate and a box of coffee creams on the way home from the hairdresser's. I ate both bars in one go but showed a modicum of restraint by saving the box of coffee creams for later.

I decided to spend Saturday evening working. It wasn't as if I had nothing to do – I needed to make notes, draw up a schedule, play with icing colours and create cake shapes. This was now my business, and I was solely responsible for its success, so I turned the oven on, opened the recipe books and began. I was still feeling nervous and a bit sad, so I put on some music to cheer myself up.

Within minutes I was singing, whisking and piping like my life depended on it. I nibbled and baked, while joining Streisand in several gutsy duets from her *Broadway Album*. I managed to lick buttercream icing and taste heavenly vanilla sponge while doing justice to those tricky Sondheim medleys (I bet even Babs couldn't do that in sync). As I was whipping up a batch of icing I thought about how often I felt like I was constantly on the edge of tears. The hurt and hate and hope were so packed down that it was hard to release my emotions onto the outside world and being on my own had sent them simmering to the surface. A lump formed in my throat as I worked.

However, just half an hour with 'La Streisand' and a mixing bowl and the dam burst. My salty tears began falling into soft caramel and whipped cream, and paddles swirled them into butter, turning the mixture into fluffy yellow clouds. By *Send in the Clowns* my heart had exploded like a bag of flour over everything and I felt a deep, deep calm flood over me. Icing sugar rose from the bowl like magic smoke, rising high into the ceiling and filling every part of me with sweetness. By midnight I was red-eyed with a sore throat from singing and weeping, but strangely happy. I collapsed in a heap, my head resting among the rubble of Rocky Road, snowy pavlova and twenty-four pastel-coloured, polka-dotted handbag cakes.

On Sunday morning, I woke up feeling better than I had in a long time. Last night's session with Barbara had brought everything to the fore and for the first time since Tom left, my heart felt light.

At six o'clock, Tom dropped Grace off and the first thing she said was, "Mummy, have you been OK? You weren't lonely were you?"

She seemed concerned, and I said "Darling, I've had a lovely weekend on my own, and I haven't been lonely at all."

26

Hard Macaroons and Wobbly Handbags

I spent the week toying with hard macaroons and wobbly handbags and felt preparations were going well for my first big event. I still hadn't perfected the finer details of the polka-dots and the handles, though. They looked wonky and whilst homemade was good, some of these looked a little *too* homemade for divas to devour. I was also up to my neck in décolletage and sugar-frosting as I was giving the basque a dry run. I needed it to be more 'fashion as art,' and less 'supermarket Busty-Boobs cake', so I decided to have a dress rehearsal and invited Al, Sebastian and Lizzie round for a tasting.

I phoned Al and Sebastian answered. "Between you and me Stella, Al's still upset about losing his job," he said.

"Well, hopefully a few glasses of wine and a girls' night in will cheer him up?" I suggested.

"Sounds perfect. We'll be around at six."

Lizzie arrived first with a huge Indian takeaway, followed by Al with Sebastian and two bottles of Pinot Grigio on his arm. I couldn't help but think how great they looked together. Al grabbed Sebastian's arm and linked him into the house, balancing the wine between them.

"Sebastian's needed at the restaurant tonight, he's only staying for a quick Pekora," announced Al, "so it's important that we tell our news straight away."

Lizzie and I looked at each other and ushered them in. We all sat down and I started to open a bottle of wine. "Go on then,"

I demanded, "what news?"

"Yes, tell us," urged Lizzie. "You can't just announce that you have news and then just sit there."

Al put his arm round Sebastian and they looked at each other; "We're getting married," he said, looking from Lizzie to me for our reaction.

We were both a bit surprised but I gathered myself together quickly. "Wonderful news!" I said, rushing to hug them both.

"I suppose it might seem a bit soon," said Al "But when you know, you know." He was beaming from ear to ear.

"You have to stay for more than just a starter," I said to Sebastian, kissing him on the cheek. "We need to make sure your intentions are honourable."

"Oh I do hope not. Come and tell Auntie Lizzie all about it," squealed Lizzie, grabbing him by the arm and patting the seat next to her.

We talked about a date for the wedding and convinced Sebastian to stay and share some of the curry with us before heading off to work. I went into the kitchen to plate up the takeaway and he followed me through to help.

"Al's a very special person," I ventured, spooning steamy, aromatic curry onto warmed plates.

"Ha, yes I know," he said, smiling "and it's now my job to make sure he's always happy," he smiled. Then Al walked in with Grace and I saw Sebastian's face light up. I think my hormones must have been at it again because my eyes filled up with tears and I had to wipe them discreetly with a tea towel.

Sebastian found knives and forks and Grace and Al moved blocks of sugarpaste and bowls to sit by the warmth of the oven and eat at the kitchen table. In between mouthfuls of chicken tikka and poppadoms we shared snippets of Grace's day at school and the drama of Greek Tragedy proportions at the monkey-bars during playtime. Emma had fallen out with

Gemma because she was going off with Ruby and Katie took umbrage when no-one would let her play, then Gemma pushed Emma playing tig and they'd all ended up in the headmaster's office.

"Sounds just like a day at Media World," laughed Al.

Sebastian reluctantly left about 9pm, hugging us all and leaving Lizzie, Al and I to catch up on our own gossip now that Grace was in bed. Lizzie kicked things off nicely with; "Al, is there any chance that Sebastian would go straight? Because I want him for myself." Al smiled like a proud parent.

"He's obviously crazy about you," I said, swallowing hard and trying not to let my hormones get the better of me again.

Lizzie was still picking at the remains of lamb tikka and rice, and whilst there was a lull I thought it a good opportunity to ask about her love life.

"So, Al's in lurve," I started, "what about you? I heard you and Barry?" She stopped eating and looked straight ahead, avoiding my eyes.

"What *about* me and Barry?" she went back to her lamb but I wasn't being fobbed off, so I tried again, "Lizzie I'm your friend and I know he's married, but it doesn't mean you can't talk to me about him."

"I saw a picture of him in *The Mail on Sunday Review* with his wife and kids. 'Barbecue Barry and his Brood,'" added Al, "I nearly died. I mean the man behaves like a teenager, shags everything that moves, yet here he is playing 'Dad'." I tried to catch Al's eye. This wasn't the time to be doing the Al thing of tactless, insensitive friend.

Lizzie put her fork down and her head in her hands. "Oh God, I don't know what to do. I can't help how I feel." I abandoned my food and put my arm round her.

"Lizzie, we're not judging you," I said, giving him another 'look', "we just want you to be happy, as long as you don't get hurt." Lizzie took a big gulp of wine.

"He's just so kind and so funny," she said. "What worries me the most is – I don't even feel guilty that he's someone else's husband. I know I'm being selfish, but he's everything. He's a wonderful lover and Stella, you'll understand this...he makes me feel young, and thin and gorgeous."

"I'd like one of those," I laughed, in an attempt to lighten things a little.

"People are saying it won't last," Lizzie continued, "I know he's had affairs before, but this is different. He really *does* love me."

"He and Mischa live separate lives," she continued. "I know I sound like a naïve young girl, but I trust him."

"Trust's a big word," I said. I didn't mean to make her feel bad, but she looked hurt. I felt guilty forcing out a confession from her then appearing to throw it back in her face but it was too soon for her to trust this guy. Al stepped in, for once showing some tact and finally realising it was time to move on to something lighter and safer.

"So Stella, when we spoke on the phone earlier you mentioned handbag disasters? Share," he demanded. "I need to see." I got up and retrieved my fairy-cake tin, opened it and reluctantly revealed one of the misshapen, wonky handbags. "Darling, it looks like something Mrs Overall would have served up in *Acorn Antiques*," he squealed, putting his hand over his mouth in horror.

"It's not that bad, is it?" I asked, beginning to feel a little panicky and studying the wonky handbag close up.

"My darling," he squealed, snatching it from my hand. "It's hardly a fashion statement in cake," he huffed, putting it on the table like it was a used handkerchief. I opened the tin and laid out a few more little cakes for inspection, hoping that he might see a redeeming feature in at least one. He scrutinised more closely, stroking the icing and looking like he had a bad smell under his nose. "Mmm, I'm not saying they're bad, but I haven't seen anything this ugly since Britney shaved her head." (He'd been watching *Ugly Betty* again.)

"Ooh Al...you're just too sensitive. Please tell it like it is," Lizzie said sarcastically, tinkering with one of the handbags.

"I know they're not great but I used my own handbag as a template – it's hard to make something that's immediately recognisable," I said feeling slightly defensive; I'd worked hard on those.

Al then suddenly clutched at the table with one hand, stifling a scream with the other. Lizzie and I looked at him in alarm. "That's it! You know what we need to do? We don't want generic – we need *iconic*," he announced. "We need an *iconic* handbag. That way it's immediately recognisable."

At this point, like fate had intervened, Lizzie had grasped her box of ciggies from her *iconic* Chanel handbag and abandoned it on the table, moving outside to the patio for a fag. Al and I looked at her bag, then each other at the same time.

"Perfect," yelped Al, lunging at Lizzie's bag and inspecting it close up like a precious diamond. He laid it on the table and began drawing the bag on a piece of kitchen paper. We were very excited now and in between puffs of smoke, Lizzie kept popping her head back round the French windows, barking instructions at him.

"Don't just think, 'fashion statement', think quantities, think simplicity." She was starting to sound like scary Sangita, but she wasn't stopping. "Think 500 identical cakes – and think about the timeframe," she added over her shoulder.

"Lizzie, think putting fag out and coming back in and shutting door, the place is full of moths!" I complained. Lizzie stuck out her tongue, threw her fag to the floor, twizzled it round under her *iconic* Gucci boot and waltzed back in.

"Look at this baby," said Al, passing me the kitchen paper revealing the outline of a small but perfectly formed Chanel handbag. It was a simple shape, with the trademark iconic entwined Cs and *very* Chanel gold-chain strap.

Al then took an abandoned lump of sponge cake from the kitchen worktop and played with it, shaping and twisting the gold foil from my most recent packet of Rolos into a chain strap and a C. It was like magic: suddenly the cake had 'the look.'

"I remember doing some wall art with Justin and Colin for one of our art bedrooms on *Home Dreams*," Lizzie said. "They had this great idea to use Quality Street wrappers on a gold background creating an effect like Klimt's *The Kiss*. It was truly amazing."

"Oh yes. You wouldn't believe what those boys can do with a bit of sticky-backed plastic and a sweet wrapper," Al added, winking at me. Lizzie picked up the cake and held it by the chain, marvelling at Al's handiwork.

"Come on," she said, getting up and washing her hands. "Let's make a fresh batch and we'll let the cake fairy show us his own brand of alchemy – how to turn base cake into pure Chanel handbag."

It was tough trying to get everything just right, from the marzipan Manolos to the Chanel handbags with gold-leaf chains and glossy black icing. As well as the handbags, I was having some problems getting the basque right (wobbly boobs, cream ruffles not adhering to cleavage, etc).

"Babes, can I just show you what I would do with that," said Al, putting down his coffee and straightening the boobs. He then went on to fix the cream ruffles and created the best white chocolate flounces I'd ever seen.

"Al, will you marry *me*?" I said, gazing at perfect, creamy décolletage.

"I love you darling but I can't marry you – I would find it

just impossible to lie back and think of England," Al laughed.

"Well I think you're wasted on the dole. Why don't you come and join me in my hopeless paradise of wannabe cake-maker to the stars." I said. Though it was said with a smile, the minute the idea came out of my mouth I knew it would be brilliant for Al and me to work together, officially. I held my breath and watched his reaction. His eyes widened as he considered my offer.

"Are you serious, Stella?"

"Al, it would be brilliant. You are creative, you have a business brain and you're one of my best friends. I'd love it. Of course, there might not be much money in it to start with." After all, this was the first big order we'd had – who was to say there'd be any more?

Al became quite emotional. "Stella, I'd be delighted. I'd love to be your partner."

"That settles it!" cried Lizzie. "You two will be great together. It's the perfect match!"

That night, Al stayed over and after Lizzie left we got out his iPod. He had over 300 upbeat tunes to keep us going and we started work singing at the top of our voices. We whisked cream, moulded gold leaf and created life-sized breasts from semicircles of sponge. I for one was completely engrossed in sponge cleavage and sang along full tilt to George Michael.

As George was giving his all on *Wake Me Up Before You Go-Go* Al suddenly screamed, "What was it Lizzie called me earlier?" He was clapping his hands together and jumping up and down on the spot.

"What? The Cake Fairy?" I said. He grinned and I knew just what he was thinking.

"How about it, for the name of our business?!" He said.

"Yes, yes I love it," I squealed, then he stopped jumping up and down and looked serious.

"Do you think it's a bit camp?" he asked, biting his lip, head to one side.

"Not at all," I lied, and went back to slapping cream on my cleavage.

27

Naked Fairy Cakes and Flouncing Fashion Queens

A week later, the Fashionista Feast was almost upon us. By Thursday, Al and I were reeling from the sheer magnitude of work we'd done and the amount we still had to do. In the final 48 hours, we filled the kitchen with enormous piles of flour bags, butter, sugar and tins. You could barely turn around without falling over a sack of something or knocking a cake tin onto the floor. I really would have to think about this in the future. With Al's help and my double oven we could just about do it but if we ever got a bigger order we'd need a bigger kitchen and probably more help.

I'd worked long and hard before, but the cake thing was physical. It involved standing continuously, whisking incessantly and working nocturnally. When 50 cakes were in the oven, another 50 sat naked on the kitchen table waiting for their sugary coats of adornment and another 50 sat dressed and waiting to be packaged. There was also shopping, planning and not forgetting the full-on singing throughout which was done with feeling and had given us both headaches, hoarse voices and sore throats.

I was even managing to handle Sangita; probably because I'd worked with the most evil, stressed and warped managers in the world, she was a walk in the park. When she screamed words like 'deadlines', 'schedules' and 'NOW,' I just calmly agreed with everything she said and answered with her favourite words; 'yes' 'OK' and 'that's fine'. She always called when I was running late, in the middle of something very delicate or needing to turn the oven down. Instead of screaming what I wanted to say ('*If you get off the bloody phone I can get back to doing it*') I just managed my feelings, remembered that it was my business and said 'really?' and 'thanks for that'.

Throughout the whole week, Grace had been wonderful. In the evenings she sorted through all the crystallised rose petals and gold leaf so we could 'dress' the fairy cakes as soon as they were iced and before they hardened. Now more flower-power than vampire, Grace had come through her gothic phase of black lipstick and leather cuffs since her father had left taking his punk record collection. Every cloud had a silver lining.

By Thursday, we were tired, tearful and exhausted but nearly ready for our first big event. We manically worked into the night and at about 2am, Sebastian arrived with dinner. He came in looking fresh and handsome, despite the late hour. He picked his way over bags, avoided trays of cake and cleared a space on the table. Looking at Al, he said, "Hello beautiful."

I rolled my eyes and shouted, "Enough! You're making me want to vomit."

Sebastian smiled and began hunting around in my cupboards for plates. As Al and I put the finishing touches to a batch of handbags, Sebastian served us up some beautiful French food from his restaurant. "Here you go people," he said, placing the food in front of us. "The finest Sebastian's has to offer – enjoy!"

Al and I gratefully wolfed down the delicious garlic chicken (with little toasts to spread the soft, hot garlic cloves across). This was served with the lightest duchesse potatoes and followed by the best chocolate mousse I'd ever tasted. Sebastian rolled up his sleeves and unloaded kilos of icing sugar and paste, dozens of eggs and several sheets of edible gold from his van; he had been to his catering suppliers earlier in the day and bought the goods at a discounted rate.

"Thanks so much, Sebastian," I said, through a mouthful of hot chicken. "You're a real lifesaver."

He flashed me a smile. "No problem. Al, I'll see you at home later." He blew Al a kiss and disappeared quietly out of the door. Then Al and I got back to work. We whisked, blended, baked and tasted later and later into the night (or should I say, earlier and earlier into the morning). It was wonderful and exhausting.

At 5am on Friday morning, we finally finished the Vivienne Westwood basque which was a triumph. The creamy ruffles were magnificent, draped across the left breast and dotted with huge, wet, scarlet cherries, the red ribbon icing tied in pretty bows all the way down. Al created a black lace-effect from the finest feathery, bitter-chocolate icing and designed the Westwood trademark bustle with the precision and fine-tuning of an aircraft engineer. Thanks to Al's cake engineering nothing would droop or fall off, regardless of cloggy climate or flouncing fashion queens.

"Stella, I think you need to start making notes," Al suddenly said, sitting back and admiring the 'installation'.

"What do you mean 'notes'?"

"Well, we are both using your ideas straight from your head when it comes to recipes and – if you wanted a holiday and weren't here well..."

"Or if I died," I said pulling a face.

"Too early for drama," said the original drama queen; "but you really need to start writing your recipes down properly – like in a book."

"Ooh yes, like Nigella – mmm I like that idea."

"It's not a chance for you to swish around the kitchen like Nigella love – it's about being organised and writing

EVERYTHING down. OK?"

"Ok...but if anyone can swish around a kitchen it's you my sweet." I grimaced at him and blew a kiss.

Grace came down in her pyjamas at around 6am as Al and I were having a break and a well-earned cup of tea. The house was still quiet and the early morning light streamed in through the kitchen window. I watched as Grace got out three bowls, cereal and milk and placed them all carefully on the table. She looked up and smiled at me, watching her. "What?"

"Nothing," I smiled back. "I was just thinking how you've changed and how the pink flower in your hair looks so much better than the fake tattoo skulls used to."

"I think you've really grown up," commented Al. "You've had a tough time sweetie, but you are turning into a lovely young lady." He was right. When Grace was little and I worked long hours, I'd bribe her with presents and sweets, rarely saying no to any of her requests. She'd become spoilt and selfish, only thinking about the next gift or treat. It wasn't her fault; she was a product of two, very busy parents who were working too hard and gradually falling out of love with each other.

Al put his head on the worktop and closed his eyes. The phone rang. Al jolted, but didn't wake.

"Stella. Erm, it's me, Tom," he announced, quietly.

"Yes?" I said, frostily, still smarting from the Diego rebuke.

"I was just phoning to say I'll pick Grace up at 7am tomorrow as I know you've got a busy day," he offered.

"Thanks," I said, in a clipped voice.

"Look, Stella, I'm sorry." He said. "I shouldn't have said what I did about you and the doctor. The truth is, things aren't so good with me and Ra...well, anyway, I just overreacted."

I was surprised and, I have to say, rather pleased. So things weren't going too well with the 'good sort' then? What a shame.

"That's OK Tom," I said, magnanimously. "I decided he wasn't good enough for me anyway." A small lie, but never mind. I hung up the phone feeling relieved. It would make things easier when he picked up Grace, at least. And maybe, just maybe, things would get easier between us, too.

On Saturday morning, after another frenzy of work, everything was ready for our first big gig and nothing had been left to chance. The cream had been kept in the fridge and the chocolate icing stored away from radiators and when the Vivienne Westwood life-size basque was finally lowered into the rented van, along with 300 marzipan Manolos and 500 sponge Chanel handbags I wept with joy and relief.

As we waved the van off, Al and I smiled nervously at each other and Sebastian appeared in the doorway with a bottle of pink Champagne.

"Congratulations both of you – this is The Cake Fairy's first event and we must celebrate," he said, popping the Champagne and filling three glasses. The pink bubbles tasted good on my tongue, but in my tummy I felt bubbles of fear and anticipation. We had a lot riding on this, emotionally and professionally. We'd worked so very hard and invested so much time, money and love. The success of the Fashionista Tea Party was the only thing standing between me and the Job Centre. I wasn't religious but as I sipped Champagne in my icing and flour-covered kitchen, I prayed that the divas would dump their mineral water and fags to devour our fashion fairy cakes with gusto.

Al and I had drunk the best part of the bottle when my mobile rang.

"Stella? Sangita."

"Oh hi, the cakes are all on their way – we're not late, are we?"

"Tea Party – come if you like – some spare tickets on the

door for you, 8pm tonight."

I put the phone down and Al was beside himself with excitement; "Stel, we HAVE to go," he said.

Sebastian smiled, "Mmm, I've always wanted to watch supermodels at play. I can probably get cover at the restaurant and drive you there."

"Yes, let's *all* go and we can see those skinny bitches chomping on couture cakes – then spewing them right back up," laughed Al.

I had mixed feelings about being present for the actual party. What if no-one liked the cakes and it was a big flop? On the other hand, I was as keen as Al and Seb to observe the beautiful people and had a twisted desire to put myself in the very vulnerable situation of finding out for myself if the cakes had passed the test. After two sleepless nights and half a bottle of Champagne I was feeling more than a little light-headed so I said "Why not? Let's go. Grace is with Tom this weekend and who knows – it might be fun."

By the evening I was too nervous to worry about what to wear so I found something at the back of my wardrobe that covered everything and consisted of two hundred yards of black jersey. Wrapping a colourful scarf round my neck, adding long glass earrings and slicking 'Red for Bed' across my lips I made a vain attempt at 'bohemian'.

Seb drove us at breakneck speed to London and Al chatted animatedly whilst I sat in the back with nausea rising up my throat.

"I feel sick," I said, like a child, opening the window and gulping cold air like water.

"Yes, it might help if you slowed down, Seb," Al smacked him playfully on the arm.

"Sorry Stel, I'll try to slow down but you know I'm just Jeremy Clarkson in a gay man's body," he laughed.

"I still may need to vomit," I announced weakly.

"Ohh, mind our posh frocks," warned Al. "I don't want Kate spotting me in crushed-plum and puke."

By the time we arrived at the hotel I was really, really nervous, feeling very sick and trembling with fear.

The event had been designed around the small fashion collections being showcased by new designers and the Fashionista Afternoon Tea was what Sangita had described as: 'a spectacular fusion of Laura Ashley florals and pastels with an oriental flavour of Willow Pattern'.

We'd arrived early because we wanted the opportunity to oversee the cake-setting and walking into the enormous, high-ceilinged room we all gasped at the sheer loveliness of it all. Pastel walls and delicately painted murals of oriental tea pots in pinks, greens and florals adorned the walls, with lots of tiny tables in different styles and colours dotted around the room. Ornate gold chairs sat at small shiny tables next to wrought-iron chairs with embroidered silk cushions. The tables were dressed in pure linen and lace – and all of afternoon tea was here, the air warm and heavy with rich Orange Pekoe and fragrant Earl Grey. Even the waitresses looked stunning in high heels, elegant fitted dresses in Willow Pattern and tiny white cotton pinafores tied at the back in huge bows.

White platters of crustless sandwiches sat under cellophane and were placed next to mountains of pastel macaroons. Tiny, vibrantly-coloured wraps with fillings I'd only dreamed of were brought in and laid side by side near our glossy handbags and baby-pink, polka-dot confections. The salty tinge of savoury, mixing with the icing was sweet on the back of my throat and took me back to birthday parties as a child. I was suddenly eight-years old and waiting for everyone to arrive.

It wasn't long before our beautiful sanctuary was invaded by voices, the loudest of which was Sangita's ordering the silent, beautiful waitresses to open bottles and pour tea. Plates began to clatter quietly, glasses clinking elegantly as Champagne and Earl Grey were poured into fine crystal or delicate china. Steam and bubbles rose along with the chatter, which started low and reached a clanging, laughing climax as more guests arrived. The fashion divas arrived en masse and were a sight to behold with impossibly long limbs and porcelain skin. Despite their thinness they all alighted on our cakes, enthusing about the look and the taste unaware that the creators were within earshot and glowing with pride. 'Ooh, these are daahling!', 'I'm eating a whole one!' and 'OMG, these cakes are DIVINE!'

"I feel like I shouldn't be here. Like they're talking about us," I whispered behind my hand to Al.

"Don't be intimidated, they're just fat girls in thin bodies," he breathed, never taking his eyes from the celestial creatures. He's so right, I thought, watching them lick perfect lips and stare in awe at the cakes while moving elegantly around the room like sleek, shiny racehorses.

Suddenly, a loud voice pierced our ethereal moment: "You two are stars, stars!" It was Sangita, and I think she was actually smiling. She seemed so pleased that I thought she might hug me, but after an awkward moment where we both faced each other – she obviously thought better of it.

"These cakes are better than anything I've ever seen. And everyone is talking about the basque. Vivienne is overcome. It is a work of art." Then, without another word, she was off.

"I'll call," she said over her shoulder, sweeping across the room waving and shouting; "Kate, Naomi... try the DARLING cakes."

Staying at our model-watching vantage point, I could see that Al's theory about some models not keeping their food in their tiny tummies might be right. The orgasmic consumption of each irresistible sweet treat appeared to be followed by a quick exit to the loo. I liked to think that these beautiful girls were retouching their lip gloss but Al clearly had other ideas. Al and Sebastian had been researching fashionista files on the internet and were a mine of model information. When I reached for a micro-sized smoked salmon bite Al held up both hands and screamed, 'canapé embargo', which apparently meant, 'don't eat too many calories.' It seemed, in the fashion world, food was merely there to be visually admired. "It's an aesthetic experience to be enjoyed by the eye and not the gob," Al pronounced, while Seb advised; "Just rise above it all and think thin."

Of course I didn't and the smoked salmon tasted wonderful and salty and sharp, washed down with prickly, cold Cristal – pure heaven on the tongue. For once I was glad that I wasn't a supermodel who had to make do with a leaf of rocket and a fag behind the kitchen bins. So I chewed on delicious, crustless sandwiches and cakes whilst looking on in awe at the lean-limbed bodies swishing and strutting past. As the towering beauties sashayed straight off the catwalk and into the party, I suddenly became aware of a not-so-super model approaching our table. It was none other than Mary-Jane Robinson, wearing a tight-fitting white trouser-suit, her twisted smile growing bigger as she came nearer to our table.

"Fuck," I said, nodding my eyes in her direction. "Don't look now Al, but MJ's here, and she's coming over." Of course he turned round and looked straight at her and as I got up to leave, she pounced on me, grabbing my arm.

"Stella, how are you?" she gushed.

"Fine thanks," I said, unsmiling.

"You made these cakes, didn't you?" she gestured towards the magnificent cakes that Al and I were so proud of. "I'm so glad you've found something you can do. I think it's great when people can use their domestic talents to make their living." She took a tiny, frigid bite of cake and shuddered. "Oh dear, back to the drawing board I think," she said turning up her lip and wrapping the beautiful, nibbled cake in a napkin. She screwed it up, crushing the cake, all the time staring directly at me.

"Are you finding it hard to swallow, MJ?" I smiled.

"How dare you!" started Al and my heart sank. He had jumped up and was standing chest-to-chest with MJ.

"Al, Kate Moss wants to speak to us about her next birthday bash," I lied, grabbing him by the arm and dragging him away.

"But Stella, how can you let her..." Al said, as I swept him through the room.

"Look," I whispered as we walked away, "do you want to risk throwing our business down the toilet? She'd love to cause a row and ruin everything. Imagine Sangita's face if she discovered her cake-makers, brawling with guests on the fashionista floor like dogs."

He nodded: "But oooh, she makes my blood boil!"

"There's a time and a place," Seb said, joining us and handing Al a glass of Champagne. A bit shaken, I urged Al to carry on enjoying the evening and to put thoughts of MJ from his mind. I needed to take my own advice because I was conjuring up those old images of a mangled MJ – this time, face-first in the canapés.

I am a complete label whore when it came to luxury, and MJ was soon a distant memory when a waitress came round with beautiful goodie bags. Thanking her profusely, I leapt with undignified haste onto the lace bag and immediately lighted on a special-edition bottle of Chanel perfume, a Zandra-Rhodes miniature teapot, a willow patterned silk scarf and a voucher for afternoon tea for two at the Wolseley. Al and Seb peeked in theirs, and watched amused as I lovingly caressed each gorgeous little goodie plundered from the Willow-Pattern tissue paper.

"You are such a Goodie-Bag Hag", Al laughed at me and rushed off with Seb to find the bag lady so they could ask for another one to take home for Grace.

Alone at the table, I continued ferreting around in the bag, sipping my Champagne and gazing about me when, through the tangle of long-limbed lovelies I saw the second surprise guest of the day walking headlong towards me. This was a much more welcome one, with a smile that filled my tummy with sparklers. Immediately pushing away the half-eaten sandwiches and cake I held my stomach and chins in and with the confidence of someone who had just downed half a bottle of good Champagne, crossed my legs and flashed a full-on smile.

"Stella! How are you? Where've you been for the last twenty years?"

"Is it Dave?" I asked, knowing full well it was. And my heart flounced like a fashionista as Dave Kennedy embraced me.

Dave and I had worked together at a local radio station early in my career and I'd had a massive crush on him. I would have heart palpitations and breathlessness every time I saw him. He was good looking, with wavy brown hair, hazel eyes and an amazing crinkly smile and I'd believed it was a matter of time before things moved to the next stage. I'd dropped endless hints, engineered situations he'd find impossible to resist and one desperate night as he chastely kissed me goodnight I had even politely enquired if he was gay. He assured me he wasn't, kissed me on the head, missing the point completely and we carried on in the same vein for another six months. We grew apart as friends when I fell in love with Tom but over the years I'd thought about Dave and had sometimes wondered what might have been.

Feeling the familiar breathlessness and tight chest (even after all these years), I smiled up at him and felt myself becoming the vivacious, laugh-a-minute, flirty girl I used to be when he was around.

"I can't believe that after all this time you're here tonight and as gorgeous as ever," I laughed, throwing my head back, hoping this might simultaneously hold in my double chin and defy gravity with the wrinkles.

"I've thought about you a lot over the years," he said, placing a familiar arm around my shoulder. "I heard you were working at Media World and called not long ago, actually, to ask if I could speak to you, but they said you'd left and there wasn't a contact number for you." *Hmm, I wonder who that was*, I thought. Of course there'd been a contact number for me – but I bet MJ's instructions had been clear on that one.

"I'm still in telly too," he went on. "In fact, I'm here tonight because we're planning to film a documentary about the reality of life as a catwalk model and I'm planning the programme and meeting people."

"How exciting, and all those gorgeous women," I gushed.

"I've never been one for the skinny types," he smiled, "but the major channels love the idea of a doco about them. There are about three companies here tonight who are gagging to get hold of *Fashion Weak* – spelt W-E-A-K."

Maybe that was what MJ was doing here.

We sat down and sipped more Champagne and he filled me in on the last twenty years. As I'd suspected (and maybe secretly hoped), Dave was divorced. After three years of marriage and a son called Max, his wife Toni had turned out to be gay and left him for another woman (who loved cats and hated Dave). Max was now six and Dave saw him on alternate weekends; I made sure to ask *him* lots of questions, after the Diego disaster.

"Are you still married to that, er, cameraman?" he asked, pretending not to remember Tom's name.

"He's called Tom and no, we're not together anymore," I said. I still found it hard to talk about my life because the Tom stuff still hurt and I wasn't so sure about laying myself bare to an old flame just yet. However, as we talked, I felt his concern, his humour, his gentleness – and I had drunk quite a bit of Champagne, so the floodgates opened. I told him all about being bullied at work, about my life as a desperate housewife, how Tom had left me for someone else so I'd concussed him with a turkey and all the other stuff in between. He laughed in all the right places, showing those beautiful white teeth, his eyes as crinkly and twinkly as they always were. We talked about life twenty years ago and giggled about some of the people we'd known and the things we'd done. After about an hour, one of his researchers came up to him and indicated to Dave that they should leave.

"Stella, can we get together sometime for a drink, or dinner?" he said, with his head to one side, smiling.

Fireworks exploded in my chest and I nodded, basking in the warmth of his smile. For the first time in ages, I felt sooo good, until...

"Hi Dave. Why, I didn't realise you and the lovely Stella were friends," it was MJ, on the prowl again.

"Oh, you two know each other?" said Dave, completely unaware that the skinny, bullying super-bitch I'd just been telling him about was now standing in front of us.

"Look MJ, I'm sorry about the documentary but you can't blame me wanting to take it straight to ITV, I mean, no hard feelings, eh?" Dave said, holding out his hand for her to shake. She took it limply and turned to me. I was intrigued. So, MJ had been chasing Dave's fashion doc, had she? I smiled triumphantly, glaring at her from Dave's side like the First Lady.

"Just remember, pillow talk is dangerous, Stella," she smirked, the saccharine of her smile giving way to the usual bitter aftertaste.

Dave's eyes didn't leave mine and as she walked away he

said, puzzled; "I'm not quite sure what that was about. What did she mean about pillow talk?"

"Oh she probably thinks I'm behind your decision to reject her offer for the fashion doc."

"But I hadn't even met you again when..."

"Oh I know that, Dave. Who cares what she thinks! She's the one I was telling you about, who made my life hell but she can't touch me now," I said with confidence. He squeezed my arm and looked into my eyes and I realised that not even MJ could ruin my mood. The tea party was a success, Sangita was over the moon and it looked like I might have a date.

28

Nude Espresso and Sizzling Pheromones

We finally left the Fashonista's Tea Party at about 2am. Seb had booked us into a cheap hotel near the party. I slipped gratefully between the starchy sheets and slept like the dead. After three days with very little sleep and lots of Champagne I was very glad to have a bit of a lie-in before breakfast on Sunday morning. I woke up still on a high, from the wonderful comments about the cakes – then I remembered running into Dave Kennedy and felt a warm jolt in my stomach; it had been lovely to see him again. I wondered if he would ever call, or if after Alex and Diego it was going to be three strikes and then out.

I didn't have to wonder for long. He called me at about 12pm just as Al, Sebastian and I were sipping coffee in the Nude Espresso in Spitalfields (the boys were hoping for naked baristas while I wanted good coffee and homemade brownies. Sadly for them, only *my* wish was granted).

Dave asked if I'd like to get together for a late lunch and suggested an Italian restaurant near Leicester Square. After another round of coffees, I left Al and Sebastian at the tube station and tried to navigate on my own, which didn't go too well. I arrived late and flustered, having got horribly lost. The night before was beginning to feel unreal after all the years in between and I wasn't even sure if he'd actually be there.

I needn't have worried. As I walked into the garlic and basil-scented warmth, I saw him sitting at a table gazing at his mobile. Unobserved, I was able to rewind twenty years and drink him in all over again. The eyes were even twinklier than the night before, accentuated by a crinkling around the eyelids that along with the greying temples made him incredibly attractive. I was surprised at the way he made me feel after all this time and gathering my courage I lifted my head and swept over to his table. "I'm sorry I'm late. I, er, couldn't find the restaurant," I stammered. With no Champagne courage, I was suddenly feeling very tongue-tied. I was twenty-two again and as he looked up and saw me his face broke into a beautiful smile.

"Stella. Glad you're finally here. I thought I'd already lost you again," he joked. He rose from his chair and gave me a firm, delicious hug. I sat down, bathing in his eyes – the most amazing hazel-flecked eyes – and when he smiled his teeth were incredibly white like someone in a toothpaste ad. He was so very, very cute. I could feel my tummy turning to warm, melted chocolate.

I nibbled on a breadstick, avoiding his stare and feeling like Celia Johnson in *Brief Encounter*. Suddenly the waiter arrived, fussing around us like a bluebottle. "Drink, Signora?" We reluctantly pulled away from each other and I ordered a glass of red.

"It's so nice to see you, after all this time," I said, sipping daintily on warm Chianti.

"And you haven't changed," he replied as enormous, unmanageable menus were thrust in our faces by the stalking waiter, who announced dramatically "My name is Pietro. I am at your service, Signor," and bowed with a flourish. Once we'd ordered and Pietro had eventually bustled off, we both leaned forward across the table and I attempted eye contact around the tower of breadsticks. Dave dipped his head to the side of the bread skyscraper enquiringly, and we both started giggling.

I detected an air of confidence in him that hadn't been there before and I thought my heart was going to stop when he reached into his upper pocket, put on a pair of round glasses and read the wine list. "Shall we get a bottle of Barolo?" he asked, looking over the rims in an authoritative fashion.

"Ooh. Get you! Dave Kennedy, wine connoisseur," I giggled.

"One of my many talents," he smiled, looking straight at me over the glasses. I was a sucker for a man in glasses – they particularly suited Dave, making him look intelligent and bookish.

Pietro returned with the Barolo, theatrically pouring the wine for Dave to taste (being a woman I apparently don't have taste buds). Once he moved on, Dave sipped his wine and said: "Well, Stella. It looks like last night was a big success for you – so where do you go from here?"

I looked at him coyly. "Well, Dave" I started, "that just depends." He raised his eyebrows and smiled. We continued chatting, about nothing and everything. Things were different now, I was grown up with a sophisticated line in small-talk and a fledgling business while Dave now wore glasses and knew about wine. It felt so good sitting across the table from him, I could almost feel the air sizzling with an undercurrent of unsated passion – then I realised it was Pietro at our elbows with the 'Sicilian Sizzler'.

I barely touched my lunch. My chest was heavy and my tummy filled with warm gloop. "I'm not very hungry," I said, fiddling with my food. "I'm feeling very 'Posh Spice' regarding the pasta."

He chuckled. "You're so funny, Stella," he said, "you always made me laugh."

The wine was mellow, the lighting soft, apparently I was hilarious and it just felt so right. The heat from the 'Sicillian Sizzler' and something to do with pheromones suddenly urged me to lean across the table. *I'm a big girl now* I thought and suddenly I felt strong enough to make my desires known. I made the move and leaned into him, narrowly avoiding my breasts brushing against the food. He was also moving towards me and I suddenly felt his warm, red-wine breath on my lips as his mouth moved against mine, softly at first, then stronger, his tongue pushing slowly into my mouth. I pulled away gently – things were going very fast and I wasn't sure that here, with Pietro's constant attentions, was the place to start ripping each other's clothes off.

I opened my eyes, pulling away and sitting back in my chair. I was horrified to discover my breasts had submerged in the as-yet uneaten Sizzler. The sexual tension dispersed temporarily as we pawed at my greasy, tomato-covered boobs with our napkins, both laughing but a little embarrassed. It was starting to look like bad porn by the time Pietro returned with more napkins, lightly swabbing me down and enquiring of my still-full plate; "Had enough, Signora?"

"Not yet," I answered, looking straight at Dave, who gave me a secret smile and ordered another bottle.

"Mmm, I'm suddenly hungry and this is delicious," I said, not taking my eyes from his as I picked up my fork and plunged it into the dish, my tongue slowly savouring the sweet tang of tomato. Even in my heightened state of sexual arousal I fully appreciated how the backcloth of black, Mediterranean olives complimented the garlic and chilli kick and my groans were genuinely culinary.

Dave took a big gulp of wine and I was flattered to note, desperately tried to avert his eyes. "I'll get the bill," he said, clearing his throat and pulling himself together. I smiled, wondering, *what happens now?*

Dave had it covered. "Stella, there's a little hotel I sometimes stay at when I'm on business here – it's out of the way and..." I looked straight at him. No point in feigning surprise or reluctance now – I'd already behaved like a porn star on Viagra. And so what – we were both divorced with afternoon childcare.

"That sounds great," I said, feeling like a woman of the world and not even giving a second thought to how I'd look naked in daylight.

Once he'd paid the bill, we got up from the table and walked out of the dark restaurant together. Stepping out onto the pavement we were almost blinded by the bright, shimmering heat of the afternoon. My legs suddenly felt shaky from the wine and he grabbed my hand, leading me across the road and through the winding streets. We pushed through the throng, passing several theatres and posters but I didn't take in any of it.

We arrived at the hotel and headed for the lift. "I feel like we should be in school, it's like playing truant," I said. As the doors closed we were suddenly alone together for the first time and I looked up into his eyes. He took my face in both his hands started to kiss me again, gently pushing me into the lift wall, my handbag dropping to the floor, his hips pushing against mine.

Once at the room we fumbled with the bloody card-key (they never work) and fell into the room, giggling. He was still kissing me as he pulled at the straps and slipped the dress from my shoulders. It fell to the ground, floral chiffon swirling in a pool on the boutique, tiled floor. This was quickly followed by matching M&S lingerie from their cheap yet chic Parisian Collection...

After the storm we lay there, side by side on the cool tiles surrounded by discarded clothes and both slightly stunned from all the hot passion and red wine.

"I always knew you'd be good in bed," he said, turning to look at me with a big grin.

"That was the floor. You don't actually know what I'm like in bed – yet," I rolled over, resting my head on his chest. It felt good to hold a man again.

"Give me five minutes and we'll do the bed test then," he said, stroking my hair. "It's a tough job, but someone's gotta do it."

I reached out and poked him on the nose. "I'm not sure. I'll get back to you on that," I joked. He grabbed my arms and we rolled around the floor pretending to fight (yes – *me* rolling around the floor of a Soho hotel room on a Wednesday afternoon after sex with a man. What had I become?!).

After more kissing and giggling I slowly stood up, gathering my clothes from around the floor. As I bent down to pick up my dress I brushed against him and his hand caught me gently by the wrist.

"I think before the bed test I need to re-examine your floor technique," he said pulling me down again.

29

Strictly Cupcakes

Things with Dave continued in a whirlwind. We spent wonderful evenings in fancy restaurants and, when Grace was staying with Tom, these were often followed by equally wonderful nights of passion. It was like we were just taking up where we'd left off twenty years before and I felt like that young, excited woman again. I flushed easily, bought new underwear and agonised over the right shade of lipstick for the first time in years. As the nights began to get shorter, Dave and I cosied up together and I started to really relax around him. The only thing that was missing from all this girlie joy was that Lizzie wasn't around to share it because she was filming in Oz with Big Barry. I sent the odd text, but she was busy and I was happy to wait because I wanted the pleasure of telling her all the details over a few glasses of wine when she got back.

The best thing of all was that I was starting to feel young again. Being with Dave meant revisiting those days when I had plans for a future with so much life ahead of me that anything was possible. He had such a great imagination and ambition; he wanted to make bigger, better programmes and start his own TV company.

"I'll build up a company, retire and sell the business for a song. We'll move abroad, somewhere warm. Or buy an old farmhouse by the sea," he said one afternoon as I iced cakes for Grace's school fête.

"I don't want to live anywhere too remote," I said, thinking about Tom's Scottish isle and holding a red-iced cake parcel up to the light for scrutiny. "I need a Marks & Spencer or a Waitrose within spitting distance. That will be written into my contract." I loved imagining a future with Dave but the only slight problem was business. Since our debut in London, The Cake Fairy had received steady orders but nothing on the scale of the Fashionista event, and Al and I weren't saying it but we were starting to get a bit worried about how long we could survive on lots of small, local orders.

"What else will be written into your contract?" he asked, with that twinkle.

"Well, Grace is at her friend's, sleeping over tonight..." I said.

"Oh yeah?" he answered absently, reading the *Guardian*.

I feigned a theatrical yawn; "And I think sex on demand would be a good thing to have in a contract," I said provocatively.

"Come here," he said, throwing the paper to the floor. He gently pushed me back onto the kitchen table, where all thoughts of school fete fairy cakes left me. Here, among the icing sugar and papercases, we performed a dramatic reconstruction of the sex scene in *The Postman Always Rings Twice*.

Dave was making coffee and I was just putting my clothes back on and contemplating a post-coital scone, when the doorbell rang. "Oh no," I said, laughing and quickly pulling my sweater over my head as Dave buttoned himself up.

"I'll go, you straighten your hair and make like you're icing," he said, smiling to himself and walking out of the kitchen. I heard the door open and lots of squealing.

Arriving in the kitchen in a hysterical frenzy, Al screamed from the doorway: "Doll, I've had a call from Sangita. She wants us to provide all the cakes for the launch of the new series of

Strictly Come Dancing. If we make this rock, it could lead to all sorts of work; not only does this company cater for BBC events, they also organise red-carpet premières, doll – in LA! This time next year we could be crafting cupcakes for Brangelina in La-La Land!"

"Oh wow!" I said, sitting down and taking this in.

"Two sugars please my love," Al instructed Dave. Dave dutifully sugared Al's coffee, handed me mine, then after a quick slurp of his own said he'd get off.

"That's right, love me and leave me," I joked, kissing him and slapping him on the bum.

Just as Al and I were contemplating what this big order would involve, the phone rang. "Sangita here," she was as terse as ever.

"Oh Sangita, we're so excited about the order – Al's just told me."

"Right then, let's talk business."

"Er, ok. I'll get a pen," I said, rolling my eyes at Al.

"OK? We're talking shiny floor and show-class dancers."

"I've got it, shiny floor, show-class," I repeated, writing it down.

"And not tacky, Stella."

"Not tacky, yes."

"And 500 dance-themed fairy cakes. Clear?"

"Yep, thanks I..."

"This is at TVC. Shep Bush. Big job. If you do it well, it's future work for you. I'll send details on email, no time now. Bye."

I spent the rest of the evening planning various cakes around the featured dances and Al demonstrated them, humming the tunes and singing instructions while I worked out the aesthetics and prosthetics. Later, when the restaurant had closed the multitalented Sebastian came over and was soon knee-deep in computers and costings. The email from Sangita with all the details had finally arrived at about 8pm and once I'd read it I had to restrain Al, who was beside himself with delight. It turned out that the cakes were for the glitzy, red-carpet event where the celebrities would meet their dance partners for the first time, which was filmed well before the show began in the autumn. And they wanted all the celebrities depicted on the big ballroom-dance cake – which meant we would have to know who they were before nearly anyone else in the country.

"This is AMAZING doll, wait until François hears about this!" Al squealed, jumping around the room.

"Al, Sangita says we'll have to sign non-disclosure agreements, so no gossiping, OK?" I said.

"Yes, yes I know, it's just so exciting!"

I smiled. I was excited too and the Cake Fairy might well be dancing her way to success.

30

Barry's Smokin' Barbie

Up to our necks in dancing cupcakes Al and I were busy for a couple of weeks with our colossal order and though this was great business, I hadn't had much of a chance to see Dave so I gave him a call. I knew he'd been busy too but I didn't want this relationship to suffer like mine and Tom's had through spending too long apart. I had some free time coming up at the weekend and I thought it would be the perfect opportunity to make some time for each other.

"We could go to the coast or somewhere," I suggested, remembering the seaside cottage idea. "Tom has Grace at the weekend so we could have some time alone together."

"Sorry Stella. I'm so busy with this new project, I can't spare the time," he sighed.

"I know we've both been up against it recently," I said, "but we really need to make some time for each other."

"I just have to get through this," he replied, like he was talking about an operation or something. I put the phone down feeling a little uneasy. I was also very disappointed; I thought he'd be as keen as I was to get together and more importantly – I'd missed him.

Instead I invited Al, Seb and Lizzie over for a special dinner, to celebrate Lizzie's (albeit fleeting) return from Australia. She'd flown in a couple of days before and I couldn't wait to see her. Al and Seb had been so supportive with all the Cake Fairy stuff and I wanted to hear all about MJ from Lizzie. Apparently, MJ had been out there, 'working' with the team and I knew she'd have loads of gossip for us to bitch about regarding the Queen of Mean.

Grace and I went into Birmingham to buy gifts for these friends who had helped me through what had probably been the toughest time of my life. We decided to shop in the curvaceous Selfridges, a silver-studded spaceship juxtaposed with the neighbouring, gothic St Martin's Church in Birmingham city centre. "Mum, it looks like it's covered in thousands of silver Smarties," Grace yelled, running across the paving and down the stone steps. I smiled, wondering how I could achieve the same look on a cake and planning a bulk buy of Smarties and edible glitter.

Once inside, we fingered luxury fabrics and wafted ourselves in profanely-priced perfume. We finally chose fluorescent pink swimming trunks for Al, a pair of blue for Seb and a beautiful, jewelled lighter for Lizzie. I also allowed Grace the best present of all: to have her ears pierced. She'd wanted this since she was five years old and I'd held out until now. As the gun pinged in her ear, I felt a ping in my heart; my baby was growing up.

After the ear-piercing we went back into Selfridges for coffee. "Cappuccino please, Mum," she said, sauntering over to a table and making like a world-weary eighteen-year old. She'd never had coffee before but seeing as I'd just paid someone to punch two holes into her ears, what harm could a frothy coffee do?

Al and Lizzie arrived about 8 o'clock; unfortunately Seb's chef had called in sick so he had to work. We all drank pink Aussie sparkly, to celebrate Lizzie's return from Oz and Grace showed off her new ears and joined in with pink lemonade.

After Grace had gone to bed, Al and I tried to prise out what was happening with Lizzie and Barry. "I've been dying to know how everything's going with Barry and his smokin' barbie – and you never text me back," Al wailed. "What's going on?"

"Oh it's just been tough out there, with MJ breathing down everyone's necks," she said, rolling her eyes at the thought of it all. "It's been a gruelling shoot and I've been tied up in edits since I came back. Sorry I haven't been able to text much."

"How's it all going?" said Al, carefully.

"Fine," she replied, tersely. "We've finished editing the first show, which will première to the industry soon. There are a few more bits to film so I'll have to fly back tomorrow, for about a week. But on the whole, we're done. Thank God."

"It's a long way to go just for a week, doll," said Al, watching her.

"I know," she fired back. "But I can't leave MJ to wrap on her own, can I? She's incompetent." Al and I looked at each other. I had a feeling that there was something else she wasn't telling us and Al and I both suspected things weren't going well with her and Barry.

"Has his wife found out?" Al asked, straight to the point as usual.

"Found out what?" she said. Lizzie wasn't one to easily share every aspect of her personal life but as her best friends, she'd always give us a big hint and in the end we'd tease it out of her. This time was different and I was intrigued and just a little worried.

"We're your friends Lizzie. We know you and Barry are together, *were* together? What's going on?" I said, touching her arm.

"Stella, trust me, you don't want to know," she snapped. "I'm sorry, but he's just not worth talking about," she answered firmly, taking a big gulp of wine and draining her glass. "Now let's open another bottle and talk about someone who is worth talking about. How's delicious Dave?"

"It's going well I think – I'm behaving like a bloody teenager – what's wrong with me?" I said.

"Sounds like Dave's doing you the world of good," she said, reaching for her wine. 'You go, girl!'

"The only problem is, he won't talk about work or his family," I said, "and sometimes when we talk on the phone he seems...I don't know, distant."

"Uh-oh! Here we go again," said Al, filling our glasses.

"What's that supposed to mean?" I asked.

"I hope we're not in Tom territory. Dave hasn't suddenly found some bit of stuff and lost interest already has he?"

"Nicely put, Al" Lizzie said, incredulously. "Dave's probably busy working all the time Stel – in fact I saw him at Media World when I popped in yesterday."

"Did you? Well, he's really busy with this new project – I think it's about MI5 – all very 'hush, hush'. He was probably using the editing facilities," I confirmed.

"Mmm. But it is a bit odd that he's using Media World, given that he rejected MJ's advances on the fashion doc," Al said.

"Yes. I must admit that *is* a bit stupid. If he's not careful, MJ will torture the editor to try and find out about his secret project then knowing her, she'll blow it wide open just for revenge," I joked.

"Oh yes. Old MJ never, *ever* forgives – or forgets," Lizzie added chillingly. We all looked at each other and pulled a face.

"Ooh Lizzie, you're scaring me now," said Al, "let's open another bottle."

The evening continued and we teased each other and swapped safer gossip while eating my homemade crab pâté followed by chicken risotto and tangy lemon mousse, washed down with Amaretto coffees. Frustratingly, Lizzie wasn't going to elaborate and provide any real gossip we could get our teeth into about our old enemy. Thinking about it, I'd go as far as to say Lizzie had almost appeared uncomfortable earlier when we'd bitched about the Queen of Mean. Her comment about MJ not forgiving or forgetting was loaded and I wondered what she meant. I just hoped she hadn't let her guard down while they were in Oz.

The following morning I was working hard on my 'American Smooth' dance cakes (red velvet with cream-cheese frosting and a sprinkling of showbiz glitter) when Mum rang. She was banging on about Facebook again. Whenever she was bored Mum loved to surf the net and Facebook was now her latest craze.

"It's better than that eBay – and Twatter," she said, then went on to talk about her great Facebook friends, the Hi Hi tribe, who she had stayed with on her last jaunt. "They base their philosophy on a strong belief in things happening in threes," she went on, while I put her on loudspeaker and whisked.

"In their culture, everything has an animal to represent it – hence the Monkey of Revenge. Oh and fate is an elephant."

I thought she might have been a bit confused because she'd said fate was a rhino last week. I tried to say goodbye when she suddenly moved on from elephants of fate to ask; "What happened with Diego? You know, Diego the doctor?"

"Yes I know who you mean. I've heard exactly nothing, Mother," I said, bored now and wanting to get on with my life. "He never called me again. Sorry, I thought I'd told you."

There were a few seconds silence where I suspected Mum was doing that séance thing, of trying to channel spirits in an attempt to remember.

"Did you make him a cake?" she asked. If she hadn't been my mother I'd have just turned the phone off.

"No Mum, I *didn't* make him a cake," I said in monotone sticking my finger in buttery, sweet batter and slurping hard.

"He didn't stick around long enough for me to make him a cake. What *is* this with you and Diego and cake? I'm really very busy." I said, desperately looking for an escape.

"I gave him your card so he could call you about the cake. You know, for his daughter's birthday? Don't you remember dear? Katerina, I think she was called."

I started to feel very warm, too warm in fact. "Mum, hang on a second. You said he was going to call me to ask me out on a date?" I almost whispered, dry-mouthed, willing this to be so.

"Oh. Has he asked you out on a date?"

"No."

"That's a shame. It was her birthday, Katerina – he wanted a cake for her birthday. I told him how you make wonderful cakes."

I suddenly felt the ground move beneath me. Either a) we were having an earthquake or b) I had the wrong end of a messy stick and had made a complete fool of myself in a faux-Australian bar in front of a very eligible South-American doctor.

"Mum, have you seen him at the hospital recently?" I wheezed, losing my voice.

"No dear. I took Beryl with her leg last week, but no sign. Such a nice chap, over here to be with his daughter. Don't know what's happened to him."

I thought I might.

"Sorry Mum. Lovely to chat but I've really got to go, the other phone's ringing." I said shakily and turned her off.

Once I'd sat down with a hot cup of coffee and a piece of warm ginger sponge, the sweet spicyness offset by sharp lemon frosting, I calmly retraced the evening in my mind. "Did he at any time mention cake?" I asked myself out loud, realising the truth as I said it. Fuck! He did – he was obsessed with it, but I had thought that was because he was obsessed with me!

I called Al and he shrieked in horror when I told him what

had happened. Later he and Sebastian turned up wanting all the gory details about my horrible discovery, clutching their stomachs and falling around the kitchen as they laughed hysterically.

"All that poor man wanted to do was order his only daughter's birthday cake but every time he tried to bring it up, I talked over him with too much information about my tragic life-story." I wailed, putting the kettle on and cutting them some sponge.

"He must have been very surprised when you arranged to meet in a rowdy wine bar covered in kangaroo pelts and corked hats," laughed Seb.

"Surreal I know but I thought we were on a date! As he was a guest in my country, I took the lead." I said, defending myself.

"I meet an Engleesh lady to order my Katerina's birthday cake," started Seb. "She wouldn't speak of cake but drinks wine and talks of husband and some *beetch* person. She swears a lot, falls out of bar and lies in gutter until taxi driver takes her home," he continued, on a roll.

"Well, now we know why he didn't call," screamed Al, red-faced and breathless from laughing.

"And the writing on my wrist," I sighed, head now in my hands.

"Oh doll," Al yelped, through fresh hysteria and reminded Seb that I was going through my 'change your life with a ballpoint pen' phase. He couldn't tell him all the details for laughing, and he and Sebastian were now holding each other up.

"Babes, he thought he was there to order a cake and within half an hour she's lurching towards him, lips puckered and 'bunny boiler' scratched on her wrist in biro," he screamed. I thought they would both need resuscitating, they laughed so hard.

"Christ," I said, shaking my head in disbelief and utter

embarrassment.

"He must think you're a bloody savage," concluded Al in his usual, sensitive way.

I didn't know what to do – I should probably contact Diego but it would mean trying to get the number from Mother and confessing to her what happened. I couldn't go there yet; it was too embarrassing and way too confusing. Knowing Mum, she'd inadvertently publish the whole bloody story on Facebook, or 'Twatter' it everywhere. The woman was a cyber-menace.

Once Al and Seb had left, I tried to put the whole incident from my mind. Poor Diego might be scarred from our encounter and not look at another woman for a while but in time he'd move on. I decided to take the philosophical approach and know that it was a sign that I was never meant to be with Diego.

Tom called later in the afternoon. It turned out he had to fly to Australia later that evening with Lizzie. "It's all very dramatic," he said. "The cameraman on *Barry's Barbie* has been bitten by a crocodile and rushed to hospital." Tom was a freelancer so Lizzie had called him to step in. "It's really serious," he said. "It doesn't look good for whoever's in charge – someone's head will roll."

"I hope Lizzie's head's safe. Because I guarantee it won't be MJ's," I spat. Tom knew all about our recent dealings with MJ and I think he disliked her almost as much as I did.

"MJ went out on the pretext of making sure everything went smoothly and it's her responsibility – she *has* to take the rap. Even *she* can't squirm her way out of this one," he stated. I wasn't so sure. Al had told me recently that she is being touted for a big TV award and her career is going from strength to strength.

"I dread working with her, but I can't afford to turn it down, there's no work around. I'm really sorry I won't be able to see Grace this weekend. I miss her so much," Tom continued. I got the feeling he was saying he missed me too, but ignored the subtext and assured him that Grace would understand and stay with him as soon as she could.

"Look after Lizzie. She's at the mercy of MJ..." I added, but he'd already gone.

Lizzie called me soon after. "Sweetie, I hope you don't mind that I asked Tom to come out to Oz. After I got the call I knew I needed to find someone quickly, he's a freelancer and he *is* one of the best. I need someone I can rely on and well, he may not be the most reliable husband, but he's certainly a great cameraman."

Tom was paying for Grace and we needed the money, and this type of contract could be very lucrative so I was fine with it. I was also glad because even though Lizzie was my friend, I knew he'd look after her.

"Not a problem Lizzie, hope you'll be OK out there. What happened?" I asked, but she was gone.

I put the phone down, worried. I didn't like to think of her in the jaws of the Elephant (or Rhino?) of Fate. I just hoped Tom got there before the Monkey of Revenge turned up.

31

Dinner at Nando's not
Breakfast at Tiffany's

Dave was late for another date. It was raining and I was soaked by the time he arrived outside the shopping precinct. He appeared through a curtain of cold, lashing water, his raincoat turned up at the collar and hair plastered to his head. "Stella, I'm so sorry I'm late. It's work, I..."

"It doesn't matter. Let's just find somewhere warm and dry," I said, smiling. "This bucket-of-water-over-the-head-look just isn't working for me." Suddenly overcome with pleasure at seeing him, I grabbed his hand and he squeezed mine as we ran through the cobbled backstreets of Worcester, splashing through puddles, stopping briefly to gaze urgently at menus in windows and eventually finding a Nando's.

Glad of dry sanctuary, we walked into the dimly-lit, pseudo-Portugese restaurant and were efficiently escorted to a seat. Dave smiled apologetically as he studied the menu. "I'm sorry Stella, but I can't do a late one tonight. Have to be up early tomorrow for a vital recce, it's really important."

My stomach lurched. "Oh, I hoped we'd be able to spend some time together," I ventured. "I wondered if you'd be coming home with me. Grace is on a sleepover and..."

"Sorry Stella, but I can't. I just have to finish this project and then I promise I'll be all yours again," he said. For the first time with Dave, I felt a little twinge of anger.

"I'm not sure you've *ever* been all mine, Dave," I said, feeling like I was being put on hold.

He reached his hand across the table and looked straight into my eyes; "Stel, I am all yours and I care about you, but I'm not ready for a big commitment yet. I love spending time with you and I want to make this work but I am tied up with work and Max...I need to spend some time with my son Stella"

"I understand," I said, trying to be reasonable, "but apart from Max, it would be nice to be put first *sometimes*."

He let go of my hand. "I don't need any pressure at the moment, I just need you to support me. This project is really important for my career and I can't fuck it up."

"I'd love to support you Dave, but you don't tell me anything."

"I hate it when you do this." He pulled his hand away, his face coloured up.

"You hate it when I do what?"

"Look, there's heavy shit going down at the moment and if I'm not careful I could lose the contract."

"You should have told me," I said brushing the back of his arm with my hand. I felt like a vet, calming a wounded animal, he was pink and clearly quite stressed. "*Tell* me all about it," I continued.

"I can't tell you, can I, because it's fucking *secret*," he hissed, jabbing me with the words and moving his arm away quickly.

I sat back, numbed by his reaction and the waitress saw her cue to wander over and take our order. I was smarting from his attack and I wanted to leave; this wasn't how Dave Kennedy was supposed to act. When the waitress left with our subdued list of food he leaned forward, his head down, running his hands through his hair and avoiding making eye contact.

"Stel, I'm so sorry. I just feel very isolated at the moment."

"I understand, I suppose it's just the nature of your work," I said, sipping my Diet Coke.

For the rest of the evening we talked about the past, which always seemed a safe harbour and was far enough away from any sparks of reality. Then Dave and I parted with a chaste kiss outside Nando's and went our separate ways.

"I'll call you tomorrow Stel," he promised, not even offering to walk me to my car. I knew as I rushed to the car park in the freezing cold that he *would* call tomorrow but was beginning to wonder whether he *wanted* to, or if it was something he felt he should do.

When I arrived home alone I realised it would be morning in Australia – so I called Lizzie long-distance. She'd only just arrived and had the crocodile nightmare to deal with, but I knew she wouldn't mind.

I told her about the evening; "It seems like he's disengaged and only with me out of duty. It's almost like he's on autopilot. He suddenly doesn't listen or pay attention, like he's a robot who's been programmed to do what a human would do. There's no passion or spontaneity or feeling at the moment."

"You know Stel, they're all pretty similar. I reckon the 'right one' is a myth. It's not about finding the one you love the most – it's about finding the one that annoys you the least," she laughed.

"Yeah. I can see that in time Dave would join the compulsory male chorus, telling me I was too old to wear pink bunny-ears or combat-trousers."

"Mmm, and he'd watch endless TV, clutching the remote control like a pacemaker for hours on end."

"But Lizzie, I wanted candlelit suppers and twinkling eyes and shared jokes. Life with Dave should be perfect. It should be *South Pacific, Breakfast at Tiffany's* and *From Here to Eternity*." I lamented.

"Dream on, girlfriend," she said, "most men have never seen

Breakfast at Tiffany's and if they have, they're on Al's bus. I think
you need to stop thinking Hollywood and start thinking
Coronation Street. Or just enjoy the sex and forget the rest."

Part of me was beginning to wish we'd never met again and
I'd just kept Dave Kennedy as a youthful crush, preserved in the
jewellery box in my head. That way I could have taken him out
and held him to the light every now and then to enjoy his shiny
perfection. I suddenly felt achingly empty and attempted to
soothe the ache by baking a batch of 'better in the morning'
banana cakes. Made from soporific, overripe bananas which
helped you sleep, the cream-cheese and peanut butter provided
protein repair while the pinch of salt replaced what was lost
from the shedding of tears. After about three of these delicious
sweet, salty, creamy confections, I was feeling more
philosophical.

The next morning, Grace inadvertently let slip some gossip as
we got ready to go to the park. It was gloriously sunny and she
was talking about when she'd been to the ice-rink with her dad a
few weeks before.

"Will you come next time Mum?" she asked. I knew what
she was up to – she'd been watching *The Parent Trap* again and
imagining she could get Tom and I back together with a Lindsay
Lohan-style cunning plan, without the identical twin.

"Oh sweetie, I can't skate," I said.

"Rachel can." she stopped, suddenly, and looked at me.

"It's OK, sweetie," I said, stroking her hair, "it's nice that
Rachel came with you and Dad."

I felt a hot rush of anger rising through my face, *so, bloody
Rachel was there too was she*?

Then, as kids do – Grace chatted about new skates and
dropped another bombshell that she'd been sitting on for weeks

halfway through the story. "I'm glad she's gone." This was said in passing, like it was of no consequence.

"Who's gone? Rachel? You mean she's not living with Daddy now?" I said, trying hard not to pounce and fire questions.

"No. Dad said they aren't friends anymore and she's gone to live somewhere else," she said, looking up at me for a reaction.

"Oh dear, that's a shame," I said, aiming for responsible-role-model-mummy and resisting a deep urge to jump up and down shouting 'Yess! Ding dong, the bitch is dead!'

I was still feeling smug later that day when I met Al and Seb at the tailors, to help pick out their suits for the wedding which was approaching fast. Having decided to get married, neither of them could see the point in delaying it and Al was already getting very excited. As he crooned over various shades of blue and pouted in front of the mirror, I told him of Grace's revelation: "I know it's not mature or sophisticated, but I'm delighted to know that Tom and the tart have split. I'm over him, I think...but I still can't stand the thought of him with *her*," I said.

"It's cause for celebration," announced Al and he snatched up the glass of fizz he'd been given when we arrived. "Let's chink to her demise." Al, Sebastian and I chinked glasses. (Mine was actually a plastic cup of water, but the thought was there.)

"Stella, there's something Seb and I wanted to talk to you about," said Al, smiling.

"OK."

"We wondered...well, we wondered if you'd be our 'best woman'. You and Lizzie have been amazing to us and we'd love to have you both and – well it would mean a lot to us," he finished

"Oh Al, I don't know what to say. I'd be honoured!" I managed, before my eyes filled up and I had to find a tissue.

"That colour is wonderful, Al," said Sebastian, sensing my collapse and changing the subject.

"Yes it is." Said Al, holding the sample up against himself. "Almost as wonderful as the thought of Bitch Rachel alone in a bedsit," he laughed.

32

Panic on the Streets of Worcester

I baked a spectacular St Clement's cake with dried oranges and lemons the following Monday whilst Grace slept peacefully in bed. It was a treat to myself, before I got stuck into the final stages of our *Strictly* order, the biggest and most important order we'd had so far. If we provided exactly what they wanted on time then we could be looking at a secure baking future for The Cake Fairy. The timing was going to be very tight but with all hands on deck I was sure we could finish everything in time for the event on the following Saturday. Al arrived early and we unloaded several huge bags of flour from the boot, dragging them up the drive and into the kitchen. "All good exercise," Al shouted as we sweated and staggered to and from the car. "They drop...10 pounds a week...on *The Biggest Loser*...doing weights like this...doll," he panted, trying to convince himself as much as me.

"Yes...but they haven't...just eaten...a whole St Clement's cake...have they?" I panted back with straining limbs and dripping sweat.

We were creaming tons of flour into tons of sugar when Sebastian arrived to help. "You two should be finalising your wedding preparations now. Don't you have tailor's appointments?" I said, sifting flour from a great height into the creamy batter.

"This is too important not to be here," Al said. "Even my love has to get into the queue behind *Strictly*."

The three of us spent all morning working to schedule, making basic mixes for the huge centrepiece ballroom cake and all the smaller fairy cakes. The top of the big cake would be covered in extra shiny, super smooth brown chocolate so it looked just like the polished dance floor and Al was creating (with fondant and bare hands) each dancer and their celebrity partner, in mid-step.

Our dance-themed fairy cakes were all planned. There was the 'Cha Cha', which was chocolate sponge infused with a hint of chilli and adorned in shiny, chocolate buttercream ruffles and red spangles, and the 'Foxtrot', a delicate vanilla sponge clad in pearls and blue, silk-like icing to represent the swish of the gown. Finally the 'American Smooth', my red-velvet cake with cream-cheese frosting was dressed in glitter and infused with a kick of lime zest, a symbol of the exciting moves this dance brought to basic ballroom steps. It was going to take us several days, but we were on target and everything was going well.

"Why don't you two take the afternoon off," I suggested when we stopped for lunch. "I can start the salsa without you and I shall foxtrot alone. Go and have a nice lunch and spend the afternoon, sorting things out for the wedding. Go on," I made a shooing gesture.

After a little bit of: 'we couldn't' then 'are you sure?' they agreed and set off. I grabbed some lunch and was just about to embark on icing the first of the 500 dancing cakes when the phone rang.

"Stella. We have a problem." This was followed by silence. It was Sangita.

"What?" I started to sweat.

"An incriminating email, Stella."

"Sangita, what is it? What does it say?"

"Very damaging Stella, libellous in fact, if not true." By now I was almost hyperventilating. "I'll read it shall I?" she said.

"Yesss! Please." *Why does everyone I know play out the suspense instead of getting straight to the point? I'm surrounded by bloody drama-queens.*

"Dear Madam," she started, "it has come to my attention that you are involved in a new business venture involving the procurement of cakes for corporate events, establishments and individuals. I feel it's my duty to inform you that this 'business' is being operated from a domestic kitchen and as such, contravenes Food Safety Regulations. I have informed the Environmental Health and Food Standards Agency of this clear breach of hygiene and food preparation laws."

"What the...?"

"It's an anonymous email, but whoever they are it looks like they are in possession of relevant information. Is this true?"

I was stunned. Who would do this and *why*?

"Stella, I'm not going to ask you whether this is true or not. I'm sure you have all the paperwork and won't let me down. It would be such a shame if you did. Just remember we are potentially about to sign a huge contract with one of my regular clients, an events company that only work with the best – and this could ruin everything. You need to sort it asap, or I will have to go somewhere else. I will need all the regulation paperwork from Food Standards by 5pm today Stella – OK?"

The phone was banged down before I could respond and in my shocked state I wasn't sure what to say anyway. All the long days and nights of hard work and building a reputation, not to mention a solid customer-base and money to live on; it suddenly all felt so fragile. The majority of our orders, and certainly all the big ones, came through Sangita. That one email had the potential to destroy us. It was 12pm and I needed everything in place by 5pm – I wasn't sure if that was even possible, and I only had five hours.

I really didn't want to call Al, he'd be about to down a large carbonara while gazing at Seb across lunchtime candlelight. Besides, he'd turn it into a Broadway production with dry-ice and dancing girls and I didn't have the time for all that. I called Dave instead, hoping he would know what to say.

"Dave, you won't believe what's happened," I started.

"Hi Stel. What's going on?" I explained about the email.

"I'd planned to hire larger commercial premises as soon as we had more orders and could afford it – but now it looks like we may have lost everything, Dave," I was now in tears, "I...don't...don't know what to do."

"Mmm...that sounds awful. I don't know what to say. Erm, I'm a bit tied up actually. Is there a website?"

"A website?" I sobbed. "For what?"

"I er...Sorry, I mean something that will tell you what to do."

"No Dave, there isn't a 'www your business is about to go bust because of some vindictive bastard dot com'. I thought it might be nice to talk to a real person, who might just care."

"Look Stel, I do care. It's just that I'm really busy at the moment, I've got something important to deal with."

"Don't worry Dave, my livelihood, my *life* isn't as important as your work, this can wait," I spat angrily.

"Oh good, I thought so," he answered, completely missing the sarcasm. I slammed the phone down and called Lizzie, who would have literally just landed from her last stint in Australia. I didn't even ask her about the crocodile attack, or Tom, I just spilled out the conversation with Sangita.

"Oh Stella, that's scary," she said, sounding genuinely shaken.

"I'm so upset I don't know where to start."

"But who? Why? Oh well, no use wasting time thinking about it. You need to get onto an estate agent that rents out commercial properties and view them immediately. You can't sit on this honey, get on the phone today. Surely in these hard times, there will be somewhere available." Unlike Dave, she had bothered to spend several seconds offering advice so I took it. I logged on to my laptop, which was sitting on the floury table surface next to the mocha cake which was inviting me to take a slice. Hastily scanning the colourful websites of estate agents, I made a note of properties that looked vaguely promising, all the time thinking about the anonymous email.

I had to let Al know, so I called him as I looked but he had taken me at my word and switched his mobile off. Just after I'd left him a message, I saw a 'reasonably-priced office rental with kitchen' and jotted down the number. Then I had a quick look on the council website to see if I there was any chance of getting my own kitchen accredited. It seemed that it might be possible, but that 'preparing food in domestic premises' had lots of hygiene implications and there were multiple forms and possibly inspections. I could take a Food Hygiene test online which I would do later but in the meantime, my best option was to find somewhere already accredited – and fast.

I made a call to a Mr Smooth, of Smooth Operators Estate Agents, who offered 'light and airy prestigious office space in a newly-refurbished listed building of excellent structure and quality'.

"Is there a big kitchen? It's kitchen space I need." I stressed, drooping at the thought of paying for unnecessary office space.

I was in a complete panic, so when Mr Smooth (real name Nigel) said, "The property would be perfect for your requirements; you need to view as soon as possible though because we have several interested parties. I'm available in half an hour," I leapt in the car and head down the M5 towards Worcester, where salvation in a suit would hopefully be waiting.

Arriving in the city centre I parked the car and ran through the high street, arriving at Worcester Guildhall, our arranged meeting place. Walking through the iron gates I noticed the stone Queen Anne adorning the entrance. She was staring at me, obviously not convinced this was the best use of my limited time. And as Mr Smooth slid towards me in full three-piece suit, with slicked grey hair and a dickie bow – I reckoned she had a point.

"Mrs Weston, I presume," he slimed, predictably, reaching out a limp, oily palm for me to shake.

"I'm tight for time," I said, shaking the wet fish, trying to be polite and at the same time making moving gestures in the desperate hope he would move his arse as quickly as possible. "I need to see the property immediately because this is a business emergency. I also have to pick my daughter up from school at 3.30."

We 'strolled' through the streets towards the Cathedral area, Mr Smooth pointing out various points of interest like I was a bloody American looking for Shakespeare, or Jesus. "It's a little-known fact that Worcester Cathedral has a history of organs dating back to 1417," he prattled pointlessly. I smiled and broke into a power-walk, in the hope he'd get the message, but still he made like a wannabe tour guide.

"In 672, Worcester became the centre of five new dioceses," he marvelled. He went on to cover The Benedictine Rule and the Danes in some detail but enough was enough and just as he embarked on a new diatribe involving the Norman Conquest of Worcester, I shot him a look of pure hate, which silenced him.

By the time we reached the property in the shadow of Worcester Cathedral and only metres from the Swan packed river Severn, I was feeling nauseous.

"Here we are," he announced, trying to get the key in the lock. I stood behind impatiently, almost shoving him through the door as all sense of dignity washed away in the panic of losing my business and leaving Grace alone outside school, prey to God-knows-what.

"Oh dear...did I leave the correct key in my office-drawer," he pondered. I was about to force open the door with his head when he suddenly discovered the key 'hilariously' hiding in the folds of his suit.

As the door opened on the 'light and airy prestigious space in a newly-refurbished listed building of excellent structure and quality' I was elated. The kitchen was a perfect square, about 30 feet by 30 feet with the most amazing huge, flat worktops that would be wonderful for icing. Three enormous ovens sat proudly against the wall under shelves and storage space to die for.

"How much?" I said, almost panting with desire.

"Well it will work out at approximately eight hundred pounds a month," smiled Mr Smooth, who I now wanted to kiss with gratitude and delight.

"OK. That's fine," I said, feeling a little faint, but believing that we could get the orders to cover this. "I'll need to start moving my stuff in straight away," I started. "There's so much equipment I'll need to hire a van, but I'll pay you up front so..."

"Oh dear, didn't they explain when you called?" He said, kindly. "The property is still in use I'm afraid, it belongs to a bakery and they can't give it up until September, at the earliest."

"This is ridiculous!" I almost shouted. "I asked to view available property and I can't wait that long. Don't you understand? *I have less than two hours*."

Desperate not to lose money in these tough times, Mr Smooth paled and made a couple of frantic calls on his mobile – to no avail. We immediately said rushed goodbyes; there was nothing here for either of us – and I ran back towards the car in a panic. As I raced past Nando's I was reminded of Dave and how he chose an early night instead of me. This made me fill up and by the time I got to the car I was crying with disappointment, stress and the fear of losing everything. I collected Grace (alone at the school gate) and arrived home to more messages from Sangita on the answer phone (I'd turned my mobile off).

"Stella. It's almost 4pm and I haven't heard from you. I'm thinking you're not able to provide me with the necessary paperwork. I'm thinking, sadly that the order for the party will need to be pulled if you can't provide the requirements asap."

I sat amongst the naked fairy cakes and cried. "What am I going to do?" I said to Grace, who looked on, horrified.

"Shall we speak to Uncle Al?" she offered, handing me a glass of water, "he'll know what to do."

"I've left a million voicemail messages – he's not getting back," I said. "I think we have to face it, Grace – we have lost the *Dancing* contract, we aren't going to the ball...and The Cake Fairy has just died."

"Mum, you mustn't give up. That's what you always say to me," pleaded Grace.

"Come on, let's go to the restaurant and see if Uncle Al's there – he'll think of something, I know he will."

I couldn't think of anything else to do, so in a weird *Freaky Friday* role-reversal scenario I did as Grace suggested, and reluctantly washed my salty face, pushed a comb through my hair and climbed into the car. I tried to stay calm as we snaked through the agonisingly slow, busy homecoming traffic and headed for Sebastian's restaurant. On the way it started to rain, which seemed to slow everything down even more and stopping at a zebra for a rainbow of opened umbrellas to cross, I thought I saw a familiar face.

"Is that Auntie Lizzie?" I said to Grace, about to beep her.

"Yes it is! And there's Dad, he's with Auntie Lizzie...yay," shouted Grace, waving frantically and trying to wind down the window to call them.

"Don't Grace, you'll get all wet. Are you sure that's your dad with Auntie Lizzie?" I said, puzzled and convinced Grace was mistaken.

"Yes, it's definitely Dad, look he's wearing that awful red jacket we hate," she giggled. I screwed up my eyes trying to see him through the rain and brollies and rushing pedestrians. She was right it was Tom – with Lizzie.

"That's funny." I said.

"Lizzie's Dad's friend too," added Grace, still waving.

"I know but..."

"She's always phoning him up," she added.

"Is she?" I said, even more puzzled. "Well they've been working together. I suppose they probably had things to sort out. To be honest, I don't think Lizzie likes your dad much."

"Oh she does," answered Grace with feeling.

I let it go. It's only right that Grace believes they are friends. I knew exactly how Lizzie felt about Tom. She hated him for what he did to me but she was such a good friend she'd sucked it all up and offered him the work in Australia so he would be able to support Grace and I. It's strange that they were together though – after all, they'd practically only just landed.

Having fought through the rain and the traffic we finally parked outside Seb's restaurant, half on the pavement, abandoning the car to whatever fate the traffic warden decreed. The restaurant hadn't yet opened for dinner so I started banging hard on the glass door. "Al!" I shouted, at the top of my voice. After a few seconds I saw Sebastian rummaging for keys and rushing to the door to let us in.

"Stella, what is it?" he asked looking very concerned.

"Oh Seb, it's awful. Where's Al? He's not answering his phone. All our hard work, for nothing..." I spluttered, eyes brimming.

"Calm down, sweetie. We had a lovely romantic lunch then Al went swimming. You know what he's like when he's in the

swimming zone. Sit down and tell me what's happened. Just sit."
he lowered me gently onto a chair at one of the tables and asked
one of the staff to bring us some coffee and lemonade for Grace.

Seb was so kind I burst into tears, telling him about
Sangita's call and the anonymous email. Throughout this I
gulped coffee and wiped at my face with a paper napkin, feeling
about five years old. Sebastian listened and nodded and shook
his head in all the right places. Then he said, "I thought it was
something terrible. Let's get this into perspective. Grace is OK,
you're OK. This is about a kitchen." I half-smiled through my
wet napkin.

"But Sangita won't work with us anymore if we can't prove
we have a proper kitchen and she's our main contact. With her
we were going places, but now..."

"But now, you have a kitchen," he said, like he hadn't heard
a word I'd just told him.

"No, Seb. I work from my own kitchen, that's the problem.
I'll need inspections and I don't think you understand."

"I understand perfectly," he said, taking a sip of black
coffee, "and the solution is simple. There is a working kitchen
here," he waved his arms in the general direction of the
restaurant kitchen.

"What...what do you mean, Seb?" I asked, confused. "You
are a restaurant and so your kitchen's always busy, there'd be no
room for us."

"I mean that you and Al often work through the night – I'm
sure we could organise your schedule so that when we finish in
the restaurant, you begin. I have all the necessary paperwork
and if anyone asks, this is where you've always worked."

Grace squealed and jumped up and down and I burst into
tears again. I lunged towards Sebastian, kissed his face and
hugged him so tight he screamed. Then he added, looking at
Grace; "And let's not forget you, Princess Grace. We have a spare

room that I will paint 'princess-pink' and you can sleep in it at night while Mum's working."

"Cool," she said with a big grin.

I called Sangita straight away with the good news. I then faxed through the restaurant paperwork immediately, pointing out that we hadn't had the chance to add our business name to it yet, but were in the process of doing so.

"Great, Stella," she barked, "I have to say, I was thinking 'curtains' for the Cake Fairy. However, I need proof that you do actually operate from this address, in case of further complaints. How soon can you send?"

"Er, we should be able to get that to you before the event," I improvised, feeling sick all over again. "Now, let's talk tangos." As I hung up from Sangita, Al returned carrying a boxful of sample wedding favours. I quickly explained to him what had happened and stood back as his face turned bright red.

"Who the hell would send an email?" he started.

"I don't know, Al. The only truly evil person I know is MJ," I said thoughtfully.

"Sweetcakes, how can it be her? She doesn't know anything about your business." Then his eyes widened.

"OMG!!!" he exclaimed. "Think, Stella, who else would know that you work for Sangita and operate from your own kitchen? Think *Fatal Attraction*, honey!!"

It slowly dawned on me. "Rachel?" I said.

"Yes yes!!! Of course it's her! Younger lover who can't live up to older, successful, chunkier wife?" he said

"Thanks, Al. But maybe you're right."

And he didn't stop there. He ranted and raved, pacing the floor, waving his arms and finally climaxing with, "The home-wrecking, life-destroying slut. She makes Glenn Close look like Mary Poppins." I wasn't completely convinced, but he was infectious.

"Nothing could be further from my mind than getting back with Tom. But if Rachel is angry about her split from Tom and blames me, who knows how far she'd go to destroy my life?" I added, starting to sound like Al.

During Al's tirade, Seb had wisely escorted Grace to the kitchen to 'help' Claude the sous-chef and returned quickly to change the subject before our Rachel frenzy hit orbit.

"Look guys, let's not get hung up on who it was or why, let's just move on and prove them wrong," he said.

33

Spangled Salsa and Chocolate Cha-Cha

"Have you said anything to Tom about his ex-girlfriend's little email yet?" Al asked the next morning, as we worked on the 'Cha-Cha' cakes. It was Tuesday and with the *Strictly* deadline looming that Saturday, we were both feeling the pressure. The morning sun was streaming through the restaurant kitchen window and I felt that strange sensation of time being suspended, which was less about magic and more to do with working through the night and having no sleep.

"No. He's only just back from Australia and I know it's been a stressful shoot. I'll tell him all about it soon," I said, dreading the conversation because it would no doubt cause trouble between us.

"Don't worry, Stel. Seb is sorting out all the paperwork we need today so we should have everything done by the weekend."

"I know Al – it's just hassle that we don't need," I said, slurping on strong, black coffee.

Al smiled and held out what he'd been working on. "This will make you smile," he said.

"What is it?"

"It's an 'exploding macaroon'. I thought we could add a little 'Hip-Hop' to the proceedings."

I took a bite from the light, crunchy disc and it literally exploded in my mouth like a thousand fireworks popping with sweet-yet-tart strawberries and sugary crystals.

"Wow Al it's aaghhh!! Wonderful, but aaghhh!" I giggled.

"That's just the reaction I wanted," he said proudly. "The secret ingredient is Space Dust – it always made me laugh when I was a kid. I think it's fiery and fun, just like the dance."

"You are so clever Al, for a moment there I was ten years old again," I smiled.

Al's phone beeped. "It's Seb," he said. "He'll be here in ten minutes."

"I'll get some brunch on, then," I said, relieved to finally have an excuse for a break and opening the fridge. We had the restaurant to ourselves until the staff arrived at ten, so there was just enough time to whip up some smoked salmon and scrambled eggs.

Lizzie appeared at the back door. "One child safely deposited at school," she reported. "She had a lovely night with Auntie Lizzie and went to bed really early – honest," Lizzie winked. "Crikey, you two look like two rough old slappers who've spent the night on the street."

"Thanks a lot!" I retorted. "That's what comes of having to work through the night because some malicious bastard has reported you to the FSA. I could be in bed right now," I sighed. "And it's not over yet." I began beating eggs with feeling.

"Hard times all round then," said Lizzie gloomily. "It's such a relief to be with my friends and away from the bloody *Barry's Barbie* edit but that's not over yet either. I haven't got too long now – I just have to stick it out."

"No you don't have to stick it out," said Al. "Look at me and Stella, we didn't stay until the bitter end – we abandoned ship before we became human husks. OK – I was made to walk the plank, but I went didn't I? Go now, all that stress will ruin your skin, girl."

"Yes, but I'm not you and I need to stay at work."

"Lizzie, I know you're a trooper but it's not like you're desperately short of money. You could walk away now and live for about twelve months without work if you stopped buying designer gear. What's going on there? Why has it been so awful?" I pressed. She flashed me a thin smile.

"Enough boring work talk!" she declared, dismissing me and turning to Al. "Where are you and Seb planning to go for your honeymoon?"

I frowned. All this drama and secrecy was getting a bit boring, especially if she wasn't going to actually talk about it. I placed some smoked salmon, eggs and plates on the table.

"Well, we're torn between Paris and Rome," he said, grabbing a plate and piling it high, looking far away like he was imagining the gorgeousness of it all.

"Do both," said Lizzie. "Do it all. Do a Grand European Tour."

"That sounds lovely," I said, then my mobile started to ring.

"Hello, can I speak with Stella?" the voice asked. It had a familiar, Spanish-sounding tone to it and I felt my stomach lurch.

"Is that you, Diego?" I asked reluctantly, trying very hard to sound lucid.

"Yes, Stella it's me Diego. Stella I... "

Oh God, I thought. It had to be something to do with my mother, she'd called him, blabbed and he was now ringing me to ask for an apology.

"Diego I'm so very, very sorry. I didn't realise you only wanted a cake for your daughter. I thought we were on some kind of date and I drank too much wine on an empty stomach and a broken heart and I...am...so..."

"Stella," he raised his voice over my bleating, "I'm phoning from Accident and Emergency, I need to speak to you about someone I think may be your friend."

"Who?" I asked, confused. "I'm sorry, I don't understand."

"He has ID, his name is Sebastian Girard. He has had a road

accident. Do you know him?"

"Yes...yes." I heard myself whisper.

"He needs you here, at the hospital. Stella, it's not good."

"Oh God!" My stomach hit the floor as I glanced over at Al who looked puzzled and had now put down his fork.

"We're on our way," I threw the phone down and grabbing my car keys, said as calmly as I could: "Al, Seb's at the hospital, I don't know any details, but I think he's OK. We need to go there now."

We all jumped in the car. Lizzie sat in the back holding onto Al who couldn't speak and I saw in my mirror that he was deathly pale. "He'll be OK, we just need to get to him," I could hear her saying. "He'll be fine once he sees you. It'll all be fine, hon." It was ten minutes away and as my car flew along the dual carriageway my mind flew faster. I kept hearing Diego's words: 'It's not good'.

When we arrived at the hospital I had to park and frantically rummaged in my handbag to find a bloody one-pound coin. "Go on Al. Lizzie, just get him in to see Seb, I'll sort this."

They leapt from the car and started running, jumping over the grass verges and diving into the entrance. The more I rummaged, the more panicky I became and I could feel myself filling up with fear and blinding frustration: *my friend could be dying and I'm late because I can't find a fucking coin. I might never see him again -and all because I need a pound to park.*

Realising that it didn't matter I abandoned the car in its space, unpaid for and ran across the tarmac faster than I'd ever run in my life. Stumbling over the endless grass verges, I eventually hurled myself through the glass doors of Accident and Emergency, breathless from running and fear. After much frantic to-ing and fro-ing through the department I was eventually led through some heavy, double doors into a room filled with equipment and people. Sebsatian was lying motionless on a bed, a network of tubes coming out of him and a team of people around him, the buzz of machines providing an intrusive backdrop of sound. Al and Lizzie were standing to one side, out of the way, clinging to each other. Al's face was wet with tears and I looked on helplessly as Lizzie rocked him like a mother would a child.

"Sebastian's really bad, Stella. He might die," Al croaked, reaching out to me as I walked robotically towards them.

"But...he can't. You're going to get married. And what about your honeymoon?" I could hear myself saying stupidly. "What happened, Al?" but he was shaking his head, too distressed to speak.

I turned to Lizzie, who was talking to one of the nurses. "He's been stabilised, the doctor will be along to see you soon," the nurse was saying "but you should know that he is very seriously hurt." Lizzie covered her face with her hands.

"I was always telling him...his bloody driving...He was going too fast – he crashed the car, Stella." Al sobbed, inconsolably. I reached out and held him. I didn't know what to do, I was so numb with shock. I just held him and willed myself not to cry because I needed to be strong for Al. Then the doctor arrived.

"Hello," he said looking at us with kind brown eyes; it was Diego. "I have been looking after Sebastian since he came in. We need to move him into the Intensive Care Unit very soon. We are doing everything we can."

"It's so awful," I said, a sob lurching in my throat. "Will he be OK? What exactly is wrong with him?"

Diego put his hand on my back. "Your friend has broken some bones but the main worry is the trauma he suffered to his head. He is in a coma and his brain is very bruised and swollen." He looked at Al. "The swelling might not go down. I am very sorry my friend, I wish I could offer you better news. We need to move him now."

"Oh...er Al, this is Diego," I said, rather inappropriately. I felt a pang of guilt for reverting to social niceties in this cataclysmic moment, but what else could I do? We were lost.

Al looked up and smiled. "Fancy you two meeting again, in the middle of all this. Isn't life funny?" And he started to cry again.

In the midst of all the awfulness, something occurred to me. I turned to Diego. "How did you know to call me?" I asked, putting my arm around Al.

"He had your business card. I recognise the name and number," Diego said. "And Stella – this was found in the car, on the front seat." Diego reached across to a trolley, picked up a small, white package and handed it to me. It was a card, with my name scribbled on the front. My eyes met Al's and with shaky hands, I opened the envelope. I slowly pulled out a bright pink card and as I lifted it up, something fell to the floor with a clank. 'Welcome Home' was emblazoned on the front of the card in sparkly letters and as I looked inside, I saw Sebastian's beautiful script. 'Dear Stella' it read, 'welcome to The Cake Fairy's new home. May you create magic here'. My eyes filled with tears and as I looked up I saw that Lizzie had retrieved what had fallen out of the card.

"Here," she whispered, holding her hand out. In it was a set of keys to Sebastian's restaurant, on a beautiful fairy keyring.

At that moment, a team of porters came in.

"We need to transfer Sebastian now," said Diego gently. "Perhaps his partner would like to accompany him?"

"Yes," Al sobbed. "I'm not leaving."

"We'll wait in the café, Al. We'll come up as soon as we're allowed," said Lizzie, and took my hand. In a flurry of white coats, drips and nurses, Sebastian was wheeled away with Diego and Al following behind. As they walked away beyond our reach

I saw Diego place his hand on Al's shoulder, which finally brought the sob that had been threatening in my throat to the surface.

"Let's get a coffee, Stella," Lizzie whispered, putting her arm in mine and gently trying to move me forward. I stood rooted to the spot, clutching the keys, watching as Sebastian's bed disappeared from sight and Al's forlorn figure faded from my view. Then I allowed Lizzie to lead me away, down the stairs and into the sunlit cafe, where people queued for coffee and chattered, unaware that life for us might never be the same again.

34

Love and Worry

I found a table near the window, which was stupid because the sun was shining directly in my eyes, making them water even more. I stared ahead, waiting for Lizzie who eventually returned with two comfortingly-steamy mugs of coffee. I took mine gratefully, holding it with both hands, watching the steam rise into the air and disappear.

"I popped out and called work," she said, practical and calm as always. "I can stay as long as I need to." She pushed a large Kit Kat towards me. "Eat this, sweetie." I shook my head and moved it to the side, unable to face it. "Come on Stel. You haven't eaten yet."

"Look I'm not exactly borderline anorexic. I won't pass out because I haven't eaten a bloody Kit Kat," I answered sharply, then immediately regretted it. "Sorry, Lizzie. Thanks."

"It's OK hon," she said, "We're both on edge. It's been a rotten few months for all of us and now this."

We sat for a long time; the sunlight moved across the canteen and coffee turned in to sandwiches and hot lunches. I called Emma Wilson and arranged for her to pick up Grace after school and Lizzie and I both kept staring at our phones. As the serving ladies dished out food and talked about 'last night' we both silently lived through the possible outcomes, unable to share even with each other.

Eventually Lizzie spoke. "I told Al to text me but I doubt he'll be able to use his phone in the ICU. I'll pop to reception see what's happening."

"I'll come too," I said, worrying that if I stood my legs may give way.

Lizzie sensed my reluctance. "Stay here. I'll be back in a minute." She threw her bag over her shoulder and walked through the canteen. I watched her go, sipping my coffee and feeling like a child whose mother had left her. I half-smiled; Lizzie was good at taking care of things – she'd battled through life alone, so she'd had to."

Within a few minutes, Lizzie was back, rushing eagerly through the door and beckoning me to move. I gathered my jacket and my bag and stumbled from the table, "What? What?" I said, joining her.

"There's a message at reception for us to go to ICU, come on." My breath caught in my throat and I stumbled after her, eventually running to catch up with her long-legged strides.

"Outpatients," she yelled, running past a blue sign.

"That's Orthopaedics," I shouted back like it was a relevant response as we whizzed past another doorway, looking everywhere and seeing nothing. Every door looked the same, every turning just like the last and we just ran and ran, completely lost in a blind panic of blue signs and white walls. Eventually, Lizzie had the presence of mind to ask someone the directions to ICU. As we entered, the thing that struck me the most apart from the occasional bleeping and whirring of machines was the blanket of silence. I saw the back of Al, slumped over the bed and was aware only of my noisy heart, beating with exertion and dread.

As we walked in Al looked up. He'd been crying and his skin was grey. "Hi," he said weakly, mustering a smile.

"How is he?" Lizzie ventured, walking gingerly round the bed.

"No change, doll. It's just about waiting now. You guys

should go home. There's no point in us all being here. Go home
and I'll call as soon as we know anything."

"You are kidding right?" Lizzie started. "We are your best
friends and we are staying here with you, end of discussion."

"Typical," he said, with his voice breaking. "Mine and Seb's
moment of drama and we have to share it with you two fag
hags." Lizzie and I both smiled and I could see tears welling up
in her eyes. I looked away.

"Have you called Seb's mum?" Lizzie asked, brushing her
face with her hand.

"Yes, Rosemary's on her way."

"Well, Stella and I will go to reception and wait for her
there," she said, "to show her the way." Al nodded, and Lizzie
and I went back downstairs.

"God, imagine the call to say your only child is being kept
alive by a machine and no-one knows what's going to happen," I
said to Lizzie. I thought about Grace and shivered.

"Poor Rosemary," I added in a whisper. I thought about the
new baby in her arms; the first words, the first day at school,
grazed knees, leaving home and years and years of love and
worry. All could come to nothing in just one day.

Suddenly, a well-dressed woman rushed towards the
reception desk.

"Sebastian – Sebastian Girard," she said to the receptionist,
"my son." And her voice broke.

"Rosemary?" Lizzie said, gently. Rosemary nodded. "I'm
Lizzie, this is Stella. We're Seb's friends. He's this way."

"The cab," Rosemary said, "I need to pay the cab. He said
there was a cash machine in the hospital. I didn't have time,
when I got the call…" and she broke off, unable to finish.

"I'll deal with it," said Lizzie. "You just get to Seb."
Rosemary flashed her a thin, grateful smile. I put my arm
through this stranger's arm. We had barely met, but we were

already united, by the event and the person.

"He's all I have, since his father died," she said, like I could make it all go away. I squeezed her arm, *what could I say?*

"On the phone they said something about Sebastian's brain swelling?" she said, as we hurried down the corridor, trying the words out like she was talking about someone else. I wanted to tell her it wasn't real, that Seb was fine. I wanted to say 'it's all a misunderstanding and he's back at the restaurant waiting for you' but of course, I couldn't.

"He's in the best place," I said, managing to discover yet another stupid cliché from what was beginning to look like an endless hospital collection.

Arriving at Seb's bedside Rosemary went straight to her son, kissing him gently on the forehead.

"Sebastian, darling – it's Mum," she whispered, tears dripping onto his face. Al stood up and put his hand on her arm and I realised I shouldn't be there. I made a gesture to Al that said I would leave them alone and he nodded.

I headed back to the main entrance and found Lizzie outside, on her hundredth fag.

"Oh Stel, that woman's face – I couldn't look at her." She said, shaking her head and sucking hard on the smoke. For a moment, I almost envied her addiction.

"We need to talk to the staff at Sebastian's restaurant," I said numbly.

"Christ of course," she said, "they have to be told." She was just stepping on her cigarette when her mobile rang. She clicked it open. "Hi. I can't talk, but I won't be in today. No. I don't think I can finish it, sorry. I know it's really bad timing – I'll explain later." She hung up with a sigh.

"Is everything OK?" I said.

"Yup," she replied shortly. "Come on. Let's go."

I didn't ask her any more, we just climbed into the car and

we set off towards the restaurant. The early autumn sun had made the seats warm and we were both silent throughout the journey. Arriving at the restaurant, we could see that Seb's loyal staff had opened up without him. Candles were flickering on the tables and the restaurant looked busy.

"Stel, What are you going to do about this *Strictly Dancing* stuff?" Lizzie asked, as I turned off the engine and reached for my bag.

"I don't know Lizzie. If something terrible happens...I couldn't face it. If Seb's OK then we'll still need a business and I think it's up to me to keep things going until we know."

"Mmm, I think you're right. But you can't do this on your own. Look I will sort it with work and take the couple of days I'm owed after all the bloody long hours I did in Oz."

"Lizzie, I couldn't ask you to do that," I said.

"Stella – we're friends and that's what friends do. But I have to say, after today we're both too stressed and tired. What do you say we both have a good night's sleep then tomorrow after the restaurant's shut, I'll come and help you for however long it takes, until the order's finished?"

"That's really kind Lizzie. I should start tonight, we've only got three more days until the party. But I really want to go home and see Grace," I said, suddenly seeing a vision of poor Rosemary at her son's bedside.

"OK. That's sorted then. You can collect Grace from Emma's and spend the evening with her, then get an early night. You need it."

"Yeah. Thanks Lizzie."

"And why don't you call Tom and ask him to look after Grace for a few days? We're almost ready for the *Barry* launch next Monday, so I'm sure he'll be free."

So I drove off while Lizzie did the difficult bit of going into the restaurant to tell them the news and to ask Claude, the sous-chef, to take charge until we knew what was happening with Seb.

I broke the news to Grace, who was upset and wanted to see Seb immediately. "I'm sorry darling but he's very poorly, we don't know when he'll be better, but his mum's with him."

"Oh well, if his mum's there he'll be OK, I'm sure," she said with a naïve confidence I longed to share.

Later I called Tom, told him the news and asked if Grace could stay with him. "Of course Stella. God that is awful, I'm so sorry. Tell Al I'm thinking of him. Is there anything I can do?"

I was strangely warmed by his response. "No, there's nothing anyone can do but wait and see. You having Grace is a big help, thank you," I said.

"Well if I can do anything more, let me know. Are you OK? Would you like me to come round?"

"I don't think so Tom," I said firmly, thinking that was all I needed, adding to this emotional mix.

We made arrangements for Tom to collect Grace after school the next day then come to the house and pick up her things. I put down the phone, feeling very alone. I couldn't talk to Tom so I called Dave; he was still supposed to be my boyfriend, after all and he should know what to say. I dialled his number. It rang, and rang, and rang. I made a cup of coffee, unable to even think about sleep even though I was so tired. I dialled again, but no answer so I left a message. "I need to talk to you," I wailed down the phone. I put it down and dialled again, but after a fourth time worried that Dave might think I was stalking him. Reluctantly, I stopped calling, turned off the lights and went to bed.

I was awoken the following morning very early by the phone ringing. My heart lifted slightly, thinking it might be Dave, but the shrill, efficient voice on the other end was like a splash of cold water.

"Stella. I need to talk with you re the event." It was Sangita.

"Sangita, can I just stop you there." I sat up in bed and shook my head as the torrent of yesterday's terrible events began to flood into my mind. I slowly explained about Seb's accident and how we were now waiting for news. Sangita was, well, Sangita.

"Oh I'd like to extend my concern. So sorry Stella. Tell Al the same. Sebastian is a very good businessman – great with money."

"Yes. He is a wonderful *person* too," I added, knowing my sarcasm was lost on Sangita, whose admiration extended only to one's business acumen or accounting skills.

"Now Stella, I don't want to seem heartless at this time, but I NEED the paperwork. I am in a very difficult position here, we need proof that you operate from Sebastian's kitchen before we progress any further."

"Of course, I understand," I said, thinking about how stupid this all was in the light of what was happening. "I'll have the paperwork to you soon, I just need a bit more time."

"Asap, Stella," she responded sharply, "and I am hoping that all this won't put a delay on the order. Three days left, I am counting on you." Then she was gone. Feeling like I'd been slapped I tried to push it all from my mind and called Lizzie to find out if she'd heard from the hospital.

"No change, but he had a 'comfortable night' – whatever that means." I put the phone down and woke Grace, dropping her off at school on autopilot, trying to imagine anyone having 'a comfortable night' attached to all those tubes.

I spent most of the day worrying and phoning everyone I could think of while waiting for news from the hospital. I tried to work on the accounts but I was distracted and without Seb, the numbers might as well have been in Chinese. I was relieved when I heard the front door at about 4pm and the sound of

Grace's high-pitched squeal.

"Muuuum! We're here!" She appeared in the kitchen doorway and rushed into my arms, which felt so good.

"How's Seb?" she asked.

"He's still hurt but it may help if we send lots of good thoughts his way," I said, not really believing it.

"And how are you?" said Tom's voice. He was walking into the kitchen and smiling at me in the way he used to long ago. I was taken aback.

"I'm OK Tom," I said tightly, forcing a smile.

I had been unusually organised and packed a bag for Grace, which was waiting in the hall but after a brief discussion about her requirements for several nights at her dad's she rolled her eyes. "Mum, I NEED these too," she yelled from her bedroom, dashing around the house, filling another bag with yet more hair scrunchies and lip balms, without which she apparently wouldn't survive the first night.

With Princess Grace's bags finally packed to her specifications I walked them both to the front door. "Tom, I can't thank you enough. I know you have the launch next Monday; I hope it won't be a problem with the school run." I said, opening the door.

"Don't say that, Stella. She's my daughter too. I love being with her and if I can help you, then, well..."

"Thanks," I smiled and looked into his eyes. He looked right back and for a few seconds standing together on the doorstep, the possibilities seemed endless.

"Stella, I was wondering," he started "erm, I mean if..."

"Hi," a voice suddenly butted in from nowhere and I was surprised to see Dave suddenly emerge from behind Tom.

"Hi, I didn't know you were coming over," I said to Dave, embarrassed that these two were both on my front step at the same time.

"Well, I got your message and it sounded urgent," he said.

"Er, Tom, this is..." I started.

"Dave Kennedy, isn't it?" he said, glowering at Dave. "I remember you."

"Hi Tim," said Dave, with a grin. "Long time no see."

Tom went pink with rage or embarrassment or both and with great reluctance shook Dave's hand. "We'll be off now," he muttered, walking away. "Give mum a kiss, Grace," he called and she bounded up the steps almost knocking Dave over. Tom nodded from the car and Grace leapt in waving manically at me as I blew kisses to her. I walked into the house, followed by Dave, suddenly feeling very lost and alone.

"That was tricky," I said, putting the kettle on and feeling like I wanted to cry.

"Don't feel guilty about *me* turning up," Dave said, taking his jacket off. "It's about time he had a taste of his own medicine. Now, what's the matter?"

I opened my arms and walked towards Dave and falling into his chest told him all about Seb, letting out the gigantic, hysterical sobs that had been sitting inside my chest since yesterday. His arms were tight around me and I felt so safe, and in that moment I didn't ever want to be alone again.

"Dave, I'm so glad you're here. It's been awful. I can't get upset in front of Al or Grace and Lizzie's just on autopilot."

"I'm here for you, Stella."

"What shall we do? I haven't eaten, I could cook something? Or we could get a takeaway? I don't want to go anywhere in case Al rings." I rummaged in the kitchen drawers for 'The Balti Spice' takeaway menu.

"Erm, that would be lovely. Er, we could do that...tomorrow night. It's just that tonight I don't have a lot of time."

I looked up, slowly shutting the drawer. "Oh? I thought

you'd come for the evening?"

"Well, I came to see you, I was concerned. It's just that I have to leave at six. I've got an invite for a black-tie telly dinner."

"Oh Dave, after what's happened do you really have to go?"

"Afraid so. I'm really sorry. You know I hate all this networking stuff, I don't want to – but I have to."

"Of course you need to. I'm being selfish," I said, coming over all Stepford-Wife.

"It's important for my career, and for *our* future," he said, kissing my face and making me feel better for a few seconds.

"I know, I understand. You must go."

"I *could* stay with you if you really want me to," he offered, now safe in the knowledge that I wouldn't allow that.

"It's fine Dave. Honestly," I said, thinking the opposite and willing him to stay. "I'm working at the restaurant after-hours tonight anyway. Call me later, I'll have my phone with me." He kissed me again and this time it was longer, with more promise.

"Are you really sure?" his voice was husky with desire and despite wanting to forget everything and just fall into his arms I had too much on my mind. I pushed him gently down the hall and out through the front door and said "You'll be late – GO." And he did.

I closed the front door and leaned on it. I didn't really want to think about it, but I had to ask myself – if it was his friend whose life was hanging in the balance, could I leave him alone and upset to go to a career dinner? I knew the answer. In my heart I secretly hoped he would cancel everything and be there for me. I couldn't resist peeping through the hall window to see if he was rushing back, having realised what was important. He wasn't.

I didn't have time to dwell. It was at least an hour since I'd last called the hospital and I needed to know how Seb was. I'd sent texts to Al's phone because I knew he left ICU every now and then to collect them. This time I called and he answered straight away, I caught my breath. "How is he?"

"He's still critical," Al answered. "I just feel so helpless, Stel. It's the waiting that's so hard. I'm not actually doing anything to make him better, just sitting by the bed."

"I'm sure he knows you're there. He can probably hear you and that will pull him through," I grimaced, spewing out what even I recognised as another ill-informed and pointless cliché. I put the phone down and wandered in to the kitchen to get something to eat. In a few hours, the restaurant would be clear and I could carry on with the *Strictly* Order – for what it was worth.

On Thursday morning I woke to find myself propped against a kitchen work-surface, my head resting on my arms. Lizzie and I had worked since eleven the night before and now the sun was throbbing through the restaurant kitchen window. I felt weighed down by a tiredness I'd never known. I slowly sat up and spotted Lizzie on the battered staff sofa, fast asleep, her phone clutched to her chest in case Al called.

The previous night Lizzie and I had beaten and whipped and whisked like our lives depended on it. The ovens were hot and we didn't sit down once, constantly moving to try and work through the bulk of the order. If we didn't reach the targets I'd set for us on that night then there was no hope of making the *Strictly* launch. By 6am, we both flopped, exhausted, promising ourselves we'd 'just have forty winks.'

We'd worked our way through most of the stuff we needed to but I couldn't create the dancing figures that Al had designed and would have made beautifully. I made several attempts but became frustrated with myself which wasn't helped by Lizzie being sulky and quiet. I'd tried several times to start up a conversation (primarily to keep me awake) but she was monosyllabic and the harder I tried, the more strained the atmosphere became. By 3am, I lost it with her; "Lizzie we are both worried about Seb, but you being like this isn't helping," I announced into the silence, slapping a huge wedge of butter into a large bowl with feeling. "Surely at a time like this we should be able to share how we feel?"

She looked at me and nodded; "Sorry, I don't mean to shut you out. But there are things I have to deal with on my own, too." I was hurt that she wasn't prepared to share her worries with me, but I put it down to a difficult day visiting Seb and trying to keep Al's spirits up and we were both exhausted.

I went to the Ladies', splashed some cold water on my face and quietly put the kettle on. I'd decided to make breakfast and a drink for Lizzie.

Just as I was making the coffee I had a text from Tom.

TXT: Hi Stel. How r u? Any news on Seb?

That was nice I thought and texted him back as Lizzie rose from her slumber and staggered outside for her first fag of the day. I made the coffees and found some croissants which I popped in the oven to warm and when she returned we ate them in silence.

"Thanks Stel," she said.

"I had a text from Tom," I volunteered, hoping to engage her in conversation. "He asked about Seb." Lizzie raised her eyebrows, clearly impressed at his concern. "I haven't heard from Dave though," I said, sadly. "He was supposed to call last night but obviously got caught up in 'networking'."

She sniffed with disapproval.

"This is all the wrong way round! Tom's being supportive and Dave's giving me nothing. I thought he was better than that, that I meant more to him."

She looked up from her croissant. "Don't waste your time on that one, Stella. Something or someone else will always come first."

"He's just so driven, Lizzie, and he loves his work," I said, defensively.

"Stella, I think he cares about you, but face it hon – he doesn't love you *enough.*"

I was surprised and a little taken aback by her brutal honesty. "Whoa Lizzie, tell me what you're really thinking. Stop dressing everything up in flowery language," I tried, hoping she'd laugh and say she didn't know what she was talking about and that he was crazy about me.

"Sorry, but you deserve better than being second best. Or worse."

I didn't respond. I was hurt, even though a part of me had to admit she may have been right. I was also annoyed – she wouldn't tell me a thing about Barry, yet she was happy to dispense advice about my love life. I finished my coffee in silence. I gathered the crockery and washed the cups and plates in the big metal sink. And it didn't matter how hard I tried, I couldn't stop thinking about what she'd said.

I turned the taps on full to drown Lizzie and the rest of the world out, but as I eventually turned them off, I was aware of voices across the kitchen. Al had arrived and was talking to Lizzie. I rushed to them, eager for news.

"Seb's having an operation," he said, almost in a whisper. "They need to relieve the swelling in his brain. It's just more waiting and I'm so tired. Rosemary's with him. She said for me to go home and change, get some sleep. It'll be hours before we know anything."

"Then why are you here, Al?" Lizzie said, gently.

"I'll drive you home."

"I did go home, but I couldn't rest and anyway I wanted to

bring these over. I found them in our study, on the printer," he said, handing me pile of papers. I took the bundle from him and written across the top of the page was 'The Cake Fairy' in silvery, fairy writing.

"It's the headed paper Seb designed – it's beautiful," I said, running my palm across the cool, silky paper surface.

"And look, he's printed invoices out with our new address on." said Al.

"The business cards are here too," Lizzie said, flashing a card in pink and silver, beautifully written, the same tiny fairy on the logo.

I suddenly felt a rush of elation. "Invoices?" I said, "This is all the paperwork with the restaurant address on the top – this is the proof Sangita needs that we have approved premises."

"That's great doll," Al said with little enthusiasm. "We can go ahead with the order and with the business now. I'm here now, so I can help." I suddenly felt really selfish.

"No way Al. Lizzie and I can manage. It's not important." I said.

"Yes way. Let's close the restaurant tonight, give the staff a night off and get that order finished. Before you say any more, Stella, it's what Seb would want." Lizzie and I both protested, but Al insisted he needed to concentrate on something, so we indulged him, called the staff, made a gallon of black coffee and set to work.

We fulfilled a large part of the order that afternoon, but the atmosphere was strained. Even with a Lady GaGa accompaniment our spirits were on the floor. I looked up from clouds of icing sugar to see that the three of us were working independently with no communication between us and no warmth. I kept checking on Al and when he looked like he was about to cry I'd glance over at Lizzie for support, but she looked tearful too. I always relied on Lizzie to know what to do and say;

she was the sensible one who took charge but here she was completely lost in her own world. I walked over to where she was working, icing frills on chocolate cha-cha cakes and I gently put my arm around her. "Look, I know this isn't easy for any of us, especially Al, but what is it, Lizzie? You've been edgy for ages. This isn't like you."

"I'm fine Stella. And please don't tell me what I'm like," she responded sharply, walking to the sink and slamming down her bowl of icing. Stung, I walked back to my worktop, looking over at Al to see if he'd witnessed what had just happened. His face was screwed up and he was holding the chunky, Ann Widdecombe figure in both hands like he wanted to strangle it.

"I just can't get this right," he said angrily almost to himself. I was wondering whether to lighten things and make a joke like I normally would but the look on his face told me 'no'. I opened the oven to bake the final 'foxtrots' and pushed the cake tray in, suddenly feeling a scorching pain as my arm caught the inside of the oven. I leapt back, giving a yelp, which made Lizzie jump causing her piping bag to squirt bright pink icing all over her new, Diesel jeans.

"Ah my new jeans, fuck! Stella, you scared me," she shouted and promptly burst into tears. I ran to the tap and shoved my burnt arm under some cold water. Then, with an almost animal howl, Al hurled Ann Widdecombe across the kitchen into the stainless-steel fridge. She smashed into a million tiny pieces, never to cha-cha again. Al slowly crumpled to the floor.

I looked at Lizzie who was sobbing and manically trying to wipe icing from denim. She stopped what she was doing and for a second, we both just stared at Al.

"I can't take any more!" he said, rocking backwards and forwards. Lizzie and I looked at each other in alarm and both rushed over to comfort him.

"Al, it's OK," I said, kneeling on the floor and wrapping my arms around him.

"Seb's going to pull through," Lizzie offered, wiping her eyes and kneeling down too.

"I feel like I'm on a tightrope between life and death," sobbed Al. "Every time the phone rings it could be someone telling me he's...he's...well, you know," he said, great sobs wracking through his body. "Rosemary's devastated too. I've tried to keep strong for her but I can only hide so much. I thought being with my best friends would help but now even you two are falling out and crying. What's happened to us?"

"Well for me, it's Barry!" wailed Lizzie. "He's dumped me for someone else!" And she too burst into tears.

"Let's just get out of the kitchen." I said. "We are going mad in here. Let's sit in the restaurant, away from all this. We need to talk." So we staggered into the dimly-lit room and sat around one of the tables, which was all laid up for the next diners. Lizzie toyed with a wine glass and Al wiped his face on a napkin. Then Lizzie spoke.

"Look, I know I'm not myself. You're right Stella, it's been tough for me at work and Barry and I...well, now you know it's over. But in the light of everything with Seb, I can't just go on about myself."

"I understand that Lizzie," I said, squeezing her arm, "but you need to talk to us. We're your friends and it's upsetting for Al and me to see you like this, on top of everything else."

"It's just his new girlfriend is really rubbing my nose in it. It's caused problems at work and the call I took the other day was about that. The launch party is on Monday and there was something I really needed to do, and now it looks like it won't be done. It doesn't really matter, but it's made everything harder," she finished.

"Oh Lizzie, I thought they didn't need you at work!" I said, feeling doubly guilty. I'd been annoyed with her and she'd been putting her career on the line helping me. "I thought everything was ready for the launch? You said the first programme was edited ages ago."

"It's not about the programme," Lizzie sighed, "that's all still going ahead. Look, I am really sorry to be cryptic but I can't say any more at the moment, but you'll know all about it soon. I just need you both to know that I'm OK and Al, you need to know that Stella and I are here for you." She reached out and held Al's hand. I grabbed his other between mine.

"Look, I think we're all being a bit silly here," I said. "We're exhausted, we're all upset and the reason I bake is to make me happy – but the magic's not working."

"Yes and however hard I try, Ann Widdecombe still looks like something from *Lord of the Rings*," agreed Al.

"There's more important stuff happening and we should be dealing with it," I said. "We shouldn't even be here. It doesn't matter about the order. None of it matters without Seb. We should be at the hospital. We'll go together," I said, getting up and grabbing the car keys.

We all pushed back our chairs, got up and headed for the door. As I was locking up, Al stopped and put his arms round Lizzie and I. "I just want you to know that the only thing getting me through this is knowing if it all goes horribly wrong, you'll both be there to catch me." Tears sprang to my eyes and I hugged them both hard. We headed for the car, and just as we were climbing in, Al's phone rang. My heart stopped. Lizzie was already in the back seat and I caught her eye in the rear-view mirror.

"OK...OK..." Al was saying. Lizzie and I held our breath.

"Oh God," he whispered. He was still standing outside the car and I couldn't see his face, so turned to Lizzie in the back. Her face was white and she was very still. "OK, well thank you. I appreciate you calling, we're on our way." Al took a few seconds to compose himself, then climbed into the car.

"I am scared to say this," he said solemnly, "but it seems that Seb's improved. And girls – he's AWAKE!"

Lizzie screamed and I rested my head on the steering wheel, squeezing back tears. I started the car, and we set off on the same journey we all took only days earlier – only this time, we had smiles on our faces and hope in our hearts.

Arriving at the hospital we headed straight for the ICU. Seb's eyes were open and he was smiling weakly. Al rushed towards him, arms outstretched. Rosemary was sitting by the bed holding Seb's hand, a bundle of ragged tissues in her lap.

Lizzie and I gave Seb a gentle hug. "Welcome back," I whispered, "I'll bring you a cake as soon as you're well enough."

"Enough, you two, it's my turn again," said Al, pushing Lizzie and I aside. He took his seat next to the bed opposite Rosemary and took Seb's hand.

"Oh Seb, I thought I'd lost you," Al said, welling up. I had to look away or I'd start blubbing again, so I started rummaging in my handbag for a tissue. Instead, I was delighted to find a long-forgotten bag of chocolate truffles and suddenly felt overwhelmingly peckish. I discretely put a couple into my mouth and turned away from everyone, lest it be deemed disrespectful to be chomping on chocolate at a time like this. So it was with bulging hamster-cheeks that I was forced to greet Diego, who suddenly appeared smiling in the doorway.

Desperately chewing and swallowing, I gestured for him to go to Seb's bedside (which probably looked strange – especially as I couldn't speak). Holding the rest of the chocolates in my clenched fist, I took a good, long look. Now that Seb was improving and things were coming together I was able to give the doctor a proper check-up. Oh, how he was working that white coat! The stethoscope slung nonchalantly round his neck was both professional and provocative and as he made a little joke and smiled, dimples appeared on his cheeks and I had an uncontrollable urge to touch him. I resisted of course; apart from the inappropriateness of me lunging towards him, my fistful of chocolate was starting to melt and that wouldn't be pretty.

I finally finished the chocolate in my mouth and was able to join the conversation. "So the operation went well?" I asked.

"Well, Sebastian looks good to me, Stella, but I'm an A&E doctor. We need to talk to the specialist. I'll see if there's anyone about."

I watched him leave then caught Seb and Al looking at me. "What?" I said, opening my eyes wide in mock-innocence, finishing the truffle mush in my hand and licking chocolate from my palm.

Within minutes, Diego returned to tell us that someone would come and speak with Sebastian shortly, but in the meantime, he could confirm that the operation had been a complete success.

"You are a very lucky man my friend," Diego announced, shaking Seb's hand. He turned to leave.

"Good to see you again, Stella." Our eyes met and as he grabbed my hand to shake it, I felt the connection. He was looking at me with some intensity. "You came straight from your kitchen?" he smiled, wiping sticky chocolate remnants from his hand. It wasn't attraction in his eyes, it was alarm. I tried not to blush.

"God, what is it about that man?" I said when he'd gone and everyone started laughing. "He makes me do such stupid things."

"Hello?" said Seb quietly, obviously still in some pain. "Can we move on from Stella's love-life, please. Don't you two have a business to run?"

"Sorry Seb, she stuffs chocolates in her gob then tries to get off with your doctor while you lie there incapacitated – and I call her a friend," Al joked.

"Forget chocolates and dishy doctors," Seb said, wincing as he tried to sit up. "What about foxtrots and cha-chas? Have you finished the order?"

"It doesn't matter. What matters is you," Al replied, plumping his pillows.

"It *does* matter, Al. If you don't finish this order it could be the end of the business. We're just building it and it's going so well. Please don't let my bad driving ruin it."

"Sweetie. You come *before* the business," I heard myself say, thinking with a little jolt of pain about Dave.

"Look, I need to sleep and you need to get that order out," he said. "If The Cake Fairy fails now I'll feel responsible and I can't live with that. Please?" Al and I looked at each other.

"Truly," Seb continued, "I'm going to be fine now and you guys have a lot to do."

"Well doll," Al said, slowly, "I can feel some of that icing magic returning to my fingers..."

"...and we're nearly there anyway," chipped in Lizzie.

"OK," I said, looking at the others. "If you are sure, Seb – let's do it." We stayed until Seb fell asleep then headed back to the restaurant with a new burst of energy. On the way back, Sangita called.

"Stella, have been looking through everything you sent. All seems fine. Will you be able to deliver the order?"

"Yes, Sangita," I said with a smile, "we most certainly will."

35

Dave's Dirty Dancing

That night we worked with renewed vigour on the order. All buoyed up by Sebastian's imminent recovery we even laughed about Ann Widdecombe and Lizzie's Diesel jeans. We honed and created satin icing, blended chilli with chocolate for cha-chas and scattered sweet sparkles over moist mango 'salsa' cupcakes. By 2am, Al formally declared the order complete by placing the last, perfect figure on the large, shiny, cake dancefloor.

"Oh God, I can't believe how hard it's been," he said, "not to mention nearly losing my future husband mid-order." He slumped onto a chair and stretched out his arms. Lizzie's work phone rang.

"Hi there," she said. "Really? Are you sure? I can't believe it, that's great news. So it's all ready?" She visibly sank into her chair in relief. "Thank you," she whispered. With that she put her phone down and put her head in her hands. I looked at Al in alarm, worried she was upset. But when she looked up again, she was smiling.

"I've been annoying I know," said Lizzie. "I've been distracted with the whole Barry thing but there's other stuff I can't talk about at the moment. I'm aware I seem like a complete drama-queen but trust me, all will become clear."

I shrugged. "It's your life Lizzie. We're not going to judge you. I just wish you'd told us about Barry when it happened, we could have supported you."

"Well I'm sorry. I will get over Barry. But there's another matter I have to deal with." She wasn't going to spill, so we didn't ask. "Are you two free on Monday night?"

"Yes, probably, but Grace will be back from Tom's so I'd need to sort out a babysitter. Why?"

"Just keep Monday night free, both of you," she said enigmatically. "There's something I'd like you both to see." Al and I looked at each other, both intrigued. It was the press launch of *Barrie's Barbie* on Monday, so it would have to be something pretty major for her to miss it.

"OK doll," said Al. "Count us in."

"Sounds intriguing, Lizzie," I said. "Look, it's late and I've got to deliver this order tomorrow so we should get to bed. What do you think about still going to the event?" I said, remembering how excited we had been when Sangita sent us the tickets.

"I think we should go," said Al, firmly. "Sebastian was longing to come and he'd be upset if we all missed out. As long as he's OK, I think we should all be there." Lizzie nodded slowly.

"In that case, why don't you all come back to mine and sleep," I said. "It's close by, Grace isn't there and we can pick your outfits up in the morning on the way to see Seb. Then we can all drive there together. And for some reason, I really don't want to spend tonight without you two."

Lizzie was smiling. "I'm in," she said. "And I'm exhausted. Let's go".

When we got back to my house, we were all suddenly ravenous. On arrival I checked the fridge and finding only eggs and cheese, made omelettes.

"We have a pass that includes Seb for tomorrow's launch," Lizzie said, placing three mugs of hot tea on the table. "It's a shame he can't be there."

"Would you like Dave to come in his place?" Al offered.

"Oh, no thanks Al," I said, without hesitation.

As Sebastian's van had been totalled in the accident, Lizzie headed off the next morning to hire a new one to take us and the cakes to London for the *Strictly* launch. Al wanted to see Seb so I went with him. As much as I wanted to see my friend, I have to admit I didn't want to play gooseberry, so secretly hoped Diego might make an appearance. When we arrived we were delighted to discover that Seb had been moved out of ICU and was now on a ward. He looked older and tired, but happy.

"I'm not sure about leaving you to spend the night in London," Al was saying. "Stella and Lizzie could go without me?"

Seb was adamant. "No Al, you all need to be there. Now off you go...and good luck, Cake Fairies."

So, after lunch the three of us set off for London, with a van full of cakes and posh frocks. Lizzie drove, looking quite impressive behind the wheel of the van in her designer shades. We got to the hotel where the after-party was being held at about 5pm and Sangita was already there, screaming orders. This was a huge night for her – the *Strictly Come Dancing* launch was such a big event in the TV calendar; everyone tried to blag their way in along with the press to find out which celebs were dancing and who they were dancing with that year...and to spot all the celebs attending the huge industry party at the hotel afterwards. The uninvited press were camped outside as the celebrity dancers made their entrances via the red carpet and the buzz around this event was massive. Once the names of the celebrities taking part had been announced, the secrecy over the celebrities would be over and we'd no longer be among the select few in the know.

We set out the cakes and whilst the celebs were being interviewed and photographed we changed into our outfits.

"So how is everybody feeling?" said Lizzie, slicking on expensive red lipstick.

"OK," said Al.

"Yeah, OK," I agreed. And that's exactly how I felt. A few weeks ago I would have expected to be terrified right now, but I wasn't. I was happy. The cakes were good, but more importantly, my friends were OK. Al and I looked at each other and smiled. I think we were thinking the same thing. Once we had finished getting ready, we went into the big hall to wait the arrival of the celebrities and invited guests.

The huge hotel function room was decorated beautifully with a dance theme and our glamorously dressed fairy cakes, exploding hip-hop macaroons and the centrepiece cake (which was to remain covered until everyone had arrived) were all arranged at one end. We waited patiently for the interviews to be over whilst Sangita checked and double-checked that everything looked perfect. Then finally, in a flood of chatter and cha-cha the celebrities and other invited guests flowed into the room. As they quaffed cocktails, our centrepiece cake was unveiled, drawing gasps of admiration from the throng. Resplendent on its own table, which even had special lighting it was almost a metre wide. With its polished surface and fondant dancers, this was certainly a talking point and warranted another photo opportunity for the invited press.

Al was soon chatting with Graham Norton about his new show as Brucie complimented me on the lightness of our sponge. Tess worked the room with Anton and other showbiz luminaries while eating our delicious cakes and in the background, glamorous, spangled women sipped white wine and chatted animatedly.

"The newsreaders look the weirdest when they do these dancing shows," observed Lizzie from her position near the centrepiece. "Look at those two over there – they look positively sexed-up in their open-necked shirts and micro-minis."

I had to agree, I wasn't used to seeing them smile so

frequently and they looked very strange from the waist down, lurking over the canapés. "It all started with *Children in Need*. Whoever put Andrew Marr in a basque and stockings on that night wants flogging," I murmured under my breath.

"Honestly, Graham's not nearly as camp in real life," said Al as we came together over the macaroons. He looked happy – the colour had returned to his face and he was networking with enthusiasm. "I'm almost running out of business cards Stel, celebrities are coming out of every nook and cranny."

I grabbed a glass of champagne from a passing waiter (just like they do in films). It was after 8pm, the cakes were being eaten and enjoyed and I was just thinking about starting out for home when Sangita leapt to my side. "Stella, the events people are saying 'fabulous', they're saying 'outstanding', they're saying 'we will be discussing a long-term contract with this company'." she practically screamed.

"Sangita, that's amazing," I said, looking at Al who was beaming with joy.

"Well, you haven't let me down and for that I thank you," Sangita said, calming down and reverting to her usual understated presence. She swept off as always without a 'goodbye' or 'see you', leaving Al and I to breathe in a cloud of financial relief and Champagne bubbles.

"Well, that's good news, doll," said Al.

"Yes, but more importantly, have you called Seb tonight?"

"Yes. He's doing well and he's pleased that we seem to be a hit. We are lucky Stella, aren't we?" he said, with shining eyes. He was so right – we were lucky. Not only had our hard work paid off, we had come through something really tough, and been stronger for it. Suddenly, I was bored of all the glitz and glamour and celebrity. I just wanted to go home, with Lizzie and Al, to see Grace and to start our lives again in the morning.

"Al, can we go?" I suggested as soon as she'd moved on. "I

think our work here is done 're cakes', to borrow from Sangita. And I have a real urge just to spend the evening with my friends and be normal. What do you think?" I said.

"Well, it *is* the new series of *The Real Housewives of New Jersey* tonight – and I know none of us would want to miss *that*." He said with a smile.

"I'm glad we have things in perspective," I giggled. "I'm already in the van."

"OK. Let's grab Lizzie and tell her we have a hot date in NJ with Danielle and the gals…" He trailed off as something caught his eye.

"What?" I asked, bemused.

"Erm, Stella don't look now but isn't that Dave over there?"

"Dave? It can't be" I said, still smiling. This was the last place Dave would be seen – too public, not good for his MI5 credentials.

"Yes that's definitely him, hanging out by the exploding macaroons," he said, peering through the celebrity throng.

"Are you sure it's Dave, *my* Dave?" I said, squinting into the distance and then suddenly spotting him in a good suit I'd never seen him in. "I'm surprised to see him here. So much for his spy doc," I said, my heart lurching. *Why hadn't he told me?* I hadn't heard from him since he came round to the house. He was too busy to support me when one of my friends could have been dying but clearly not too busy to hobnob with celebrities. I screwed up my eyes and I saw Dave more clearly. He was talking animatedly to someone and laughing.

"I wonder who he's talking to? I haven't seen him so engaged for some time," I said.

"Yes doll, he's been so tied up with MI5, he isn't allowed to *engage*," Al said sarcastically. "He's worried he might be bugged but I'd love to bug the conversation he's having with that twisted old slapper."

"Who?" I looked back through the familiar faces and there she was. Dave was talking and laughing: with Mary-Jane Robinson.

"Stella, there's something I think you should know," Al said, moving me round the buffet table out of Dave's eye line. "I met François from Fashion earlier tonight by the piano. He said that Dave's come in from the cold."

"What do you mean?" I asked, puzzled.

"Well, I wasn't going to tell you until we'd got out of here but apparently the spy doc collapsed. Oh doll, you should probably hear this from Dave..."

"Al! Please tell me!" I said, worried now.

"François says Dave couldn't get any real spies to take part. There's a surprise, I could have told him that and saved all the time and money," he sniggered.

"What else did François say," I asked, still reeling from what I had just seen and trying to piece everything together.

"He said, 'the eagle has landed'."

"Al, will you stop with the spy stuff and tell me exactly what you mean?"

"He's sold out, love. It seems that after his spy stuff collapsed he gave his fashion doc to MJ who, according to François, paid him pots and bestowed 'Executive Producer' on his pretty little head. He's now working at Media World. Cyclic, isn't it?"

"I don't think cyclic is quite the word I'm looking for," I said, beginning to feel a rising chill.

I looked at him across the room; Dave Kennedy, with those crinkly eyes and twinkly smile? "He wouldn't do that," I said firmly, recalling everything he'd said about integrity being more important than money. "He would never sell his fashion doc to Media World, he said they'd wreck it and he'd have no control. He always said he wanted a stylish, cerebral approach. That's why he said no to MJ in the first place."

"Oh darling, I'm sorry. So much for principles, eh?" Al put his hand on my arm. "It seems he has a price, Stel."

I couldn't quite believe it. Surely if it was true, he would have told me? I needed to hear it from Dave before I decided what to do next.

Al was putting on his jacket to leave. "Come on girlfriend don't waste your time on him. Those table-flipping Jersey gals are waiting."

"Hang on Al, I'll just be a minute," I answered, and calmly walked across the room, parting the sea of B-list celebrities and ballroom dancers. When I reached Dave I could see the shock on his face.

"Stella, how lovely to see you," he stammered. "I didn't expect you to be here." He turned on the charm and smiled that big, open smile.

"You knew I had the cake order for this," I said without smiling. "You might have guessed that I'd deliver them myself. You could always have called me to check and by the way, thanks for your support over the last few days."

At this, I glanced over his shoulder to see MJ smirking, one ear in our conversation the other pretending to listen to some poor, defenceless dancer. Dave manoeuvred me away to a small table filled with screwed-up paper cases and spilt Champagne.

"Stella, I'm really sorry I haven't been there for you. Work has been so busy. I just haven't had time."

"I understand, Dave," I said, coldly. "It's nice to see where your priorities lie. Sebastian will be fine, by the way – not that you care."

He looked hurt. "Stella, I need to talk to you. I'm sorry for everything that's happened. It's just that the spy doc hasn't worked out."

"So I gather – but I heard about it from someone else. Not

from you."

"I've been at my wits' end. I sunk everything I had into that project. I had no choice; it was for our future, Stel. You know? That lovely house by the sea – you and me?"

I was unmoved. "I can understand that having no job and no money is bloody hard and I can see how you could be tempted to work with a company you don't believe in," I began. "But after everything you said about needing to work with people you respect, in a company with the same values, I honestly can't believe that you'd do it. That you'd let MJ..." I trailed off, lost for words.

"I know, I know. I understand how you feel. I'm so sorry, I had no idea she'd do that. I can't believe she sent an email."

"What email?" I said. And then the truth hit me, square between the eyes. Bitch Rachel had never tried to wreck my business – why would she? We'd never met and it was over between her and Tom. The email had come from someone else entirely.

"MJ sent the email to Sangita about me running the company from home, didn't she?" I said, slowly and carefully. Dave shifted uncomfortably. "I'd discounted her because I assumed she didn't know anything about my business, but it all adds up now. She heard it all from you, didn't she?" I felt tears spring to my eyes. Boy, could I pick 'em! Different man, different betrayal, but a betrayal nonetheless. He didn't answer, he just dropped his head and stared at his shoes.

"You are so weak. Why didn't I see it before?" I said almost to myself, too hurt for anger.

"I didn't know she'd try and hurt you. She asked about you and I told her, in all innocence. I was just being nice. I had to, she's my boss Stella."

"You 'being nice' to that vindictive, hateful woman almost cost me my business," I spat.

"Stella, I love you. I'll resign. I know I've been bloody stupid. I just panicked," Dave said, clutching my hand.

"I'm sorry. I can never be with a man who would sell me to the highest bidder," I said, pulling away from him. "And I can never be with a man who can't support me when I need him the most. I have finally learnt that I'm better than that. Goodnight – and goodbye, Dave."

I got up from the table, leaving him just looking at me with tears in his eyes. I walked towards Al and Lizzie who were waiting with my coat.

"Are you OK doll?" Al said, helping me on with my coat and looking very concerned.

"It's over. I don't need him. Actually, I don't need any man," I said. "Now, where were we?"

"Headed for New Jersey and those real housewives?" suggested Lizzie.

"You bet," I said.

36

Starlets, Twiglets and Lizzie's Revenge

All of us had a quiet day on the Sunday after the party. Al spent time with Seb who was keen to hear all about the event and over the moon it had gone so well. He was very weak, but making good progress. Lizzie had to disappear off somewhere and I collected Grace and spent the day with her. We went shopping and watched movies – it was wonderful to spend time with her and I think we all breathed a sigh of relief that the events of the last few days were over.

I had just put Grace to bed when I heard a little tap on the front door. When I opened it, Lizzie was standing in the chilly darkness holding an envelope.

"This is for tomorrow night, babe," she said with a grin. "Al's coming too. Your mum is going to babysit, it's all arranged."

"What is it, Lizzie?" I asked, puzzled.

She winked at me. "You'll see. There's a cab coming to pick you up tomorrow at 6.30 – see you there!" and with that, she disappeared off into the night.

I took the envelope back into the kitchen and opened it. Inside was a ticket to the première of *Barry's Barbie*. I stared at the glossy print on the front, puzzled. I couldn't believe that Lizzie wanted me to attend the première of Media World's latest project and I didn't understand why she wanted to be there, either. But after the events of the last few weeks, I knew I had to go – she needed our support.

I was thinking about this when Al rang. "Stella, can you believe it?!" he squealed, sounding almost like his old self. "I mean *hello?* This show nearly ruined both me and Lizzie!"

"I know," I said, "I don't understand it, but we need to support Lizzie. She's been there for both of us and now we need to be there for her."

Al sighed. "You're right doll, of course. I'll see you tomorrow then. Seb sends a kiss."

"Send one back," I said, and hung up. If I was honest the last thing I wanted to do was go to *any* awards party, let alone one where MJ would be present – but it looked like that was exactly what I had to do. I went upstairs and raked around in the wardrobe until I found the navy 'date dress' I had worn to see Diego. It was still in its polythene from the dry-cleaner. *That'll do*, I thought and then climbed exhausted into bed.

The taxi picked up me first and then Al and we arrived at the venue on a cool October night to be greeted by paparazzi gathering round our taxi like coiled springs. Big cars stopped ahead of us to unload their Z-list celebrity cargos at the tiny doorway into the cinema. Footballers and girls 'who'd once slept with a footballer', soap stars and ex-*Big Brother* contestants all jostled for position in front of flashing cameras in the early evening sunshine.

"You couldn't actually put a name to most of the faces, but you sort of know who they are," Al commented as we sat in our taxi waiting. When we finally pulled up outside and stepped out of the taxi, photographers were shouting 'over here luv' and snapping wildly on the off-chance either of us were famous, or 'had once slept with a footballer'.

I felt quite sick but gathered together all my courage, held my stomach in and walked on wobbly heels. My magic pants were digging in under the dress, but I thought 'tall' as I swished into the viewing room with Al on my arm and, as my eyes became used to the light, I was disappointed to see how small the venue was. In the cramped dark, young waiters approached with corks in their hats offering pseudo Aussie-style canapés from trays and addressing everyone as 'sport'.

"G'day!" Al said, taking a barbie titbit from the tray.

"No canapé embargo here," I whispered. "No," said Al, wrinkling his nose at the morsel he'd just taken, "and it's a shame."

I felt nervous about what lay ahead as we watched the hungry Z-listers fill up on miniscule kangaroo-burgers and crocodile-kebabs. There was no Cristal but we were soon furnished with lukewarm white wine in cheap glasses and were asked to take our seats for the viewing, which we were told would consist of several highlights from the programme to be followed by a speech from Media World's owner, Fast Frank.

As we waited in the black stillness for the curtain to move and the screen to flicker into life, I looked furtively around the viewing theatre, hoping no-one could see me. I noticed a few familiar faces from Media World – I think I spotted Denise the vicar's wife – but I didn't see Lizzie. Then I turned round and saw Tom standing alone at the back. He smiled at me and nodded, lifting his hand in acknowledgement and I waved back. It hadn't occurred to me that he would be there – but of course, he'd filmed a lot of it so he would be invited.

People took their seats, the lights were lowered, the hissing and giggling ebbed and the curtains opened. Suddenly we were faced with a big screen and a series of glossy shots of Barry chopping salads and marinating meats. This was what Lizzie referred to as 'pre-barbie meat prep', which always sounded vaguely coital to me. As Barry spread his Aussie charm like thick, sweet ketchup, it was soon evident that this programme would be a winner. A fast-paced, well-filmed (thanks to Tom), well-scripted (thanks to Lizzie), life-affirming programme (thanks to Barry), which epitomised good times. The trail played out with a montage of feel-good days on the beach and family holidays, evoking memories of endless summers and warm sand between the toes.

"That was televisual sunshine," Al said with some disappointment as the lights came up.

"Mmm, brilliant ratings and spin-offs for years to come," I said with a hint of bitterness. It would keep MJ in work for the rest of her mean, media life.

There was then a fifteen-minute break where starlets munched on Twiglets and TV execs networked like their lives depended on it as mere mortals looked on. There was still no sign of Lizzie.

"Where do you think she is?" I hissed to Al.

"If I was her, I would have started on the vodka, doll," he said gloomily. "With this series she's made MJ look great."

Finally we were back in our seats and Fast Frank was mounting the small makeshift stage for his big moment. Frank thanked Barry for a wonderful performance and, being a hard-headed businessman, he couldn't resist a little PR for Barry's books, T-shirts, barbie aprons and mugs, the fruits of which would all come Media World's way. He went on to thank the production team including Tom, who'd stepped into the breach when the other cameraman was injured. He was obviously unaware that the crocodile attack had happened under the eyes of his star exec and head of the company whose official reason for being there was to ensure there were no accidents.

"Now, last but not least, I have a very special thank you for a very special person," he announced.

My heart sank.

"She has turned this whole Barry barbecue brand into pure

gold. Come up here, Mary-Jane Robinson," he announced and
clapped so hard the audience joined in. I exchanged a horrified
glance with Al. MJ mounted the stage, as wiry and hard as ever
but attempting 'girlish', hiding her face with hair and fake
modesty. Frank hugged her gratefully, saying over and over
again; "You're the one who made it happen." He went on to
thank her copiously and credit her alone for saving the shoot
and Media World.

Wearing a smug, self-satisfied smile, and a figure hugging
white Chanel dress, MJ stepped forward to the mic. "It's been
such hard work and I'm exhausted," she said in clipped tones
with tight, red lips. "But I would do it all again, it was just so
rewarding. Frankie," she said, turning to him, "you are the most
wonderful boss and Media World is lucky to have you."

"This is obscene – like a drag version of Marilyn singing to
JFK," commented Al, loudly.

Frank approached MJ with a huge Jane Packer bouquet of
deep pink roses and an overblown cheque. So, MJ was not only
taking the credit for the whole programme, she was also getting
a bonus. I wondered why on earth Lizzie had wanted us to
witness this. Frank was about to hand the roses and cheque to a
drooling MJ when he whipped them away at the last minute,
grinning all over his face.

"But first, members of your team have a little surprise for
you!" He said. "They have made a special film in honour of your
achievement. Now I haven't seen it yet, but I'm assured it's a
testament to your hard work. Lizzie!"

Suddenly, Lizzie swept onto the stage and positioned
herself at MJ's side. Smiling broadly, she took the mic from
Frank and gave MJ a huge, open smile. "I know Mary-Jane wasn't
expecting anything from the crew, but we just had to do this.
MJ, you leave us all truly speechless. Everyone who worked on
the project wanted to give you a special gift," Lizzie said.

"My cameraman Tom and I have been busy recording and editing those off-diary moments I think you'll find amusing. They reveal how hard everyone's worked and just how tough it's been for MJ on these foreign shoots. Enjoy!" With that, Lizzie bear-hugged a smiling but bemused MJ, and added in lip-synch with hand actions; 'from me to you'.

Suddenly on screen, there was MJ dressed up to the nines, drinking Champagne and laughing with Barry on his balcony. This was followed by fly-on-the-wall reportage shots of MJ with a clipboard, having meetings, discussing scripts with Barry and generally being the boss. The next scene was a wide shot – taken from a distance – of MJ emerging onto a balcony wearing a towel and looking a bit the worse for wear. I looked around for a reaction and in the darkness I could see the glint of fake white veneers, people smiling in anticipation. Then suddenly, into the silence, MJ was shouting over her shoulder on the balcony: "Fucking hell, I need another drink...where are my tabs?"

Al shot me a look, the audience gasped and uneasy giggles staggered across the silence as everyone waited for the punch line; but there wasn't one.

In the next shot, MJ was joined on the balcony by Barry wearing only boxers and holding out her pack of cigarettes. They each took one and lit up, laughing and drinking Champagne from half-empty glasses on the table. This was obviously filmed with a telephoto lens, because neither of them seemed aware of the camera.

There was a low rumble in the audience; this was starting to feel uncomfortable and I could see by MJ's frozen smile that she was horrified. The next shot was MJ kissing Barry, climbing all over him and saying in a drunken slur: "I don't care, I want you again, now, sod the filming." When Barry protested, she raised her voice: "Look, Frankie'll pay for extra days on the budget. He won't even know he's spent it. Stupid bastard's rolling in it. I want you, NOW!"

At this point, there were audible gasps and mutterings from the audience and, judging by the look on her face, MJ wanted the ground to swallow her up. Panic-stricken, she began pawing at Fast Frank's arm, vainly trying to talk at him, moving him away from the screen but he was stuck to the spot, wide-eyed, as the next scene appeared.

The camera was on the ground but voices could be heard and someone was shouting. Despite not being able to see anyone, I could tell MJ's voice anywhere. "You tell Barry's wife about this and I'll deny everything. And don't even *think* about going to fat Frank. I'll tell him you're jealous because I'm with Barry now. One word and your career will be over," she ranted.

Suddenly, Lizzie's voice: "My career was over the day you came on this shoot."

The next scene showed MJ drunkenly telling a young runner, "I shaid I wanted vodka and DIET Coke, you cretin. Get me another!" Then the sound of sloshing liquid, followed by a gasp from the doused runner. "Shtupid bitch," MJ slurred in the darkness. Cut to MJ smoking more fags, feet up, talking about the cameraman attacked by the crocodile. "Shtupid bashtard stepped straight onto it. I wash in the wine bar, nothin to do with me." she said, giggling as she reached for her vodka, taking big swigs and wiping her mouth with the back of her hand like a trucker.

This was followed by a montage of shots put to music (Elton John's *The Bitch is Back*) of MJ in various states, snogging with Barry, drinking Champagne from the bottle and screaming at junior staff while lounging on a director's chair. This was all happening during filming, while everyone else was working. We heard her shouting at runners, swearing at researchers and bullying anyone who dared to disturb her drinking, hair appointments, or afternoons of delight with Barry.

I tore my eyes away from the screen as it ended, desperate to see the look on her face again but she'd gone from the dark, empty stage, where only Frank and Lizzie now stood. Fast Frank looked lost, still open-mouthed, but had enough wits about him to put the envelope containing the big, thank-you cheque for MJ discreetly but firmly behind his back. He wasn't that 'shtupid'.

Al and I looked at each other, wide-eyed. "That was bloody fabulous," he whispered. I couldn't speak I was so surprised and still transfixed on the stage area.

"I'm soo glad you two came," screamed Lizzie, rushing over and hugging us both at the same time. "Did you see it? Wasn't it fab?" At this point, Tom joined us and they smiled and hugged each other and suddenly it all made sense.

Al was almost jumping up and down with excitement. "It was brilliant. MJ will be *toast* after that! Why didn't you tell us? When did you make it? How did it happen?!"

Tom put his hand on Al's shoulder and said: "Come on everyone. I think we all need to have a proper chat somewhere, away from here." We went straight to the nearest pub, where, over a bottle of wine, Lizzie and Tom told us exactly what had been happening.

"Almost the first time I met him, I fell for Barry," Lizzie confessed. "And yes, we were lovers but I realise now that Barry was always looking for the main chance. MJ offered more airtime and threw money at him, saying she could do wonders for his career. She arrived on the scene and treated me like dirt, giving me all the worst jobs and blaming me for everything that went wrong. I just put up with it – that's how she is with everyone and I knew I was doing my job well. But once she'd started to make a play for Barry I was sunk. One night I discovered them in bed together and was devastated. I stupidly said I'd tell Barry's wife, though I had no intention of doing that. I just overreacted. Later, as you saw in the footage, MJ said if I told Barry's wife or Fast Frank got to hear about the affair she'd deny everything and say I was jealous. Then my career would be over." Lizzie took a gulp of gin and tonic. "She also said she knew who my friends were and that she was prepared to do whatever it took to destroy your business." I knew my career was over once she'd got her claws into it – but I couldn't let her ruin you two.

"What a bitch!" Al hissed, leaning closer and sipping hard on his chilled white wine while Tom poured more from the second bottle he'd just brought back to the table.

"Then the crocodile incident happened. It was the icing on the cake and I knew there was no way MJ would take the rap for it. I knew you were having a tough time Stel and didn't want to add to the stress so I called Tom. I thought he could help me."

"Yeah, Lizzie told me everything and we came up with a plan for me to film MJ on the next shoot. Funny because we weren't going to be out there for long and we were worried we wouldn't have enough footage. We ended up with plenty!" said Tom with a smile. "I wanted to get MJ back for all the stuff she put you through when you worked for her, Stel, and I was worried about the business. You've worked so hard and it means so much to you." Tom added.

Lizzie continued: "When I heard about the vicious email I just knew it was MJ and I felt so guilty, like The Cake Fairy would fail and die and it would all be my fault. I knew you were hoping to sign a contract with the big events company and MJ was flavour of the moment in the fickle world of TV. A word in the wrong ear and it could have been curtains. I called Tom and said: 'let's do it'. So we booked an edit-suite in Birmingham, away from prying eyes and made our own film."

"Wow. I can't believe all this was going on and we had no idea," I said, putting my arm round Lizzie. So Grace had been right when she spotted them together – but they were doing something for me.

"Then everything happened with Seb," said Lizzie, somberly. "We only had a short time to finish the film and as soon as I heard what had happened, I knew that I had to be with you, Al. It meant Tom was left to do it on his own, and he wasn't sure he could juggle work, Grace and editing in secret."

I looked across at Tom, fiddling awkwardly with his wine glass. Lizzie took a gulp of wine and carried on.

"I'm sorry that I've been so down. It's just that every time I went into work, MJ would try her best to make things difficult, just like she did with you, Stella. I'm just glad it's over," she said.

"Thank you both for everything," said Al, hugging Lizzie and smiling at Tom. "But why on earth didn't you tell us?"

"For a start Al, you'd have been so angry you'd never have kept quiet, which would have blown the whole plan," said Lizzie. "I know what you and François are like. If MJ had got wind of any of it she would have just sacked us and we desperately needed to be at the launch tonight so we could play the film publicly, and for Frank especially. As it happens we'll no doubt be sacked now anyway for embarrassing Frank and Media World but I think we've all just about had enough of that company."

"Hear, hear," said Tom. "More drinks I think," and he stood up to go to the bar, which gave Lizzie the opportunity to talk to me.

"Stella, I felt so guilty working with Tom. I felt bad even *speaking* to the man who had broken my best friend's heart. Apart from not wanting to worry you with more MJ stuff I thought you'd feel betrayed if I told you I was making this film with him. I was dying to tell you everything. Then everything happened with Seb and MJ was making my life so hard, I didn't want to burden anyone. And it seemed so unimportant compared to what you were going through, Al."

"I'm sorry I put pressure on you," I said. "It must have been awful, dealing with all that on your own," I said, welling up.

"It was all worth it in the end. MJ's got enough to worry about in her own career now without trying to ruin yours – and anyway, her credibility after this is zero. She's been proved a liar and that's enough."

"Well, I'll drink to that," said Al, holding up his glass. "Here's to the end of the Queen of Mean – and the rise of The Cake Fairy. Cheers!" We all chinked glasses. I could see Tom watching us, from the bar. Al saw me looking at him, and took my hand.

"Stel," he said softly, "you will always be my best friend along with Lizzie, and if you don't want to its fine. But I was wondering if I should invite Tom to the wedding? Just for the evening? He's really helped out here and I know Grace would love it."

If Al had asked me only a few weeks ago, I would have been outraged. But as it was – it felt right. I had moved on and after all, Tom was the father of my child.

"Yes. I think that would be nice, Al. Thank you," I said.

"I propose another toast," said Lizzie. "To Al and Seb. May their marriage be long and happy."

"To Al and Seb!" I echoed. "To having your life back and the different things that means to all of us."

EPILOGUE

Wedding Cake and Wishes

A month later, the wedding day had finally arrived.

Lizzie, Grace and I helped Al and Sebastian get ready in the afternoon. I don't know who was more nervous. When we arrived, their house was, as always, immaculate, all chrome kitchen and clean lines. However, within about ten minutes of 'preparations' it was an exploding disaster. Unusually, I was the first one ready in my sequinned, 'best woman' swimsuit of deep scarlet, with a matching silk sarong.

"Cake, Stel. Is the cake OK?" Al demanded from their en-suite bathroom. "It hasn't gone droopy or anything?"

"Noooo Al, it's looking fabulous in place of honour poolside, where you should be NOW. Hurry up!"

To top Al's nerves, Grace was having hair issues and demanding something 'more cool,' each time I styled her hair. Torn between seahorse and sea-fairy for her bridesmaid outfit, Grace had plumped for the latter and was in diaphanous glittery wings, mermaid's tail and, apparently, 'uncool' hair.

"Grace, I'm sorry but this is about the fourth time I've tried and I can't do a Lady GaGa, so you will just have to live with it."

"But Mum, when Charlotte's mum puts her hair up she looks way cool."

"Well then perhaps I'll talk to her mum about adopting you – AFTER this wedding. We are now all very late and you're still half-dressed. Not to mention the groom, who's still in the bath," I muttered to myself.

"I heard there was a celebrity hair-emergency," Lizzie said from the doorway, gin and tonic in one hand and hairbrush in the other. "Come on Grace my love – it's clear your mother doesn't care. Allow Auntie Lizzie turn you into something fabulous!"

Grace smiled and pulled a 'yeah Mum' face at me while I ran to the bathroom to knock once more on the door. "Al, my sweet, you are now in serious danger of missing your own wedding," I announced, just as the doorbell rang. "And the cars are here now to whisk us to 'water wonderland'," I tried, hoping this would move him. There was no sound, so I slowly opened the door.

"Have the flowers arrived?" he asked, standing in front of a bank of metrosexual, male beauty products, his face covered in a white lather.

"Yes Al, they're at the pool all ready and waiting for you. Like everyone else."

"And the lifeboat favours?"

"Yes Al."

Knowing it would be some time before Al emerged from the bathroom, shaved, toned and well- moisturised, I peeped over the banister to see Seb, who was trying to fix his tie in the hall mirror – not easy with one arm in plaster.

"Let me help you with that," I said, "seeing as I have clearly failed as a hairdresser."

Seb smiled, his face filled with light. "I'm feeling so wonderful Stella. This really is the best day of my life."

I arranged his tie, blew him a kiss and went back into the bedroom were Lizzie was playing Charlie Le Mindu to Grace's Lady Gaga. "Mum, this is sick," Grace said, smiling.

"Don't be rude, Auntie Lizzie's doing a lovely job," I said, slightly affronted on Lizzie's behalf.

"Mum, sick is good," Grace said, rolling her eyes at Lizzie who winked at me.

"Oh. Well, I actually feel sick and that's not good," I said, plonking myself down onto the bed. "I'm nauseous – all excited and nervous at the same time."

"And on top of what you've eaten this morning that could make one big mess on the carpet," squealed Al, rushing into the room half-dressed, pulling on socks and combing his hair at the same time. He eventually straightened, held out his arms and gave us a twirl in his bright blue, fish-tailed suit.

Grace giggled. "Uncle Al, you look awesome."

"And I feel awesome," he smiled, slipping his feet into blue patent-leather. "Come on girls – what you waiting for? It's showtime!" he leapt out of the room and down the stairs, swiftly followed by two best women and an excited sea-fairy. Climbing into the waiting taxi we passed Seb, who was holding open the doors and chatting to the cab driver.

"At last!" he said locking the front door, admiring Al and piling into the back with Lizzie, Grace and I. His Majesty, Al sat proudly in the front and instructed the driver to "Please drive slowly, I am gorgeous but nervous. It's my wedding day." We all giggled and Seb shook his head in mock despair as the taxi driver smiled uncertainly and set off for the ten-minute journey to aqua-married bliss.

Once at the Splash Centre we all piled out of the taxi and a handful of people – including Al's parents – waved animatedly, greeting us like film stars and snapping away with their cameras. After the photos were done, I hugged Al's mum, Jean, who wiped a tear while his dad Brian shook Seb's hand. "Ooh you both look sooo handsome," Jean said, squeezing Al's arm. Al linked his mum and started to walk her into the building, she was in her seventies and a little wobbly on her feet but feisty like her son. "Now where's Seb?" I heard her say, "I need to give him instructions about the way you like your cauliflower cheese."

"Don't worry Mum, he wrote it all down last time we saw

you, remember?" Al answered, kissing the top of her head.

The heat and chlorine hit me in the face as we arrived poolside and walked into the adjoining aerobics gym which had been transformed into 'Seaworld' for the occasion. Human seaweed jostled with Neptunes of various sizes, sexualities and genders, like the cartoon cast from *The Little Mermaid*. Lizzie and I stood together, dressed in our matching beachwear and dark sunglasses

"That red suits your blonde hair," Lizzie said, looking me up and down.

"Thanks sweetie," I said, appreciatively. But as I looked around and eyed the younger girls in tiny bikinis and mini sarongs, I couldn't help but feel I was less 'Pammy from *Baywatch*' and more 'Shelley Winters: the fat years.'

Suddenly, the music started. Lizzie and I ushered everybody into the pool area to stand along both sides of the pool, facing the deep end. Then we took our places near the celebrant. The happy couple appeared from the changing rooms at the shallow end in matching, sea-blue suits with satin fishtails. They were smiling, looking at each other and holding hands. My heart lurched and my eyes filled with water. I kept my head down and tried to concentrate on the pale blue, mosaic-tiled floor, determined not to burst into uncontrollable sobs at this early stage in the proceedings.

"They look fabulous, don't they?" Lizzie hissed. I nodded, unable to speak.

"Yes, they do. They do look fabulous," a voice whispered behind us. It was Sebastian's mum Rosemary, dressed in a classy, deep-pink costume with matching beaded sarong.

"It's so nice to see you under happier circumstances. You must be very proud of him," I said, discreetly wiping my eyes and making room for her to stand between Lizzie and I.

"Yes. As I'm sure you know, Sebastian's an only child," she

said. "This is the day I always dreamed of."

At that point the music started and Al and Seb walked to the side of the pool, followed by my sea-fairy and a vivid collection of sea urchins whose day job was being Al's nephews and nieces. They were escorted by Al's sister Linda, who was busy tucking in scales and arranging seaweed hair. The boys, followed by the unruly gaggle walked slowly round the pool in front of the guests, who moved back to let them pass. Their celebrant, friend and men's 200-metre champion Tristram was waiting at the deep end with a cheeky smile, a just-worked-out six pack and Speedos.

"Nice," whispered Lizzie, under her breath.

"Forget it – he's in the cocktail lane," I sighed.

"Today we are here to witness these two people making a public declaration of love and a lifelong commitment to each other," Tristram started. "The couple have written their own vows to truly reflect how they feel about each other." Then the boys started to recite their vows. I noticed that Al was shaking slightly and I got my tissues ready.

"I vow to love Al all my life. I will dance with him, swim with him and protect him from the sharks in open water," Sebastian concluded.

Al looked up at him, his eyes shining. "And I vow to love Sebastian all my life, to hold his hand when he's scared, never put his swimming trunks on a hot wash, and never push him in the deep end."

Then I stepped forward, passing Al the white-gold wedding ring he had chosen and Lizzie did the same for Seb, both trying our best not to cry. Everyone laughed and clapped and cheered as Ella Fitzgerald sang *Ev'ry Time We Say Goodbye* over the PA system. Al and Seb then stripped off and dove into the water, coming up holding each other's hands in the air and hugging.

"So much for not getting the plaster cast wet," Lizzie

chuckled, wiping a tissue across her eyes.

The guests showered the happy couple with confetti whilst they were still in the water. Grace and the urchins especially enjoyed throwing the coloured paper into the water and Lizzie and I watched in silence for a few seconds as it floated then swirled into multicolour madness. I think we were both contemplating the lack of love and confetti in our own lives.

"Come on babes, let's get started on the buffet," Lizzie said, grabbing my arm, linking me and heading for the groaning table in the gym, stacked with seafood, shell-shaped cookies with white-chocolate pearls, sea-horse fairy cakes, mermaid-shaped meringues and the swimming pool wedding cake.

"This looks dee–lish!" Lizzie announced, forgetting about men in trunks and filling her plate. "You've done an amazing job Stella," she said, looking at the cake and gaping in awe at the detailed little sugar people diving into sea-blue icing. "Ooh that's you, and there's François from Fashion. Oh, and Denise up to her neck in blue icing and boys...oh and there's me, I've lost a few pounds," She giggled.

Plates piled high we made our way to one of the circular tables which had been set out in the gym. Covered in swathes of sea-blue material, each table was sprinkled with sparkly fish confetti and had a glass bowl with floating blue flowers and lit candles in the centre. Al's lifeboat favours were laid carefully at each place and we sat on blue gossamer-covered chairs. In between mouthfuls, Lizzie was running up and down to video the lesbian synchronised swimming team doing their Esther Williams bit and then filmed Pete from Graphics dressed as Carmen Miranda as he started off the karaoke at the other end of the gym.

When 'Carmen' had finished his rendition of *Three Little Fishes* Sebastian, with Al at his side, took the mic. "Hi everyone, can I have your attention?" Gradually, guests stopped chattering and made their way into the gym. "Firstly, thank you sooo much for coming. We didn't really want any speeches today – we just wanted everyone to enjoy the pool and the food and..." at this, Al couldn't contain himself any longer and grabbed the mic.

"Thanks to Mum, Dad and Rosemary for being such wonderful parents and producing two gorgeous boys." He said with a wink. "Thanks also for the lovely buffet," Al continued. "The cauliflower-cheese flan is lovely, Mum." He then went on to thank Tristram for being the cutest ever celebrant, along with sea urchins and the sea-fairy bridesmaid, who was dripping wet and eating ice cream in a very un-fairylike way.

"And now we come to the cake," Al said, looking at me with a smile. "Well, what can I say? It's just amazing. Thank you, Stella – and not just for the incredible pièce de résistance. Thanks to both you and Lizzie – for truly being my 'best women', for always being there for me and for being such dear friends to both of us. The events of the last few months have taught me a lot about true friendship," he said with a smile, and then turned to Sebastian "and about true love. Now let the celebrations begin!"

Lizzie wiped her eyes then put fresh batteries in her video camera. "Sebastian," she shouted, "come and speak to the camera."

Sebastian swept Al across the dancefloor and rushed over. "What can I say? I'm the happiest man alive!" he shouted, dragging Al behind. "We've chosen blue as our wedding theme today," he said directly to the camera. We want to celebrate our maleness. Yes, we're reclaiming blue, not borrowing pink from the girls anymore, they can have it back."

"It's not any old blue either," added Al, "it's the blue of the ocean because we met in very blue waters," his arm now firmly round Seb.

I felt moved by their mutual joy and when Al staggered

towards me later in the evening holding a glass of blue champagne, I put out my arms and he sat on my knee. "I'm so happy Stella," he said. "I've never been this happy. He's so good for me you know." I hugged him.

"You're so lucky, some people wait all their lives for what you two have," I said kissing him on the cheek.

Later, I sat alone watching Al and Seb dancing the last waltz in their matching suits. *Two blue penguins dancing in a sea of happiness*, I thought, overcome with pink prose and blue Champagne. I vowed then, with chlorine in my nostrils and hope in my heart, that I would only spend my life with another man if we could be as happy as they were tonight.

I glanced across to see Tom slipping through the door. He'd arrived for the evening celebrations and as I watched him thread through the guests I thought about our wedding day. We'd been so happy, we thought it would go on forever and I suddenly felt a sob in my throat and needed some air. "I just need to nip out for a sec," I said to Lizzie, getting up. "I'll be back in a minute." I walked through the beautifully decorated hall unnoticed as everyone carried on dancing and drinking.

I found my coat and pulled it on over my bathing suit, then stepped out into the icy cold. I shivered and walked across the pavement towards my car. Slipping into the driving seat, I stared back at the municipal pool building where so many happy people were celebrating and thought about how I'd changed in the past year.

I thought about Tom and Grace inside. Tom had found Grace just as I'd left and was laughing at something our daughter had said to him. I thought about the way he had leant down and touched her face with such tenderness and tears sprung to my eyes. For a moment in the chilly darkness I looked up at all the stars and wondered if Tom could figure in my future of pink and green fairy cakes. Then I remembered the past and how I'd changed and how Tom wasn't my match anymore.

I loved my new independence and knew that, whatever happened, I had out grown my old life and could now only share my future on my terms. I wanted real, passionate, uncompromising love and all the contradictions that came with it. I wanted to be close to another person but still be me and most of all I didn't want my dreams swallowed up in another marriage of money-worries, guilt and game-playing.

There, in the starry blackness, with the muffled sound of laughter and happiness in the air, I realised there were things I had to do.

It was colder now; there'd be a frost tonight. I slid out of the car and started heading back to the pool. Wrapping my coat around me I heard my phone ringing in the pocket but before I could find it the ringing had stopped. I checked the number; it was Diego's, and he'd left a message. I fumbled with the buttons to hear what he said.

"Hi Stella, I been thinking about you – perhaps we could go for a drink sometime? This ees not about cake. Please call me." I felt a catch of excitement in my throat and smiled, putting my phone back in my pocket and holding it there like a secret. I would call him back later.

So much had changed in the past year. I didn't know what would happen next but that's what made it so exciting. I gave a little skip and walked back into the wedding. Welcoming the warm blast of air, heavy with love and chlorine, I made a wish and dared to hope that one day, I could have my cake – and eat it.

The End

Cake Fairy Recipes!

Dear Al,

As requested, here are my notes, poured straight from my disorganised unruly head onto paper. If anything should ever happen to me (knocked down by a bus/run off with a millionaire/am scouted by 'Models One' and am jetting around the globe on assignments) then it's all here – everything I know – knock yourself out boyfriend!

You won't need much stuff for small amounts – 1 large, roomy bowl, 1 whisk (I use hand held but any will do), weighing scales, and a spatula to scrape every last bit from the bowl.

May I also suggest you accessorize with a bag of Maltesers and the latest celebrity mag? It has been scientifically proven that chocolate and salacious 'A' list gossip stops you from opening the oven door to see if the cakes are ready – which could lead to a flat cake disaster zone.

Hints and Tips

Just a few pointers before you get mixing. Baking is my business and it is a deeply pleasurable experience that fills me with something akin to chocolate. There's nothing lovelier than escaping to the kitchen and that calm heartbeat of the whisk, creating fluffy, sweet, creamy batter – a blank canvas to flavour or colour depending on your mood or whim.

Cake-making can be calming, elating, inspiring and therapeutic, but in order for it to be all that – you mustn't be stressed sweetie. Life is hard enough and when you've had a long day dealing with everyday problems and painful people, you don't want to be managing temperamental fairy cakes. So to keep this loveliest of pleasures intact my recipes are very simple, extremely easy and so impressive even you won't believe you made them. I used to bake these cakes at the end of a long day with a small child and trust me they are foolproof. These babies can be made any time of the day or night and they always work – even with a toddler running round the kitchen (or 'helping').

Another tip; when doing the all in one mix (as illustrated in my fabulous notes), I put all the dry ingredients in the bowl first then wait a few seconds and check that all is calm before I add the wet ingredients. That way if there's suddenly a child/mother/goldfish emergency or a telephone ringing, I can abandon for as long as I need to. But once you add the wet ingredients you need to stick with it through to the end (whatever's happening) because the 'rising' process begins and you need to get them in the oven ASAP. If you don't, your fairies will be flat. And no-one wants a flat fairy!

Talking of which, try not to keep opening the oven door until they're ready as this can also cause sinking (you know you can be impatient!). Once you do get them out (oo-er!), if you are unsure whether they're properly done, just insert a skewer. It should come out completely clean if cakes are cooked.

Ooh and Mum asked me to mention sieving action. She always taught me to raise the sieve high when sifting flour to allow as much air as possible into the bowl an make the lightest fairies. Make sure the bowl is really large too so you can get plenty of height without dusting the kitchen (or the cat) in flour.

There are no fancy or unobtainable ingredients in my recipes Al...and as you know I'm not very exotic (more's the pity!) so all the ingredients can be found in a girl's kitchen cupboards. However, the time to hit the icing emporiums and specialist shops or websites is when you want a rich colour – like violet for the punk fairies or deep red for the red velvet cupcakes. Colour paste comes in small tubs, is inexpensive and available in a rainbow of wonderful shades and colours. It can be added to basic icing, including buttercream, or the cake batter for red velvets or even green and purple for 'scary fairies' at Halloween.

Finally, know your oven! The cooking times in all recipes can vary depending on how hot your oven is and can make the difference between light and golden and...let's not go there. So adapt accordingly, if your oven is hot, bake either at a slightly lower temperature, or for a few minutes less – and vice versa.

Good luck!

Violent Violet Punk Rock Fairy Cakes

Inspired by Gerald's Vicarage Garden!

The anti-establishment buttercream frosting is bright purple and swirly and sweet – but if baking for hardcore punks the batter needs to be ultra violet too. I like to dress mine in black 'skull and cross bones' paper cases – often used more innocently for children's pirate parties – but hinting at something darker here. Makes about 12 "kick ass" fairy cakes.

<u>Ingredients</u>
110g or 4 oz self-raising flour
1 teaspoon baking powder
110g or 4 oz softened butter
110g or 4 oz lavender or plain caster sugar (you <u>may</u> be more organised than me – ok...ok, you <u>will</u> be, and might even have a jar of caster sugar with a few sprigs of lavender already in the kitchen cupboards?)
2 large eggs
12 rebellious paper cases

<u>Violent Violet Buttercream Icing</u>
250g or 9 oz icing sugar sifted
60g or 2 oz softened butter
A whole load of violet food colouring (ideally a paste from a cake decorating shop or from a cake craft shop online)
Rainbow dust edible bling in violent violet to scatter everywhere (and over yourself too)

<u>Method</u>
Pre-heat the oven to 170°c/325°f/ Gas Mark 3 and fill a cake tin with the paper cases. Sift the flour, sugar and baking powder

into a large bowl. Don't forget the height!

Add the butter and eggs then whisk on a slow speed (yes you can sip your coffee now) until everything is combined. Now add the purple droplets – you can be all arty Al and swirl it for a marble effect – or work at it until it's pure punk purple.

Spoon the mixture into the paper cases (remember they will rise so don't fill to the top). Bake in the oven for approximately 20 minutes or until risen and springy to the touch.

Once out of the oven and slightly cooled, take the cakes from the tin and cool on a wire rack... Al don't... oh too late, you've burned your tongue!

For the Frosting

Beat together the icing sugar and butter on a medium speed with a hand held whisk.

Turn the whisk down and add purple colouring (make like Johnny Rotten and splash it in until it can't take any more!). Continue whisking until the frosting is light and fluffy – this may take at least five minutes, bear in mind the longer you whisk the topping the lighter and fluffier it will become... and I know how much you like 'fluffy.'

Now top the cooled cakes with the blindingly violet frosting with a knife or the back of a spoon with a very camp swirling movement (you know you can do it).

Then scatter edible rainbow dust on top of the Punk Fairy Cakes while pogo-ing round the kitchen (Al, don't even try to pretend you're too young to remember the pogo!)

Yummy Mummies' Organic Victoria Sponge
(or Stepford Sponge!)

To be made by Mummy before the school run so she can impress the other mummies at the school gate by announcing to her perfect offspring (with a serene smile – not induced by drugs) that "there's organic homemade sponge for tea darlings!"

Ingredients
220g or 8 oz organic self raising flour
2 tsp organic baking powder
220g or 8 oz organic butter
220g or 8 oz organic caster sugar
4 large organic eggs
Seeds of half an organic vanilla pod
2 x 20 cm or 8 inch lose bottomed sandwich tins (these don't have to be organic)
6-8 tablespoons homemade (absolutely!) organic strawberry jam
Several fabulous dollops organic double cream

Method
Put on a pink polka dot apron and pre-heat the oven to 170°c/325°f/Gas Mark 3. Now grease the cake tins with organic butter and a serene, organic smile. Sift the flour, sugar and baking powder into a large bowl, lifting the sieve high to the heavens.

Now add the butter and eggs and whisk on a slow speed until everything is combined. Add the vanilla pods and mix. Spoon the mixture into the two cake tins. Bake in the oven for approximately 25-30 minutes or until risen and golden and springy to the touch.

Once out of the oven and slightly cooled turn the cake tins upside down and place on a wire rack.

When completely cooled, spoon on the organic homemade jam and organic cream and sandwich together in an orgasmic organic rush of pleasure. Dust carefully with organic icing sugar and stand back in the afterglow to enjoy the sight of Stepford Wife perfection.

Now apply pearly lipstick and collect organic children smugly from the school gate.

Inebriated Christmas Tarts

Tipsy and gorgeous for Christmas, these classy tarts are impressive yet sooo easy to make. They have a wonderful boozy glow with a faint echo of almond paste which is just so Christmassy it makes you want to sing! To make these tarts and truly embrace the season, you will need Christmas music and a glass of Amaretto on the side as you bake. This makes about 12 tarts.

<u>Ingredients</u>
350g or 12 oz mincemeat (homemade or from a jar)
2 tablespoons Amaretto
200g or 7 oz plain flour, sieved
40g or 1½ oz caster sugar
80g or 2¾ oz ground almonds
125g or 4½ oz diced butter
1 large egg, beaten
Milk for glazing

<u>Method</u>
Ok so put that Christmas compilation disc on (the one you got free with *Cute Cupcake* magazine). Grease a twelve-hole cake tin and put aside. Add the Amaretto to the mincemeat and stir, leave aside then pour yourself a small liqueur to inspire that Christmas feeling. As George Michael opens with 'Last Christmas I gave you my heart..." wiggle your hips, sing loudly and put flour, butter, sugar and almonds into a bowl and plunge (cool) hands into it. Rub the ingredients together with your fingertips and when they're all combined, add the egg. The CD should now have moved seamlessly on to Johnny Mathis' 'Going Home for Christmas,' which indicates it's time to gather the mix

together in those cool hands, make a ball, wrap in cling film and pop in the fridge. This needs to be left to chill for half an hour which will give you enough time to trawl through the latest gossip in *Heat* magazine.

Now thirty minutes later – you're celebritied up and the haunting tones of East 17 start their (old but good) Christmas anthem, try not to cry as you roll out the pastry singing 'Stay Another Day.' Roll the pastry out onto a floured board. Then cut out twelve pastry circles with a fluted cutter (7.5cm/3ins) as the E 17 boys reach a bell-pealing climax – and place all the pastry circles into the prepared, greased tin.

Add a large teaspoon of liquored mince-meat to each pastry circle and then cut 12 more circles, place them on top of the mince filled bottoms and seal all the edges to prevent the tipsy mincemeat escaping. Pre-heat the oven to 200°c/400°f/Gas Mark 6, cut a small slit in each pastry top to let the steam escape, brush with a little milk and chill for another 30 mins (time for *Hello* and a forensic scrutiny of festive photo shoots). Once you've spent a whole 30 mins studying TV soap stars dressed in Santa suits you can pop the pies into the oven.

Bake for 20 minutes, serve warm and let the sweet, Christmassy aroma fill your kitchen and your heart.

Volcanic Fairy Cakes

Aloha! Now a call could come anytime from a global celebrity planning a Hawaiian themed birthday bash (luau) and wanting volcanic cupcakes. My advice is to keep this hot little recipe up your floral sleeve! This makes about 16 fairy cakes.

Ingredients
120g or 4 oz plain flour
140g or 5 oz soft light brown sugar
1½ teaspoon baking powder
2 teaspoon cinnamon
40g or 1½ oz butter (softened)
120ml coconut milk
1 free range egg
8 slices of tinned pineapple rings chopped up into very small pieces
Paper cases? Well...I'm thinking metallic blue for the sea – but you could go for Hawaiian shirt floral – after all it's a luau!

Hawaiian Frosting
300g icing sugar
175g cream cheese
12 cocktail umbrellas and edible sugar flowers

Method
Pre-heat oven to 170°c/325°f/Gas Mark 3.

Place floral lei around your neck and sift the flour, sugar, baking powder cinnamon into the bowl then add the butter and mix well until it looks like golden rubbly sand on a sundrenched Hawaiian beach. Next, beat in the coconut milk and egg with a whisk.

Now remember that pineapple upside down cake your mum always made? As homage to that, put a couple of pieces of the chopped pineapple into the bottom of each paper case and top with the cake batter. Pop into the oven and sigh as the scent of pineapple wafts across the kitchen, reminding you of those endless summer nights when you were 18 and drank Malibu and your upper arms didn't resemble old porridge.

For the Frosting

Whisk the icing sugar and cream cheese until light and fluffy then apply to cooled cakes. Make a cone-like volcano-shaped topping and stick a cocktail umbrella in and dot with lots of little sugar flowers. Mix an exotic cocktail, sit back, enjoy the cupcake view and make like you're lying on that beach in Honolulu!

The 'American Smooth' Red Velvet Fairy Cake

From the 'Strictly Come Dancing' collection.

Dance the night away with this red velvet cake covered in cream cheese frosting, dressed in green glitter and infused with a high kick of lime zest. Named after the ballroom dance, this is basically a simple dance recipe with a few exciting moves. This fairy cake is *Sex in the City*, it's the whole cast of *Glee* singing together...it's you and me in high heels...this is how we roll! Makes about 14-16 cakes.

Ingredients
110 g or 4 oz cup self-raising flour
1 teaspoon baking powder
60g or 2 oz cocoa powder
110g or 4 oz softened butter
110g or 4 oz cup caster sugar
38ml bottle of red food colouring – (using liquid colouring can affect the consistency, but I've used it in emergencies and it's fine. However, for a really blingy red sponge use a whole pot of concentrated red paste instead).
2 large eggs
12 metallic paper cases (shiny dancing shoes)

Cream Cheese Frosting
300g or 10 ½ oz icing sugar
60g or 2 oz cream cheese
2 tablespoons lime juice
Zest from 1 lime
Edible green bling

<u>Method</u>

Pre-heat the oven to 170°c/325°f/Gas Mark 3, fill a cake tin with shiny paper cases and start that music (may I suggest a favourite ballad). Shimmy as you sift the flour, sugar, cocoa and baking powder into a large bowl. Height, darling – make those cakes light on their feet!

Add the butter, eggs and red colouring (a whole 38ml bottle of colouring will give your sponge a real rich, red shade). Now with a slow rhythm, whisk until everything is combined and your mix is so red it's dancing in the bowl! If the mixture is a little dry, add a splash of milk. Spoon the mixture into the paper cases and bake in the oven for approximately 20 minutes or until risen and springy to the touch.

Once the cakes are out of the oven let them chill out on a wire rack.

<u>For the Frosting</u>

Now mix the cream cheese, icing sugar, lime juice and zest in a bowl with a whisk or a wooden spoon and a muscular arm. Once it's light and fluffy apply to the cooled cakes and while getting your breath back, do a little cha cha cha with your arms and sprinkle that green bling all over your fairy cakes baby!

Take a bow!

Coffee Fairy Cakes

Inspired by nude espresso and naked baristas, these coffee fairy cakes will keep you up all night baby!

I know you love your coffee strong and hot – so here is my special recipe and there's nothing fairy-like about these cute little caffeine bombs. We're not talking 'a hint' of coffee – we're talking caffeine fix in a cake, which BTW will increase one's metabolism, thus allowing more cake to be eaten. If you can't take the pace and are looking for something more mellow put less coffee in the mix – you wimp!

My recipe makes 12 fairy cakes or 30 baby fairies. The mini versions are a sophisticated companion to enjoy with after dinner coffee (much like yourself Al). The big babies are great for coffee mornings, bake sales and random social gatherings of coffee enthusiasts and naked baristas. Chocolate covered coffee beans are a great little topper – but being a bad girl I like to sprinkle a little gold fairy cake dust and give it some bling.

<u>Ingredients</u>
110 g or 4 oz self-raising flour
1 teaspoon baking powder
110g or 4 oz softened butter
110g or 4 oz caster sugar
2 large eggs
1 tablespoon of coffee granules dissolved in 1 tablespoon of hot water

<u>Coffee Frosting</u>
200g or 7 oz icing sugar, sifted
1 tablespoon of coffee granules dissolved in 1 tablespoon of hot water (add more or less to taste)

Chocolate-covered coffee beans or party glitter – both optional depending on your mood and who you're baking for.

Method

Pre-heat the oven to 180°c/350°f/Gas Mark 4 and fill a cake pan with paper cases. Sift the flour and baking powder into a large bowl. Add the eggs, the caster sugar and the softened butter. Now completely dissolve a tablespoon of coffee granules in a tablespoon of very hot water. Add this to the other ingredients in the bowl and whisk until soft, creamy, coffee heaven emerges. I bet you can't resist a little slurp. Delicious? Told you so. Now put the mixture into the paper cases. Bake in the oven for approximately 20 minutes and make yourself a well-earned cup of coffee while allowing the scent of sweet coffee to permeate the air (multi-sensory coffee experience) while leafing through various celebrity mags.

Once out of the oven and slightly cooled, take the cakes from the tin and place on a cooling rack.

For the Coffee Frosting

When cakes are completely cooled, sift the icing sugar into a bowl and dissolve the coffee granules in hot water. Combine until the mixture forms a soft, thick paste. Taste the icing and if you want a stronger coffee flavour then 'bring it on' and add a dissolved teaspoon of granules. If you just can't keep up and want less coffee taste, add more icing sugar and a little hot water. If the icing is too thick, add hot water and/or coffee to taste!

Now top the cakes using the back of a teaspoon or a knife. Eat the first one and make sure it's all utterly gorgeous – you can still adjust icing accordingly. If you're not sure – eat another one and keep this up until you know exactly what flavour you want.

If the icing thickens too much while you eat and ice, put the spoon or knife in hot water and continue.

Now make another cup of coffee and consume more coffee cakes for more multi-sensory coffee bliss.

Chocolate Chilli Fairy Cha Chas with Spangly Frills

These simple-to-make cheeky little fairies are lively, sweet and just a little bit spicy. The heat is in the buttercream, so if you are baking for children or don't like chilli, just bake the cakes as directed and leave the chilli out of the buttercream...they are still cha chas, just a little more restrained.

Now before you begin just let your hips sway very slowly, feel that music and just let those Latin rhythms pulse through the body as you cha cha round the kitchen collecting the ingredients. Makes about 12 cakes.

<u>Ingredients</u>
2 free range eggs
110g or 4 oz caster sugar
110g or 4 oz self raising flour
110g or 4 oz butter, melted
½ tablespoon cocoa powder
12 red metallic paper cases (they remind me of strappy scarlet dancing shoes).

<u>Chilli buttercream</u>
70g or 2 ½ oz butter, softened
140g or 5 oz icing sugar
25g or 1 oz cocoa
1-2 tablespoons milk
¼ level teaspoon chilli (or to taste)
½ teaspoon cinnamon
½ tablespoon milk
Red sparkly bits and edible red glitter

Method

Cha cha over to the oven and turn it to 180°C/350°F/Gas Mark 4 and fill cake tins with paper cases.

Now whisk the eggs and sugar together in a bowl until light and fluffy – all the time swaying those hips and taking little cha cha steps (it improves the texture, trust me). Slow down the tempo now and <u>fold</u> in the flour, cocoa and melted butter.

Spoon mixture into scarlet stilettos (or paper cases) and bake for 20-25 minutes until springy to the touch.

For the Frosting

When the cakes have chilled out on their wire rack – they will be ready for their dancing dresses.

Beat the butter in a large bowl until soft. Add half of the icing sugar and beat until smooth. Add the remaining icing sugar, chilli and cinnamon and the milk and beat the mixture until creamy and smooth. Check the taste and add a little more chilli if you fancy something hot, hot, hot and beat in extra milk, if necessary, to loosen the mixture.

Now top those cha cha fairies and throw on some red sparkles and bling, take a big chocolate chilli bite and dance the night away.

English Rose Fairy Cakes

These fragrant fairies are perfect with a cup (china of course dear) of Earl Grey tea and a Jane Austin novel. You will recall we baked these for the 'Fashionista Afternoon Tea' and they went down very well, albeit some of the skinnier ubermodels munched only on rose petals and avoided the calorific cake. So if baking these for fashionistas I would recommend baby cakes because a whole one would be far, far too much! This recipe makes about 12 standard size cakes.

Ingredients
115g or 4 oz butter
115g or 4 oz caster sugar
2 free range eggs
115g or 4 oz self raising flour
1 tablespoon rose water
12 pretty pink paper cases

Rose Icing
200g or 7 oz icing sugar
4 tablespoons rose water

Frosted Petals
12 freshly plucked rose petals
1 egg white
1 tablespoon caster sugar

Method
Pre-heat the oven to 180°c/350°f/Gas Mark 4 and fill a cake pan with 12 large paper cases – or 24 small ones (if fashionistas or little girls are coming to tea). Now beat the sugar and butter

together until light and fluffy, add the eggs one at a time and keep beating. Now sift the flour and fold it into the mixture using that lightness of touch you are famed for! Open the rosewater and stop and smell the roses for a minute ah...that's better. Now stir in the rosewater and put the heavenly scented batter into the fairy cases and pop into the oven for about 20 minutes until golden and springy to the touch.

As the cakes bake, filling the kitchen with divine fragrance, imagine you're in a rose garden and pluck petals from a (preferably pink) rose and brush each rose petal with the egg white, covering it completely, but lightly (don't soak it.*) Now with a fragrant flourish, sprinkle with caster sugar and leave to dry.

NB* I find garden roses are great for crystallizing but tend to wrinkle more than bought, cut roses so be very light with the egg white.

For the icing
Once the cakes are cooled, begin on the icing. Mix the sugar and rose water together to form a thick paste and add the tiniest drop of pink food colouring (to match the rose petal colour or perhaps a little lighter). Apply icing to the cooled cakes and top with a sugared rose petal. Dig out your best china, place exquisite rose-topped fairy on the china, make a pot of pale golden Earl Grey and enjoy a little Jane Austen under a willow tree in the garden.

Cranberry and White Chocolate Christmas Fairies

These sweet little fairies are so easy to make you'll be able to whip up a batch between Christmas shopping and festive partying. I know you don't like anything too tarty – therefore the white chocolate icing counteracts the tartness of the dried cranberries. This delicious but not-too-sweet treat is perfect to serve with sherry when the gay swimming team arrive unexpectedly after a vigorous Boxing Day breast stroke down the cocktail lane. Makes about 12-14 cakes.

Ingredients
150g or 5 oz self raising flour
150g or 5 oz butter, softened
3 free range eggs
150g or 5 oz caster sugar
2 tablespoons milk
Several drops of vanilla extract
75g or 2 ½ oz dried cranberries
12 gold paper cases

For the Icing
60g or 2 oz white chocolate, chopped
Edible gold stars and glitter

Method
Set the oven to 180°C/350°f/Gas Mark 4 and first sift the flour into a large bowl from a great height. Then add all the ingredients and beat until smooth...and that's it! Yes it's as easy as that. Don't forget to stir in the cranberries! Now divide the

mixture between 12 gold cases, and bake in the centre of the oven for 18-20 mins, or until the cakes have risen and are just firm to the touch and springy. While this festive fairy feast is baking, pour a glass of egg nog and find some hymns on the iPlayer.

Take the cakes from the oven and transfer them to a wire rack to cool.

For the Topping
When the cakes are cool, simply melt the white chocolate in a heat proof bowl over a simmering pan of water – or if in a real rush in the microwave. When melted, spoon the white chocolate onto the Christmas Fairies and bling it with some edible gold stars and glitter. Serve to hungry boys.

About the Author

Sue Watson was born in Manchester long ago and after attending Manchester Polytechnic and hanging around the Hacienda for far too long, moved to London to seek fame and fortune. She found neither, but had a wonderful time working as a journalist on tabloid newspapers and women's magazines.

Moving into television, Sue became a producer with the BBC and worked on garden makeovers, kitchen takeovers and daytime sofas – all the time making copious notes so that one day she might escape to the country and turn it all into a book.

She still has the notes and now writes novels in Worcestershire, where she lives with husband Nick, daughter Eve, two cats and a rather glamorous goldfish.